WORLD ∝ OF THE ∞ ORB

Adventure Awaits!

Michael Thompson

RavenCon 2017

MICHAEL THOMPSON

THOMPSON ORIGINAL PRODUCTIONS LLC
BRISTOW, VA

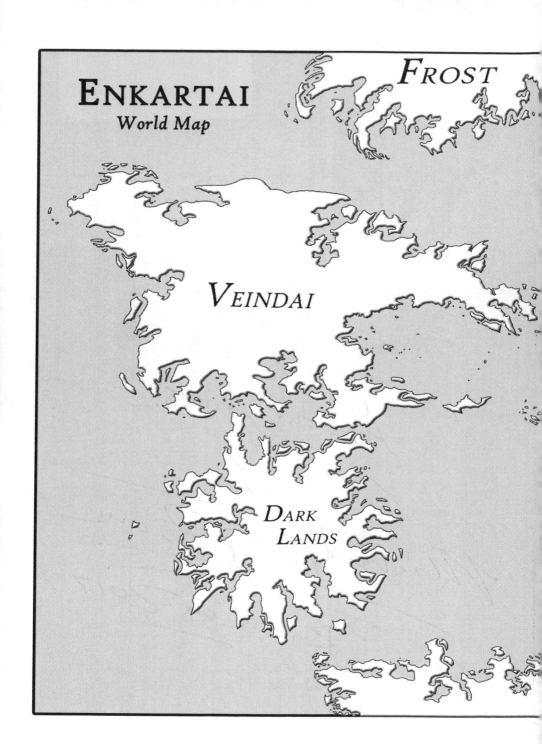

ENKARTAI
World Map

FROST

VEINDAI

DARK
LANDS

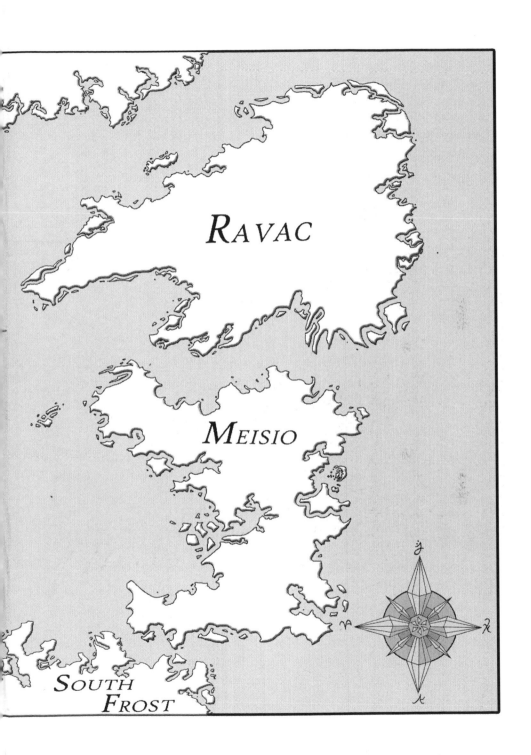

RAVAC

MEISIO

SOUTH
FROST

Published by Thompson Original Productions LLC
Bristow, VA 20136

Library of Congress Control Number: 2016910996

ISBN 978-0-9799216-6-7

Written and Illustrated by Michael Thompson

Printing History

First Printing, October 2016

Printed in the United States of America

For

Lawrence Schoonover

My Great Grandfather
& My Greatest Inspiration.

Contents

Prologue
The Master and His Student

"All the world is elements," the Master spoke. "Elements in their righteousness and depravity. Water, with its life, and its bitter cold. Weather, with its breaths, and its fury. Land, with its foundation, and its quakes. Fire, with its warmth, and its destruction. The light that guides us, the spirit that binds us, and the darkness that tears us apart."

The Master gazed up at the stars, then continued, "Indeed, these attributes have spilled into other worlds, invisible to our own. Separate, and yet connected. All the worlds are elements. And we, we are the greatest elements of all, because we can choose our own power. Directed by light or deceived by shadows. The path you take is up to you."

"How will I know which path is right to choose?" the Student asked.

The Master smiled. "Your path has already chosen *you*," he explained. "It is the noble, virtuous path that chooses us all. All you must do, is decide to follow it."

1

The Field Trip

A wad of paper struck me in the back of the head and laughter poured from the rear of the bus. I ignored it and continued reading my book. I was too focused on the new novel I borrowed from the library to care about who the culprit was. I just can't get enough of books, especially science fiction. The way authors create new worlds fascinates me. The book I was buried in that time was called *The Adventures of Captain Galloway*, and was about a rookie space captain who crash-lands on an alien planet and has to find his way home. I guess I would consider myself somewhat of a nerd. I'm not good at many physical activities. I really only excel at schoolwork and computers. *Nerdy* stuff.

Many distracting sounds cluttered the vehicle: the laughter and shouts of my classmates, the loud music blaring from their earbuds. Even the bus itself made clunking and sputtering sounds as it blundered down the road. The squeaking of its shock absorbers joined the ruckus whenever we hit a pothole, which happened regularly. I had to constantly push my glasses back into place.

It wasn't just the noise keeping me from reading; my excitement pulled my attention to the window to see that we were getting close to our destination. We were on a field trip to the Museum of Natural History. I'm also a bit of a geek when it comes to history and science. I returned to my book and tried desperately to ignore the irritating sounds around me.

Once I finally tuned the noise out, I was snapped back into the commotion by another paper wad. I turned around to see Eddie Seaver, a jock in my class, laughing and slapping his buddies high-fives. He had a freckled face and curly, red hair. As usual, his attire consisted of our school colors, red and gold, as displayed on his letterman jacket. An emblem of our school mascot, the lion, was depicted roaring ferociously on the right side of the outfit. The jacket was a little too big for him. I guess he thought it made him look tough or something. He'd like to think he's the most popular guy at our school. I'd like to think he's the most delusional.

My view was dragged up the aisle when the sound of loud, fast talking overwhelmed the chortles of Eddie's posse. It was none other than the 'Acy Sisters, Macy and Stacy. They weren't related, nor did they bare any resemblance to one another, but everyone called them sisters because they dressed the same, acted the same, and spoke in the same manner. Today, their speech was especially hard to understand, since it seemed like they were talking at the same time, and their voices melded into one boisterous sound.

I tried again to return to my book, when Andy, my best friend, leaned over the back of his seat and said, "Dude, do you ever do anything other than read?"

I looked up at him.

"I mean seriously Marv, it's been like, thirty minutes!" he continued. He brushed the bangs of his shaggy, light blond hair away from his eyes.

"It's a good book," I murmured as I continued reading.

"You should do something more important," Andy explained, "like play video games!" He waved a handheld game in front of me. The screen read, *Alien Hunt: Ultimate Destruction*. "You know you *want* to!" he urged.

"No thanks, Andy," I said. "I just want to read."

Andy sighed, "You're hopeless, Marvin," as he began playing his game.

"Ha ha ha!" I heard him laugh moments later. "Die, aliens, die!" The noises from the game made it hard to concentrate. I found myself reading the same words over and over.

"Could you please turn that down?" I asked him quietly.

He glanced back at me. "You say something?"

I repeated myself and he adjusted the volume. I thanked him.

With the feeling of being watched, I turned to my right and saw Alison Adair, glancing quickly at me and then looking away.

"*Dude*, she totally likes you," Andy said in an excited whisper.

"Maybe," I said. I looked back at her. She had dark brown hair and dark eyes, similar to me, and light freckles scattered across her nose and cheeks. She wore a violet hoodie and dark blue jeans, and was drawing something in a sketchbook. I recognized the sketchbook from an art class I had taken with her;

4

its black cover was decorated with calligraphic, Korean lettering painted in white—an expression of that half of her heritage.

I've had a small crush on her ever since she moved into my apartment building, and Andy always tried to tell me that she felt the same, but no girl would like *me*, I decided, and I had never even talked to her. I turned my attention away, and within seconds Andy whispered, "Look, she's looking at you again! See?" I spun around and her eyes widened in shock, before she returned to her sketching.

"You like her, right?" Andy asked.

"Well, yeah," I answered hesitantly.

"Then you should ask her to prom!"

"I... I don't know."

"C'mon, it's the end of the year, you won't see her for a whole summer! The worst thing she could say is '*no*'."

That's what I fear most, I thought.

"You can't succeed if you don't try," Andy shrugged as he returned to his game.

I decided Andy was right. Fueled with confidence, I turned to Alison. "Hey," my voice came out in a rasp.

She locked eyes with me. "Hey!" she spoke elatedly through a big, beaming smile.

I cleared my throat and ignored the nervousness churning in my stomach. "So, what'cha drawing there?"

She lifted her sketchbook and revealed a beautifully detailed picture of a hummingbird drinking nectar from a flower.

"That's amazing."

"Thanks," Alison said. "It's not finished yet, I still have to color it."

"It looks great already," I told her as I studied the flower in the lower left corner of the masterpiece. "What type of flower is that?"

"It's an Iris," she explained. She grinned again and placed the sketchbook on her lap.

"Anyway, there was something I wanted to ask you," I said.

She kept her happy expression and nodded as I talked.

"So, I was wondering if maybe you'd like to—"

Suddenly, another wad of paper whizzed by and hit Andy in the back of the head. With no hesitation, he spun around and cried, "Who threw that?!"

5

Eddie Seaver and his crew started laughing again. Andy found the paper and tried to throw it back at them, but it slipped through his grasp and flew out to his left, grazing Macy's shoulder. She and Stacy gasped at the same time.

"*Who* threw that?" Macy questioned.

"It was Andy. I bet he did it on purpose," Stacy accused.

"It was an accident!" Andy argued.

"Pretty bad arm ya got there!" Eddie called.

"Pretty bad *face* ya got there!" Andy snapped.

"Children, children, *please* calm down," our World History teacher, Mr. Barber, implored. He stood up and raised his hands to quiet the bus. He was a short, pudgy man with a bald head, brown mustache, and thick glasses that magnified his eyes and took up most of his face. Once everyone had quieted down, he continued, "That's better. You all are juniors in high school and you act like a bunch of preschoolers! You better shape up, 'cause your teachers next year aren't going to tolerate this." He glared around the bus full of silent, spooked faces, then added, "Alright, we're almost at the museum. I want all of you on your best behavior, and *no talking* until we get there."

The whole bus was silent. I turned to Alison and whispered, "Like I was saying—"

"*Sh!*" Mr. Barber shushed.

Alison mouthed the words, *We'll talk later*, and I nodded and slumped down in my seat. Andy and I exchanged troubled glances.

I found my Captain Galloway book beside me and tucked it in my backpack as the bus hissed to a stop. The doors flew open, and everyone exited the vehicle. Mr. Barber followed us out.

"Okay, line up everyone," he commanded. Mr. Barber was very orderly, and called role more than any other teacher I've known. "Alison Adair." he called.

"Here!" Alison sang.

"Andy Bailey."

"Yo!" Andy answered.

He continued down the alphabetical list, and my name was called last, of course. "Marvin Wessel."

"Present," I replied.

The class of twenty-seven students flowed up a flight of steps and into the open doors of the Museum of Natural History. I trailed behind them, and stopped at the base of the steps to stare up at the huge, ornate structure. Much of the building was constructed from whitish stone and marble, and supported by giant pillars. It reminded me of Greek architecture.

I took a deep breath and slung my backpack over my shoulder before adjusting my dark green, collared shirt and tucking in the pockets of my khaki slacks. Andy appeared on my right.

"Let's go, Marv," he said. He was wearing a white T-shirt, old worn jeans, and his favorite: a bright orange jacket. He shook my shoulders as if gearing up for a game. "This is gonna be awesome."

"I didn't know you had an interest in this sort of thing," I said.

"Oh I don't," Andy replied, "but I'm hoping they have a gift shop."

We entered the museum to see a tall man with graying dark-blond hair, wearing a dark suit, and standing with his hands behind his back.

"Welcome," he spoke, "to the Museum of Natural History, in which you will all witness an assortment of the most astounding aspects of our world. My name is Mr. Connley, and I will be your tour guide this morning." He began walking into a hall with a sign over it that read, *fossils*. He continued, "If you would follow me, we are about to venture back in time to the era of the dinosaurs."

"Man, this guy's really into it," Andy whispered to me.

We followed Mr. Connley into the hall of fossils. He stopped in front of one and said, "Here is everyone's favorite monster, Tyrannosaurus rex. His name means the 'Tyrant Lizard King'. You may be surprised to find out that T-rex's closest relatives today are chickens and ostriches."

"So, he's the Tyrant *Chicken* King?" Andy blurted out.

The tour guide waited for a few students to stop laughing before he responded, "Raise your hand when you want to make a comment, and believe it or not, you aren't too far off. You see, recent findings suggest that T-rex might have been covered in

7

feathers, more closely related to its avian descendants. ...It's a bit humorous, don't you think? T-rex began as the world's most feared predator, and now he's the world's favorite food." A few people laughed as we continued through the exhibits.

We made our way through prehistoric times and the dawn of man, Mr. Connley telling us interesting bits of information and Andy whispering sarcastic comments in my ear all along the way. Our group walked under an archway framed by ancient vases on either side, and entered a hall bedecked with archaic paintings mounted on the walls. Beneath each piece was a paper sign that read, *DO NOT TOUCH* in massive, bold letters.

Our tour guide approached one of the pictures and said, "Here is an excellent example of Aboriginal artwork—" I lost track of his voice when my eyes drifted to see a door at the end of a shorter hall stemming from the one where my class was standing. The door looked old and wooden, and seemed out-of-place with the rest of the museum. I studied the door further and found the words, *Artifact Room* carved into it.

"Are there any questions?" Mr. Connley asked. His eyes scanned the group for hands from behind his gold-rimmed specs. I glanced back at the Artifact Room, then raised my hand. Mr. Connley nodded and gestured for me to speak.

I said, "I was wondering if we could check out the Artifact Room."

He raised his eyebrows. "What was that?" The tour guide leaned forward to hear me better. I repeated my question and he responded, "I'm sorry, I can't hear you from back there. Why don't you come to the front?" I muttered *Excuse me's* as I worked my way through the crowd of students.

Suddenly, a white sneaker hooked over my foot and I tripped and fell to the ground. I grunted upon impact with the cold, tile floor, as my glasses flew off and my vision went blurry. I squinted upward to see a hazy blob of red and gold. It let out a short laugh and spoke, "Better watch your step, there."

I went back to the floor and started feeling for my glasses, when a violet figure approached. It knelt and placed the lenses back over my eyes. My surroundings came into focus to reveal Alison, her dark eyes filled with concern, her pretty face radiant with genuine kindness, as she asked me, "Are you okay, Marvin?"

I think that's when I realized just how much I liked her. "Yeah," I heard myself say as a grin spread over my face. "I'm fine." Alison beamed her big, white smile, and all my embarrassment melted away. She helped me up and gave Eddie a sneer.

Andy dashed to my side. "You alright, buddy?" he asked.

The tour guide peeked over the crowd at me. "You okay there?" Mr. Connley called. "These floors had been waxed, they may still be slippery."

Eddie tried to act concerned as well, but his crooked smirk gave him away. "Yeah, the floors are slippery, Marvin."

I ignored him and told the tour guide I was fine, as I walked on through the crowd.

I stood in front of Mr. Connley. While his hair and attire lacked any color, his eyes were bright, emerald green. They narrowed at me as he grinned and asked, "Now what was your question, sir?"

"I was just wondering if we could take a look in the Artifact Room."

His expression became sullen, and his green eyes rolled to view the unusual door, before returning to me. "That room is off-limits," he said simply, as he turned away.

The class started to follow him.

"Wait!" I choked out, a bit louder than I meant to.

He and my classmates stopped and stared at me. I glanced at them all, then questioned, "Why not?"

Mr. Connley approached me, his face stern, and stated, "Because, that room is not on our tour. It is not on *any* tour. The Artifact Room isn't open to the public."

"Why?" I asked.

The irritated tour guide took a deep breath through his nostrils, stared at the door, then replied, "Because it is not meant for you to see."

He hardly answered my question at all. "Let us continue," he declared as he walked back to the front of the group.

The tour slowly came alive again, the wave of students lurching forward as Mr. Connley took the lead. He gave me a studying glare before turning a corner and escorting the class deeper into the museum. I walked slowly, keeping my eyes locked on the mysterious door. I hadn't realized that I ended up at the back of the group until Andy nudged my arm.

"Hey Marv, check it out."

I broke my trance and looked ahead, seeing one of the *DO NOT TOUCH* signs had been stuck to Eddie's back.

I laughed, "Nice."

Eddie rounded the corner.

"C'mon, I wanna see his reaction!" Andy urged. As much as I did too, my fascination with the door was unshakable. My attention drifted back to its secluded, shady hall.

"I want to see the Artifact Room," I told him, my eyes not straying from my target.

"Why?" Andy asked. "It's just a bunch of old, dirty crud someone dug up."

"No, it isn't," I told him. I stopped walking and turned to Andy. "I think he's hiding something."

"Who, the tour guide?" Andy let out a laugh. "You've been reading *way* too much science fiction."

As the last of our class turned the corner, I dashed down the opposite hallway. Andy fidgeted and stammered in protest briefly, but followed close behind anyway as I rushed down the passage and met the old door. I turned the knob, but found that it was locked.

"Ha!" Andy voiced. "You see? This room isn't open to the public, just like Mr. Connley said."

I tried to open it again.

"Sorry, *detective*," Andy said. "The door's locked." He took the knob and jiggled it back and forth to prove his point. I was about to abandon my pursuit, when Andy turned the doorknob once more, and a clicking sound filled the air.

Andy's mouth fell open and he tore his hand away. Immediately, I gripped the knob one more time and turned it. The doorknob squeaked and clunked as it rotated all the way to the right, and the door moved slightly. Excitement buzzed within me as I pressed my shoulder against the door and pushed with all my weight. It barely budged, and I turned to Andy.

"Help me out here," I said.

"Just forget about it, Marvin," Andy implored. "We can probably sneak back into the group and forget this whole fiasco before anyone notices."

I shook my head. "It's almost open, see? Just help me open the door so we can see what's inside, and then we can leave. It'll be like an adventure."

"Fine," Andy huffed as he placed his hands on the door. "*I don't know what's gotten into you,*" he mumbled under his breath.

"On three," I commanded. "One... two... three!" We heaved all our might against the anchored piece of wood. Finally, with our combined strength, the sticky film between the door and its jamb snapped, and the door creaked open.

A small, dusty room, with dirty tan walls and rotting wood floorboards revealed itself. The room was poorly lit, with only the light from a small window streaming in through its tattered, black curtains. A single light bulb hung from the ceiling as well, but it was old and burned out. The room's walls were mounted with shelves that held countless remarkable artifacts. I stepped through the shadowed opening and cautiously placed my foot on the floor, cringing when the loud squeaking of the boards broke the silence.

Andy quickly looked out into the hallway, then joined me in the room and shut the door so no one would see us. The door clicked shut and I strolled around the room less fretful.

"This place gives me the creeps," Andy muttered.

"Anything that has to do with *learning* gives you the creeps," I said. "This place is amazing..." I wandered toward the first row of shelves, set at eye level. A collection of figurines was the first to greet me. There were statues of wizards and warriors and fantastic creatures. Some of the figures appeared to be part animal, part human. The shelf above held ancient pots, pans, and other antiquated items. The display of the farther wall held other interesting artifacts, but the centerpiece of the room was the one to capture my gaze.

I approached a shiny, Tyrian purple orb that was displayed on a silver, three-legged stand.

"Wow," I breathed.

"Wow, a big marble," Andy said sarcastically.

"It's not a marble," I told him. "It's an orb." The orb absorbed incoming sunlight that made the inside of it glow, almost swirl, in a vortex of mystic light. "It's beautiful," I whispered.

"Yeah, this was *totally* worth detention. Can we go now?"

"Not just yet," I voiced, not taking my eyes off the tantalizing light patterns within the relic. I scanned some unusual markings around the rim of the orb's stand. "Oh, cool!" I said.

"What?"

"It's got some weird writing on it," I replied. "I can't tell what language it is. What do you think it says?"

"I bet it says, *'Don't let Marvin touch this'*!"

I wrapped my hands around the orb and picked it up.

"What are you doing?!" Andy clamored.

It was smooth and crystalline, large enough that my fingers couldn't quite wrap around the diameter. It was dense, but not quite as heavy as I expected, and was very warm. My eyes glinted as the light inside of it intensified and spun faster, like the countless stars of a whirling universe.

"C'mon Marv, put that thing down," Andy said.

The dazzling display of swirling light within the orb turned into a rapid spin, followed by a blazing, white flash and a burning sensation upon its surface.

"Ow!" I cried as I dropped the artifact.

Andy's face twisted in fear as the orb landed with a *thump* and rolled across the floor. "I meant put it down on the stand!" he shouted.

"The orb burned me!" I retorted.

"You wimp," Andy said as he strolled to the corner of the room to retrieve the orb. "You probably just held it too close to the window and it heated up." He knelt down and placed his hand on it. "*Yow!*" he wailed, jumping backward and shaking his hand. "What the heck?!"

Another flare of white light surged in the orb, and Andy and I stepped back in disbelief. A radiant, white glow overtook the object, and the entire room began to rattle.

"Okay, we can go now," I stated.

Andy darted to the door and twisted the knob. "It's locked!" he screamed.

"What? How?!"

"I don't know!"

Our shouts became muffled by a wild, whirring sound generated by the otherworldly artifact. It began to levitate, and the Artifact Room shook with increasing intensity. Pots, pans, figurines, gems, all crashed to the floor. The orb's glow magnified, and my heart throbbed violently inside my chest when I realized it was pulling us in.

My sneakers slid along the floor, slightly at first, then a powerful, invisible force tugged fiercely at me, sweeping me off my feet. I grasped the bolted-down leg of a display table, as my body drew upward and flailed in the air.

This has to be a dream, I thought. *This can't be real.*

I shut my eyes and tried to stay calm, tried to wake up from this nightmare, but reality delivered a brutal strike to my being as a shrill cry erupted from Andy's mouth. I gawked in terror as my friend flew backward and was absorbed into the orb's radiance. I stared wide-eyed into the brightness, frozen in fear, unable to scream. The white energy spun faster around the orb in a violent, deafening flurry of sound.

Beads of sweat that rolled from my forehead and palms were sucked into the object. The unyielding pull grew unbearable, and I could hold on no longer. My grip tore free and I soared helplessly backward, as the hot beams of energy engulfed my body.

I felt dizzy at first, and my vision was blurred, but when my eyes adjusted, I found myself throwing about in a cyclonic tube of Tyrian purple energy.

"M-*ar-ar-ar-ar-vin-in-in!*" a distorted, echoing cry of Andy's resonated through the portal.

I couldn't tell which direction I was going, whether I was falling or flying, but I knew there had to be a destination. My body plummeted like a rag doll through the aggressive ride, and was met with another searing flash of white light, before everything faded to black.

2
The Forest

I woke up to a stinging sensation. My eyes fluttered open, and bright sunlight streamed in. I winced at the light and shook my head. Sound and sight were both blurry. A loud, unknown yowl hurt my ears, and sudden impact stung my face. My surroundings pulsed with the cloudy light before fading to a distinct fuzziness that indicated my glasses had fallen off, and the distorted yowl became Andy's voice yelling, "Marvin!" Another wave of pain. Another. I found my glasses askew on my chin and frantically positioned them over my eyes. Things came into focus, and I nearly jumped at the sight of Andy leaning over me, hand drawn back.

"Marvin!" he wailed again as he slapped me in the face. *SLAP!* "Wake up!" *SLAP!*

I scrambled to my feet. "Stop it!" He waited a few seconds, then lightly slapped me again. I shoved him away and he laughed.

Andy brushed his hair back, grin fading, and wondered aloud, "Where are we?"

I thought the same question. Huge trees towered all around us, their massive trunks stretching higher than I could see, and smaller leafy plants hugged the ground around the trees, hiding all hints of our whereabouts. Ferns and shrubs sprouted from the moist, reddish brown soil. I reached out and felt the thinly ovate leaf of a fern. It was stiffened from a glossy, waterproof covering that made it feel plasticky, almost not real. I released my grasp on the frond and small bits of rainwater flung from the leaves and sprinkled onto my forearm. It was definitely real.

"Are we behind the museum or something?" Andy asked.

"I don't know," I replied.

My feet started to carry me through the maze of trees, and Andy followed. Our shoes sank a little with every step we took through the damp soil. I couldn't tell which direction we were going. I didn't know where we were. I didn't know what happened in the Artifact Room. But all these worries were overwhelmed by the instinctual urge to return to civilization.

Droplets of condensation formed on the lenses of my glasses, but I didn't rush to clean them off. The air was fresh and moist. Cool vapor wisped over my face as I moved. Aside from a bit of mud sticking to the bottom of my sneakers, it was a very refreshing walk.

"This place is disgusting!" Andy groaned. I looked back at him. He was struggling to shake the mud from his shoes. He continued, "Everything's wet and gross."

"It probably just rained," I noted.

"I don't remember it raining," Andy muttered.

We journeyed onward. I kept thinking we would find a path back to humanity, kept hoping there would be a road or a walkway beyond the next passage, but there was nothing but plants.

"How deep in the woods are we anyway?" I heard Andy ask.

I scanned the area. There were no signs, no recognizable landmarks, no clues of our location whatsoever. I shook my head, frustrated, and walked on. My foot suddenly jerked sideways into a depression in the earth, and I lost my balance and flopped into the mud. The cold, mucky substance clung revoltingly to my arms, knees, and abdomen.

"Wow," Andy chuckled. "I give that a ten." I sat up on my knees and was about to complain, when an unusual footprint caught my eye. Andy saw it too. "What do you think made that?" he asked, suddenly worried.

I stood up and wiped the mud from my arms and shirt. The footprint had three toes and looked like it belonged to a bird, except it was much larger.

"It's probably just a bird's footprint that got distorted by the rain," I explained.

"Or not," Andy said, pointing to a trail of identical tracks. Whatever animal made the prints appeared to have a near five-foot stride. I shrugged, still sticking to my distortion theory, and continued through the wood.

We traveled and traveled, and still came nowhere near our destination. Terror struck me. Andy and I had been walking for what felt like an hour. I wanted to check my watch to know for sure, but the hands had stopped moving. My eyes darted around the area. Nothing but trees, and beyond the trees were more trees. We were lost. All the worried thoughts were hitting me now, infesting my mind. *What if the museum was in the other direction and we were walking away from it? What if we never found the museum again? What if this is all a dream...?*

No. This wasn't a dream, I knew. I was there, experiencing it all. All the unfamiliar sights, sounds, smells, and feelings. This wasn't a dream, as much as I wished it was, so I had to stay focused and find my way out. There's always a way out.

What happened in the Artifact Room?

I shook the last thought from my head just as a rustling sound entered my ears. Andy and I turned around to see movement behind a wall of undergrowth. A sense of salvation washed over me and I ran toward the sound, but Andy caught me by the loop of my backpack.

"What do you think you're doing?!" he questioned in a stern whisper.

I shook myself free. "Maybe it's someone who can help us."

"People don't just lurk around in the woods."

"Isn't that what we're doing?"

"No, apparently *you're* trying to get us killed! There's probably a dangerous animal over there!"

"We have to find out, don't we?"

"Not necessarily."

"C'mon Andy, it might actually be someone who can help us. We can't be far from the museum, right?"

Andy sighed, "For a smart guy, you're really dumb."

I crouched down and snuck behind the bushes, motioning for Andy to follow.

More rustling filled the air. Andy's expression was troubled as he approached. I pried the foliage apart and kept my breathing quiet and steady as I peered through the opening. There was nothing, and the rustling sound had subsided to an eerie silence.

"Anything?" Andy whispered.

"No," I told him.

"Great. Now let's get moving."

I turned away. "Alrigh—"

A slight crackling of twigs resonated from a nearby location. I spun around, separated two clusters of greenery, and peered through once again. Nothing in front of me, but the sounds of soft shuffling and meat tearing turned my attention to the right, toward a small clearing splattered with the blood of a slain, stout pachyderm. The thick, wine-colored substance streamed from a fresh bite mark on the creature's neck. I stared in terror, mouth agape, breathing silently heavy, as the gruesome image suddenly became more grotesque when a monstrous foot plunged three sharp talons into the fallen beast's torso and ripped it open.

A primordial animal feasted on the innards of its defeated victim. She was a fearsome mixture of bird and reptile, about the size of an ostrich. Gray and dark green feathers covered her body. A long serpentine neck wielded a head whose pointed tooth-lined beak gobbled up meat, and bulbous, bright red throat swallowed it down. Similar lumpy red flesh covered areas around the bird's nostrils, face, and snake-like eyes. A long, swaying tail with a feathery flair at the end of it counterbalanced the creature's upper body, and strong padded legs with clawed three-toed feet supported her weight. A pair of short, two-fingered arms hung below her chest, the razor-sharp claws slicing at any bits of meat that refused to detach from the rest of the prey's body while the bird ate her meal. Fringed feathers, the precursor to wings, edged the underside of the animal's short arms. The predator chewed hungrily at the pachyderm carcass, as Andy and I stared in disbelief through the bushes.

"What is that?" Andy breathed.

In a circular motion, I took the glasses from my face, wiped them on my sleeve, and placed them back in front of my eyes. There stood the monster, a blend of blood and drool rolling down her jaw. I looked at Andy, my eyes filled with dread, and said without speaking that we had to get out of there.

Staying low to the ground, I took one step back, but my foot set itself on an old decaying branch, and snapped it in half. The massive bird's head shot up, and feathery frill flapped open.

My heart jumped. Andy and I watched in horror as the creature strutted toward us, her forked tongue tasting the air. The bird stood tall and stared down at us. She cocked her head side-to-side, refraining from attack. She looked confused.

"Maybe it can only see motion," I suggested.

Andy and I remained still, as the bird's ferocious head snaked down to face us. I shivered as she flicked her tongue at me, then sharply exhaled a humid, fusty breath. She brought her head back and screeched.

"Maybe not," Andy said. "Run!"

The bird lashed out, but missed and bit into the bushes, as Andy and I scrambled away. She spat out a mouthful of twigs and leaves and chased after us. My heart pounded in unison with the creature's rapid footsteps. We weaved through trees, hopped over logs, and ducked under branches, as our attacker screeched and pursued us with untiring vigor.

I turned to Andy and panted, "Let's split up. That'll confuse it."

Andy nodded, and we diverged in two directions.

The crazed bird paid little attention to our maneuver, however, and sprinted on after me. Of *course* it went for me. Like all predators, it zeroed in on the weakest one of the group. It didn't help that I still had my backpack on either. I should have tossed it aside but my terror only allowed me to focus on running, running significantly slower than I could have.

My heavy book bag fwomped about as I navigated through the brush in a zigzag pattern, hoping to lose the bird, but this monster was made to run after prey. She dashed around a line of trees and closed in on me. The bird's vicious head appeared on my left. The fearsome jaws opened, and red throat throbbed as it released another piercing wail. Like a wrecking ball, the beast swung her skull into my stomach, knocking me off my feet.

I grunted as I flew backward and slammed into the ground. The bird approached, snarling and looming over her new prey. She placed her foot on me and dug her talons into my side. Searing pain jolted through my body, and a short scream escaped my mouth.

I tried to get free, but the more I squirmed, the more her talons sank into my flesh. The creature lowered her head to feast. I shut my eyes in fear and clawed at the dirt beneath me, bracing for pain, when a sudden thumping sound and shriek made me open my eyes.

Andy was throwing rocks at the bird.

"Lay off my pal!" he cried. He threw a stone and it landed on the monster's head with a *thud*. She shook the ache away, then opened her beak as her fleshy throat pulsed and released a terrible screech. The bird stepped off me and poised to strike at Andy. She darted toward him.

Without warning, an arrow whizzed through the air and stuck between the animal's neck and shoulder blade. She squealed and fell over on her side. I stood up, holding my wound, and approached the fallen beast alongside Andy. We stared down at the body in both relief and confusion, then looked to the right where the arrow had come from. There was a girl, a crossbow clenched in her hand, and riding atop a strange, yak-like animal.

The girl clicked a button on the left side of the handle with her thumb, and the two ends of the bow folded in. She slid the weapon into a quiver strapped around her back, then dismounted the yak-like beast and approached us.

She had brown hair and bright blue eyes, and was wearing earth-colored, handmade clothes, bracelets, and necklaces. I guessed she was about our age. She stopped and studied us. Her sharp, periwinkle blue eyes stared into Andy and me. They were both dazzling and frightening.

"You all okay?" she asked.

"Yeah," I voiced. I cleared my throat. "Thanks for saving us."

Her expression became more relaxed. "You're welcome."

Andy stepped toward her with a big, stupid grin on his face and beamed, "Well howdy-do to you!" I could tell he was interested in her. "The name's Bailey," he said, making his voice deeper as he reached out his hand. "Andy Bailey."

The girl took his hand and shook it. "Veronica Blaire." She turned to me. "You are?"

"Marvin Wessel," I told her.

"Pleased to meet you both."

"How'd you find us?"

She laughed. "How *couldn't* I find you? I was hunting a few spans from here when I heard you two screaming your heads off, scaring all the thornbill away, so I decided to see what the fuss was about."

"Well, you really saved our butts!" Andy said, smiling and continuously shaking her hand again.

Veronica glanced at me, then back at Andy and said in a short, fake laugh, "Okay, that's enough of that."

"Right, right, of course," Andy said through his smile as he released her hand.

"So, how'd you two get lost in the first place? You aren't that far from town," Veronica said.

"I know!" I answered exuberantly. I was overjoyed to *finally* come across some sense on this nonsensical journey. Things were *finally* becoming less strange. "We just aren't from around here."

"Obviously," she replied. "Just look at your clothes. There isn't a ronk or ruftaram in the whole region that can spin material like *that*. You must be from Veindai, yes?"

Things were strange again. Andy and I glanced at each other.

"Uh, no," I said.

Andy gestured behind him with his thumb. "We live over in Gloryfield County."

"I've never heard of it," said Veronica.

"We go to Van Schoonhoven High School," Andy clarified. "You know where that is?"

Veronica shook her head.

A worried feeling pulsed through me. "Do you have a map we can look at?" I blurted out.

"Sure," Veronica said. "I just bought a few from the best cartographer around. They cost me quite a few siv, but quality isn't cheap, you know?"

We didn't reply.

She watched us for a moment, then stepped back to the yak-like animal.

Her pet snorted as she patted the side of his face. The bovine was covered in long, shaggy, tan fur, with a few dark brown markings on his chest, ears, and around his eyes. A bushy tail of the same dark color swung behind him. He had a blunt face with gray skin covering his snout and mouth. The huge creature was armed with four horns, a pair on his head, and a pair sprouting from his cheekbones. Also, two short fangs protruded from his mouth. Standing almost seven feet high at the shoulder, the beast's giant body was supported by four strong, hoofed legs. The animal's dark eyes stared at Andy and me, and his nostrils flared and let out another snort.

With stunning agility, Veronica leapt up, got her foot on a stirrup, and sat backwards on a saddle that was positioned between the beast's shoulders and attached to a large basket-like structure atop his back. She sifted through a small supply case at the front of the basket in search of her maps.

With a furrowed brow and confused expression, I circled and studied her enormous pet. I had never seen anything like it. I asked her, "What type of animal is this?"

From high atop the animal she looked down at me and smiled. "This is Boris," she said proudly. "He's a Mountain Ronk, a rare breed."

"Oh..." I said, bewildered by the immense bovine. "Okay, thanks."

"That's one big buffalo," Andy murmured.

"Ronk," Veronica corrected. She returned to her sifting and found what she was looking for. "Here we go." She tossed me a rolled-up map. I caught it and frantically opened it up. My eyes widened.

"What is this?" I asked Veronica.

She leapt back to the ground. "What do you mean?"

"This can't be right," I said. "This place doesn't exist. This can't be right..."

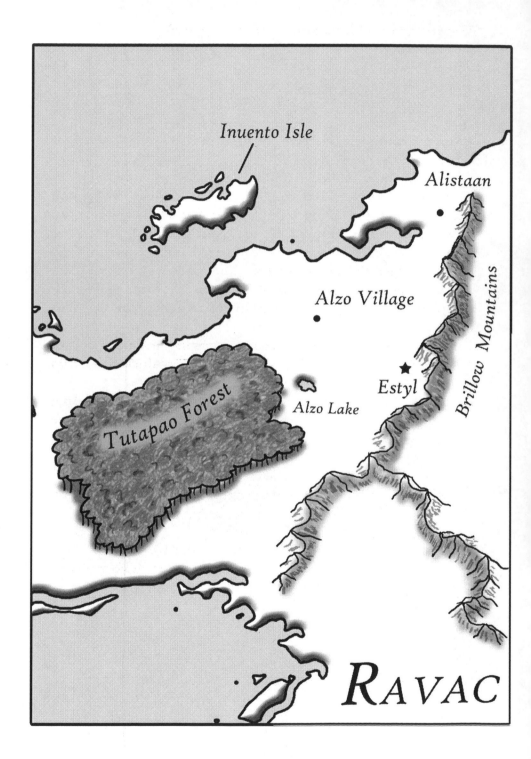

Inuento Isle

Alistaan

Alzo Village

Tutapao Forest

Alzo Lake

Estyl

Brillow Mountains

RAVAC

"*Ravac?*" I heard Andy say. "What's a Ravac?"

"The name of this continent," Veronica said in a baffled laugh. A crinkle formed in the middle of her brow as she stared at us in confusion.

Andy turned to her. "Is this a fake map?"

"What are you talking about—?"

They were talking back and forth, but I lost track of their voices. This place, everything was so similar that the slight differences had remained imperceptible until now. The atmosphere was different, the gravity was different, I felt different. Even the air entering my lungs was different. Everything was just slightly awry, slightly dissimilar to what I was acclimated to, and being aware of these minute changes was unsettling. Queasiness overwhelmed me. My legs felt wobbly. My surroundings started to spin. I threw up.

Andy and Veronica immediately stopped their banter.

"You okay, Marv?" Andy asked.

I coughed and nodded. Reaching toward a pain in my side, I discovered a stream of blood seeping through my shirt. I held up a handful of the red fluid, and Veronica gasped.

"You're hurt!" She darted to me and lifted my shirt, revealing three deep puncture wounds. "Ooh, that's a nasty cut." She retrieved some bandages from a supply case and wrapped up the gash for me. "I'll take you to get healed," she said as she mounted her massive pet.

She grabbed my hand and helped me climb into the basket on the animal's back. Andy was hesitant to join.

"Let's go, Andy!" Veronica called.

"Do I *have* to ride that thing?" Andy questioned.

"No," Veronica said. "You can walk. Just follow Boris' footprints, okay?" She flicked the reins, and Boris started to stomp away.

"Alright, alright, I'm comin'," Andy griped as he walked up to the bovine and struggled to climb into the basket. Veronica and I helped him aboard, and Boris carried us off.

Enormous tree trunks grew tall and diverged with branches whose leaves overlapped and provided shade from the sun. I was lying in the basket, my head propped up by a bag of supplies, and watching the light gleam through spaces in the scrolling canopy. My legs ached from walking through the forest and being chased by that crazy bird. I was glad to finally be off my feet.

Boris walked slowly, his huge body swaying side to side with each heavy footstep. This combined with a soft breeze and relaxing animal sounds made for a reposing ride. At least, I thought it was.

"Can't this thing move any faster?" Andy complained.

"*He* can move faster, but *he* doesn't want to right now," Veronica replied.

Andy let out a long sigh of boredom and sank down in his seat.

Veronica rolled her eyes and asked me, "How's your cut, Marvin?"

I lifted up my shirt and glanced at the bloodstained bandages. They seemed to have stopped the bleeding. "It's good." I said.

"How much farther is it?" Andy asked.

"Quit whining," Veronica said.

"This is taking forever."

"Would you rather me drop you off here and let the furadons get you?"

I asked her what a furadon was.

"That thing that attacked you," she answered. "Giant, predatory birds. Real nasty creatures."

Andy sat up. "Hm... get eaten by the ugly turkeys, or die of boredom," he pondered, moving his hands as if weighing the options.

Veronica sighed, "Just be patient."

"Too bad I left my game on the bus..." Andy muttered. "Hey Veronica, you know how to play *I Spy*?"

"No."

"It's easy. I say, 'I spy' and then describe something, and you try to guess what it is."

"...Okay."

"Alright. I spy with my little eye something... green!"

"Is it a leaf?"

"Yes, but *which* leaf?"

"I'm not playing this game."

24

Andy chuckled, and I shook my head, struggling to force off a grin.

Once Andy had calmed down, Veronica instructed, "Keep your eyes peeled for a lake."

"Gotcha," I said, retrieving the map. I unrolled it and found a feature called *Alzo Lake*, and just beyond that was a dot labeled *Alzo Village*. I didn't know why I was looking at the map, since I had no idea where we were. All I could tell was that we were somewhere in the densely wooded area called *Tutapao Forest*.

I asked Veronica approximately how far we were from our destination and she responded, "Almost a megaspan."

I didn't know what that meant, but I nodded, thanked her, and continued studying the map. Out of the corner of my eye, I thought I caught a fleeting glance of something moving behind us. I placed the map beside me and scanned the area. Nothing.

I laid myself down and shut my eyes. The trees were becoming less abundant now, so the enlarged gaps in their canopy allowed for more sunlight to shine through. The warm rays tingled my face, but the sound of footsteps on leaves sent a chill through my body. I sprang up and listened intently for the sound again.

It was a quiet noise, but distinct enough to make the hair on the back of my neck stand on end. For a moment, I could vaguely make out some rustling, but I couldn't tell for sure, since Andy was passing the time by making popping sounds with his mouth.

I hushed him and stared into the foliage behind us, listening for the noise. Obnoxiously, Andy made another loud pop.

"Quiet, seriously!" I whispered.

Andy slid into a laying position with his hands behind his head. He started rambling about how I need to calm down or something, but I was too focused on finding the source of the rustling to identify what he was saying. After I didn't reply to whatever he was talking to me about, he started a conversation with Veronica, as I continued to squint into the brush.

Suddenly, I found it. My mouth fell open and made a small gasp. There in the distance, a pair of yellow, snake-like eyes gleamed brightly through the shade of tangled greenery. My body stiffened in fear. I tried to speak, but no words came out. Frantically, I started tapping Veronica's shoulder. She didn't turn around right away, and continued talking to Andy.

The furadon revealed its face as it took a slow step into the light, keeping its head close to the ground, and body poised to strike. I forced out a word, "V-Veronica..."

She glanced back at me, halted her discussion with Andy for a moment, and asked, "What is it?"

I wanted to scream. I wanted to yell and tell them we had to get out of there, but my fear prevented me. I just stared, wide-eyed at our attacker lurking in the forest.

"What is it?" Veronica repeated.

The creature took another step toward us.

"*Fuh...*" I sounded.

"Huh?"

"*Fuh...*" I let out another trembling noise.

The predator snarled, then sprang from its hiding place and dashed. Finally the word erupted out of me, "Furadon!"

Veronica and Andy looked back, as the hungry bird stormed toward us, and Boris continued along the path at his slow pace. Several more furadons burst from the forest and joined in on the chase.

"Great!" Andy said. "The big turkeys are chasing the world's slowest animal!"

Veronica flicked the reins, "Yah!"

Boris took off at an unbelievable speed that caused Andy and me, who weren't restrained by any form of seatbelts, to go flying backward into the far end of the basket. We glanced behind us at the horrific pack of furadons. At first, the birds loped slowly and showily, their bodies upright, head-frills unfolded, feathers puffed out, and fang-lined beaks wide open to warble cries, like they were trying to scare us. It definitely worked, but Boris was moving incredibly fast, leaving the birds in the dust.

Andy and I breathed a sigh of relief. As Boris trotted on, Veronica called over the blustering wind, "They gone?"

"Yeah," said Andy. "Boris outran 'em."

Suddenly, in the distance, we saw the furadons tuck their heads, fold in their frills, flatten their feathers, and sprint after us with increasing speed.

"Strike that," Andy yelled. "Go, go, go!"

The furadons caught up quickly, and one of them whipped past the others and ended up directly behind us. She snarled, baring her pointed, grisly set of teeth. The creature ran with her body close to the ground, then slowed for a moment before leaping into the air. Andy and I screamed, as the beast soared toward us, her three clawed toes reaching forward.

With one hand gripping the reins, Veronica drew her crossbow and spun around, her intense blue eyes gleaming through her long, wind-tossed hair. She took aim as the bow folded out, then pulled the trigger, casting an arrow at the loathsome bird. The furadon let out a garbled squeal and tumbled backward, tripping another member of her pack. Andy and I glanced at each other, our eyes still wide with terror, before looking back at the rest of our pursuing adversaries.

The furadons' red throats swelled and released loud, shrill cries.

"Duck!" I heard Veronica yell.

Andy and I turned and narrowly dodged a low branch passing over us.

"Here, hold this," Veronica commanded, handing me the reins.

"Who, me?"

"Yeah!"

I gulped and clenched them tightly.

Veronica stood up and started to edge her way to the end of the basket on Boris' back.

"Duck!" I screamed.

Immediately, she dropped the floor and Andy covered his head as another large branch passed over them. Veronica looked back. Seeing that the path ahead was clear of any more obstructions, she stood again and loaded her crossbow.

Veronica fired at the next closest furadon, sending it toppling backward. I marveled at the huntress' accuracy and the efficiency of her weapon. A central gear whirred, simultaneously drawing back the string and rotating the next of three preloaded projectiles into the crossbow's rail. The weapon clicked. She fired again. She repeated this a few times, taking out three of the five creatures left in the chase before reaching into the quiver on her back to replenish her ammo.

It was astonishing how well Veronica was keeping her balance during the bumpy, jostling ride; I was having trouble staying seated. I continued to steer the massive, stampeding Boris, glancing back only occasionally to ensure everyone was okay and to see how many furadons were still after us.

Two of the vicious birds remained, leaping, missing, falling behind, and catching up to us again. Suddenly, a third one emerged from the forest and dashed out in front of us. Out of shock and terror, I let out a short yell. The monster was too close for me to steer away from, but Boris wasn't fazed at all. He ducked his head, aiming his horns at the bird, and upon impact with the creature, reared himself up, launching the furadon into the air. The bird squealed as it soared over us.

"What do ya know? These birds *can* fly!" Andy laughed.

Veronica nudged him with her foot. "Hand me that multiweapon."

He looked at her in confusion. She sighed and pointed to it. Andy picked up a short cylindrical handle and asked, "This?" Veronica nodded, and he gave it to her.

The huntress took a deep breath. "Hope this works."

With the click of a button, the handle extended into a long staff, and a spear sprouted from either end. She pressed another button and one of the spears shot out, revealing the chain it was attached to, and imbedded itself in an upcoming tree on the right side of the path. Veronica then fired the second chained spear into another tree on the left.

As Boris ran past the two speared trunks, Veronica released her grip on the handle. The multiweapon snapped into position between the two trees and acted like a tripwire, knocking the remaining furadons off their feet.

"Yeah!" Andy cheered, as Boris carried us away from the creatures. The fatigued furadons stood and shook away their aches, before abandoning the chase and hobbling into the forest.

We stayed atop Boris for a while as a precaution before backtracking so Veronica could retrieve her multiweapon. I released my death grip on the reins, awkwardly slid off of the saddle, and tiredly sat on the dirt against Boris' front right leg. I let out a long breath of relief and patted the side of the bovine's face.

"You did good," I panted.

Boris snorted.

Veronica leapt to the ground and Andy scrambled after her. "That was awesome!" he exulted.

"We almost got killed," Veronica stated as she walked toward her multiweapon. "I'd hate to see what your definition of *dangerous* is."

"But you! With your crossbow and that spear-shooting staff thing, you were amazing!"

A slight smile etched her face. "Thanks." She grabbed the handle of her multiweapon and retracted the two spears. She flipped the staff around and clicked the center button, transforming it back into the compact cylinder that she clipped to her belt.

She brushed a strand of hair from her eyes, which sparked at the sight of something just beyond the clearing. "Well what do you know? We're right where we need to be."

I looked up, past an opening in the trees, and voiced, "*Wow.*" Before us lay a gorgeous lake with clear, shimmering water that reflected the surrounding landscape like a mirror.

Beneath the surface of Alzo Lake, a small hexapoid narrowly escaped the hungry jaws of a giant salungrahl. A spray of ink clouded his path as his funnels released a jet of water to propel him away in the nick of time.

The salungrahl flailed through the haze of ink. His beady eyes scanned the waters for the hexapoid, and a trail of bubbles caught his attention. The amphibious predator's shovel-shaped cranium surfaced for a breath, before sinking back down to pursue his prey. The beast uttered a resonating growl and took off.

His bulky, yet streamlined body sliced through the water, forced forward by the strong swipes of his finned tail. Recognizable dark orange scales with reddish stripes sent all animals cowering at the sight of him, the apex predator of the lake.

Frenzied, the young hexapoid was nearing the edge of the lake. The roar of the Salungrahl reverberated around him. Running out of time, the cephalopod hatched a bold plan. He swept at the sand beneath him with his tentacles, forming a small depression in the ground. Another roar. Quickly, the hexapoid nestled his body in the hole, and buried himself. He waited, prepared to fight if necessary.

We joined Veronica as she knelt by the water's edge and filled up a canteen.

I asked her, "Shouldn't you filter that or something?"

She snapped the lid closed. "No need." She pointed toward some odd-looking plants at the bottom of the lake. "You see those plants?"

I nodded.

"Those are called *poriflora*, they naturally filter the water."

The vegetation was dark green with pores that sucked in water, swelling the leaves, before releasing the liquid and shriveling up. They looked like they were breathing.

Some small crustaceans used the plants as cover from the larger multicolored fish patrolling the depths. The water was so clear it looked like the glass wall of an aquarium. Only the slight ripples wrinkling the surface reminded me it was liquid.

"The water's so pure, you could drink straight from it if you wanted to," Veronica explained.

I glanced at her with suspicion, then cupped my hands and drank. The water was perfectly clean and refreshing as I gulped it down. I released a chilled breath and felt revitalized. "That's really good."

Andy tried some also. "Wow," he said. "It's so... *watery!*"

"I gotta have some more," I stated.

"Nope. One sip per person," Veronica said.

"Oh. Sorry I didn't—"

"Marvin, I'm joking. There's plenty."

I blinked. "Oh..."

Veronica chuckled lightly as she strolled over to Boris and placed her canteen into the basket on his back. Andy grinned at her, then laughed and whispered to me, *"I kinda like her."*

I nodded. "I noticed." I submerged my hands, deeper this time, for another drink. All of a sudden, a creature emerged from the sandy basin and latched onto my hand. *"Yow!"* I wailed as I tore my hand back.

A cephalopod with light blue skin, six coiling tentacles, and a tan cone-shaped shell clung tightly to the back of my hand and repeatedly bit me with a circular saw-like maw. The creature snarled, then stared up at me with big dark eyes, and abruptly stopped, becoming calm.

His tentacles tightened when a giant salamander-like monster the size of an alligator swam toward the edge of the lake. After a moment, the beast turned and thrashed back into the deeper waters. The cephalopod relaxed.

Veronica drew her crossbow. "Hold still!" she said. The frightened creature shrieked and scampered up to my shoulder.

"Don't shoot it!" I shouted, shielding the creature as he trembled and hid halfway in his shell, terrified from the commotion.

Veronica retracted the bow of her weapon and slid it into her quiver. "We've got to get that thing off of you," she protested.

The creature chirped happily and crawled up and down my arms and across my torso. I laughed as he moved about, his tentacles tickling me. "I like him," I said. "I've never had a pet."

"Yeah, he's cool!" Andy said. "Let's keep him!"

"He should be released," Veronica stated.

"*Awww!*" Andy and I groaned in unison.

"Put him back," Veronica instructed. We sighed, and I placed the creature back in the water. He stared up at me for a second, then swam away.

We turned back to Veronica. "Okay," I mumbled. "Let's get moving—"

FWAP! The creature leapt from the water and clasped onto the back of my head, knocking me forward in a heap. I stumbled to my feet, the animal chirruping and purring, refusing to let go.

"I think he likes me," I said.

"He *can't* come with us!" Veronica said.

"Oh, come on," Andy begged.

"Please?" I added.

The cephalopod chirped, as if pleading as well.

She glared the three of us, then groaned. "Fine."

"Yes!" we cheered.

Boris carried us down a dusty path, and the entrance of a village started to peek over the horizon.

"We're almost there," Veronica told us.

"Thank goodness," Andy stated.

I adjusted the new bandage protecting the bite mark on my hand, making sure it was tight enough, and checked the other one around my side.

"Sheesh, Marvin, you're a disaster," Andy joked. "First the furadon, then your new pet. Is it me, or are you like, an animal magnet?"

"Yeah, yeah," I muttered as I petted the cephalopod's spiraled shell.

He purred.

"I think I'll call him Scooter," I announced.

"Cool," said Andy.

"Wonderful," Veronica grumbled.

3
Alzo Village

"**W**e're here!" Veronica called.

Andy and I gripped the edge of the basket and took an inquisitive look around as we passed under a large archway and entered Alzo Village. The community was bustling with people, all buying or bartering for items from vendors in the market stands that lined the street. Animal-drawn vehicles passed us by as we navigated the crowds and ventured deeper into the village.

As we made our way through the town, the clamor of shouting villagers, desperate to purchase and sell the best items, subsided. I watched buildings scroll by and found myself intrigued by the fascinating architecture around us. The buildings were all made of sand-colored rock, and the craftsmanship was so fine, there were no visible brick seams anywhere.

A larger-than-life statue of a man made of smooth, dark brown stone suddenly caught my eye. The depicted individual was holding a compass and a rolled-up map. Armor covered most of his body, and a sheathed sword hung out to his side.

"What's that?" I asked, pointing to the sculpture.

Veronica glanced at it, then said, "That's a statue of Alzerus Rufroy. He founded a bunch of settlements in Ravac a long time ago, including this one."

Andy sighed, "Marvin, do you _have_ to bring history class with you? The field trip is the one day of the school year we don't have to do any legitimate work, and yet you can't seem to contain yourself."

"How can I with all these historical landmarks around me?" I asked, just to annoy him. He groaned and lay back down.

Far from the village I spotted an immense stone castle, its tall towers topped with dark green, cone-shaped roofs reaching for the clouds.

"What's that?" I asked, pointing to it.

Andy let out another audible groan.

"Empress Rholana's castle," Veronica said. "Greatest ruler Ravac has ever seen."

Boris stomped down the cobbled road and brought us to a residential area. The dwellings were all dome-shaped and constructed from the same sand-colored rock as the other buildings in the area.

"Where are we going again?" Andy asked.

"We're visiting a friend of mine. He's going to heal Marvin." Veronica gave the command for Boris to stop in front of one of the many houses in the vicinity. She dismounted her pet and tied his reins to a hitching post near the house. She lovingly patted his head and kissed his snout. "We'll be back." Boris snorted affectionately and nuzzled his nose against her face.

I joined Veronica on the ground and was about to ask how her friend was going to heal me, when I noticed someone watching us from across the road.

A nearby vendor was pushing a cart full of produce and scowling at us, his intense, grayish eyes studying our group. His upper lip curled and revealed that he was missing a few teeth. He wiped some sweat from his brow, but kept his angry expression. The thin man's skin seemed tanned from being out in the sun too long. For shade he donned the hood of his cream-colored garment, then drew a tool from a pocket of his dark brown vest and began wrathfully peeling a piece of fruit, while keeping his eyes locked on us.

"Hey, Andy," I murmured.

"Uh-huh?" Andy answered as he struggled out of the basket on Boris' back.

"That guy is looking at us."

Andy landed beside me, glanced at the man, then said, "Well what do you expect, Marv? You stick out like a sore thumb."

"Huh?"

"Yeah, you're wearing your fancy-schmancy, green collared shirt and everyone else is wearing more casual threads."

"Me?" I let out a short laugh. "Why would they be looking at me? If anyone, it's *you* who's attracting attention with your bright orange jacket."

"Well, it's *obvious* they recognize that I'm more *fashionably apt.*"

"Whatever," I said, as Andy chuckled.

"Come on, you two," Veronica called as she took a key from her pocket and unlocked the front door.

We stepped inside the tiny house. It was a quaint, one-story home with tan walls and an old wooden floor. Most of the rustic furniture was stacked with books and scrolls and coated with a thick layer of dust. A cool breeze flowed in from a nearby window, but quickly dissipated in the musty atmosphere.

"Where's this friend of yours?" Andy asked.

"He might be sleeping," Veronica whispered.

I touched my hand to my bandaged side. I winced at a dull soreness that burned in the wound. I took my hand away and the pain subsided.

Veronica noticed my achy expression and assured me, "He's an expert at this sort of thing."

We made our way into the main living area of the home to see an old man snoozing in a rocking chair. He had long, grayish white hair that extended just past his shoulders and an equally long mustache and beard that covered most of his chest. He wore a ragged brown robe and slippers. Like the house, the man's hair and clothes were unkempt and disheveled.

"Hi Murry!" Veronica beamed when she saw him.

The old man snapped out of his slumber. "Wha? Who's there?" he babbled. He turned around and saw us, as Veronica smiled and walked up to him. "Oh, Veronica! Good to see you," he greeted, as Veronica gave him a big hug. He caught sight of Andy and me and asked her, "Eh... who are those two?"

"That's Marvin and Andy," she said.

Andy and I waved at him.

"They lost or something?" Murry whispered.

"I guess. They keep saying they're from *Gloryfield*."

"I've never heard of it."

"Me neither, but Marvin got hurt in the forest and he needs your help."

"Alright, bring him here. I'll see what I can do."

Veronica returned to me. "Murry will fix you up, Marvin."

"C'mere, let's see what we got," Murry said, tapping a stool beside him.

Nervously, I walked toward him and took a seat. A loud squeak sounded as I shifted my weight on the old, straining stool.

"Wow, excuse yourself, Marvin," Andy had to say.

35

I glared at him with an unamused look, then turned back to Murry as he spoke, "I understand you were hurt in the forest."

"He got attacked by a giant turkey," Andy interjected.

Murry looked at him strangely. "Turkey?"

"He *means* furadon," Veronica corrected.

"Oh, *furadons*. Vicious creatures, those birds."

"Yeah." I lifted my shirt and showed him the bloody bandages. "It's wrapped up pretty well now. I'm not sure what else can be done, unless you have some antibiotics or something."

"*Tsk tsk tsk*, yep, that furadon did a number on you." Murry stood up and went to a drawer. "Go ahead and take off the bandages."

I looked back at Andy and Veronica. Andy shrugged, but Veronica motioned for me to go on.

"But it'll start bleeding again," I said to Murry, who was preoccupied rummaging for something.

He replied, "Don't worry, I'll be quick."

Confused, I unraveled the bloody fabric.

The three claw wounds stung as they met the air. Murry returned with a strange tool in his hand. I wondered how he planned to fix the gash with nothing more than a stick-shaped instrument.

But, as quickly as the question entered my mind, it was answered, when a ray of light blue energy flared from the tool and illuminated the wound. In an instant, new flesh had covered the once injured area, and all the pain had dissipated. I couldn't believe my eyes. I was healed. The tool he used was a wand.

"There we go. Good as new," Murry smiled.

Andy plodded toward me, brow furrowed, mouth agape. He stared at the mended wound, then at Murry. "How did you do that?!"

"He's a wizard," Veronica explained.

Murry huffed, "*Was* a wizard."

"*Is*," Veronica insisted.

Murry raised his hand to quiet her, then asked me, "You have another one?"

I snapped out of my shock long enough to say, "Yeah, uh, just this one from where Scooter bit me."

"Scooter?"

Scooter peeked out from behind my head and chirped.

"Oh, you've got yourself a hexapoid! Fascinating little creatures. Did you know they can live in or outside of water? I suppose they'd have to since they migrate from time to time."

Murry shook his head and laughed, "I'm sorry, I'm babbling. Let's see this cut."

I unwrapped the bite mark, and Murry healed it with the same spell. Blue light seeped through my flesh and flashed. As it dimmed, I moved my fingers and watched the skin regenerate.

"Wow," I stated. "Thank you!"

"Sure thing."

"This is impossible!" Andy said with a frown as he examined my hand.

Murry laughed, "You act like you've never seen magic before."

Andy looked really confused and distraught. "There's no way," he said. "There's no way you're a wizard."

The old man sighed, "Well don't worry 'cause I'm not... not anymore."

"Murry—" Veronica started.

"Veronica, please," he stopped her.

A tapping sound suddenly drew his attention.

"Excuse me a moment." He strolled to the other side of the room.

Andy continued studying my hand. He gawked at it from all angles and shook it side to side.

I yanked my hand away. "Cut it out."

Murry followed the tapping sound to a window. He opened it, and a large bird flew into his house. It touched down on the dining room table and cawed. The bird was about the size of an eagle and covered with white feathers, along with some blue ones patterning his chest and the tips of his wings and long tail. The bird's deep blue eyes were framed by a staunch brow of flaring, yellow wisps that extended past his face. That, along with a shallow crest of stiff feathers at the top of his head gave him a regal, powerful look. His blue beak opened and released another caw, exacting Murry's attention.

"Oh, Klype," Murry said, stepping toward the bird. "What've you got for me?" Murry unlatched a lightweight pouch harnessed to the bird's front and retrieved a rolled-up piece of paper. He unrolled the note and read it. He smiled. "Well, how about that? Shmileah's birthday is tomorrow. I should send him a gift."

"Maybe you could give it to him in person?" Veronica suggested.

The old man glanced at her momentarily, then muttered, "Yes, that would be nice."

Murry set the note down, then took a pinch of seed from a nearby bowl and held his hand out to the bird. "Thank you very much, Klype." Klype gobbled up the generous portion of seeds. The messenger bird cawed, then flew out the open window.

Andy and I realized that we had both been watching the peculiar bird. We looked at each other. Andy shook his head, and started rambling about the cut on my hand again.

"There's no way," he repeated.

"No way of what?" I asked.

"Your hand can't be healed like that. There's no way. It has to be some sort of an illusion."

"Illusion?"

"Yeah, you know with mirrors and stuff—no one can heal that fast. Maybe the skin is fake—"

"No Andy, it's real. I can *feel* it. It's *there*."

"Then how?" Andy whispered.

I stared past him for a moment, then felt myself say, "I don't know... It has to be magic."

Andy threw his hands up in the air. Infuriated, he cried, "Earth to Marvin! There's no such thing as—"

"Earth?" we heard Murry say.

Andy and I looked at him, then at each other, before Andy replied sarcastically, "Yeah, Earth—the blue planet, third from the sun—ever heard of it?"

Murry held a blank stare at the wall, before finally responding, "Yes." He gazed at both of us, eyes glittering, then asked, "How *exactly* did you two get here?"

Murry gave us food and tea, as we all gathered around a dining table and Andy and I tried to recount what had happened.

"It was strange," I explained. "One minute we were in the Artifact Room, and the next we weren't."

We took a brief intermission to snack on the delicious morsels Murry had provided. I hadn't realized how hungry I was until I started chowing down. I bit deeply into a flaky roll topped with a creamy, fishy spread. I asked Murry what the topping was made of, and he said it was *freshwater crimfish* with some *gualov* zest. I finished the roll and took a sip of the refreshing, neutral-tasting tea to wash it down. Scooter was given a pile of berries and some bread. He finished his meal in no time and chirped gleefully before crawling back up to my shoulder.

We gave Murry compliments on the food and thanked him after we finished.

"I'm glad you enjoyed it," he said. "Now, tell me more about how you got here."

We told him everything, or at least we tried to. The details of what happened between finding the Artifact Room and finding ourselves lost in a forest were hazy. It was like trying to recollect the minutia of a dream. We did our best.

"What color was this artifact?" Murry asked.

Andy frowned as he tried to remember. "It's sorta between burgundy and purple..." he thought allowed. "It's..." He snapped his fingers. "It's burgurple!"

"Tyrian purple," I said, "and it was on a silver stand."

Murry stroked his beard and took a sip from his cup of tea. Veronica, Andy, and I sat at the edge of our seats waiting for him to say something.

"I don't believe it," he finally spoke. "You've found it."

"Found what?" Andy asked.

"The Orb," Murry replied. "The Orb is the most powerful relic in our known universe. It holds the power to travel between the Realms."

"What do you mean, *Realms*?" I asked.

"There are more worlds in existence than simply what you can *see*, Marvin. This universe is but one of many, in a limitless multiverse. The Orb allows its user the ability to travel between our world and the world of another universe. *Your* universe."

"But... how?" Andy questioned.

Murry told him, "The Orb is constructed from five crystals, each of which grows on a different continent of the globe. The gems inherit unique qualities from the elements that surround them." Murry retrieved five seeds from the bowl he fed the messenger bird with and placed them on the table. "Let's say these seeds are the crystals that make up the Orb." He held up two of them. "Perhaps *this* crystal forms on Veindai, obtaining electrical properties since it grows at high altitudes in the midst of thunderstorms. And *this* crystal forms on Frost, obtaining the property of ice since it grows in freezing temperatures." Murry placed the two seeds side-by-side. "Now, as the crystals come in contact with each other and are exposed to each other's elemental power, they once again begin to inherit the qualities of the elements around them." Murry hopped the two seeds over one another a few times. "So the crystals are constantly switching attributes." Murry gathered the remaining seeds into a pile. "Add more crystals to the mix..." He switched all the seeds around a few times. "And we have a never ending cycle of power-swapping."

Murry looked at us, waiting for a response, but we were speechless. He continued, "It is said that upon the Orb's creation long ago, it emitted a blast of invisible energy so fierce, it rattled the stars. Then, it disappeared. Your world is very similar to ours; it is comprised of all the same elements. That is why the Orb appeared there. Our worlds are simply different *versions* of each other, and the Orb is a bridge between the two. Your version is known as Earth, ours is known as Enkartai."

Andy and I sat there, soaking up the information. As crazy and unbelievable as it was, I actually started to understand it.

"Does that make sense?" Murry asked.

"No," said Andy.

"A little," I said. "But I don't understand how it can... you know, *teleport* us."

Murry turned around and found two more objects for his demonstration, a gold coin and a button. "Alright," he said. "This coin and this button are you and Andy."

"Ooh ooh!" Andy raised his hand. "I want to be the coin!"

Veronica rolled her eyes.

"Very well," Murry said. He looked up at us. "I assume you touched the Orb, yes?"

Andy and I nodded.

"You see, when you come into contact this..." Murry searched for the right words, "this amalgam of elements... it distinguishes *you* as an element as well, and you become a part of it." He switched all the pieces of the model around a few times before continuing, "After that, a portal opens, connecting your world and ours. And here you are."

"That's incredible," I said.

"No, it's not!" Andy snapped.

"What do you mean?"

"Well for starters, how do we get home?"

My heart skipped a beat. "Oh shoot, your right," I said, turning to Murry. "How *do* we get home?"

Murry's eyes were wide, and he took a deep breath before he spoke. "Did you—" His voice rasped. He cleared his throat and started again, "Did you manage to hold on to the Orb as it transported you?"

We shook our heads.

There was a long pause. "Ah," the old man finally said in a distressed tone. "That is unfortunate."

"What?" Andy shot out of his chair. "What's unfortunate?"

"Well, without the Orb," Murry started.

"Yeah?"

"...I'm afraid there's no way of returning you home."

A deathly silence fell on the house. Veronica's blue eyes filled with dread as they darted between Andy and me. We were both frozen, petrified. I couldn't even bring myself to think I was so shocked. The brief moment felt like an eternity, but was finally disrupted as Andy exclaimed, "That's just *great*! A few weeks away from the last day of school, and I get teleported to another dimension!"

"Universe," Murry corrected.

"Whatever!" Andy barked. "Just my luck. I have to start my summer trapped in another world."

"Actually, the summer just ended here," Veronica said.

Andy let out a long growl and buried his head in his hands. "Not helping!" He stood up and started pacing across the room. "I don't believe this!"

I stood up to catch him. "Calm down."

"Calm down?" Andy uttered. "Are you insane?" His wild, light blue eyes locked with mine, as he struggled to contain his hysteria and tell me, "Dude, we are stranded. No one knows where we are... and I'm pretty sure our cell phones won't get reception in an alternate universe."

41

I searched my mind for answers—possible solutions to our dilemma, but all I came across were unnerving thoughts. I didn't know what else to say, so I just forced out the words, "There's always a way out."

"And what might that be, Marvin?" Andy asked, still hysteric. "*Ooh*, wait, I know, don't tell me..." He scooped up the five seeds from the table. "Maybe that messenger bird will deliver the Orb to us in exchange for these seeds."

Murry's eyes glinted. "You may be on to something."

Andy looked at him strangely.

Murry clarified, "Not about the bird, but about the seeds—the five crystals." He brushed a strand of gray hair out of his eyes. "We could build another Orb," he stated. "It has happened once before."

Andy took his seat again and we all scooted in closer to listen to Murry's story:

"His name was Areok. He's the one who first discovered the Orb back in your world and arrived here."

"How did he get back?" I asked.

"He traveled across all of Enkartai and collected a crystal from each continent," Murry said. "He was quite an inspiration. Wherever he went, he bettered the lives of those who needed help. In fact, he's the one who led the resistance against Shamaul and helped contain him in the Dark Lands."

"Who's Shamaul?" I asked.

Murry let out a long sigh.

"You don't have to tell them," Veronica said.

"No, they should know," Murry stated. He shut his eyes and inhaled deeply before he began. "He's a warlock. His real name was Mahlgrador Marko," he recounted. "He was once a great wizard, very skilled with magic. He knew every spell there was, but it wasn't enough for him. He wanted to know more. He became greedy and started studying the dark arts, trying to learn all aspects of the world and how to control them." Tears started to well in Murry's eyes. "He found these books... and then he... he..." Murry's face paled and twisted in sadness as tears streamed down his cheeks. He struggled to choke out the rest of the story, "He... oh, he had such promise!" He beat his fist against the table and broke down and wept.

Veronica patted his back. "You don't have to say any more."

The old man sniffed, "I'm sorry," as he dried his eyes with his sleeve. "Let's just say Mahlgrador learned some things he shouldn't have that day. His knowledge alone killed him." Murry took a breath, then continued in a shaky voice, "He died, but that wasn't the end of his life. He was resurrected by another wizard, who, at the time, was unaware of the horrible evil that had corrupted him. Mahlgrador Marko rose from the dead and unleashed an age of destruction and chaos. From then on, he called himself Shamaul.

"After Ravacan forces finally drove him away, he went on to raze a different continent. No one even remembers its name; it was warped into a place of unspeakable horror, populated by Shamual's monstrous horde, and became known simply as the Dark Lands."

Murry blinked his tired eyes and gazed out the window. "It wasn't until Areok came and imprisoned him there, that people could breathe easy again," he concluded in a whisper. "The wizard who resurrected him was hated for what he had done." The old man looked at us all, as his eyes began to well again. "That wizard was me. Mahlgrador Marko is my son."

Andy and I exchanged stunned expressions, as Murry cradled his head in his hands and sobbed, "It was all my fault; I shouldn't have done it."

"You didn't know," Veronica said.

"I knew the Spellcaster's Code," Murry replied. "Raising the dead is taboo."

"But Murry—"

"The Code's the Code, and there's no way around it. It's right there on the wall."

He pointed to a framed document behind Andy and me. I stood up and went to read it:

I, the spellcaster, vow to use the powers I have obtained nobly, for the betterment of life. I pledge on my honor and title as a spellcaster that I will never perform the following actions: I will not use magic to harm the innocent, I will not use magic to steal, I will not use magic to raise the dead...

The list went on and on. I read through it and eventually came to the last line:

I will not use magic to perform these, or any other actions out of spite.

I pondered the Code, and read it over once more.

"You're the greatest wizard in Ravac," I heard Veronica say to Murry. "In all of Enkartai even."

"I cannot call myself a wizard," Murry protested. "I broke the Spellcaster's Code."

I examined the document further, analyzing every word, and felt myself say, "No you didn't."

Murry lifted his head and stared up at me from across the room. "What are you talking about?" he questioned.

"The Code contradicts itself," I explained as I pointed to one of the lines. "Here it says, 'I will not use magic to raise the dead.'" I slid my finger down to the final line. "And here it says, 'I will not use magic to perform these, or any other actions out of *spite*.'" I turned to Murry. "You didn't bring Mahlgrador back to life out of spite. It sounds to me like you brought him back out of love. He was your son. You were afraid and you missed him."

Murry was silent for a while. He sat there, deep in thought for a long time. He shook his head, having not come to any conclusion, and spoke, "I... I don't know." The old man stood, stretched, then wandered into another room. "I don't know," he repeated.

Veronica, Andy, and I joined in the middle of the kitchen.

"That was nice of you," Veronica said to me.

I shrugged. "That's just what it says in the Code."

"It was still nice."

Andy admitted, "I'm still kinda in shock about this whole thing."

"Yeah," Veronica agreed. "It's not every day you stumble across a couple of guys from another universe lost in a forest."

"Being attacked by those homicidal furadons," I added.

"I still think we could'a taken 'em," Andy joked.

"Sure you could've," Veronica said.

"They're just lucky I was in a good mood today." Andy dramatically flexed his arms and Veronica covered her mouth to hold back a laugh.

Our conversation halted as Murry stepped back into the kitchen wearing a violet, hooded cloak. Veronica's face lit up. "I haven't seen you wear that in a while!"

The wizard smiled. "I know." He tugged at the rope belt around his waist, but his round belly prevented it from tightening any further. "I guess I've put on a few pounds since the last time I wore this." He chuckled lightheartedly.

Murry gathered some supplies into an old rucksack: a small book, a sack of coins, a bag of dried food, and several other items. He slung the rucksack over his back, then found his wand and tucked it in his cloak's pocket.

"What's going on?" Veronica inquired.

"I'm going to get these two home, that's what," Murry replied.

Veronica's eyes brightened, and an excited smile spread across her face. "We get to travel around the world?"

"This is a mission, not a trip. And I'm afraid I can't bring you without your father's permission."

"What? If it wasn't for me, these two would be in a furadon's gut right now!"

"Veronica, I can't just take you on a long—and possibly dangerous journey without your father's consent."

Veronica let out a growl. "I *can't* get his permission. He's up in Alistaan training the troops, you know that!"

"I'm sorry Veronica—"

"Murry please! I've always wanted to travel; I've never been out of Ravac. Besides, if my dad trusts me enough to stay in the village by myself while he's gone, then he *must* trust me enough to make my own decisions."

"Your reasoning's a little far-fetched."

"Murry, I think of you as a parent. Would *you* let me to go?"

Murry's expression softened. "You know I would, but I'm not your parent. Unless you can get your father's permission—"

"I'll send him a letter! That way he'll know."

"I'm not sure..."

"It's fine, trust me. And there's no way I'm leaving you with these two. Especially Andy."

"Hey!" Andy interjected.

"C'mon Murry, please?" Veronica folded her hands and blinked her twinkling, pleading, blue eyes.

Murry resisted her heartbreaking stare for as long as he could, but he eventually caved. "Oh, alright!"

"Yes!" Veronica exulted, wrapping her arms around him.

"But you better write your dad a letter, *at least*!"

Veronica agreed, "I will, I promise. Plus, now that I'm coming, Boris can carry us anywhere we need to go! It'll cut our travel time in half!"

"*Or multiply it by two*," Andy whispered to me.

Veronica punched him in the arm.

"Ow!"

"Settle down now," Murry said. "We have a long journey ahead of us. Does everyone have their things?"

Veronica secured the quiver around her back. "Ready!"

I retrieved my book bag and echoed her. "Ready."

Andy raised his hands. "Hold on a sec." We turned to him as he spoke. "Lemme get this straight. We're gonna go to *every* continent?"

"Essentially," Murry answered.

"So we're travelling around the *entire* world?"

Murry pondered his statement for a moment, then nodded. "Essentially."

Andy groaned, "I *really* regret leaving my videogame on the bus."

4
The Journey Begins

"**E**veryone set?" Murry asked us.

We started to nod, when shouts from outside drew our attention.

"What's going on?" Andy asked.

Murry listened to the racket for a moment. He shook his head, confused, then took a small, silver rock from a shelf and gazed into it. I was surprised to see an image moving beneath the sphere's sleek surface.

"What is that?" I asked him.

He raised an eyebrow at me, as if the answer to my question was common knowledge, then remembered I wasn't from Enkartai and explained, "Oh, well this here is an *optirock*. There's another one above my door. I can look through this one, and see what's happening in front of the other."

A smile spread across his face as he noticed the wonderment in my eyes. I was intrigued to learn as much as I could about his world, and he seemed delighted to teach me.

Murry took another glance at the optirock, then balked. "Ooh, quick! Everyone down!"

We stooped to avoid a round fruit that burst through Murry's half-open window and splattered against the wall. A voice from outside yelled, "Shadowlover!" as another fruit soared into the house and smashed onto the floor.

"What the heck was that?!" Andy screamed.

"It's Kip the fruit vendor," Murry sighed. "He throws things at my house from time to time."

"What? Why?" I asked.

"Because," said Murry, "he blames me for Shamaul's reign of terror long ago."

"But that wasn't your fault."

"Tell that to Kip," Veronica grumbled as she stood in the window.

I peeked over her shoulder and saw it was the same person who was watching us when we first arrived in the village.

"Shadowlover!" he shouted again. Veronica scowled at him, then slammed the shutters closed before the next fruit hit.

"We should get moving before he starts throwing melons," Andy suggested.

Boris was dining on a pile of hay near the hitching post to which his reins were looped. He took a break from his snack and looked our way, as we all snuck outside. Murry came out last, trying to shield his face with his purple hood, as we headed for Boris.

"Shadowlovers!" Kip stopped us in our tracks. We rotated to face him, his features contorted in hate, silvery eyes aglint and gap-toothed mouth spitting: "Marko! Hidin' as usual. Ya tink I can't tell who y'are? And whadda ya tink yer doin' wearin' bright robes like dat? Y'ain't got the right! Ya goodfernothin' shadowlover!"

"Pay no attention to him," Murry whispered. "Let's just go."

We tossed our stuff into the basket on Boris' back, ignoring the rambles of the enraged vendor: "How dare ya show yer face out here? Yer a disgrace! A fiend! Why don't ya just go live in the Dark Lands wit dat wretched son o' yers ya loved so much? Ya certainly loved him 'nough to plunge the rest o' the world into chaos!"

Veronica's face twisted in rage as she stopped packing and approached the fruit salesman.

"Veronica wait—" Murry tried to stop her.

She stood before the vendor and glowered menacingly at him.

"What?" Kip questioned. "Yer defendin' dat old shadowlovin' fool?"

Veronica drew her crossbow and answered, "I'm *telling* you to stop yelling at my friend!"

"Veronica!" Murry gasped, as the huntress gripped her weapon.

Kip's eyes grew wide and his body stiffened. "Ya shouldn't be carryin' dat ting around, girl. The Empress don't approve o' dat!"

"I *have* my hunting license. I can carry this anywhere I please," Veronica retorted. "And I'm sure my friends would back me up if I had a *misfire*."

"*Veronica!*" Murry roared.

"You see?!" Kip hollered into the air, trying to attract attention. "The shadowlovers are takin' over!"

"Put that away this instant!" Murry demanded.

"Listen to the shadowlover, girl," Kip sneered. "Respect your elders!"

Veronica frowned and resentfully holstered her crossbow. "You should follow your own advice."

Murry ran a shaky, distressed hand through his hair and took a breath of relief, as Veronica marched back to us. As soon as she was a good distance away, Kip began yelling again, calling us all shadowlovers. Veronica struggled to contain her anger as she rejoined the group.

I looked to the left of me, expecting Andy to comment on the situation, but noticed that he was gone. My eyes darted around the area and I suddenly spotted him, sneaking up behind the shouting fruit vendor.

"Oh no," I murmured, as Andy appeared directly behind the man's cart of fruit.

Veronica and Murry traced my anxious gaze, and watched, as Andy placed his foot on the cart.

"Shadowlovers!" Kip exclaimed. "Yer all shadow—"

WHAM!

The cart tipped over. Fruits scattered everywhere and rolled across the dusty ground. Kip's jaw dropped as he knelt to gather his produce.

"Run," Andy advised as he jogged past us and clambered into the basket on Boris' back.

Murry, Veronica, and I exchanged stunned glances, before a large fruit splattered near our feet and sent us fleeing.

"Shadowlovers!" Kip screamed at the top of his lungs, as we took off atop Boris and evaded another barrage of fruit. "*Sha-dow-lo-vers!*"

Boris stomped down the road, swiftly carrying us out of Kip's line of fire.

"I had to do something," Andy explained.

"Did you see the look on his face?" Veronica laughed.

Murry held a reprimanding glare on both of them. "You both should practice a bit more restraint," he recommended.

"I did practice restraint," said Andy. "I practiced how the fruit was restrained to the cart." He shrugged. "Apparently it wasn't."

He and Veronica shared another laugh. I almost did too, but I fought the urge away when I caught sight of the disapproval in Murry's face. He wasn't angry with them, but he definitely wasn't pleased. The wizard shut his eyes and shook his head, forgetting the situation.

Veronica briefly stopped by her home, saying she wanted to pick up some extra clothes and supplies for the journey.

"Girls and their clothes," Andy commented to me. "*Uff!*" he grunted as a huge sack of supplies knocked him flat, and Veronica climbed back into the saddle and smiled.

We turned a corner, riding out of the residential district and back into the marketplace.

"You can stop right here," Murry said.

"Huh?" Veronica voiced. She noticed we were nearing a tent with three messenger birds resting on their perches in the shade. A sign atop the tent read, *Aviary Message Delivery.*

Murry stared at Veronica until she remembered she had to send her father a letter.

"Oh," she finally responded, "right."

We dismounted our ride and stepped under the tent. I remembered the white-and-blue messenger bird from earlier, Klype. His name was written on a sign that hung below his designated perch. The same went for his two counterparts. Next to Klype, a bird with mostly red feathers, some black, and a black beak was named Rynn. Beside Rynn was an all-black feathered bird with a bright yellow beak named Jupree.

Klype cawed at us, alerting someone to the front of the tent.

"Coming!" we heard her call. A lean woman ducked under a flap and appeared behind a table. Her clothing was baggy on her thin body: a dusty T-shirt, suspenders stretched over her shoulders that held up her pants, a pair of old boots, and a pair of padded, bird handling gloves that covered her forearms. She had frizzy, gray hair that was kept out of her face by a bandana, and huge, dark goggles that covered her eyes. She moved her oversized eyewear to her forehead, and an enormous grin spread across her face.

"Murry!" she said, hugging him. "Haven't seen you out here in a long while. How are ya?"

"Doing just fine, Deedee. And yourself?"

"Great! The birds have been getting quite a workout today too. Lots of mail to deliver." She scratched the birds' heads and spoke in a loving tone, "Isn't that right? It's been a busy day, yes it has." She returned to Murry. "So what brings ya this way? Got something to send?"

"This one does," Murry said as he moved aside, and Veronica stepped forward. She had been hastily scribbling something down that whole time. She rolled up her letter and handed it to the woman.

Deedee took the paper and placed her goggles back over her eyes.

"Where's this heading?" she asked.

Veronica told her, "To Cliff Blaire, in Alistaan." Veronica looked over at Murry, then added, "And I'd like it to get there as quickly as possible, please."

"Well alright," said Deedee. "I'll send Rynn, he's the fastest."

Rynn hopped onto Deedee's gloved forearm, and the handler slid Veronica's note in his tube-shaped carrying pouch. Rynn's eyes shut. Deedee whispered instructions to him, and his fiery eyes shot back open. A powerful gust of wind rattled us, as Rynn's wings flapped and carried him skyward, disappearing against the gleam of the falling sun.

Deedee let out a laugh and held on to her fluttering bandana as the current hit her. "Magnificent creatures."

We said our goodbyes and climbed back atop Boris. Andy sat in the front of the basket this time, closer to Veronica's saddle. He started a conversation, "So, you think your parents will be alright with you going with us?"

Veronica glanced at him, then back to the road. "Parent," she corrected.

Taken aback, Andy replied, "Oh... I'm sorry—"

"It's alright," Veronica said quickly. "My mom passed away giving birth to... who would've been my little brother. He didn't make it either."

"I'm really sorry."

"It's fine. It happened a long time ago."

Veronica refrained from making eye contact, or any expression, and focused intently on steering us down the road. A tense silence fell on us. Andy glanced at me, his worried eyes displaying his discomfort. Veronica was rigid, making no movement unless it involved adjusting Boris' reins to turn a corner.

I moved closer to her, and said, "I know what it's like."

She looked at me.

"My dad was a soldier. He died fighting in a war when I was very young."

Veronica's glistening eyes linked with mine. Her lips parted, trying to craft words. She turned her head away and let her hair fall in front of her face.

I talked while she gathered herself, "These were his." I opened a compartment of my backpack and showed her my dad's dog tags. "He wore them in battle. I feel like, I can sense him when I hold on to them. So he's always with me." I moved one of the metal tags with my thumb, letting the sunlight reflect off the letters of his name. Samuel T. Wessel.

My eyes moistened, and I shut them to quench the tears. I felt a hand grip my shoulder, and my eyes reopened to see Veronica. She took a shuddering breath, then spoke, "Your father died a hero."

I nodded, and told her, "So did your mom."

An uneasy smile formed on her face. "I know."

The road narrowed as we grew closer to the exit of the village, and the clamor of shouting street vendors slowly returned. There was a brief pause when the merchants first saw us, then a deafening uproar as they held up their merchandise and demanded our attention.

Veronica groaned, "This is my least favorite part of town."

The one-way road was framed by shacks, carts, and tents of rowdy merchants trying to sell their goods. The entire street was one giant bazaar. We tried to stay calm as we passed by the salespeople, each of them pitching their products:

"You there, with the beard, you look like you need some delicious guallovs. Only three siv!"

"I have plenty, thank you," Murry replied.

Another one called, "Young lady! I see you have a crossbow. These arrows are the highest quality, handcrafted—"

"I make my own," Veronica said.

A merchant said to me, "Hey, you look smart. I bet you need one of these!" He held up a simplistic wooden cube with rows of tabs that could be slid side-to-side.

"What is it?"

"Well it's a counting box o' course! That'll run ya just five siv!"

"Uh, no thanks."

"Four siv!"

"He isn't interested," Veronica interjected.

Another salesperson called to Andy, "Hey kid."

"Huh?" Andy turned to him.

A stout, reptilian humanoid with markings inked across his red-scaled body held up a needle. "You look like you're going on an adventure. Y'know what the perfect thing is to document your voyage? A tattoo! Whaddaya say?"

"Sure!"

"Andy, no!" Veronica scolded.

We were nearing the exit of the village when I noticed Murry sniffing the air. "Veronica, stop here," he said.

We slowed to a halt, and suddenly became aware of a decadent aroma fuming from a fresh batch of pies. A tiny, kind-looking old woman with snowy white hair rolled up in a bun was seated on a stool. She wasn't yelling or demanding attention. She just sat there, grinning gently at us.

Murry asked her, "Excuse me ma'am, what type of pies are these?"

"Mouryll pie," she answered in a rickety voice.

Murry smiled. "That's my friend's favorite. How much?"

"One siv."

"I'll take one."

The lady handed him a pie and Murry gave her two coins.

She looked at them and said, "You gave me an extra."

"I know," said Murry. "You keep it."

She grinned and waved at us as we left.

Stone roads became forested paths, and our journey began. The sun was nestling in the west, only delivering traces of light through the gaps in the trees. The sky was swathed in thick clouds, hued red by the sunset, with the silhouettes of massive winged creatures gliding overhead. I used my backpack as a pillow, watching the sky slowly darken as time went by.

We went quiet as the night came alive. Nocturnal animal calls resonated around us.

How is this possible? a worried thought suddenly crept into my mind. *How are we going to travel around the entire world?*

I forced the thought away and instead distracted myself with the unfamiliar animal sounds, trying to guess what type of creatures could make them.

Distinct bird calls echoed in the distance, followed by screeches, grunts, and hollers that could've belonged to any number of beasts. Next, a buzzing noise. Definitely a flying insect. And it sounded close. I followed the noise to a giant, ugly bug that had landed on the rim of the basket, staring at me with its huge, red, fragmented eyes.

I shooed it away and it zipped over to a tree trunk, tilting its head side-to-side and watching me still. The creature resembled an oversized fly, except its mouth was a sharp beak with two thin, curved fangs.

I lost interest in the unusual animal when I saw Murry studying the sky. He declared, "I've misjudged the time. I thought we'd be able to make it to the shore before nightfall." He observed the sky further, then announced, "We'll have to make camp here."

Veronica guided Boris to a stop, and we climbed out.

Andy didn't look too thrilled. He blankly watched Veronica and Murry pass in front of him, carrying supplies from the basket to the site. "Camp?" he uttered.

"That's right," Murry replied.

"*Camp?*" Andy repeated.

"Quit whining and set up a tent," Veronica ordered.

Andy groaned and got to work.

As Murry gathered firewood, I helped Andy construct one of the shelters. We set the last component of the tent in place, then stepped back to observe our handiwork.

"I think we did it wrong," I admitted.

The tent was all bent up and sloping down on one side. Andy took another step backward and found that his pant leg was caught in a string. He pulled himself free, and the entire structure collapsed.

Andy grumbled, "Even in a different universe these things are impossible to set up."

Murry noticed we were having trouble, so he shot a spell at the demolished abode. Within seconds, the pieces levitated and moved into their correct positions, and the tent constructed itself.

"Why didn't you do that in the first place?" Andy questioned.

Murry shrugged, "I couldn't leave you two with nothing to do." He finished aligning the sticks of his fire bundle into a teepee shape, then pointed his wand at it. "*Inferna*," he whispered. A red beam surged from the wand and ignited the wood.

Andy clapped his hands together. "Alright," he said. "Let's get out the rest of the tents."

"They're all out already," Murry responded.

"Wait a sec, you don't mean we're *all* sleeping in that tiny thing."

"No, of course not."

"Oh, okay good."

"Veronica brought her own tent."

Andy and I glanced over at Veronica and her enormous shelter. It was twice as big as ours, and even appeared to have mesh vents that could be opened or covered depending on temperature. Veronica smiled devilishly and waved at us with her fingers, before putting the finishing touches on her *mansion* of a tent.

Andy stammered, "But... but..."

"What's the matter?" Murry asked.

"We have more people! Shouldn't we get the huge tent?"

"No, no, that's hers. She wouldn't want three smelly guys and a hexapoid stinking up her tent."

Scooter chirped.

Andy took a deep breath through his nostrils and held it. He pushed his fingers through his hair, strolled away, and let out an agitated growl.

I asked Murry, "Is there some sort of spell that can make the tent bigger?"

"Oh, sure," he answered.

Andy dashed back to Murry. "Perfect! Do that!"

Murry shook his head and raised his hand. "Oh, no no no—"

"Why not?!" Andy wailed.

"This tent is already very fragile," Murry explained. "The spell will give it size, but in turn become even weaker. The slightest breeze would disintegrate it." He noticed our apprehensiveness and assured us, "It's not that bad."

Almost immediately, Murry fell asleep and started snoring. Andy covered his ears and rolled over, trying to block out the racket. With his cushion wrapped around the back of his head, he rotated to look at me from the other side of Murry. I started to shrug, when a loud *clunk* outside caught our attention. Andy and I glanced at each other, then crawled out of the tent to see Veronica sitting by the fire and dropping another log into it.

We stepped outside to join her. She stared, unblinking into the flame, the orange glow flickering against her still features as she took a bite from a piece of fruit.

Andy appeared on her left. Her eyes lifted toward him, then returned to the fire. He sat beside her.

"Why're you up?"

She looked at him skeptically, then took another bite of fruit. "Thinking."

"About what?"

"Just thinking."

Andy's brow furrowed. "You're thinking... *about* thinking?"

Veronica blinked. "What? No. I'm just thinking."

Andy seemed dissatisfied with the answer. "You're just thinking."

"Yeah, that's right."

"About nothing in particular."

"About a lot of things."

We sat in silence for a brief period, before Andy rejoined, "It's late. Why can't you 'just think' in the morning?"

"Gee, I wonder why."

We all smiled, and Veronica tossed us each a piece of fruit. We lounged, watching the fire. My eyes followed a couple embers that popped upward and caught a breeze, spiraling into Enkartai's night sky.

My gaze fixed on the firmament. I had never witnessed an array of clearer stars before. They were incredible, like a thousand glimmering gems against a pitch-dark blanket. I switched from a sitting position to a laying one and rested my head on my hands.

When I was young, I used to stare up at the stars with my dad. I remembered how they always made me feel small, just one tiny speck in the vast universe. Once I learned there was more than *one* universe, that feeling returned, amplified. The worried thoughts cluttered my mind again. I tried to keep occupied by looking for constellations, but I instantly realized that there weren't any—not any that I knew anyway. The unfamiliar stars peered down at me, like I was a microbe under a microscope. All the curious eyes blinked as they clustered around the viewing lens, eager to catch a glimpse at me and see how I'd adapt to my new environment.

There I was, one tiny speck in a new universe invisible to my own. To get back, Andy and I would have to embark on an impossible quest around the world. A loud sound jarred my thoughts.

Andy let out a long, reverberating belch, then raised his hands in triumph. Veronica's face curled in disgust. She shoved him and he laughed.

I smiled. At least I was in good company.

A creature crawled out from his hiding place behind a tree limb. His head cocked to the side, and bulging eyes blinked, observing that the travelers had entered their shelters and fallen asleep. His beak released a chattering sound, as he cocked his head again, then unfolded his wings and flew.

The furious beating of his wings carried him rapidly through the sky. A hungry growl gurgled from his abdomen. He groaned and flapped harder, averting his awareness to the ache in his joints. A creature like himself was not accustomed to flying such long distances with so little to eat.

He was a vermic, a fowl-smelling insectoid avian from a species of detritivores, used to gorging themselves on decaying animal tissue.

This was a different kind of vermic however. Dark magic coursed through him, making him more aware and responsive, sentient. Another hungry growl. The vermic snarled and muttered something angrily, flying faster and faster.

Food is near, he told himself. *Complete the task.*

While many cultures often associate the vermic with cunning and trickery, this one was outwitted himself, and plunged into a difficult mission.

The scent of saltwater stung the creature's nostrils and sickened his empty stomach. Not until wave water sprinkled on his underbelly did the vermic realize he was losing altitude, and falling dangerously close to the wicked currents of the Jaiveh Ocean. The vermic's beak let out a frantic chatter, and his sore, tattered membranes fluttered, struggling to climb higher.

Exhausted, the little animal's body hung limply beneath his wings, which beat sluggishly, barely enough to keep him from plummeting into the ocean. He was falling asleep as he flew, he had forgotten how long he was flying, and was questioning to where, and why? He was losing his grip on direction, time, and reason, but the dark spell took care of that; it carried him onward like instinct.

Food there... the spell convinced him. *Only there.*

The air felt thicker. It clogged in his lungsacks and weighed him down. His vision hazed. He shook his head wearily and blinked several times. He was inches from the water: dark, murky liquid laced with infectious pathogens and encased in dead algae, unable to thrive in the nauseating air. A sudden breeze delivered its revolting scent to the creature's nostrils. Damp, sour fumes flowed in, coated his throat, and lingered there, growing increasingly fowl as it festered. The stench was enough to make the vermic, an animal known for its awful odor, cough.

Though putrid, the air was somehow familiar. The vermic raised his head to the sound of crashing waves. The seemingly endless Jaiveh Ocean came to a vicious halt against a shoreline of jagged rocks. An immense stone wall appeared before the vermic's red, fragmented eyes.

The destination, something hissed.

The Dark Lands, he realized.

He snapped back to reality. He remembered everything. But he had to hurry. His master beckoned him.

The pain in his wings numbed as he took on the most grueling part of his flight, a sharp ninety-degree ascent to scale the towering Dark Lands barrier. The vermic was not from that continent, so the spell that contained the beasts inside did not affect him. The magic manifested in a dome of dark energy that flowed up the barrier and encased the entirety of the land.

The vermic felt a chill run through him as he passed through the dome. There the night sky became blacker, unnaturally dark, and the stars disappeared behind a thick, smoky quilt of clouds. His antennae twitched at unfamiliar howls and cries. Another bellowing groan startled him briefly, before he distinguished it as that of his own stomach. The vermic chattered, then accelerated into the night, veering around a twisted maze of branches and trunks. As the tired creature zipped through the dead forest, the keen eyes of terrorwolves shined from their lairs. The vermic's dry throat swallowed. The route he had selected was the fastest, but also the most deadly.

Emaciated gargoyles circled in the skies above, eager for a potential meal such as himself pass by. The vermic focused on keeping his body above the dangers of the ground, but below the dangers of the sky. As he flew, bricks became visible beyond the wiry web of branches. He burst through them and flew at the structure. Several screeches from above made him quicken the beat of his wings and slip through a small fissure in the building's façade.

The tiny animal shuddered in the castle's frigid air, then scaled the spiraling staircase to the highest point. His heart throbbed, as a horrifying rhythm resonated all around. It echoed off the walls, penetrated his body, and rattled his insides. The vermic uttered a shrill squeal, before clearing the top of the staircase and passing beneath an archway.

A set of long, armored fingers drummed against the stone arm of a throne, and sent a chilling echo throughout the castle. The vermic landed before the ruler, and the drumming ceased.

The vermic fretfully rubbed his front legs together as he faced him. The Dark Warlock was draped in tattered, black robes over black armor. A hood concealed his head while allowing his twisted horns to sprout through a pair of crude openings, and an eerie, silver mask hid the rest of his countenance, except for his eyes. His eyes were those of a serpent. Piercing yellow with wriggling radial fibers and slit pupils.

Singed, scaly skin was visible through the large eyeholes of the mask. Whatever scorched him had burned away his eyelids, and destroyed the muscles which enabled expression. However, as he tilted his head downward, the brow of his mask came over the tops of his eyes, simulating a frown.

"What have you found, vermic?" he bellowed. The voice seemed to emanate everywhere while the face of the mask waited in silence. The silver facepiece worn by the warlock was skull-like, its eyeholes and nasal cavity resembling sockets, but was toothed by two crescent-shaped fangs that gave him a fearsome, predatory visage.

The vermic bowed, as much as his stiff exoskeleton allowed him. "Shamaul," he buzzed. "Your feelings were correct. The Orb has been activated."

Shamaul sat forward in his throne. "Is it Areok?"

"No, Sire. Two children."

The Dark Warlock stood, strolled onto a balcony, and watched the Dark Lands' clouds whirl in the sky. "So, it is true," he spoke. "These... fluctuations of energy are accurate. The Realms have brought us two little explorers..."

Hesitantly, the vermic interposed, "Unlikely, Sire."

The warlock's venomous stare returned to the creature. "What do you mean?" he hissed.

"They seemed to have arrived inadvertently."

"Is the Orb with them?"

"No."

The warlock was displeased. He let out a growl as he gripped a round ornament on the railing, similar in size and shape to the vermic's head, and crushed it effortlessly.

The creature let out a fretful squeal, then stammered, "B-but Sire, I... I did hear something else."

Shamaul released the dusty remains of the ornament and listened.

"The old wizard they're traveling with... your father... he spoke of constructing another Orb."

60

The animosity in Shamaul's eyes simmered. "Another Orb," he echoed in a sinister breath. He clasped his hands behind his back and watched the clouds.

The vermic fidgeted tentatively. He raised an arm, wavering whether or not to request food from the warlock, then turned away and took flight.

5
Morning Sail

I shot awake when Andy fell on top of me.

"_Augh!_" I hollered. "What're you—"

"Sorry dude, I tripped over your big head," he laughed.

I shoved him and fixed my glasses before joining the others outside. We exited the tent to find Veronica and Murry already collapsing the larger shelter and packing supplies onto Boris' back.

"You work early," Andy yawned.

"You sleep late," Veronica replied, tossing a bag at him. He grunted, then lifted it onto Boris' back, before lethargically sliding against the bovine's hind leg and sprawling out on the ground. He groaned in exaggerated exhaustion. Boris snorted and flicked his tail at him. Murry and I took our seats in the basket, with Veronica in the saddle up front.

She stared down at Andy and shook her head. "You're like a meelrat!"

He reluctantly peeled himself off the ground. "What's a meelrat?"

"A limbless rodent."

"Gross," Andy grumbled as he clambered to enter the basket. I grabbed his hands while Murry gripped the back of his orange jacket and pulled. "How does it move?" he asked as he flopped into the basket between Murry and me.

"A little faster than you."

Andy rotated to his side and looked at her. She raised an eyebrow at him. He returned to his stomach, and Veronica flicked the reins.

Our journey northward carried us out of the thick forestry, as the crashing of waves became audible, and Boris' strides became trudges through sand. Scooter scampered up my torso to stand on my shoulder and chirp with glee at the sight of the vast ocean. The absence of strong, floral scents reintroduced the delicious smell of the mouryll pie, which taunted our nostrils. Andy pleaded for a slice, but Murry reminded him it was for his friend.

"Where are we going anyway?" Andy asked.

"Inuento Isle," Veronica replied.

"Is that a resort or something?"

"Not quite. A long time ago it was a place of exile."

Andy and I looked at each other with hesitation, as our ride slowed to a stop.

We dismounted Boris and approached an old cottage, tucked inside a frame of dry-looking trees. Murry knocked on the door. It cracked open, and an old man peeked through. He was tall and bone-thin, with a dark complexion and a pure white, wooly beard. A smile wrinkled his face, as he threw open the door.

"Murry!"

"Shmileah! Buddy!"

They hugged and patted each other's backs.

"Haven't seen you in ages," Shmileah laughed.

"I couldn't miss your birthday."

Shmileah's eyes widened as he pointed to the pie in Murry's hands, "Is that for me?" Murry gave it to him. Shmileah stuck out his tongue and laughed, before turning back into the house and calling, "Woman, get out here! We got a guest!"

"Don'tcha call me woman, ya skinny old fool!" a voice called back.

Veronica, Andy, and I exchanged amused glances with each other.

Shmileah rolled his eyes. "It's Murry."

A lady came running. She had a similarly dark complexion, but was much shorter than her husband, and much better dressed. While Shmileah's tattered, tan garbs hung loosely on his gaunt body, his wife's outfit consisted of a multi-layered, light blue dress, a pair of blue gem earrings, and a hairband of the same jewels that held back her sliver locks.

She rushed with a look of astonishment to the front door, then smiled warmly at her visitor and held her hands up to her chest. "Oh, Murry!"

"Oh, here we go," Shmileah said.

"Well, would you look at you, Murry? So handsome in your wizard's robes."

"Thank you, Dawn. You're looking beautiful as ever."

"Oh, Murry, always *such* a gentleman." She poked Shmileah's side. "Unlike *this* one."

"There you go badtalkin' me!" Shmileah said. He showed her the mourryl pie that Murry brought. "Look'ere, he came for *my* birthday; brought me my favorite pie!"

"So *now* you think about eating," Dawn said as she grabbed one of his arms and shook it. "Look at this man. If he stood sideways ya couldn't see him."

"I'm always out catchin' the fish, that's why!"

"N' ya don't catch enough to eat back what'cha lost."

"I catch plenty; you're always choppin' off all the good parts n' cookin' 'em to a crisp."

"Fine then," Dawn said, disappearing into the house. "Next time ya catch one o' those limpjawed rock suckers I'll leave the heads on. Maybe you can have a conversation with your own kind."

"I married you, didn't I?"

"Oh, hush up," we heard Dawn say from inside, as Shmileah stuck out his tongue and laughed with us, then invited us all in.

We gathered around a circular dining table, conversing for a while and sharing slices of the mourryl pie.

"That's quite a story," Shmileah said.

Murry nodded, pointing to the map in the center of the table. "This is our first stop."

Shmileah swallowed his mouthful and looked up at Murry skeptically.

Murry opened his mouth to speak, then shut his eyes and nodded. "I know."

Shmileah leaned forward, looking around as if being listened to, then whispered, "Sometimes when I'm out fishin' late at night, I see these green sparks comin' up from the isle. I think he's still—"

"I hope you're not talking about that awful man," Dawn said as she brought each of us what looked like a halved coconut shell filled with purple juice.

I decided to speak up. "Who?"

Shmileah swished the juice around in his cup, watching the translucent bits of pulp whirl around before taking a sip and shifting his attention back to the map. He stared at it a while. The corners of his mouth stretched back as he swallowed, and his upper lip curled slightly when he responded, "MoiKy Chi."

"Worst ruler Ravac has ever had," Veronica tagged on.

64

"What'd he do?" I asked.

Shmileah uttered an angry laugh.

Dawn placed her hands on her husband's shoulders and looked at me softly, "He was the emperor once and he wasn't a very nice man."

"He had this idea!" Shmileah returned. "That humans were inferior to animals! He wanted to rebirth some ancient beasts o' legend..." He shook his head. "They said the spirits had assigned him emperor, but I'm not so sure—I think he rigged it somehow. He was in cahoots with one o' them Readers, I know it!"

Dawn hushed him.

Shmileah apologized. The small house flickered with the light of a small fireplace, as the edge of the map began to recoil and roll itself. Shmileah set down his drink on the revealed wooden tabletop.

"N' you *know* his supporters followed him to the isle when they sent him away! They went in boatfuls; no one stopped 'em!"

Dawn leaned down and spoke into her husband's ear, "I think the rest o' Ravac thought good-riddens to 'em all."

Shmileah grumbled.

Dawn patted his back and stood back up. "Let's not talk about this anymore."

Murry sighed, "Unfortunately, we have to. It's the only way of getting these boys home." Dawn looked at us, her face wrought with worry. She shook her head.

"There must be..." she swallowed, strolling away, "crystals elsewhere."

"Now you know that ain't true," Shmileah said. "You know MoiKy Chi took the whole lot o' them."

"What?" Andy interjected. "Wait, how?"

"It was the only way he'd go peacefully," Veronica explained. "Ravacan forces took him and all his riches to the isle at the same time."

"That's crazy," I said.

"That's stupid!" Andy yelled. "What'd he think he was gonna spend them on?"

"He didn't want to spend them," Veronica said. "He was building something."

"Building what?"

"Something that could turn people into animals."

The fire popped and a pair of iron instruments in Dawn's hands clattered against the sides of the clay pot inside when she jumped in fright.

"Ya've got that fire too hot," Shmileah called to her.

"Ya've got no sense of temperature," she retorted.

Veronica picked at the remnants of her slice of mourryl pie, before sliding the plate to Scooter to finish and glancing up at Andy and me. We stared back at her, dumbfounded.

"What?" she asked.

Andy pointed in the direction of the isle. "There are *monsters* out there?"

She shrugged.

Andy sat back in his seat and laughed in disbelief.

Shmileah continued speaking with Murry, gesturing to the map, "That stretch o' water's a good length."

Murry agreed.

"Yer gonna need a boat."

Dawn's head shot up from the other side of the room.

"That's actually the other reason I came," Murry said. "I wanted to ask you a favor."

Shmileah was about to speak, when Dawn came back, "I'm sorry Murry, but Shmileah ain't sellin' boats no more. He's retired."

"I see."

Shmileah looked at us, then waited for Dawn to exit to the other room. He spun back around. "So, what're ya lookin' for? Something big, right?"

"Big enough for four people and a ronk."

Shmileah gestured for us to follow.

He guided us outside. "I want you to see this." We followed him to a large object covered by a tarp. He removed the veil and exposed the body of a handmade, wooden sailboat. "She's made of forzawood. Floaty and strong." Shmileah knocked on the sleek, finished bow. "I'd recommend something like this."

"That's a beauty," Murry said.

"It is."

"I don't suppose you'd be willing to sell it."

"Well, like Dawn said, I ain't sellin' these no more."

Murry nodded.

Shmileah cocked his head. "So I guess I'll have to give it to ya for free."

"Shmileah, we couldn't."

"Ah, the lady would get on my case for takin' money from ya anyhow."

Murry smiled. "You're a good friend."

Shmileah circled around to the back of the boat and got in position to push. "Come on! Help me get'er in the water afore Dawn finds out what we're doin'."

"Shmileah!" Dawn called. "Where're ya off to?! Ya better not be sellin' no boats to no one—"

"Wha-oh," Shmileah laughed. "Gotta move!"

With the boat in the water, we all climbed inside, as Shmileah continued to guide the craft from behind.

"Quick rundown," he said, stepping deeper into the water and pointing to different parts of the boat as we began to float on our own. "*That's* the mainsail. Don't leave it open all the time, only when the wind's in your favor. *That's* the jib. Same principle. Try to keep her balanced—All o' you, keep to the opposite end of where your ronk is lyin'."

Boris snorted from the back.

"Shmileah!" Dawn exclaimed, lifting her dress and sloshing toward the boat.

"Gotta go!" Shmileah saluted. He stuck out his tongue, laughing and waving to us, as he plodded through the currents.

Dawn hurried toward us and handed Murry a jar filled with a thick brown liquid strewn with chopped up meats and vegetables. "Yer not leaving without a nice, warm stew," she said.

Murry smiled. "Thank you, Dawn."

She patted his arm. "You're very welcome, Murry. Stay safe." She exchanged a caring grin with us, then ran back to the shore. "Shmileah, what'd I tell ya? I turn my back for the slightest bit, n' you're off sellin' boats again!"

"*Hoo hoo hoo!*" the old fisherman ravished in the distance.

"Be easy on him, Dawn; it's his birthday," Murry called.

"Gonna be his last birthday once I'm through with'im!" she called back in mid-chase.

We laughed, and when a sudden gust of wind blew past us, we raised the mainsail. White water splashed against the bow, Murry unrolled the map, and we set course for Inuento Isle.

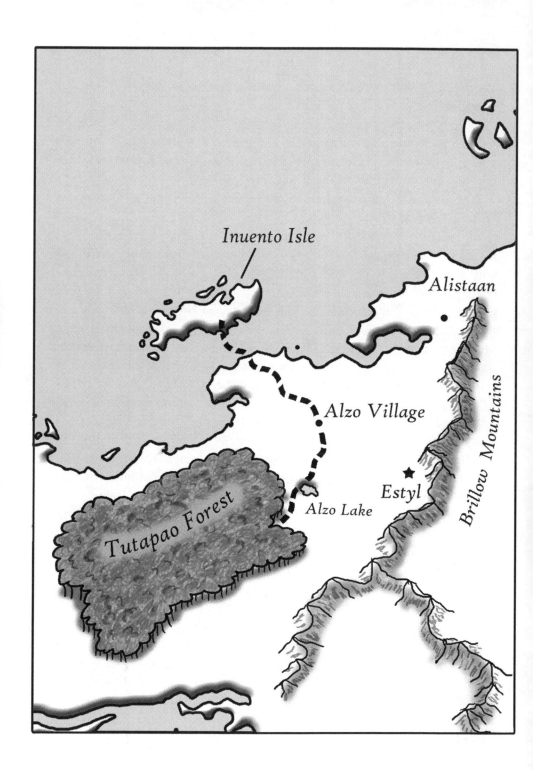

The clashing of blades rang out through the otherwise eerily silent Dark Lands, reverbing off the warped rock formations and across the barren landscape. As if drawn to the sound of conflict, a thick fog steamed and crawled across the ground, into a short pseudo-valley that housed a crude, cobbled ring designed for battle. Several intrigued creatures slinked from their nearby dens to investigate the noises, then quickly retreated to their shadows when colliding steel weapons irradiated the air.

An ork stumbled backward, shaken from his opponent's last attack. He grunted and regained focus on the white-robed warrior who stood in the center of the arena. The pale figure stood calmly, head bowed in meditation and sword grasped loosely in his right hand. The enraged beast breathed harshly through his gritted, square teeth, spitting with every exhalation, before bringing himself to an apex of fury and charging at his adversary, roaring and lifting his axe.

The warrior's fist tightened around the handle of his sword, as he sidestepped and spun in avoidance of the rampaging assailant, slicing at the creature's arm as he turned. The ork let out a distressed wail as he gripped his spewing wound, then rotated to face the culprit. The beast's beady, yellow eyes squinted at the swordsman, who stood in the center of the ring, his head bowed yet again.

The ork released an aggravated puff of breath from his dripping nostrils, then sneered and took hold of his oversized weapon with both hands, stomping toward his enemy. The warrior raised his head, as the ork stopped a stride away from him. The beast's lips pulled back in rage, and veins pulsed as the axe came down.

The swordsman dodged the ork's downward strike, leapt around the creature's massive frame, and cut at his side. He roared. The warrior hacked again, and like a hatchet into a tree's trunk, the sword became lodged in the dense bone of the ork's shoulder blade. The monster roared out as his attacker levered the sword free. The skilled fighter staggered backward, stopping abruptly when the ground started to shudder.

A second ork had invaded the combat session. He roared into the arena, wielding a mace and locked on the white-robed warrior. He swung, and the swordsman dropped down, narrowly rolling to safety, before getting to his feet to leap again in avoidance of another strike. The orks alternated, smashing at the ground with a barrage of fists and weapons, as their target rolled and flipped, evading their every attempt.

The swordsman landed a short distance away and uttered a pant. His grunting pursuers regrouped and approached, confidence curling their grotesque faces. The swordsman growled, sheathed his weapon, and straightened himself, assuming a meditative stance. The orks quickened their pace. He waited. When they reached the appropriate distance, he dropped to his knee, forced down one hand with fingers curled, and a shockwave of fire exploded around him.

The beasts shielded their faces and stepped back. The orange flames roared, spiraled, and intensified, as the white-robed warrior leapt through the whirling conflagration with his sword brandished above him. The first ork's features melted in disbelief. The slow-witted creature suddenly realized the young warrior had improved greatly since the previous exercise.

The sword sunk in between the beast's shoulder and pectoral, knocking the towering creature to the ground. The warrior pulled his bloody weapon from the sheath of flesh to deflect the second ork's mace, guiding it away from him and into the ground. The mace's speared top embedded in a fissure, and the swordsman wasted no time separating the ork from its weapon with several jabs and one hack to the leg. With a final, powerful kick, the behemoth toppled over in defeat.

The victor stood, composed himself, and steadied his breathing, as a gargoyle swooped from above and touched down on a rock at the edge of the ring. The white-robed figure spun his weapon, black ripples of flame forming over the blade to cleanse it of the orks' blood. He refused to acknowledge the gargoyle's presence.

The winged creature snarled at him, then spoke harshly, "You have been beckoned."

The warrior's fiery, orange-red eyes flared within the shade of his hood.

The Dark Warlock stood on the grounds outside his castle, a hunched goblin hobbling at his side and surveying the area. A figure stepped through the fog and approached them, his white robes easily spotted through the darkness. He stopped before his master and kneeled, placing his fist on the ground.

"You sent for me?" he grumbled, irritated. Shamaul glared down at him silently. The swordsman's eyes blazed, rising to meet the warlock's. After an eerie silence, he reluctantly concluded his statement, "Sire?"

Shamaul spoke, "I have a task for you, Grimmoch. I have recently become aware of two young travelers, from Earth."

Grimmoch's head shot up. "The Orb?"

"Yes."

"But I thought—"

"It still exists, and soon, there may be another."

Grimmoch frowned in thought, then nodded.

"I want you to watch these Realmhoppers. I want to know their every move. Their every breath."

"...Of course. Certainly—"

"And, when need be, I want them eliminated."

Grimmoch paused. "Is..." he started. "Is that necessary?"

The warlock glowered at him. "The gateway to the Realms is within my grasp. I will not allow this opportunity to elude me."

Grimmoch glanced at the warlock's goblin subordinate, Gumble, who was uttering restrained laughs. The ugly creature bounced in place while smiling fiendishly and licking at his fangs.

"Now, remain still," Shamaul boomed, his sharp fingers uncurling with metallic clicks. "It is time for you to fulfill your purpose."

"Sire?"

"This mission requires an eye beyond the wall." Dark energy coiled in his hand. "And an agreeable mind."

"You are going to force me into Anti-Ka?"

Shamaul watched his kneeling apprentice, then spoke, "Your recent behavior has proven you to be unpredictable. I cannot trust you." A horrid enmity burned in his words.

Grimmoch's fiery eyes searched the ground, as if the answer to his dilemma lay hidden in the colorless rubble beneath him. He looked up again. "You do not have to do this. I could apprehend

71

the Realmhoppers myself. I could bring them to you... and you would not have to exhaust your power."

Shamaul lowered his head at him, the brow of his silver mask appearing to furrow over his sinister, anguineous stare. "My power is inexhaustible."

Grimmoch slowly bowed his head for the final time. He shut is eyes, then responded, "You are correct, sire."

The warlock lifted his hand to commence the spell.

"You cannot trust me." A wave of orange flames shot from Grimmoch's hands and ignited the dry ground at the warlock's feet. Shamaul raised his cape to shield himself from the blast, as the white-robed warrior made his escape. He whistled for his windserpent, who flew from her perch in the mountains and swooped under her owner, carrying him into the sky.

Shamaul threw down his cape, the whipping motion extinguishing the fire and rattling the airborne embers encircling his figure. The air hummed. His scepter levitated into his grasp, and the glass sphere housed in its blade glowed blue and fired several surges of energy at his target.

The agile windserpent swerved and snaked to evade the whirring blasts as she quickened her ascent toward the dome of black energy that surrounded the continent.

Grimmoch raised his sword, and shouted a spell that generated a beam of white light. The Dark Lands' creatures hissed at the foreign element radiating from the sky. The rays cut through the eternal night of the wicked continent, and separated the energy of the dome long enough for the escapees to pass through.

Shamaul watched, as the tear in the dome writhed and closed itself, and the Dark Lands' clouds rumbled aggressively.

"Where is he going?" Gumble snarled, looking desperately to his master, who said nothing. "From where did he learn that spell?!"

Shamaul watched the smoke-colored clouds roll and separate beneath the resealed dome of magic that confined him. They began to coil again.

"It seems our resources have been limited."

6

Inuento Isle, Ravac

For the initiating stretch of our journey, we seemed to cover distance quickly, watching Shmileah's old cottage and the shoreline of the mainland drift into the background. But at the midpoint of our sail, we seemed to neither grow nearer to our destination, nor farther from our starting point. The two landmasses appeared stagnant in the ocean. I looked up in time to see a flock of several large flying creatures gliding directly overhead, their shadows providing brief respite from the hot, cloudless morning. The stinging tightness in my features began to loosen in the shade. Though shadowed, I could tell that the animals were more reptilian than aviary.

Their craniums projected elongated, toothy beaks that were flattish and sword-like, and had arched structures protruding from the snout and chin that seemed to cut through the air and guide the rest of the creature's massive, scaly body. Though they lacked legs, their outstretched arms possessed wingflaps that puffed with wind and somehow allowed them to soar long distances without having to move. I asked Murry what type of animal they were, and he told me they were called _spearbirds_.

I nodded and stared upward as the last of the flock's diamond-ended tails passed by and the sun shined in my eyes again. I winced and squinted back at Murry, who was flipping the page of a small handbook and mouthing words. I considered retrieving my Captain Galloway book from my backpack, but reconsidered—either from my restiveness, or my heat-induced malaise. I decided it was a mixture of the two.

Scooter had found a clever way to cool off by clinging to the jib and intercepting the droplets of water that sprinkled up from the bow. The boat jostled as a larger wave clipped the nose and pelted us with saltwater. A few drops landed on my lenses.

I removed my glasses and dragged them against my shirt, finding that Andy and I had been staring at each other for a long time. His eyelids slowly closed and reopened.

73

"You blinked," he told me.

"No, that was you," I corrected.

"Oh."

Veronica growled and chucked a canteen at him. "Drink some water."

Andy looked at the canteen, then smiled and croaked out, "Can't. Not... enough... energy."

Veronica rolled her eyes. "Looks like we're almost there."

"Oh, really?" Andy hopped up.

I stood as well, putting my glasses back into place to see the coast of the isle rapidly approaching.

"Land ho!" Andy declared. Veronica grinned briefly as she gathered the mooring rope, while Murry slid his book back into his rucksack and furled the mainsail. Boris started to snort and stand, which wobbled the craft and nearly knocked us off our feet. We stabilized again as the water shallowed and the front end of the boat was supported by sand. We exited our vessel and tied it to a nearby tree before stretching out and trekking into the isle.

We reached the top of a grassy hill and examined our surroundings. Aside from a few patches of green like the one we stood on and some trees in the distance, the isle was otherwise bare and hilly. I could see why a wrongdoer would be exiled here. A stale breeze flowed over our faces as we squinted into the distance. There was nothing.

"Well this is exciting," Andy said.

Veronica raised her hand at him and tilted her head. "You hear that?" We stopped and listened.

"Hear what?" Andy whispered.

The noise suddenly entered our ears: a rhonchisonant sound, something breathing. Boris grunted in response. Veronica glanced over the edge of the hill, then stepped back in horror.

"What is it?" I asked.

"Minotaurs."

"What?"

"Into the basket!"

We hurried into the basket on Boris' back as we heard the trudging steps of the creatures scaling the hill.

"Come on, come on," Veronica urged as we all piled in. She jumped in last and threw a red sheet over our bodies. "Stay low," she instructed.

Andy pointed to the red fabric above us. "What is this?"

"Boris' bath towel."

Andy covered his mouth and made a muffled gag.

"Don't move," Veronica whispered. "Don't breathe."

"Don't worry."

"*Sh!*" Veronica shushed him just as the stomping drew nearer outside, and the raucous sniffs and grunts sounded directly above us. *Don't move*, Veronica mouthed. We felt the beasts rotate above us, exchanging frustrated grunts in their wordless vocabulary. Veronica ordered us to keep quiet with her eyes. I swallowed dryly, waiting for them to turn away. We stayed glued to the floor, not moving an inch, not making a sound.

FEEERT!

We all looked at Andy with dread. Veronica's harsh whisper cracked with rage:

"*Are you serious?!*"

"*Sorry, I was nervous!*"

In the midst of the altercation, the beasts tore the blanket away. They examined it, grunting, then caught sight of us inside the basket. Andy turned his palms up, smiling uncomfortably.

Veronica snarled, "Andy, if we survive, I'm going to kill you."

The minotaurs directed us at spearpoint down the hill and over a cobbled walkway framed sparsely by spindly trees sprouting from circular openings in the path. Sunrays spat in between leaves and bothered my eyes. I squinted back at our shadowed captors as we stepped through another patch of light and their features became visible.

Each creature bore the face of an ox with the muscular torso of a man. Short tails swung behind them, and two bovine legs supported their massive frames. As they moved, long, matted, black-brown fur swayed and flung terrible odors at us. I coughed as the acerbic stench collected in the back of my throat. One of the minotaurs grunted at me and brandished his weapon. The spear resembled a medieval polearm, but was crudely constructed with an overly elaborate blade cast in the shape of a serrated, palmate leaf.

Bits of sand skittered across my lenses and pelted my face. I raised my hand at a dusty breeze and turned my head away to see Andy hacking and spitting the grit from his mouth. Veronica watched him.

He eventually caught her stare. "What?"

She shook her head and looked away, as if insulted. Andy threw his arms over his head and turned to me in befuddlement. I shrugged.

Then, as if growing from the earth, a set of towering structures pierced the horizon. I wondered how we didn't notice them before, then decided the they must have lain hidden behind tree clusters and the hilly terrain. The foremost building was comprised of familiar sand-colored stones, with darker carved rocks accenting the entranceway and windows. A wooden bridge creaked as we passed over it and entered the main chamber of the edifice. High windows were positioned over the farthest side of the chamber only, lighting a tall platform where an ornate, gold throne was secured before a wall of green crystals.

The gems glittered, refracting light over the floor in front of the arrangement. As we stepped into the green glow, we could see the shape of a man seated in the throne. He was tall and muscular, with a bald head, prominent nose, and countless pieces of gold jewelry cladding his dark tan skin. He sat ten or so feet above us, observing our group with angry, coal-colored eyes.

I whispered to Veronica, "*Is that—*"

"*Yes,*" she said.

I pointed to the wall of crystals. "*And are those—*"

"*Yes.*"

We stopped before the platformed throne.

"Who are these?" the ruler's voice boomed.

"Visitors," Murry spoke.

"Visitors? I don't recall *inviting* any individual from the mainland to my humble abode."

"We were not invited, we—"

"Ah, then you are *not* visitors; you are trespassers." He sat forward in his throne, his innumerable gold necklaces clattering together as he leaned. "I dislike trespassers." He laced his fingers. On his right hand he wore a jeweled, bronze-colored metal glove. His stare shifted when Veronica stepped forward.

"MoiKy Chi!" she called to him.

An unsettling grin spread across his face. "The girl knows my name." He looked down to a short goat-man standing guard beside his high platform. "My reputation has preceded me." He turned back to her. "It's customary to bring offerings when introducing one's self to the emperor."

Veronica said her name, then reached into her pocket and retrieved several gold coins. MoiKy Chi laughed, "I have no use for that here." The goat-man leapt by and snatched the coins anyway.

Murry introduced himself next and held out a book. "I've read it many times."

"A spell book?" MoiKy Chi said. "Magic has never interested me."

The goat-man nabbed it.

"Who are you?" I was asked, unenthusiastically. "And what pointless curio have you brought?"

"Marvin," I said as I searched through my backpack. As I sifted, my Captain Galloway book somehow found its way to the top and tumbled out.

"What's this?"

The goat-man grabbed it and brought it to the former emperor.

MoiKy Chi flipped through it. "The parchment is pristine..." he said, running his hand over the text. "But it has already been scribed on." He tore a page out and held it to the sunlight. I cringed. He added the ripped book to a pile of our things. "Next?"

Andy lifted his chin at him. "Andy Bailey."

The ruler frowned.

"Oh, uh, hang on," Andy said, searching each of his pockets and pulling them inside out. He shrugged. "Sorry dude, I'm empty."

MoiKy Chi pointed to his neck. "What's this?"

Andy looked down at his necklace. "That's a shark tooth—"

"A sharkperson's tooth, you say?"

"Uh, no, just a regular old shar—"

"Give it to me."

The goat guy leapt up, snapped the chain from Andy's neck, and delivered it to MoiKy Chi.

"Hey!" Andy yelled.

The ruler reached down to retrieve the necklace. "Thank you, Pann." He tossed the chain aside and secured the pendant onto one of his own necklaces.

Andy's arms dropped to his sides. "Come on, man, I spent like eight bucks at the gumball machine for that!"

Veronica whispered to me, "*Is that a lot?*"

"Well, it's definitely more than he should've spent."

She groaned, then called to the tyrant again, "MoiKy Chi!"

He stopped fiddling with the tooth.

"We've come a long way—"

"Of *course* you have." He sat forward in his throne, his nose cringing wolfishly. "You reek of urbanites. Where have you come from? Alistaan?"

"Alzo."

"What business could you possibly have here?"

"We want something from you."

MoiKy Chi's head rolled back in jest. "And what is that?"

"A crystal."

The former emperor rocked slightly in his seat. His cheered expression faded into a hateful half-smile. He rotated, dragged the spiked index finger of his metal glove against the surface of the crystal wall behind him, and a small chunk detached. He caught the gem and turned it in his sharp fingertips so it would sparkle.

"These are hard to come by nowadays."

Veronica's face remained unchanged, though her fists were clenched.

MoiKy Chi went on, "I understand that they are difficult to mine. They must be arduously chipped from stone, cleansed of all impurities." He held it up to his eye and gazed through it. "They have an incredible bonding property..." He caught sight of Veronica through the gem. He lowered it, still smiling, then set it aside and laced his fingertips again, "What will I get in return?"

Veronica's mouth stiffened slightly. "What do you want?"

A third minotaur appeared in the entrance, leading Boris inside with a rope. MoiKy Chi's eyes glinted.

Veronica frowned. Her hair twirled as she followed the tyrant's gaze, then spun to face him again.

Chi lifted the green gem from the arm of his throne. "You may have your crystal," he said, "in exchange for your bovine."

"No!" Veronica roared.

"What a spectacular creature," the ruler rubbed his chin, entranced. "He'll be perfect for—"

"You *can't* have him!"

MoiKy Chi eyed her momentarily. "Very well. Since you insist that you are *visiting*, you may stay, and work off the value of your crystal." He raised his gloved hand, and the minotaurs' heads shot up alertly. "Take them to their rooms."

The creatures complied, leading us down one hallway, while Boris was escorted down another.

Veronica pushed past the two minotaurs and called to the tyrant, "I know what you do here!"

He raised an eyebrow.

"Don't hurt my ronk!"

MoiKy Chi smiled. "You have my word. I am an appreciator of nature's wonders, you know."

Veronica studied him, before stepping back to our sides.

"Enjoy your stay," he said. A voluble laugh slipped through his teeth and vibrated around us. As we left, he turned to the side, revealing an unnerving pair of eyes tattooed on the back of his head.

"I don't like him," Veronica said.

"He took my necklace," Andy muttered.

As the group conversed, I noticed a frail-looking man being dragged across the floor of the main chamber.

"No... no..." he protested exhaustedly. He and a swine-like creature were pulled into a large antechamber, where Pann stood smiling beside an obelisk-shaped structure. "No... *please! NO!*" The man thrashed with his last amount of strength.

The others heard the commotion and looked back as the prisoner vanished inside the room, still fighting, and Pann pulled back on a lever. The minotaurs shoved us further into the hall, as green light flashed behind us, and the man's scream melded with the animal's squeal into a horrific, conglomerated vocalization.

I felt a numbness shoot through me. Murry leaned in to speak to us. "We *will try*," he whispered coarsely, clearing his throat, "*to minimize our time here.*"

A minotaur growled impatiently and moved us along, as the air chilled, and we marched deeper into the darkening, howling hall.

We entered our room, which was more like a cell. The metallic *clunk* of the heavy cage door resonated off the thick walls of our square cavity, as a minotaur grunted at us and twisted a key—one oversized to accommodate his huge fingers—locking us inside.

Andy walked up to the bars, "Hey, aren't you gonna read me my rights?"

The minotaur huffed in reply, launching bits of snot at his prisoner.

"*Augh!*" Andy shouted, wiping his face. "Guess not."

The monster shook the gate, growled in approval, then stomped off.

We stood there, perplexed in the center of the cell, studying the plain, sandy walls and set of bunk beds of the same color, and material.

"I call top bunk!" Andy declared, climbing up to the higher of a pair. He lay down, shifting his shoulders and stretching out. "Ooh, *comfy!*" he chuckled.

The rest of us glanced at each other, before following Andy's lead and selecting our beds. I sat down on the one beneath Andy, while Murry eased into the lower one of the second set, and Veronica climbed up to the top. She rotated to face us, one leg tucked under herself while the other swung freely over the edge of her bed.

Scooter crawled over my abdomen and chirped. In my peripherals, I thought Veronica was watching me, but when I turned I could see that her stare was blank and introverted. I sighed and let my head fall, which I immediately regretted, since my bed was a solid block of stone. I rubbed the back of my skull before lying down again with my hand as a pillow.

I glanced at Veronica, who was still deep in thought.

"Boris'll be okay," I told her.

Her eyes moved. She slid her jaw for a moment, then shut her eyes and nodded, before turning away.

I took a long breath. The air was gritty. I coughed and flipped to my side, contemplating what type of work MoiKy Chi would have for us tomorrow. The room's single, rectangular window cast a square spotlight on the floor that gradually dimmed into an orangish color. The sun was setting.

I looked up and noticed Andy leaning over the edge of the top bunk. He said, "Wouldn't it suck if this thing fell?"

My eyes widened. "Yeah. It would."

Andy nodded. "Well, goodnight dude."

I surveyed the structural soundness of the bunk beds, noting the support beams secured to each of the outer corners and how the right sides of the beds seemed to fuse with the stone wall they were positioned against. Once I was convinced I wouldn't be flattened in the middle of the night, I started to relax.

The chirrups of nocturnal animals serenaded the night. I yawned, blinking tiredly, trying to decode the odd orchestra. The noises were rhythmic and small-sounding. Either insects or croaking amphibians, I figured. But every once in a while a louder one bellowed: one of MoiKy Chi's slumbering hybrids. I swallowed fretfully, but quickly calmed when Scooter's restful purring hummed in my ears, and my eyelids finally slid shut.

When the chilled nighttime air thawed, my eyes reopened. It took me a second to realize it was already morning. As I stirred, Scooter emerged from his shell and leapt onto one of the bunk bed's support beams. I sat up and stretched out. My stiffened back made a pop as I reached. I put my hand over the vertebrae, but realized I was fine. I was surprised at how well-rested I felt. I heard Andy yawn above me, and his hand appeared over the edge of the bed. His whole arm began to dangle, and he suddenly realized that he was rolling off.

"Whoa, whoa!" he awoke as he teetered, then fell, grabbing hold of the stone with his left hand, swinging, then dropping to the floor. "Oof!"

"You okay?" I asked.

He groaned in response.

Veronica sat up, her hair disheveled, then shook her head and laid down again, as Andy peeled himself off the floor.

I lifted my backpack to my side to retrieve my Captain Galloway book, then immediately remembered it was gone. I sighed through my nostrils, unzipping it anyway and searching for something to occupy my time. In one of the smaller compartments, I located my dad's dog tags. I was thankful that those weren't taken away. I slipped them over my head and tucked them beneath my shirt as I searched further. In the main compartment I found a dull, eraserless pencil and a bent-up worksheet. I straightened out the paper and found it was an extra credit questionnaire Mr. Barber had given us regarding some of the exhibits at the museum and how they related to our current unit in class. I started filling out some of the answers.

Andy sat beside me, dragging his hands across his face. He smacked his mouth, then frowned, looking over my shoulder.

"Uh, Marvin?"

"Yeah?" I replied, filling in my answer for the second question.

"What are you doing?"

"What?"

He repeated his question, "*What* are you doing?"

"The worksheet," I held up the page, "that Mr. Barber gave to us."

He started to laugh.

"What?"

"Dude, we're in an alternate universe... and you're doing homework."

"Yeah?"

"*Why?*"

"Why not?"

Andy placed his hands on my shoulders. "Marv, there *is* no school here. There *is* no history class." He shot to his feet and opened his arms. "We're free!"

I let out a laugh. "We're in a holding cell."

Andy looked around. He shrugged. "Still better than Mr. Barber's class."

CLANG!

We shouted and covered our ears as the loud crash of metal against metal pulsed through the room.

"Wha? Who?" Murry stammered as he got up.

Pann stood outside of our room with a pole clutched in his hands. He struck our gated door again.

Andy gritted, "We're awake!"

Pann snarled, "Your presence is required outside."

A second hybrid rounded the corner and unlocked our cell. At first, my subconscious recognized it as being part walrus, but upon closer scrutiny I decided otherwise.

The abominable creature lumbered inside, its massive gut jiggling and nearly compromising its balance with each step. The beast's skin was thick and gray, like that of an elephant's. What I originally mistook for a helmet was actually one of many dermal plates growing from its flesh, especially on its head, neck, and forearms. As it worked its way closer on flipper-like feet, the stench of rotted fish fumed from its mouth. From its unhealthy gums grew two pairs of spiky tusks, the enamel of which was yellowing, especially near the roots. The monster's beady eyes squinted, and lumpy jowls puffed with air as it gurgled an internal growl and reached for us with its morphed, pinnipedian fin-hand, confiscating Veronica's crossbow and Murry's wand.

The two began to object, when Pann explained, "Can't have any *trouble*." The goat-man called back the second hybrid, referring to the creature as *Chubz*. It grunted in compliance and carried the items away. As the beast left, Veronica rotated her belt to conceal her multiweapon. "Come with me," Pann continued. "You have a debt to pay."

We were told to leave anything extra in the cell. I propped my backpack against the wall beside Veronica's quiver and Murry's rucksack and followed the goat-man out of the palace. Every few steps he took were interrupted by a fidgety half-gallop that made us adjust our speed, and upon doing so we were chastised for slowing down. The passage became brighter as sunlight streamed in through the exit, and we passed by a row of stables, in one of which Boris was kept.

"Boris!" Veronica exulted, running up to his pen. She jumped onto one of the wooden crossbeams of the stable door and leaned in to wrap her arms around his head. Boris placed his nose against the side of her face.

Pann growled, "No stopping! Move along!"

Veronica kissed the ronk twice on the snout, stepped back down, then doubled back and kissed him again before rejoining the group.

Pann's jowls raised in disgust.

As we walked outdoors, we could see groups of gaunt humans struggling to pull stone blocks across a field of dirt, while minotaurs roared and whipped at them and MoiKy Chi looked on from his seat on a balcony.

"We are building a monument in honor of the emperor," Pann said, "a statue in his likeness." The effigy so far only reached as high as the tyrant's legs. Craftspeople balanced on rickety wooden platforms were frantically chiseling and smoothing details into the sculpture. Pann grinned. "The head should be on by the end of the day."

When we hesitated, the goat-man sneered, "Go, now!"

We scrambled to our stations.

"You have twenty blocks to move before sundown."

The blocks were the size of hay bales. We were hooked up to harnesses that attached us to the massive stones, and were whipped whenever we fell too far behind. I took hold of my shoulder straps to keep them from digging into my skin and pressed forward, inch by agonizing inch, as sweat poured from my body. A bead of the salty liquid rolled into my eye, and when I reached to wipe it away, I momentarily lost my stride and was lashed. I let out a scream and was hit again. I kept my growls internal, as I felt an x-shaped wound burn on my back.

Andy was having trouble as well. He was falling behind and being whipped repeatedly.

WHIP! WHIP!

"OW! Stop it, ya dumb cow!"

WHIP!

Andy growled, tore off his harness, and confronted the former emperor.

"Hey!" he called to the balcony. "Hey! Down here!"

MoiKy Chi slowly tilted his head, upon which he balanced a tall, ridiculous-looking, horned crown.

"Listen up, *Spicy Ravioli*. I've been doing this forever! The blocks are too *heavy*, the sun is too *hot*, you're a big *slacker*, and I want a different job!"

The ruler's eye twitched. "Very well," he boomed. "You may take Taeloch's job. He is in need of a rest."

"Great. What's my new assignment?"

"Now, you will be transporting three blocks at a time."

"WHAT?!"

"Keep in mind that your progress today will affect whether or not you receive your crystal."

"Chi, you've gotta be kidding—"

MoiKy Chi raised his glove, and a pair of minotaurs lifted Andy by his arms and carried him back to his work station.

"C'mon MoiKy, we're pals, right?" Andy persuaded.

The ruler stared past him.

"...Oh, so now you're ignoring me? Are you too busy thinking of what *else* you're gonna take from your mom's jewelry box?"

Chi's nostrils flared.

Andy held his hand up to his eye and pinched his fingers together. "Look! Now I'm crushing your head like a grape! An ugly grape!"

Andy was strapped to three blocks of stone with a circular device clamped around his mouth. He muttered something angrily as he inched his way across the sandy field.

We all powered through the intense labor, and when the sun set, we dragged our last few blocks to the base of the statue. I ran my hands through my hair and swayed dizzily, trying to regain my balance. Andy unstrapped himself and flopped onto the dust. My head throbbed in pain and I decided to join him. Although the statue only reached as high as MoiKy Chi's neck, we had completed our end of the agreement and transported twenty blocks across the field. Veronica passed the canteen around. I took a sip of the warmed fluid, swishing it in my mouth before swallowing, then offered it to Andy.

He stared at me exhaustedly and muttered something inaudible, his mouth still covered. I apologized and handed it back to Veronica, as Pann approached us.

"We filled our quota," Veronica panted.

The goat-man snarled, glaring at the sunset. Andy pointed to his mouth and murmured something. Pann kicked it with his hoof and the clamp disengaged.

"Agh!" Andy yelled as he touched the red impressions on his face. "That's all it took?!"

"Do we get our crystal?" I asked.

The hybrid looked up at the darkening sky, then growled at us and spoke through his gritted fangs, "Tomorrow."

Instead of leading us back to our room, Pann directed us in the opposite direction, toward a large, circular building that resembled an amphitheater.

"What's this?" Murry asked in between pants.

"You've been relocated," Pann responded.

Veronica looked to Murry, who she was helping to walk and keep balanced. The wizard blinked tiredly and nodded.

We entered the lightless halls of the coliseum, walking past rows upon rows of cages filled with enslaved humans, many of whom had been dragging blocks alongside us this morning. "Here's one," Pann sneered, pulling open a cage door and gesturing for us to enter.

We stepped inside. The new cell made our old one look luxurious. It was half the size, with only two wooden planks hinged to the walls and held level by chains. The floor was uneven and damp, and like the walls, was built from darker, less-refined bricks than our previous room. A minotaur locked us in, then hung the key on his belt and returned to his post.

"The emperor apologizes for the lackluster accommodations," Pann said, before turning away.

Murry pointed to Andy and me. "You two can have the beds."

We shook our heads, already in sitting positions on the floor.

"No, *you* get one of the beds," Veronica said as she guided the old wizard onto the wooden surface. Veronica looked at the second plank.

"You can have it," Andy told her.

She waited a moment before accepting the offer and lying down. Andy looked at me, and then leaned back against the wall. I did the same, cradling Scooter's shell from my pocket and resting him on my leg.

The night was devoid of the nocturnal animal chirps from before. Only the growls of stomachs and drips of liquid from the ceiling were audible in the ghastly halls. I stared past the bars at a small, square window, through which two full moons gleamed brightly in the dark sky. They were incredible.

I wanted to comment on them, vocalize my admiration. But my throat was dry, and exhaustion had set in, so I faced the astrological marvel and the glittering stars that framed it, gripped my dad's dog tags through the fabric of my shirt, and fell asleep.

7
Secret of the Coliseum

My arms felt like they weighed a ton, and neck and back muscles ached as yesterday's work caught up with my body. I awkwardly reached behind me to feel long scars across my back. I sighed, then winced, covering my temples as my head throbbed painfully at a thunderous sound pounding from the center of the coliseum.

What sounded like the crashing of giant waves roared through the hallways and overwhelmed my ringing ears. I waited a moment for my senses to recover, then listened to the noise again, realizing that it couldn't have been waves due to its proximity to the shore. It was rhythmic as well, and when I shut my eyes and dissected the cacophony, I found it was composed of many different sounds: roars, grunts, snorts, and bellows. They were chants.

I slid to the cage door and looked around the corner as best I could. I could see half of an arched passageway leading outside, but nothing more. A sudden shriek of terror sounded in the distance, followed by hollers of delight.

"Poor feller," someone voiced.

"Hello?" I said.

No one answered. After a moment, I could hear the creak of a wooden plank. I cleared my throat and spoke again. "Is someone there?"

"Right 'ere," the voice returned, a hand appearing through the bars of the next cell over.

I moved closer to the brick wall that separated our rooms. "Can you see what's going on out there?"

"Yeah. It ain't pretty."

"What?"

"The arena's a mess. Looks like their pullin' him back in now so they can clean up... Ooh, he ain't too thrilled 'bout that."

A worried tightness formed in my chest. After I didn't say anything, our neighbor spoke, "Name's Zyvin."

87

I took a breath to calm myself. "Zyvin, what's going on?"

"Wait, you don't know?"

"Why are we here?"

It took several seconds for him to reply. Finally, I heard his tongue click as he reopened his mouth. "To be killed."

Dizziness seeped into my mind as Zyvin continued his explanation, almost frenziedly: "He's gonna feeds ya to the Morogma—biggest beast on the isle. He ain't even tellin' people?"

I stood, steadying myself with the wall. I could almost hear my heartbeat as it sent shockwaves through my body, hazing my vision with each thump. I sucked in some air and waited for my surroundings to straighten out. "Guys," I choked.

Andy rolled over on the floor. "Five more minutes."

"Guys, guys, get up!" I started yelling. "Get up! Get up!" I shook Andy awake, and the others started to move.

Andy squirmed. "*Gah!* Marv, what's your deal?"

"We need to go."

"What's going on?" Veronica asked.

"He's gonna kill us!"

"What?!" Andy shouted.

"He's feeding us to the Morogma!"

"Moroginga... what?"

I shook my head. "It doesn't matter. We need to leave."

"You're staying right where you are," a voice boomed.

MoiKy Chi strolled in front of our cell, Pann grinning fiercely at his side.

"Chi, you liar!" Andy cried. "We're supposed to be out of here by now!"

"Eager. Once the stadium's cleaned you'll have your turn."

Murry approached the bars, hands folded. "Your highness, these are children."

"Yes, they are too young to be transformed and you are too old," MoiKy Chi said. "The only passable being amongst you is your ronk."

Veronica's eyes widened. She stepped forward.

"Stay away from him!"

MoiKy Chi laughed.

"Let us out!" Veronica cried.

"Then what? Let you have your crystal too? Gallivant around your village displaying the treasure you've brought back?"

Veronica glowered at him.

"Did you really think I'd allow myself to be pilloried this way? Until now no travelers dared intrude on my land, and if you were to return to your *hovels* with any trace of wealth—"

"That's not what we're trying to do!"

"*Whatever* you call your pursuit, it won't be realized here. No. I think a better message to convey to Ravac would be that no one who enters Inuento leaves alive."

Veronica's face was still, and her knuckles were white. She repeated her first demand, stressing each syllable, "Let. Us. Go."

The tyrant blew a haughty, half-laugh from his nostrils, his mouth curling. "I know who you are..."

Veronica frowned.

"You're Cliff Blaire's daughter. He was an excellent general— terrible at following orders however." MoiKy Chi bent down to look her in the eyes. "Do you think I'm intimidated by you? You're just a little girl." His stare burned into hers. "A little girl whose mommy died because she wanted a little boy."

Rancor flared in Veronica's eyes. Without warning her hand shot through the cage, grabbed hold of his necklaces, and pulled back, slamming his forehead into the bars.

"Agh!" he cried out, stumbling, as beads and pendants slipped off the broken strands and scattered over the floor. "RAH!" He slammed his metal fist against the bars of our cell, sending a hush through the halls. He breathed angrily through his nose, eyeing each of us. "Your deaths will *not* be swift," he said as he left.

Veronica turned away, sinking to the floor and hiding her face. Murry knelt beside her, placing a hand on her back. She sniffed.

Andy and I looked to each other. "What do we do?" he whispered. I looked away, searching for an answer. I caught myself turning to Veronica first, but stopped halfway. My brow slanted in worry. I scanned the rest of our cell, then the hallway. There, a minotaur grunted as he passed by, a set of keys jangling on his belt.

I looked back at Andy. *We need to get the keys*, we seemed to think at the same time.

"How do we get those off him?" he asked. I looked around for the answer to our new dilemma, when Scooter peeked over my shoulder. "Scooter!" Andy declared, picking him up. He pointed to the gleaming ring of keys on the beast's belt. "See the keys, Scooter?"

Scooter seemed to understand.

"Go get 'em!"

Scooter looked at me, as if asking for permission. I nodded.

With no hesitation the little cephalopod scurried off, easily slipping through the spaces of the bars and scuttling across the stone floor. Before long, he was clambering up the minotaur's leg. We tensed as he slid a tentacle under the metal ring and attempted to move it. The hefty keys lifted off the creature's belt, but immediately dropped to the ground, Scooter still clinging to them, and landed with a loud *CLANG*.

The minotaur turned, catching sight of the hexapoid. We called him back frantically as the monster raised its weapon.

Scooter shrieked and hopped down the hall, gripping the keys with his two back tentacles and zigzagging to avoid the minotaur's blade. Sparks shot up from the floor as Scooter narrowly evaded each strike.

"Come on come on come on come on!" Andy and I kept shouting as Scooter sped toward us and jumped through the cage and into my arms, while the keys were blocked by their width and clattered outside. Andy reached through to snatch them, turning the ring sideways and pulling them in, just as the beast reached our cell. It opened its arms, threw back its head, and released a loud, pulsating roar.

One end of Veronica's multiweapon launched, clubbing the monster in between the eyes and knocking it flat, unconscious. We looked at her in astonishment as she rose to her feet and retracted the chained segment of the weapon.

"Let's go," she commanded.

Andy selected one of the keys on the ring and reached around the bars. He turned it in the lock and the gears clunked and unlocked the door.

"First try!" he exulted. We opened the cell and treaded cautiously into the hallway.

"Hey, let me out too," Zyvin called.

"Andy, toss me the keys," I said.

"We gotta go."

"I'll be quick."

I caught the keys, selected one of them, then tried the lock. It didn't budge.

"Hurry," Zyvin urged. I flipped to the next one and the door still didn't unlock.

"Marvin, more are coming!" Andy yelled.

I flipped to another key, and another. Finally one worked, and the door swung open. Zyvin stepped out. He was lanky and significantly paler than the other captives, as though he hadn't seen sunlight in a long time. He had an elongated chin and nose, and his face was framed by long strands of grayed hair that hung past his neck. His right eye was brown, while his left one was discolored and appeared to be blind. He tilted his head at me and squinted, as though expecting me to look different.

"Uh, thanks," he said.

"No problem."

We both turned when Andy shouted my name and something else bellowed a roar. I grabbed the keys from the door and handed them to an onlooker in a nearby cell.

"Here you go," I said, as Zyvin and I raced down the hall.

We arrived in time to see Veronica fending off a minotaur. She interrupted the creature's lunge with a swirling block that knocked the spear from his hands, followed by a jab to the ribs with a bladed end of her multiweapon. I jogged to Andy's side just as another minotaur joined the fray.

"Hi," I panted.

"Welcome back," Andy said. "Who's that?"

"That's Zyvin."

Zyvin waved.

"Oh. Hi." Andy slashed at an incoming spear with a rusted machete.

"Where'd you get that?" I asked.

"Found it," he replied, blocking again.

The minotaur shook his head and uttered a frustrated roar as it issued another hasty, unsuccessful lunge with its polearm that missed Andy and struck the floor. Andy chopped down on the monster's weapon, fracturing the end of the staff and severing the blade. The monster looked at its splintered tool, snorting bewilderedly, then shifted its grip and swung the broken instrument like a bat.

"Ow! Hey!" Andy protested as the beast smacked his shoulder. He sidestepped as the minotaur swung again, hitting the wall, before Murry stepped forward and took hold of the bladeless polearm. The wizard tightened his fingers, and shoved the staff toward the monster, a surge of magic, purple energy coursing over the surface of the handle and bursting into a wriggling, plasmatic shockwave that sent the two minotaurs hurtling down the hall.

Murry stepped back and brushed himself off. "*That was sloppy*," he chastised himself.

That was incredible, I thought.

Our feet clopped over the cobbled floor as we navigated the halls. We kept our guard up, glancing down every path before we stopped at a dead end.

Not being pursued, Veronica held out her multiweapon. The bladed ends retracted first, then the two outer segments slid back into the central handle that she clipped to her belt. Andy discovered a pair of what resembled cellar doors. They opened to a set of stairs leading into an underground passage.

"Where does that go?" I asked.

Veronica stared into the passageway, then out a small window, "Looks like it leads back to the palace."

"Great," said Andy. "We can pop up, wave hello, grab a crystal, and get out."

Murry pulled at his beard. "It won't be that easy."

"We can ambush 'im."

"And any guards?"

"Yeah, them too."

"Why're you after his crystals?" Zyvin asked.

"Long story."

Zyvin's throat bobbed nervously.

While the group deliberated, Veronica walked past them and entered the dim, underground hallway.

Andy glanced down the stairs, then back at us. "Guess we're going."

Our footsteps echoed and amplified off the eroded bricks of the underground passage. Two rows of angular lanterns protruded from the wall and lined the hallway. Inside of each, a hovering ball of light circled and cycled luminosities. They dimmed and brightened, their shine hued by the reddish glass they swerved

92

behind as they provided limited spots of visibility throughout the passageway.

As I stepped closer, I could tell that the lights inside came from large bioluminescent insects, ones I would later learn were called *moonbeetles*. I locked eyes with one of the grotesque bugs. Though its light was beguiling, its appearance was detestable. The crest of its lumpy forehead sloped down to give the creature a natural frown. Its slimy mandibles rotated over one another, and bristled hairs sprouting from the spaces in the creatures thorax twitched at my approach, before the bug charged, striking the inside of its glass enclosure.

I took a step away from the wall, then glanced forward as Veronica marched on. Her stride was long and hurried; I had to jog for a few steps just to catch up with her.

Andy speedwalked to her side. "So what's the plan gonna be?"

"I'm finding Boris," she replied.

"Oh." Andy's pace slowed.

We were rattled and winded, but I understood Veronica's haste. We sped down the hall, stopping only when our echoing footsteps became overwhelmed by the sound of hooves against rock. A large animal with four horns and long, shaggy fur moved into a section of red light.

"Boris?" Veronica said.

Boris snorted in reply.

Veronica ran up to hug him. "Oh, thank goodness!"

She wrapped her arms around his head and kissed him. Boris swayed slightly, staring emotionlessly ahead. Through the dim, red light I could see the color drain from Murry's face.

"Veronica, come back here," he whispered.

Veronica looked at him in confusion, still clinging to her pet. She turned back to Boris, examining his eyes.

"Boris?" she shivered. "Boris, can you—"

The ronk made a guttural huff and started to move. His front legs appeared to bend unnaturally, and his back hunched. Veronica stepped back robotically, terror-struck, as Boris rose up on two legs and clenched his five-fingered hands into fists.

The minotaur roared.

8
<u>Child of the Obelisk</u>

We started to retreat down the hall in the direction we came, when two more hybrids appeared to intercept us. In a matter of seconds, our wrists were cuffed in weighted restraints. We were escorted through the tunnel, Boris walking in between the other beasts and dwarfing them in stature. His upper set of horns were just inches from the tall, brick ceiling of the passageway. I estimated his new height was around eight feet. His bipedal gait was steadfast. As we passed through the hallway, the patches of tinted light provided brief, fleeting glimpses of Boris' new form. The same gray skin on his snout was now visible on his exposed chest and abdomen, as well as his muscular humanoid arms, although the rest of him was still coated in shaggy, tan fur. His fingers, tipped with sharp nails, curled furiously, ready to strike at something or draw his weapon from the pouch slung over his back. He was outfitted with armor plating on his shoulders. A metal belt fastened a cloth around his waist, an opening on the backside of which allowed his tail to swing freely behind him.

My exhausted muscles burned as the weights pulled my arms down in front of me. The circular stone clamps were connected by two short lengths of chain that kept my wrists close together and made it impossible to walk normally. I attempted to straighten out and a pain shot over the nerves in my right shoulder. I let my arms drop again and turned to Andy, who slogged along indignantly. I noticed that his machete was lost in the scuffle. He looked at me, shaking his head to express his frustration. I agreed with him silently.

A line of dull amber light formed above us as a pair of doors grinded against the stone floor and revealed the main chamber of MoiKy Chi's palace. We ascended a set of steps to behold the tyrant ruler waiting for us. He caught sight of our arrival from atop his platformed throne, and opened his arms in a welcoming motion. He laughed, internally at first, until the sound slipped through his toothy grin and exploded out of him.

"Isn't this adorable!" he proclaimed.

We stopped in front of the base of the platform, surrounded by our three grunting escorts. Chi raised his gloved hand to call Boris forward, while dismissing the other two. His smile grew greater as he settled into his seat and leaned right.

"*Like game pieces*," he said to Pann over the arm of his throne.

Boris halted beside the platform, his visage shadowed by the glittering wall of crystals behind him. MoiKy Chi couldn't contain his smugness as he gestured grandly to the minotaur.

"I see you've met the newest child of the obelisk. What do you think?"

We didn't respond.

"He's my greatest creation." His expression softened in admiration. "Taeloch was ready," he went on, grasping his chin. "He was the strongest. He was prepared for the next level of existence."

I swallowed hard and glanced at Veronica. She was staring at the floor, her face half-hidden by her hair.

"What is it, dear?" the ruler asked her. "Lose something?"

"You lied."

"Excuse me?"

"You said you wouldn't hurt him."

"I said I wouldn't harm *your* ronk. I kept my word." He sat forward in his throne. "The moment he entered my palace, he became mine."

Veronica's bloodshot eyes burned with hate and anguish.

Chi turned his palms toward us. "Same as you all." His stare shifted to Zyvin. They locked eyes for a moment, studying each other, before the tyrant spoke again, "I don't remember this one."

"Zyvin," he retorted.

"I did not request your name," Chi stated, agitated. "The faces of the weak all blend together." He watched us for another moment or two, before proclaiming, "Kill them."

Boris stepped in front of us and drew a spiked club from the pouch on his back. A menacing shadow stretched over our bodies, as he raised the weapon over his head.

MoiKy Chi bellowed, "Now, Taeloch."

The minotaur's massive chest rose and fell as he peered down at us, his brown eyes searching our faces. Veronica's was woebegone; her blue irises seemed darkened against the red-tinged irritation of her tears.

"Now," the tyrant repeated impatiently.

The minotaur tightened his grip.

Chi exposed the shining gem in the palm of his gloved hand. "Kill them!"

Boris let out a growl. He swung his club.

Chi went white with terror and dropped from his throne to avoid impact with the spiked weapon. It passed over him and hammered into the wall of crystals, as Boris let out a roar. Shards of the green stone shattered and detached from the formation and scattered over the floor. Murry picked one up, concealing it in his sleeve. The tyrant stumbled to his feet, eyes wild and mouth hanging open.

"How—?" he started. Boris swung his club again, bludgeoning the leader in the abdomen and launching him across the chamber.

"Ho-ho, alright!" Andy cheered.

Boris looked to Veronica and snorted. She smiled and blinked her tears away; new ones were beginning to form.

MoiKy Chi wheezed, gripping his ribs. Boris stomped toward him.

"Hey Chi, this really *is* your greatest creation!" Andy called.

The tyrant's eyes widened. "Guards!" he choked out. "Protect me!"

Two minotaurs rushed down one hallway, Chubz from another, while Pann retreated. The hybrids closed in. We glanced at each other, then scattered.

The guards broke formation to pursue us. I nearly tripped over my own sneakers as I ran, my hands still shackled and swinging gawkily in front of me. I panted, looking to see where the hybrids had gone, when I noticed an intensifying, rhythmic vibration pounding through the stone floor. One of the minotaurs charged after me at full-stride. I uttered a nervous sound as I ran out of places to go. My legs fidgeted, wanting to dodge, but I remained frozen. At the last second, Boris stormed in from the left, ramming into the assailant's jaw and knocking him to the ground.

I panted and nodded to Boris. He snorted, before another minotaur grabbed him from behind, pulling him into a new fray. My attacker started to stir. He placed his fist on the ground and shook his head with a growl. I looked behind me and found a freestanding pillar. I hammered my shackles against its surface in an attempt to break the porous-looking stone.

"*Ah!*" I sounded, my wrists pounding with ache. *Bad idea.*

I noticed a vase wobbling atop the column. The minotaur stood, shaking dust from its black fur and roaring furiously. While Boris was locked in combat with the other hybrid, the monster ran toward me again, picking up speed and tucking its head.

At the last second I jumped. The giant pillar crumbled upon impact, the chunks of stone and heavy vase burying the beast. A rush of sandy wind and debris blew over me.

"*Alright,*" I coughed. "That works." I balked when shockwaves resonated through the chamber.

Chubz grunted as he slammed a long-handled mace into the wall, missing Andy. The slow creature swiveled on his unbalanced fin-feet, corralling Andy and Veronica in a corner. He tried again. Veronica skillfully hopped over the weapon while Andy was struck in the abdomen by the handle's backswing.

"*Oof!*" he grunted as he soared, skidding to a stop on the floor in front of me. "*Arg...*" He arched his back at a pain and squinted up at me. " 'Sup?"

I helped him to his feet.

Chubz cornered Veronica. The skin around his neck quavered as he grumbled internally and reached out with one of his giant hands, lifting her by the torso to his eye level. Veronica strenuously raised her shackled wrists over her head as the beast's grip tightened around her. Chubz's jowls curled up as he roared in her face, revealing his rotting teeth. She winced at the foul fumes, shouting as she brought the heavy stone rings down on the monster's nose with a spattering crack.

The creature hollered in anguish, and dropped Veronica to cover his damaged face. The huntress landed in a sitting position. She pushed off the wall, slid under the beast, and popped up behind him, grabbing her multiweapon with her constrained hands. The two speared ends extended just as Chubz spun around, his huge, right forearm sweeping the staff from her grasp. Murry rushed to pick it up.

Veronica hopped backward as the beast regained his balance and bellowed in fury, red bubbles popping from his bloodied nostrils. We heard Boris roar, as the second minotaur guard was heaved across the chamber at Chubz. The two grunted and toppled, and were then struck by a powerful bolt of electrical magic cast from the multiweapon in Murry's hands.

Smoke rose from their motionless bodies as we regrouped and caught our breaths. Scooter clambered up to my shoulder from my pocket, as Veronica retrieved her multiweapon and retracted it. She tried aiming the handle over the back of a pin that secured the stone cuff, but couldn't. She approached me.

"Hold this."

I took the handle.

"Now tap the button once. Don't hold it down."

I followed the instruction and the spears shot from the compact handle, striking the backend of the pin and dislodging it. She freed her other hand, then helped the rest of us remove our restraints. Zyvin reappeared at our sides, looking around the chamber cautiously. He held out his wrists.

We rubbed our arms as the last set of the shackles dropped to the floor.

"We should go," Murry advised.

We started to agree, when arrows whizzed over our heads. We yelled and ducked down. One bounced off of Boris' shoulder armor. He grunted and raised his arm.

"Die!" Pann snarled as he fired projectiles from Veronica's confiscated crossbow. He shot tactlessly in all directions, and kept pulling the trigger even when the last of the preloaded arrows had been fired. He sneered at the crossbow and rotated it in scrutiny, when the chained segment of Veronica's multiweapon whipped it from his hands. "*Grah!*" he hollered.

Boris lumbered toward him.

Pann started to gallop away. "Reinforcements!" he shouted. "Rein—"

SLAM! With a single, swift kick, Boris sent Pann sailing like a flicked insect, disappearing down a shadowed hall. Our minotaur uttered an agitated growl, put his club away in its pouch, then looked alertly for any remaining threats. We followed his lead, taking one last glance around the area.

Incoming rays from the skylights of the palace illuminated swirls of dust that were just beginning to settle from the fight. Fragments of stone and crystal littered the floor, and bodies were strung out along the bases of the walls. MoiKy Chi's lay on the far side of the chamber without consciousness.

"What a dump," Andy declared. He caught sight of Veronica's crossbow and went to retrieve it.

Veronica smiled lovingly at her pet, her tender expression bright with pure exultance. She wrapped her arms around his stomach, then halted briefly when Boris knelt down and placed his nose against her cheek. She laughed, then hugged him again even tighter and buried her head in his chest.

"I love you, boy," she told him.

Boris snorted affectionately, and with his human arms, discovered he could hug her back. After a moment, he lifted her up.

"*Whoa*," she sounded, before letting out a laugh as Boris set her on his shoulder and started to walk.

"Let's go," she giggled. The crossbow under his arm, Andy continued looking around the chamber. I waved for him to follow.

"One sec," he replied.

"What're you doing?" I asked.

"Looting!" he answered, unsheathing weapons from the belts of the vanquished minotaurs. "Seriously Marv, play a videogame once in a while." He started to catch up to us, then quickly doubled back to kick MoiKy Chi once in the face.

"Andy, come on!" Veronica called.

Andy chuckled and jogged back to the group. I looked at the new weapons he had acquired. He held out two blades. One was a curved sword with a marbled, dark brown grip made of polished stone. The other was a double-edged dagger with a brassy hilt-guard and an ivory handle.

"Which one do you want?" Andy asked.

"Uh, I..." I thought aloud, shaking my head. "I don't care, really."

"Good, 'cause I wanted this one," he grinned, holding up the sword.

I let out a laugh and took the dagger.

Murry smiled, holding the crystal out in front of him. "We've got it."

I grinned back, turning the pristine-looking dagger in my hand and watching my reflection glint over the sharp, polished surface.

99

Boris led us to the entrance of the antechamber, in front of which two human guards stood attentively with elaborate, gold-colored armor and cumbersome looking spears of the same color and decoration. Their eyes widened at our approach and they readied their hefty spears, but paused to gawk at the massive minotaur we were traveling with.

We stopped a few feet away, Boris grunting. The two men stared back, awestruck. Boris threw his head back with a vociferous, echoing roar and the guards promptly dropped their weapons and ran.

Boris placed a shoulder against the tall set of arch-shaped doors and pushed. Inside, he set down Veronica, and we all explored the daunting, square cavity.

"Spooky place," Zyvin commented.

Scooter chirped in the chilly atmosphere as he scuttled from shoulder to shoulder to observe the foreboding room.

Against the far side of the antechamber stood an obelisk-shaped structure constructed from stone and accented with an ornate, brassy metal. Inlaid lettering of an unusual alphabet was carved vertically down its façade, and the characters sparkled with green. I couldn't tell if it was a statue or some type of machine. The only hint was a lever on the right side of the tower that was set to the inactive position.

Boris approached it. He carefully skirted the edge of a small pool of water at the contraption's base that flitted with emerald sheen from a crystal basin, and passed by a wall of canisters containing different colored liquids, all of which bore labels etched with the silhouettes of different creatures.

He stopped in front of the obelisk and drew his club, then grunted and smashed the front of the device. It cracked and bent. He slammed his weapon down on it two more times until the stone face had crumbled and the brass frame was nearly v-shaped, before issuing a final blow to the obelisk's zenith. The exposed, inner crystals shattered with a dying buzz, and Boris holstered his club.

"Hey, check this out!" Andy called. He had found our confiscated belongings in the corner. I took my backpack and ripped Captain Galloway book, Veronica grabbed her quiver of arrows, and Murry picked up his wand and covered the crystal in a cloth before depositing it safely into his rucksack.

Andy sighed.

"No necklace?" I asked him.

"No," he replied, muttering something under his breath.

We all filed out of the dark room and back into the hallway to make our leave, only to find MoiKy Chi smiling at us.

"Well, hello again."

We yelled as nets were thrown over our bodies. Boris roared and stormed to our aid, only to be apprehended by a pair of enemy minotaurs. They viced his arms with long-handled metal clamps, grunting and wrestling with him for control. We tried to cut ourselves free, but metal wiring coiled around the rope made escape impossible.

"There's no reversing the transformation, if that's what you were hoping," the tyrant told us. He spoke calmly, although his body was riddled with dark bruises, and breathing sounded challenged. "Taeloch and Boris are one being now," he continued. "One consciousness." He stepped closer to Boris, as the hybrids carried us away, back into the dim, eerie labyrinth that led to the prisons and arena of the coliseum. "And he is mine."

"No!" Veronica screamed.

Boris tried to shake free and pursue us, but the clamps around his arms stayed tight, and the doors to the underground passageway grated shut behind us.

MoiKy Chi peered into the eyes of the enraged minotaur as he growled and pulled at the clamps around his arms.

The human mind is always dominant, he whispered to himself.

The beast thrashed. A hybrid guard squealed, nearly losing its grip on the creature.

"Some minds require more coaxing I suppose." He held up his gloved hand, the metal fingers clicking as they opened, baring the green gem in the center of the palm. "Look here," the ruler instructed.

The beast hesitated, grunting and trying to pull himself away, but eventually his eyes drifted and locked on the stone.

MoiKy Chi grinned. "There you are, Taeloch."

The minotaur huffed. As his limbs relaxed, the other hybrids released their clamps, and the tyrant motioned for them to leave.

"Focus now," he said. "I want you to focus on your name as I say it. Taeloch."

The beast's ears twitched.

"You are mine. Forget the wizard, forget the boys," MoiKy Chi went on, reading the twitches in his creation's face. "Forget the girl."

The creature's chest rose and fell as he glared at the gem.

"Very good," MoiKy Chi said.

The monster's gaze switched to him.

"Now then—"

The minotaur's hand covered the ruler's face.

With a swift, powerful throw, MoiKy Chi hurtled against the wall and uttered a sharp wheeze, then fell limply to the ground, as the minotaur stomped off.

The tyrant remained in a crumpled heap for some time before his eyelids peeled. He blinked away a hazy film and stumbled to his feet. Hunched, he lurched forward, into the antechamber. He coughed violently and reached for a surface to steady himself, staggering into the shelves and dropping vials of animal blood to the floor. He groaned as the sticky substances blended and seeped into his shoes. Lifting his head, MoiKy Chi took in a startled, whistling breath at the sight of his mangled contraption. He ignored the pain throbbing in his muscles to canter toward the obelisk, bloody footsteps introducing red swirls to the emerald pool.

He placed his hands on the ruined structure, examining the large dents to determine if his invention was reparable. His face tightened in hatred and metal fist slammed on one of the depressions.

Taking a long breath to gather himself, the former emperor ran his gloved hand over the device. When he reached upward to examine the damaged zenith, a jolt of green light connected with the gem in his palm, followed by a thunderous surge that radiated his body.

Loose strands of energy wriggled from the main beam, coursing over the bloodied pool and pulsing with greater intensity. The tyrant ruler let out a garbled scream that resounded through the hallways, distorting. Next, a violent, squealing inhalation, followed by another panicked shriek that fused in resonance with the echo of inhuman screeches.

9
The Morogma

Everything whirred. From the terrifying howls reverberating off the walls of the passage, to the frenzied, disjointed thoughts ricocheting through my mind. The noises were penetrating. They rattled my subconscious, summoning images of my rowdy classmates hollering on the school bus. For a while, I pretended that I was still immersed in that clamor, that I was still oblivious. The bus shook as it passed over a pothole and the jocks in the back seats cheered at the springing action it created. This was a different kind of sound, however. It was menacing. It pulled me in. The image started to fade, but the cheers lingered and intensified. They weren't human.

A sudden pain in my back made me open my eyes. My fingers had gripped the netting so tightly that they had lost all feeling. I loosened my grip and freed an entangled sneaker to shift position in the cramped compartment. The hybrids carried us like garbage bags through the dimly lit hallways, occasionally swinging us and scraping our bodies against the wall.

Even our own breathing sounded distorted and ominous through the echoing tunnel. When a spot of light shined on our captors I peeked through the spaces of the netting at the creature that was carrying me: a hulking hybrid with fearsome jaws. Its slanted neck and gruesome, elongated head bobbed with each step it took. It breathed raucously through its open mouth, a long tongue frequently emerging to lick at the constant streams of saliva rolling over his grisly, external teeth. I couldn't decipher what animals it was comprised of. Its face looked reptilian, and though it had some scales, most of its body was covered in rough, cracked, gray skin, with fur of a similar dark hue coating its shoulders and areas around its neck.

The nets containing me, Murry, and Zyvin were gripped in the creature's three-fingered hands, while another hybrid, a stalky minotaur with horns sloping past his broad chest, transported the ones containing Andy and Veronica. The coarse air dehydrated my throat. I tried to swallow, but ended up hacking instead. The hybrid growled at the noise and slammed me into the wall. I winced at the pain and held in my yell so I wouldn't aggravate the beast any further. After a tense moment of silence the monster croaked a breathy hiss and swung me into the rock again anyway.

The hallway began to brighten as we approached the exit. A wave of hot air swept over our bodies when we left the chilled hallway and entered the scorching arena. The audience of monsters roared with delight as our captors flung us onto the sandy field. I let out a pained breath as my stomach struck the ground. Scooter clambered over my back, wrapped his cool tentacles around my neck, and chirped repeatedly. I groaned and lifted my head, granules clinging to my cheeks and lenses. I wiped them away and grabbed for my dagger, missing twice before taking hold of the handle and getting to my feet. Scooter continued to chirp. I steadied myself and looked ahead, as the arena shuddered, grains of sand rising off the ground with every thud. An enormous creature pulled free from its chains to stomp toward us.

The Morogma was colossal, with a fearsome head and horned snout resembling that of a rhinoceros. However, its eyes were small, yellow spheres with slit pupils, and mouth was lined with pointed, predatory teeth. A massive torso rotated with each crushing step, while four powerful arms swayed at its sides. The creature's fingers curled maliciously, and muscles in his arms and chest contracted as he threw back his head and unleashed a horrifying roar.

"Run," Murry spoke.

A rush of adrenalin glazed the strained muscles in my limbs and back, and I plodded across the arena faster than I had ever gone. A massive hand hammered into the ground behind me and a deep-toned growl of frustration sounded.

I kept sprinting. My breaths were short, infrequent inhalations. I glanced behind me at the sound of another slam, farther away this time.

"No no no!" someone cried.

I turned around in time to see Zyvin being picked up by the beast. He screamed as one of the four clawed hands wrapped around his torso and lifted him to his face.

"Hang on!" Andy yelled as he ran up to one of the beast's legs and hacked at its ankle with his sword. The Morogma turned in confusion, then swatted him away with the back of his lower right hand. Zyvin's hair was sucked forward and blown back as the Morogma sniffed him. Zyvin threw a couple ineffective punches at the beast's snout, before its lips pulled back and revealed rows of jagged, bloodstained teeth.

An arrow whizzed from Veronica's crossbow and stuck in the roof of the monster's mouth, locking it open. The Morogma gurgled and dropped his would-be meal to reach for his face, sputtering a growl. Zyvin flopped onto the sand. He frantically pulled himself forward and scrambled away, while the dissatisfied audience howled in disgust.

The giant hybrid's red tongue whipped at the foreign object. He growled and grabbed for his mouth, before abandoning the effort, forcing his jaws shut, and snapping the arrow in two. His throat writhed as it uttered a low-frequency roar that resonated across the arena. I clutched my ears as the deafening hum pounded through the earth and rattled my body.

The audience enlivened as the star of the show moved across the field, viscid saliva dripping from his bloodied mouth. Murry stepped in front of Veronica and aimed his wand at the terror. He fired several blasts of violet energy at its face, halting its approach momentarily. The creature huffed, shaking away the attack, before walking again and ignoring the blasts that followed.

Murry and Veronica sidestepped to evade a strike. The Morogma roared, overwhelming Murry's voice as he shouted a spell and sent a disorienting wave of wind at the beast. He and Veronica retreated while the Morogma raised his arms at the gust and grunted in anger, then turned to look for his targets, finding that they had relocated behind him. Murry stayed in front of Veronica, a violescent sphere shining on the end of his readied wand. He guided their backward steps while keeping his gaze locked on the behemoth. Veronica aimed her crossbow over Murry's shielding arm and fired an arrow at the creature. It sunk partially into a dermal plate, only to be brushed away immediately after. The Morogma's yellow eyes narrowed, and hands balled into fists as he prepared to charge.

A boom sounded from across the stadium, sending a hush through the audience. All heads turned toward the source, a wooden gateway. It shook, slats separating, as another forceful impact pounded from the other side. The Morogma stopped and sniffed the air. Suddenly, the wooden gate fractured and flew open, as Boris rammed through. He cantered to a stop on the dusty ground and roared. The Morogma approached his new combatant.

Onlookers began to chant as the four-armed beast rounded and studied the new minotaur, head low, blood-red tongue swirling in his maw. Without warning, the Morogma took off. His arms swung as he picked up speed and barreled down the field. Boris drew his club as the beast neared and took two half-gallops before bludgeoning the creature's lower jaw. The uppercut struck with enough force to break the beast's stampede, lift his feet off the ground for a moment, and send him toppling backward.

The stunned audience hushed as their monster lay battered. The beast rolled onto his stomach, eyes gleaming hatefully at his newfound enemy, and tongue licking the blood from his stained gums. His four hands gripped the sand, then pushed his hefty body back into a battle stance.

Boris stood readied, club clasped and fist balled, as the Morogma stomped toward him. Boris snorted and issued another blow to the side of the Morogma's face. The abomination grumbled, blocked a returning attack with his forearm, and knocked the club from the minotaur's hand. Boris threw a punch, and the Morogma caught it.

The tank-like creature took hold of Boris, raising his body over his head and roaring to the audience, before chucking him away. The crowd cheered delightedly, as their monster picked up his opponents club and roared again. Boris staggered upright, sand falling from his fur as he straightened out. The rest of us watched, petrified, unable to intervene in the battle of the beasts.

The two juggernauts circled one another from opposite ends of the field, the Morogma uttering taunting grunts and striking the earth with Boris' club. Boris ducked his head down and charged. The Morogma did the same, and when the two collided, they grasped each other's palms. Dust shot from the ground as they struggled for dominance. With the club gripped his lower right arm, the Morogma walloped Boris' leg, which impeded his might long enough for the depraved mutation to shove the minotaur away. Boris stumbled to a stop, and when he turned, his stolen club was tossed at him and bounced off his torso. The monstrous audience squealed with animalistic laughter.

Boris huffed and took hold of the weapon, as the hybrids' roars overlapped into a single, overpowering sound. And in response, the Morogma began to move. I swallowed hard as the stadium shook with the monstrous, echoing chants of the audience. They seemed to align with the Morogma's lumbering pace. As the cheers quickened, so did his steps, until the monster jogged at maximum speed across the stadium.

Boris' hooves shifted. He snorted, prepared to swing, and when the Morogma drew near him, he issued his attack.

The Morogma ducked his head down in avoidance, before rearing himself up again and driving his horn into Boris' side. Boris let out a howl as the Morogma lifted him by the wound. The awkward location of his strike caused the minotaur to twist in midair and land hard on the dusty field.

Veronica let out a panicked cry as her pet struggled to move. The audience roared with delight. Boris grunted and clawed at the ground in an attempt to stand, before two of his foe's massive hands wrapped around his ankles. The Morogma pulled him back and threw him across the arena. We watched helplessly as Boris hit the stone wall on the opposite end of the ring. Rock crumbled inward when he struck it, and a cloud of sand swirled from the crater, hiding the minotaur from view.

The Morogma's crimson tongue spiraled to lick his nostrils. He grinned fiercely at his injured competitor, then released a sharp cry when an arrow buried in his neck.

He growled and turned to Veronica as two more projectiles pelted him. He scratched the first one away, as Murry fired violet blasts from his wand at the creature, calling his focus in yet another direction. The beast wailed and raised his upper arms at the barrage, annoyed. The grotesque audience hollered irately at the Morogma. The beasts in the front row were the most outraged, throwing loose items and spitting through their teeth as they vocalized their anger. The other creatures expressed themselves with less clout, mirroring the motions of the others and mimicking their cries in whatever squeal or growl their amalgamated vocal cords allowed them to create. Andy swiveled to my left, following my eyes and scanning the onlookers. They seemed entranced.

Andy frowned at a figure in an observation balcony.

He yelled, "Is that you, Chi?"

The cloaked entity rotated. Eyeing Andy, he raised a gloved hand to the eye-level of his shaded hood and pinched his index finger and thumb together.

"Yeah, that's you," Andy grumbled.

The Morogma's muscles spasmed. He flexed every one of his arms and roared at the audience, heeding their appetite, before lumbering across the field where Boris lay immobile.

"We can't let him get to Boris," Andy told me. I nodded, then looked to Scooter, who, reading my gaze, leapt from my shoulder and clung to the wall. Andy raced toward the behemoth, sword brandished, and I followed, dagger in hand. Andy sprinted ahead of the beast, tapping a forearm with his blade as he passed.

"Yoo hoo!"

It grunted, not redirecting its path.

Andy jumped back in front and chopped at the beast's knee, before retreating to a safe distance once again.

The Morogma roared.

Andy repeated the process and hopped in and out of the line of attack, like a rodeo clown, leading the monster in the opposite direction. My senses began to cloud as I ran to join the fight. Sounds muffled and the world slowed as I closed in on the towering monster. I watched Andy leap backward as the Morogma bent down to swipe at him, and at that moment I felt myself lunge onto the monster's back and stab my knife into it.

The dagger sunk into the atrocity's thick, gray skin, and when I pulled back on the handle, the metal edge detached. As I gawked at the bladeless weapon, the shouts of the stadium resurged, shaking me back to reality.

"Marv!" I heard Andy scream, as the Morogma bucked me from its back and hammered me in the stomach. I flew into the wall, grit digging into me as I slid down. It all happened too quickly for me to feel pain. I shook my head, disoriented and enflamed.

"I'm useless!" I shouted. A shadow suddenly covered my body. The Morogma had abandoned his pursuit of Boris and selected me to finish off first. "*Shoot!*" I muttered, backing up a few inches as the drooling beast loomed over me, ignoring the projectiles lobbed at him by my hollering group members.

I caught sight of a handle to my right and reached for it. When I held it out, I realized it was just a discarded arrow—one that was broken and missing the speared end.

Of course, I thought.

A putrid breath fumed from the creature's mouth. It hissed and sucked up its own saliva as it breathed. The audience was chanting again. My friends were yelling. The pounding force of the stomping, hollering spectators and the frenzied shuffling of the group sent particles of sand airborne, and cyclonic breezes sucked them up and wisped the grains along my raw skin. The sandstorm dissipated over my glasses, as the hideous creature clenched its fists and heaved its chest. Arrows fractured off its invulnerable body.

"I'm running out!" I heard Veronica call. I heard the clanging of steel and a demanding shout of Andy's blend into the whir of noise. I blinked, breathing heavily, as the world slowed down again. Murry hollered magic words, powerful bursts of energy radiating from behind the beast and exploding into clouds of indigo smoke against the back of my attacker's cranium.

I felt a tightness form in my abdomen. A symptom of my horror, I thought. Emotions circled internally, changing. They transformed into something else, something palpable, physical. All things ceased to be real except for that feeling. It roiled and surged upward, through my chest and manifested into a single word as it erupted from my throat:

"Inferna!"

A wave of flame exploded from the end of the fractured arrow that had remained clenched in my outstretched hand. The Morogma let out a pained wail and shielded himself as the fire rolled over him. I gawked, unblinking at the firestorm as I got to my feet. I had almost lost control of the blaze as I assumed my stance, but reoriented and pressed forward, the Morogma yowling and staggering back.

The flames suddenly cut off. The Morogma's veins pulsed beneath his quavering skin. He raised his head above his shielding arms, gritting and blowing an enraged breath from his nose. But a bellowing roar that slipped through his teeth was cut short, when Boris returned, ramming into the creature's lower jaw with his horns.

The Morogma fell, sliding to the middle of the field, his body clobbered and skin still fuming. He struggled to raise himself, snapping in attempts to reposition his broken jaw. As he wobbled to his feet and Boris approached, the monstrosity let out a gurgling shriek. Boris sidestepped to dodge a staggering, unsuccessful swipe, and then brought his club down on the beast's skull.

Boris stepped back, snorting, as the Morogma's immense body collapsed, and sent a shockwave through the coliseum and the bodies of its spectators. We gathered around the center of the stadium at Boris' side, catching our breaths and gaping at the body of our defeated foe.

Andy raised his arms in an exhausted shrug.

"It's just that easy," he joked between breaths.

Veronica rubbed Boris tenderly.

"Good job, boy." Her hand levitated over the deep wound in his side, before petting him again. She swallowed. "Good job."

Zyvin joined us last, Scooter clinging to the back of his head. He cleared his throat and tried to say something, when the cephalopod clambered over his face.

"*Eh, ack!*"

Scooter chirruped and leapt to me.

"Uh, yeah," Zyvin muttered awkwardly. "That's yers."

I nodded to him as Scooter settled on my right shoulder. On my left, I felt Murry's hand come down.

"Well done there, kiddo," he laughed as he jostled me proudly before releasing his grasp. "Seems you have a knack for magic."

I grinned and let out a half-pant, unable to speak.

Murry smiled, then looked upward when the beasts of the front row began to protest and rise up from their seats. The wizard stepped back and readied his wand.

"Perhaps we should make our exit."

10
Escape From Inuento

The sickening horde writhed impetuously, like swarming insects from a disturbed hive. The innermost row of creatures stretched their limbs over the edge, producing the loudest cries and aggravating the hysteria. As I scanned the violent crowds, I noticed the empty observation tower of the coliseum.

Veronica loaded one of her two remaining arrows, eyeing the crowd.

"Stay together," she voiced, as we all moved backward as a unit. Gears turned. A metal gate behind us clunked open. We spun around, weapons brandished, expecting to see another animal charge from the passage. But instead, a familiar laugh echoed from within. MoiKy Chi's white smile was the first thing to become visible through the shadowed opening.

"Well done, well done," he applauded. "Inuento, *here* are your champions!" The audience growled in rancor and disgust. Their ruler drew nearer to us, the ground shaking with every step he took. We frowned in perplexity as the former emperor seemed to grow taller the closer he came.

He continued to congratulate us, "I am truly impressed. Not a single human or beast has conquered the Morogma. Pity he's dead—he was so difficult to create." He turned his head and sucked a breath through his fake grin. "Took a lot of *ingredients* to build him. I'll have to restock."

A barbed, scorpion-like tail emerged from the dark and stabbed the ground between us. We all gasped and scrambled apart.

"I'm sure you'd be willing to contribute."

The tail whipped around and stabbed the sand at my feet, and I jumped back in horror. The deadly appendage retracted and coiled to its owner's side.

MoiKy Chi entered the light and threw down his cloak, revealing his new, frightening form. His face, arms, and abdomen remained human, but his legs were bovine, clad in matted, black fur with massive hooved feet, and his back was covered in gray scales and exoskeletal plating that traveled over his shoulder blades and spine, and transitioned into a deformed, arachnoid thorax and swinging, scorpion's tail.

He laughed and raised his hands, the gem of his right glove sparking. Two gray, eel-like creatures, fused at the bases of their necks to MoiKy Chi's shoulders and trapezii, snaked upward from behind the tyrant. They snarled and drooled from their hanging jaws, as their lengthy forms bobbed and steadied into s-shapes. Each of his extra heads possessed a crocodilian cranium ended with a pseudo-beak and sharp, outer fangs. A tri-set of dark, spiraled horns crowned the terrors, and sinister, serpentine eyes stared us down from their high vantages.

"There have been a few changes since last we spoke," the mutated madman announced.

"I didn't think it could be done," Andy admitted. "You managed to make yourself even uglier."

MoiKy Chi laughed internally.

"I'm serious," Andy chuckled, pointing to each of the three heads. "I can't tell which one is you."

In response, the serpent to his right hacked a green ball of liquid at Andy's shoes. Andy stepped back as the acidic fluid hissed and dissolved a hole in the earth. He pointed to the creature with the dripping mouth. "Definitely that one."

The plates on Chi's back clicked together angrily, as a few members of the hybrid audience began to slip from their seats into the coliseum's battlefield.

"Your time here has expired," the ogreish ruler stated coldly. He bore his gemmed palm, curled his metal fingers, and the head of every spectating hybrid shot up. "Farewell."

The entire stadium drained, its occupants crawling over one another to tumble into the arena. MoiKy Chi laughed as his army flowed around him and closed in on us. We grouped together again to form an outward-facing ring. Veronica shouted an order that was inaudible over the cacophony. But in unison with the group, I readied my improvised wand, and we began to take steps as a single entity toward the exit of the arena.

Hybrids howled as they scrambled toward us. We efficiently fended them off. Our combat weapons deflected the assaults, and spells kept the monsters at bay. I felt absent from my body as I methodically and naturally fired blasts of flame at the beasts. I discovered that the greater intensity I gave my words and movements, the more powerful my spells became.

"Inferna!" I exclaimed, halting the hastened approach of an enraged, horned beast. I shouted the magic word once more, feeling my hand buzz with warmth. The muscles in my palm twitched, almost innocuously. I watched as particles of crimson luminance detached from the splintered end of my makeshift wand. They floated outward, like droplets of magma in an absence of gravity, before coming together and spinning wildly into a white-hot light that surged and sent an airborne fireball hurtling at our attackers.

This is amazing, I thought.

Zyvin shuddered and shielded himself, as Andy's sword crossed in front of him to block the lunging polearm of an armored minotaur.

"Keep it together, Zy!" Andy told him.

"I don't have a weapon!" he yelled.

Veronica glanced at Zyvin, then looked into the battlefield. She flipped her multiweapon, launching a speared segment at an incoming reptilian hybrid. It shrieked as the blade sunk into its scales, leaning back and clawing at its chest. Its toothy maw released another frantic wail when Veronica retracted the chain, pulling the beast toward her. When the sputtering creature skidded within reach, Boris walloped it with his club, separating the beast's body from the blade of the multiweapon and loosening its grip on a speared staff.

Veronica picked up the new weapon and tossed it to Zyvin. "Here!"

Zyvin fumbled with the hefty tool, muttering nervously.

As we continued our tactic and worked our way across the field, the mutated tyrant released a displeased breath. "This is no fun at all." He stomped toward us in a few steps, kicking past his charging minions, and dipped one of his monstrous, extra heads into the center of our ring, biting the ground.

I let out a yell, as the eely creature lifted its head, eyeing me fiercely and snapping. Suddenly, the motive behind its stare went blank, as Chi seized control. The second swooped alongside the first, and the two serpents swept forcibly in opposite directions, separating our group.

I landed hard on my stomach in the dust, grunting, and before I could lift my knee to get to my feet, a hand wrapped around the collar of my shirt. Boris lifted me from the sand and set me down. I thanked him and he snorted in response, before the two of us fended off an enclosing crowd of hybrids.

Andy and Murry were slashing and blasting through the swarm ahead of us, and Zyvin and Veronica were farther back. The huntress extended her multiweapon, stepping and spinning, twirling the staff above her head. As she picked up speed, the three sections separated, linked by chains, and spun even quicker. The bladed ends sliced at the bodies of the encroaching horde. They stumbled back. Some collapsed. The blades of the multiweapon cut into the ground, and when she halted her spin, she dropped down, plunging the two ends into the sand amid a pile of vanquished opponents.

A screeching sound made her rise again. She fired an arrow into the sky, shooting down a pale, winged, bat-like hybrid. She raised her last arrow above her.

"Murry!"

Murry turned, made a motion with his wand and shouted, "Renora!" A shimmering, yellow light shot from his wand, surrounded the arrow, and in a flash Veronica's fist was clenched with countless duplicates of the projectile.

I felt my mouth fall open in amazement. Before I could gather myself, a squeal sounded at my left, and a hoof impacted my arm. I jumped back, prepared to launch a fireball at my attacker, but stopped. A pig-man grunted, swinging his arms stiffly, against his will.

I frowned and shoved him away, before assuming a battle stance when another hybrid roared and charged for us. A blood-red tongue writhed from his long mouth, flailing as he ran. I recognized the horror as the beast that had netted me, Murry, and Zyvin. Unlike the pig-man, its beady eyes were fearsome and focused. Before it could strike, Boris swept its legs with his club. It landed, screeching and snapping, before Boris issued a final bludgeon to its face, knocking the beast out.

The felled hybrid was clad in brass-colored armor, certain areas of which were bejeweled with green stones. As I examined the skirmish, I noticed that the monsters adorned with this armor were fiercer—more exact with their attacks, while the other hybrids lumbered along, directionless and drone-like. They seemed to follow the motions of the armored beasts at the front of the barrage.

MoiKy Chi bellowed orders from his spot in the center, raising his gloved hand and exposing the gem in its palm. Whenever he did so, diminutive specks of light flickered inside the gems of the guard-beasts' armor as well, reaching the eyes of every hybrid in the coliseum. MoiKy Chi clenched his metal fingers, the green crystal in his palm shining and intensifying the vigor of his subjects.

"Veronica!" I called, pointing to Chi's hand.

She spun around, catching sight of the glow, and raised her crossbow to her eye.

An arrow cut across the field, through a brief opening in the maze of limbs and into the crease of the crystal's frame. The gem shattered, an arc of plasmatic, green current flaring from the tyrant's broken glove.

"*Argh!*" he growled, gripping his wrist, as the masses of hybrids suddenly stopped their assault.

They grumbled, looking to each other in confusion. During the brief reprieve, we all regrouped, swerving around the befuddled creatures and heading for the exit.

"Stop them!" MoiKy Chi roared. The beasts didn't budge. Some of the guards barked orders at the unmoving hybrids, who snarled back in defiance. While attempting to navigate the crowds, Chi kicked over a few hybrids with his hooves, stirring aggression. "Silence!" he snapped, to no avail.

Andy laughed, "Hey Chi, who's in charge now?"

"Insipid *peasant!*" the former ruler boomed. "Of course my mind is dominant over these filth-eaters!"

A hush fell on the creatures, including the snakes fused to his own body.

"Get them!" Chi roared.

The hybrids didn't move. His extra heads hissed, the right one locking eyes with him.

Chi's nostrils flared, as he raised his gemless glove at the serpent and breathed hatefully, "*Listen to me!*"

The snake screeched and bit into his hand. MoiKy Chi roared in pain as the creature retracted, steam rising from the bite marks as its corrosive saliva melted the metal. The second one bit into his side. Chi hollered and wobbled, sinking to the ground while the liberated hybrids overpowered his guards and moved in around him. The serpent on his right shoulder sunk its fangs into his collar, while the left one chomped down on his stomach again.

Chi was eating himself alive.

MoiKy Chi let out one more wail before he disappeared into a sea of limbs, claws, and snouts. At the same time, a heavy wooden door burst open, and a wave of enslaved humans rushed into the coliseum, overpowering the remaining guards.

We jogged for the nearest exit, turning briefly to call for Andy, who was shouting into the fray and pumping his fist in the air.

"Andy, let's go!" Veronica yelled.

"Coming!" He worked his way past the scrambling bodies and joined us.

The hybrids were not only going for MoiKy, but for the arena itself. Frames and decorations crumbled inward. Andy turned around one last time.

"Killer party, Chi! You really know how to bring the house down!"

Veronica grabbed his arm and pulled him along.

He chuckled to her, gesturing at the destruction. "Get it? 'Cause of the—"

"Yeah. Good one." She motioned him onward

The raucous cries of revolt faded into the distance, overwhelmed by the crashing of waves against our stern. The wind and currents were both moving in the perfect direction as we made our escape from the chaotic isle.

As we sailed, the sky dimmed. The thick clouds faded into a deep indigo color, almost completely concealing the sun's fleeting rays. The hidden sunset gave the spaces of the dark, cumulous ceiling a scarlet, molten hue. The clouds parted in a couple areas above us, gleaming like massive, curious eyes. They watched us as we slipped away, into the sparkling ocean, before they too retreated as nighttime took over.

I leaned back, feeling my arms hang limply, exhaustedly, over the edge of the craft. I took a deep breath from a cool, pelagic breeze. Holding in the air, I shut my eyes and attempted to direct my focus away from my aching body. Scooter's chilly tentacles graced my neck as he crawled over me. I smiled at him, and laughed contently through my nostrils when he chirped and explored the compartments of my backpack. He reemerged at the sound of Zyvin's unusual, howling yawn.

Veronica asked him, "How long did MoiKy Chi keep you prisoner?"

At first Zyvin didn't notice the question, seeming preoccupied with the nighttime expanse, moonlight glinting off his eyes. When it finally registered he fidgeted.

"Hm? Oh... I've—" He cleared his throat, thinking, sighing. "I've been imprisoned a long time." His eyes flicked at us solemnly. He shifted to avoid our concerned stares.

The isle was almost invisible, but the glow of fires was intense enough to pierce the night. As we observed the flickering, distant lights, we cumulatively caught sight of two forms floating by on a buoyant slab. The hybrid in the front was long-armed and rowing with his palms, and the one behind was stout and kicking from the back. As I squinted, I recognized the latter creature as the pig-man. He snorted and raised a hoof to our boat.

I mirrored his wave; my friends did the same. We watched the two hybrids paddle for the mainland atop what looked like a door from Chi's palace. They disappeared in the distance, as Murry stated, "Shmileah is going to be very confused."

"Hey, an island!" Andy announced. A small island started to become visible on our right. The islet looked plain and uninhabited. It was barely large enough to accommodate a single house. "We should stop for the night," he suggested.

"We should keep going," Veronica replied automatically, guiding direction of the sails.

Andy shook his head at her response. "What? Why?"

"To get *you* two to the next crystal."

Andy sat forward, listing reasons on his fingers. "We're *tired*."

"Doesn't matter as long as one of us is awake."

He raised a second finger. "We're *exhausted*."

"Same thing." She shook her head, frowning. "You don't even have to move—"

"*And* we're hungry."

Veronica growled. "We *have* food. Murry brought some with him."

"There're fruits on the island though! Look!" He pointed to the orange, oval-shaped fruits sprouting from branches. "We can eat some of those and save the rest."

"We don't know if they're safe."

"Those are guallovs," Murry reported, peering at the trees. "Guallovs are safe."

"Guallovs are good," Andy added.

Veronica sighed.

Andy urged, "I *really* need to take a bath too."

"I agree with you there."

"It would be smart to make port," Murry explained. "It's always preferable to sail at daytime." He stretched out, yawning. "And rest is always valuable."

Veronica eventually agreed, turning into the shore. We got out, and Boris dragged our craft onto land. We plodded across the deep swaths of sand to a more level area.

Andy clapped and rubbed his hands together. "Alright! Let's break the tents out—"

"Can't," Veronica stopped him.

"Huh?"

"Chi took 'em."

"Dang it! We have to sleep on the ground?"

"Better than the cells."

We agreed, as Murry circled the group to perform the healing spell on each of us. Tingling, new flesh replaced the whip scars on my back, and I let out a soothed breath. When Murry approached Zyvin, however, he protested.

"Nah, nah, I'm good."

"Are you sure?"

"Yeah, I'm not too banged up, y'see. 'Sides, magic an' all..." He cringed. "That sorta thing gives me the creeps."

"Very well."

Boris snorted as Murry healed his battle wounds, and Veronica petted him. She gave him a hug, then found a spot against a tree to sit. Boris grunted. Mirroring her movements, he bent his knees, placed one hand on the ground, and lowered himself into a seated position with a huff. Veronica scooted to his side.

Once we were all healed, Murry distributed handfuls of sweet-smelling powder that he retrieved from a jar in his rucksack. He called it a *dry wash*, and when I asked him how it worked, he told me the powder was a special type of dried mud that had incredible cleansing properties.

"You can clean yourself with *mud*?" Andy asked.

"Yes," Murry replied.

Andy shrugged and buried his head in the floury substance. When he rose, his face was covered in the white powder. Clumps of it were clinging to his eyelashes and bangs. He let out a laugh, which blew a cloud of white from his lips and made him chuckle even more.

"I swear officer, it's not mine!"

Andy and I laughed, although no one else gasped the joke. After we cleaned ourselves with the powder, we wound down and helped gather supplies for the night.

The thick overcast had cleared to reveal a perfect, night sky. The embers from our campfire twirled around each other as they rose, pirouetting for an audience of stars. I smiled at the performance, before returning to the group's conversation. Andy gestured to me with his thumb.

"Marv and I were... ten I think." He looked at me to confirm.

"Yeah, it was fourth grade," I said.

Andy continued, "So, this kid was *huge* compared to us. Like Boris-sized."

Boris snorted, and Veronica grinned in skepticism.

Andy assumed a hulking stance and imitated the bully in a deep voice, "Gimme yer lunch money! Grah!"

Veronica laughed as Andy recounted how we narrowly avoided getting beat up. He exaggerated slightly about the grandness of our escape and how I managed to outwit the brute with a riddle. Andy chuckled upon concluding his story.

"That guy was a real bozo."

"What's a bozo?" Veronica asked.

"Someone who's dumb," Andy replied.

Veronica giggled at the word.

Our tiredness seemed to fade. Andy recounted several tales that had everyone laughing, and although I could sense the dwindling presence of my worried thoughts, they seemed distant, unreachable. They were overwhelmed by a feeling of revivifying contentment, and I was more than willing to let them drift away for the night.

Zyvin sat apart from the rest of the group, shaving the end of a stick with a small knife.

"Cool knife," I heard Andy say.

Zyvin thanked him under his breath.

"I thought you were unarmed."

Zyvin looked up, defensive. "I was," he insisted, holding up the small blade. "You really think this would'a done me any good out there?"

Veronica defused the hostility. "Where're you heading, Zyvin?"

He shaved another piece of wood away. "Puerri Island."

Veronica examined the map. "Where is that?"

Zyvin reluctantly stood up. He found the spot on the map and pointed it out with his knife.

"Oh. That's pretty far."

"I know."

"We won't be down there for a while. We can drop you off someplace closer if you'd like—"

"No, no." He finally cracked a grin. "I ain't no sailor I'd get myself lost."

"Well then, you're sticking with us for a while."

He continued whittling. "That's fine."

I lay with my hands behind my head, observing the marvels in the sky. I turned when Murry mentioned, "It is fascinating."

"What?" I asked.

"Areok was also a spellcaster. This is the second time an Earther has come to our world, discovering untapped abilities."

I smiled.

"He was a master of both the sword *and* the wand," he laughed, gesturing to Andy and me. "The two of you are like another version of him."

"Hey, check this out!" Andy hollered. He threw three fruits into the air to juggle them. He caught one, but the other two fumbled to the ground. Veronica clapped her hands unenthusiastically.

Murry looked to me and shrugged. "Someone once told me that, they heard Areok say, things like magic are not present in your world... which," he shook his head, "baffles me." He cleared his throat. "But, I wonder if such properties are, in fact, present. Perhaps in a different way. Or perhaps invisible."

I asked him, "What happened to Areok?"

"I don't know. No one does, really."

I thought for a moment. "Did he just..." I couldn't construct a new question, but Murry elaborated anyway.

"He was present for a long while. He jumped back and forth, between our world and yours, earning many titles. He even mastered and taught the practices of Ka before he disappeared."

"What's Ka?"

Murry's eyebrows raised in surprise. "Ka is energy," he told me. "Spiritual energy, carrying the essence and effulgence of all things."

When I stared back more quizzical than before, he sat forward to elaborate. "It is similar in some ways to the energy you draw upon when you cast a spell. Unseen, until it is accessed. The difference lies in the origin of this energy."

I nodded, soaking up the information.

Murry brushed his fingers through his beard, gathering his thoughts to explain the difference: "Magic—you see—draws upon the innate, world-building energies of the elements. Ka instead flows directly from the lifeforces of the world's inhabitants."

"Ka is... someone's spirit?"

"Ka is a *product* of the spirit."

I leaned in when Murry steadied his hand below his chin, slowly uncurling his fingers. A small sphere of pure light flickered in his palm, its shine lightening my stunned features.

"Everything has Ka," Murry spoke. "Even nonliving things absorb this energy from nearby lifeforces." The ball of light spiraled. He smiled at it. "I believe that Ka contains the intersectional property of all the elements. The simplest and grandest quality of all. And it resides within us."

Murry raised his hand toward a rock, the white glow spreading and shining down his fingertips. I immediately spun to view the effect. The same glow appeared on the stone, activating something deep within. It lifted a couple inches off the ground, rotated slightly, and after a moment, dropped, burying partway into the sand. I looked to him, astonished.

"That's the best I can do," he laughed lightly. He sounded out of breath. "There's much more to it that I'm not capable of."

"That's amazing," I said.

He smiled, reading the wonderment in my eyes.

"Can you teach me?"

He seemed taken aback by the question. He thought a moment. "I'm not the best at it, but I can try."

I reached for the same rock.

"Focus," Murry said. "Try to feel your own energy reach out and link with the rock's energy."

I frowned at the stone, but it didn't move. I dropped my arm.

"It's very hard," Murry insisted. "A very hard skill to master." He grabbed my shoulder. "Don't be discouraged though. Most folks can't even wrap their minds around it. Besides," he stretched out, "being a spellcaster isn't too bad either, you know."

I laughed and agreed with him.

Our small island became silent, as everyone fell asleep on the beach. I wanted to do the same, but my mind was still alert, thinking about magic and Ka. I rolled over to view the rock again. I reached for it, muscles tightening, as a breeze flowed over my arm. Through the dark, I thought I saw a few grains of sand move around the base of the object. I squinted at it, relaxing my hand.

Did it move? I wondered. I watched the rock a few moments more, then decided it didn't matter.

I rolled onto my back and directed my attention to the stars. In their presence I no longer felt small. Instead, I looked upon the brilliant specks of light as they glinted over their black canvass, like an expansive, celestial masterpiece that had been painted and presented just for me on this perfect night.

I grinned delightedly, when the portrait's dazzling subjects brightened and fluxed, and an encouraging message was delivered to me through their sparkling luminance:

Good job, Marvin, they conveyed. *You're not* useless.

11
The Living Island

I stretched out, bathing in sunglow before a loud cawing drew my attention. A plump, scruffy-feathered bird with a bumpy red crest and colorful beak squawked at the morning rays from atop the bough of an old, sodden tree. I shielded my eyes to observe it, grinning at its unusual plumage, when an arrow whizzed by and shot it from its perch.

My mouth fell open.

"Breakfast!" Veronica called.

I ripped a hunk of oily meat from a thick leg bone with my teeth. The portion frayed into stringy fibers, and the clinging globs of fat dissipated as I chewed. I swallowed, and only then did the metallic, gamey taste envelop my pallet. The bird had an overwhelming flavor, but I promptly finished my portion and left the scraps for Scooter to nibble on. He chirped with delight when another bone was added to his pile.

Boris snorted, finishing a huge meal of grasses that Veronica had prepared for him. He even picked up the charred organ meats of the bird and dined on them as well. I wondered whether Boris' new hybrid stomach craved the protein, or if his diet was always omnivorous. Before I could ask, a clanging sound filled the air.

Andy filed the blade of his sword with a bumpy, misshapen rock, attempting to sharpen it. Veronica took a break from stretching and approached him. She took the stone from his hand.

"The rock has to be flatter than that," she told him. She walked over to a tree and slammed the rock against its trunk, cleaving it into two sleek pieces. She smiled, before tossing the improved tool to Andy. "Bozo."

He caught the piece, watched her leave, then beamed a huge grin.

Murry retrieved the second half of the rock, bringing it to me as he drew his wand with his free hand.

He explained, "Some spells have similar properties to light." The wizard waved his wand over the flat, mirror-like surface of the stone. "They can be reflected." He aimed at the stone, then flicked his wrist. "*Renora.*"

A yellow beam flared, bounced off the sleek exterior, and returned to irradiate the instrument from which it came. Murry dropped the rock and held out his wand. The spell danced over the polished, wooden carvings, sometimes seeping into the grains, before a faded image began to take shape. When I looked closer, I could see miniature flares on the surface of the wand, sending specks of duplicated material sideways to form into a new object.

Like mitosis, the wand replicated itself. And as the last of the particles fused with the duplicate, a new wand dropped into Murry's other hand. He gave it to me.

"A wizard requires a proper wand."

I took hold of it, examining the exact same, intricate carvings along the handle.

"Wow..." I uttered, blown away. A great smile spread across my face as I thanked him.

He chuckled.

Andy plodded over the sand, swinging his sword loosely by his fingertips as he stepped. Veronica sat secluded on the far side of the beach, running her fingers through her hair. He watched her momentarily, then looked to the ground. He sucked a breath through his nose, then dropped his sword into the sand and joined her.

"Hi there."

She looked up at him and spoke tiredly, "Oh, hey."

When Andy sat next to her, he noticed she was running blue flower petals through her locks. "What're those?"

She looked back at him. "Oh, uh—" She released her long hair, a wavy tress bouncing and freeing one of the delicate adornments. She pointed to the interwoven petals with a spiral-motion, trying to think. "They're petals," she said, shutting her eyes and shaking her head at the vagueness of her answer. "I don't remember what kind. They're good for hair."

"Okay. Cool." He sat next to her as she completed her treatment, combing her fingers through a few more times. She dropped her hands to her legs, shrugging, then looked to him again with a modest half-grin. Andy gulped. Her periwinkle eyes seemed to sparkle more radiantly in the company of the royal blue flower petals bedecking her tresses.

Andy smiled at her. "You, ah..." He was suddenly speechless.

She tilted her head and raised her eyebrow. A petally, brown lock whorled.

"You look really pretty."

Veronica's expression reset. She looked down at her hands, fiddling, then smiled softly at him.

"Thanks."

I strolled across the islet, tasked with locating extra guallovs to gather before we sailed to our next destination. In one hand I gripped a loose branch and in the other I waved my new wand. As I made circles in the air I felt the resistance of wind change, and when I focused on the sensation, I could see a translucent ripple of air form in the wake of my patterns. I let out an intrigued breath.

I tucked the tool away when I reached the shoreline and the base of a tall, dark-trunked, guallov-bearing tree. Reaching with the fractured tree limb, I tugged at a bundle of the orange-skinned fruits. I whacked the branch once and the thorny green stems popped, freeing three guallovs. One bounced off the ground and splashed into the water. I left the other two in a small pile and went to retrieve it, reaching for the bobbing object with the branch.

As I reached, the fruit jerked away, wobbling. I frowned at it, stretching again. But before I could sweep it back to the shore, it submerged rapidly, disappearing. *What?* I wondered, leaning over the shoreline and peering into the deep. I squinted. For a brief moment, I thought I recognized movement beneath the surface, but the image quickly dissipated. I kept staring, puzzled. Then, two massive, red lights shone beneath the current.

The others were completing the final few chores necessary for us to progress when I came sprinting across the islet, my pace frenzied and face drained of color.

Veronica dropped a bag into our boat and stepped toward me. "What is it?"

"Something—" I started.

The entire island shuddered. A flock of long-tailed birds screeched and took flight from their perches.

Andy's eyes widened. "What was that?"

The ground shook again. This time the rumbling was coupled with a deep, echoing hum, like the blast of a distant fog horn. It pulsed from below.

Andy frantically repeated his question. Veronica knelt down, feeling the sand. She found a shallow spot, swept the grains away, and revealed a smooth, dark brown surface.

I approached, looking over her shoulder. "What type of rock is that?"

"It's not a rock," she replied.

Before we could make it to our boat, we were thrown off balance, another thunderous tone vibrating. Water splashed over the front of the island, soaking the trunks of trees as the entire land mass rose. Streams trickled from the edges, and the ocean stretched farther and farther below us.

We staggered. Andy and I fell to our knees near the edge. I wrapped my hands around a brim and pulled myself forward to lean and peer into a deep, dark aperture where two enormous saucer-shaped eyes glowed fearsomely.

The island was the shell of an immense creature. The foliage on its back swayed as it lumbered onward with long, tree trunk-like legs, piercing the ocean floor on speared feet. Its luminescent, crimson eyes shone brightly. Two beams swept across the ocean like searchlights wherever the gaze of its fiery, orange-red pupils drifted.

"That's just great!" Andy cried. "We just escaped an island *full* of monsters—"

The behemoth lurched, sand falling from the rims of its shell.

"And now we're on an island that *is* a monster."

Four long, gray tentacles stretched from the same aperture as the colossus' eyes. They swept at the currents, curled, and whipped the air. The living island released its sonorous, guttural groan, as we struggled to maintain our balance atop the tremulous ride.

"We're being carried off-course," Veronica said.

"*Of course* we are!" Andy announced. When the beast took another quaking step, he lost his balance and fell to the ground. "*Oof!*"

The behemoth stopped suddenly. We stayed still, our pupils darting between one another. Like an enticed snake, a gray tentacle prowled upward to examine the point of impact, and snagged Andy's ankle.

His face went white. "Oh, boy."

My friend let out a yell and clawed at the sand as the creature pulled him down.

"Andy!" Veronica shouted.

We rushed after him to no avail, as the beast pulled him off its shell and dangled him before its massive, inquisitive eyes.

"Hang on!" I called.

"It's not up to me!" Andy retorted, hanging upside-down.

The monster rotated him with its tentacles, uttering popping grunts. *There has to be a way out*, I thought, frantically searching for a solution. *There's always a way out.* The titan let out a gurgle, and the bases of its two front tentacles separated as a toothy beak came forward. The mouth unhinged, and the encircling puffy, mottled brown flesh vibrated as it screeched.

"Whoa!" Andy yelled.

The tentacle wrapped around his torso and brought him closer to the beast's gullet. I searched the land, grabbed a guallov, and heaved it at the tentacle. The fruit tumbled down the long limb and hit Andy in the forehead.

He shook his head, frowned, and hollered, "Whose side are you on, Marv?"

"Sorry!"

Strings of saliva quivered as the beak opened and closed. Andy squirmed. In his clenched fist, he discovered a handful of sand, and when he was pulled nearer, he threw the grit into the monster's eyes. It let out a shriek, and the red spotlights disappeared a few times as it blinked the grains away.

Andy cheered, but the island creature loosened its grip. Its tentacle unraveled, and Andy fell. Everyone screamed.

I stiffened in horror as I watched my friend plummet, screaming, toward the violent, churning ocean. My heart raced in panic. *No!* I reached forward. *Stop falling!*

Everything was suddenly quiet. I took in a few heavy breaths through my knotted throat and, realizing my eyes had shut, I lifted my head and reopened them.

A white glow surrounded my hand, and in the distance, Andy floated in an aura of the same light. A look of terror and confusion was fixed on his face as he gawped around, suspended in midair. I got to my knees and reached forward with both hands, making large motions on instinct. It felt like I was gathering a substanceless rope.

Andy levitated toward us, and once he was within reach, I took hold of his hand and pulled him up. We both flopped onto the sand. I rolled over on my back, suddenly fatigued.

Andy gaped at me, brow slanted and breathing heavy. "Thanks."

I lay there, body abuzz with simmering energy. I nodded nonchalantly. "Sure thing."

Veronica got Andy to his feet. Zyvin and Murry each grabbed one of my hands to raise me up.

Murry gripped my arm. "Well done."

We took a moment to recover before we convened around our boat in the center of the island-shell, adjusting our balance each time the creature took a quaking step.

Andy swayed with one of the stomps and raised his arms. "Now what?"

"Why don't we wait it out?" Zyvin suggested. "Wait till this thing sets down again?"

Veronica shook her head. "It might not."

"It might."

"It's going south. We need to go north."

The group's conversation slipped away for a moment as I explored my thoughts. I looked around, shaking my head at impractical ideas.

Andy interjected, "Maybe if we all get in the boat and..."

Veronica raised an eyebrow. "And what? Ride it down?"

"Never mind. That wouldn't work."

"Definitely not. And I think you've seen enough air today."

My head rose. "No," I heard myself say. "No, that might work."

"What?"

Murry studied me.

"Everyone in the boat," I instructed.

Veronica and Andy started to protest.

"Listen to him," Murry said calmly.

We all got in. Boris snorted and joined us last on the opposite end of the craft. The far bench creaked as he lowered into a seat.

I shuddered, "*Okay.*"

"Marvin, what's your plan?" Veronica asked.

"I'm having second thoughts about this," Andy said.

"It's okay," I said. "I'm... just gonna..."

The wooden boat groaned as white energy shined over its surface. I steadied my hands on either side of me and lifted us all off the ground a few inches in an aura of Ka. We slammed back down a moment later and everyone yelled. Scooter hid partially in his shell.

"That was for practice!" I assured them.

They exchanged uncertain looks.

Once they calmed and braced, I took a breath, gathered myself, and spread my fingers again. I frowned as I attempted to locate the boat's energy. *Come on, where is it?* I wondered, still trying to detect its presence. I spread my fingers farther apart, as if the greater surface area would more effectively capture the energy. I composed, then stopped overcomplicating my search and told myself, *It's there.*

The white glow reappeared. Startled, I quickly I extended my arms and clenched my fingers, feeling my veins throb and the muscles in my forearms quaver uncontrollably. The tenseness slid to my shoulders as I straightened out. Zyvin curled up in his seat, gripping the craft as we lifted off the ground. I took a heavy stepping motion, placing my right foot forward, and leaned.

Zyvin hollered as we levitated off the edge of the giant's shell, "Oh, sweet merciful creator!"

We lingered there for a moment, my muscles seizing up. I let out a gust of air. "*Okay,*" I strained. "Going down."

The light cut out. Everyone screamed as we twisted downward a few feet in the absence of Ka. I refocused, clenched my fingers, and the boat slowed and teetered in midair.

Boris released a snort. Veronica's face was frozen in panic. She gripped her seat, leaned forward, and let out a restrained, gravelly groan.

I apologized to everyone and oriented myself. Slowly, I pushed my palms toward the bottom of the boat, feeling a resistance that reminded me of two like-poled magnets nearing each other.

I felt heavier as I did so; my feet seemed fused with the floor. A pain in my temples started to manifest. I winced at it and gritted my teeth, as I struggled to set down what felt like a massive weight. I wanted to ignore the ache, so I turned my focus inward, to the flow of Ka. It charged within me, infused with the motive I willed, before escaping through my pores to become visible, shine, and link with the energy of our boat.

As we floated down like a leaf in autumn, the waves became audible, and I could sense droplets of water spraying up, disrupting the field of Ka beneath our craft. I lowered us a little bit more, before the white glow flickered out, and the boat fell the last few feet on its own. We grunted as we touched down, water splashing over the sides and rocking our craft. We steadied out, and everyone cheered.

"Alright, Marvin!" Andy shook me.

The celebration cut short, when one of the behemoth's pointed legs plunged into the water beside us, creating a wave that compromised our balance. We shouted and leaned in the opposite direction to become stable again. Veronica dashed to the sail and unfurled it.

"Aeralisk!" Murry shouted, casting a gust of wind into the mast and propelling us forward. We swerved in the beast's shadow, navigating its massive limbs and speeding to a safe distance. The creature watched us escape, the red beams of its gaze draping our backs, before it redirected its focus and lumbered away.

Natural winds began to flow into the sails, and Murry halted his spell and relaxed on the bench. My muscles felt numb; it took me a while to raise my arm and catch Andy's high-five. I leaned back, tired but content.

Zyvin asked us, "So what exactly is y'all's goal?"

Andy explained it all in a single breath: "We got sucked through an Orb in *our* world that was made out of five crystals from *your* world so now we have to collect those same five crystals in *your* world to make another Orb and get back to *our* world."

"Oh," Zyvin said. "Well alrighty. Say, can I see that green crystal ya got?"

Murry retrieved it to show him.

His pale, bony fingers wrapped around it. "Wow." The emerald shine reflected off his brown and his grayed eye as he examined it. "That's... that's quite a rock, ain't it?" A half-smile parted his lips.

Murry motioned for him to return it after a moment. He took back the crystal, wrapped it in cloth, and placed it in his rucksack.

We skipped across the waves, the dark blue surface of the ocean glimmering beautifully. Saltwater crashed against our bow, exploding into cool mist that wisped over my skin. I grinned and raised my Captain Galloway book to eye-level in an aura of Ka, flipping the page with the same energy.

"Okay, *now* you're just showing off," Andy said.

I laughed and dropped the book to my hands.

Two dolphin-like creatures leapt from the ocean alongside of our boat, drawing the fancied attention of everyone aboard. Their violet skin was translucent enough to display their glowing innards and flashing veins that blinked and cycled myriad colors as they dove in and out of the water.

A feeling coursed through me. One of invigoration and renewal that indicated the presence of something tremendous. As I witnessed the spectacular creatures arc and dive before the rosy sunrise, I felt as though I was meant to be there. That it was fate that had guided me to this beautiful world, rather than a horrible accident.

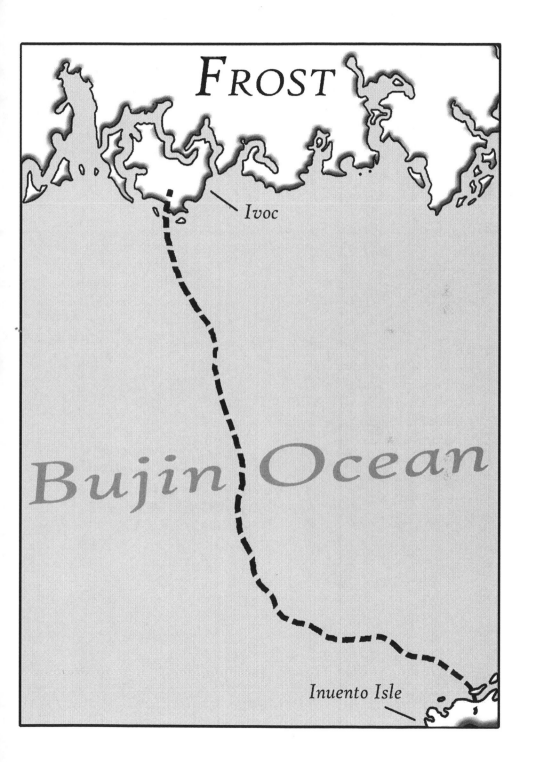

FROST

Ivoc

Bujin Ocean

Inuento Isle

12

Ivoc, Frost

Harsh winds battered us. I raised an arm to block the squall, but its stinging mists spiraled over my forelimb and numbed my face.

"How long has it been?" Andy chattered.

"Almost three days now," Murry replied.

Pellets of ice chittered over my lenses and bounced off my thick tunic. The padded outfits that Veronica provided were probably intended for a purpose other than cold weather. The long sleeves were thin and flexible, but the torso was stiffened by a denser material. I initially found it uncomfortable, but the attire somehow kept my core insulated, so I welcomed the coverage. Murry shouted over a gust that if we arrived at a harbor village he would purchase warmer clothes.

I had prepared an improvised nest-like enclosure for Scooter by stuffing my backpack full of fabrics and deconstructed carrying bags, but he frequently emerged to explore and seemed strangely comfortable outside.

Zyvin wasn't so adapted. He was shivering erratically, although he was offered the most material to cloak himself with.

"You okay, Zyvin?" I asked him.

"Fine," he shuddered, pulling sheets closer to himself and tucking them with his chin. His outermost layer was Boris' old bath towel, which everyone decided was best left unlabeled.

"How's breakfast?" Andy asked Veronica.

"Still swimming," she said, peering down the sights of her crossbow into the ocean. The arrow she loaded was fitted with a larger, multi-edged head, and was attached to a rope. A breeze flipped hair away from her attentive, blue eyes, and when a hazy shadow entered her shot, she fired.

Veronica yanked back on the rope, extracting a thrashing, foot-long creature from the water. It was a strange mixture of fish and crustacean. Veronica grasped the arrow that pierced its dark gray, segmented shell and underbelly, and lifted the alien to the center of our boat. Ovoid receptors resembling eyes were positioned on its semicircular cranium above two long whiskers, and although it possessed fringed pectoral and dorsal fins, its tail flapped horizontally, with crustaceous swimmerets fluttering underneath.

"Zyvin, lemme see your knife," Veronica said, holding the fish to the floor.

He chattered and stared forward, unaware of her question. Veronica awaited response, then held the squirming creature down with one hand and reached for her multiweapon instead. Murry intervened with a spell:

"*Sonnus!*"

A sparking, green light changed into smoke when it hit the animal, and its body eased in the mystic vapors long enough for Veronica to retrieve her blade.

The creature's body was propped upside-down. Murry held his wand beneath it and used the Inferna spell to cook the creature in its own shell. When the underside was cracked open, steam hissed and juices popped from within. Since the meat mimicked the shape of its segments, portions could be speared from the exoskeleton and easily distributed. I eyed my handful of meat. It was light-colored and darkly spotted, and when I took a bite I discovered it tasted how it looked—stringy and rich, like an oversized prawn with denser meat. To wash down our meal, Murry repeated his method to heat the remaining brothy stew that Dawn had given him.

Our satisfied breath clouded the wintry atmosphere as we completed our feast. To maintain our new internal heat we huddled up along one side of the boat. Zyvin kept distanced.

Veronica watched him, her head lying half-hidden in Boris' fur. "Aren't you cold?"

His eyes shifted. "Nah, nah. I'm good. Plenty warm—"

Boris snorted, grabbed Zyvin by the shoulder, pulled him under his arm, and squeezed him like a toy.

"Eh, ah!" He squirmed, before grumbling a sigh.

What looked like a pod of whales surfaced in the distance. Their heads were crowned by calcareous growths that grew outward into shapes that resembled coral, but were dense enough to split the ice as they rose. They sprayed water from the spaces in their ornaments, before ducking back down into the deep. I learned these creatures were called *plownoses*, and that they break up the frozen sheets whenever they rise. Recognizing that we were sailing in between fractured slabs of ice, I became suddenly fretful that one of the migrating creatures would emerge and impact our vessel. But thankfully, land became visible, and we pulled ashore without incident.

I trudged onto the snow, my steps wobbly and unstable. I ran my hands down my legs and gripped my knees, trying to push the feeling away. Veronica handed Andy the boat's mooring line.

"Moor this," she said to him.

Andy looked confused. "Isn't this enough?"

"What?"

"You said we need more of this."

"No. I said *moor* this. Tie it down."

"*Okay*, alright."

Andy awkwardly dragged the prow of the boat to the snowy bank and searched for something to tie it to.

We ventured forward, squinting through the whiteness. Murry led the group, looking for indications of our whereabouts and consulting the map, which frequently flapped over in the wind. He muttered under breaths and pointed to sets of ridges and peaks. He traced their outline with his finger and returned to the parchment to inspect their orientation on the inked continent.

Our pace ground still in the center of a sloping, bowl-shaped pass while he reasoned. Surrounding rock faces provided enough reprieve from the howling wind for Murry to decipher the map undisturbed. My eyes trailed, following the ridges of the stone peaks, until I reached an unusual shape. Through the blizzard, the jagged, rocky angles were interrupted by an organic form.

I tapped Veronica's shoulder, pointing out the shape. She frowned at it. Andy stared too. They both stepped to my sides to examine the apparition and mutter thoughts on it.

As we talked, the object moved. Limbs and pointed wings were distinguishable. It flapped up, a slender body hanging below the bat-like wings, while its head remained slanted toward us.

Veronica's features curled. She flared with anger. "Hey!"

Everyone's attention shifted skyward. When the blustery wind redirected, the looming beast took flight. My heart thudded as its shadow passed over us. Veronica trotted after the fleeing menace, pulled the crossbow from her quiver, and fired.

Hit, the winged creature spiraled into the snow, and we rushed toward it. Murry urged us to be cautious as we gaped at the frightening being.

The wounded fiend squirmed in an icy crater, snow blotted by a thick, dark substance rolling from where the arrow remained embedded. It pushed off the ground with feeble arms and lunged for Andy, who backstepped and swung his sword in front of him.

The hunching demon took a few wary, backward steps and stretched his wings out to appear larger. Faint, black energy rippled over his figure like flames, leaving dissipating trails as he backed. He kept his head low and eyes on us, his huge, dilating pupils quivering wildly from within the unnatural aura.

"A gargoyle..." Murry breathed. "How...?"

It snapped its fangs. A segment of Veronica's multiweapon launched and buried in the snow, and the beast screeched and leapt to become airborne again. Veronica retracted the segment as the gargoyle attempted to escape, its flight challenged by the arrow in its stomach. Veronica hollered at the creature as he fled. She fired another arrow that pierced the webbing of a wing and made him spin out into the rocky wall. The gargoyle grumbled and clawed for the stone behind him to lift himself, when Veronica slammed the handle of her multiweapon against his throat, pressing it forward with both hands.

"Why're you here?" she questioned. The monster fought the choking staff. Veronica pushed harder and repeated her demand.

"Kill me!" the cretin challenged.

We readied our weapons over her back as she interrogated the fiend.

"Why are you following us?!"

A dark red tongue slithered around his fangs as his pupils pulsated.

"He sent you! What does he want?!"

The gargoyle fidgeted. A whispering hiss slipped through the air as the black aura faded away. His wild pupils shrank into slits without the cover of the veil. He yowled and thrashed. Veronica battled with her grip. The flailing monster's exposed, crackling skin steamed in the brightness.

"No hope! No hope!" he choked out, sputtering ink-black fluid. "The sunseekers rot! The redbloods rot!" He frantically grabbed at the arrow with his spindly, clawed hands and pulled it deeper into his body. The gargoyle uttered a harsh, dying wheeze, then went limp against the rock face, his tongue hanging from his mouth.

Veronica stepped away, holstering her weapons and leaving the arrow in the creature's gray flesh. Zyvin's throat bobbed as he swallowed and stepped away, eyeing the beast's body with a petrified, unblinking stare. Murry's eyebrows leveled over his scrutinizing gaze. He inspected the dead body of the creature for a while more, until the last of the group circled.

Andy pointed to the corpse behind him. "That's new."

The wizard's mouth tightened as he sighed. "*That*," he blinked languidly, "is all too familiar."

"What is it?"

"A gargoyle, from the Dark Lands."

"How'd it get out?"

"Why was it following us?" I muttered.

Murry shook his head, unable to answer those questions.

A voice sounded in the distance. We all looked ahead, and another shadowed figure approached, this one human. An old, bearded man set down his walking stick on the brim of the sunken pass. He gripped it with both hands as he studied us, wind blowing over the fur on his sleeves, collar, and pelt cape. He scanned our faces, and his pale, frosty features stretched in shock when he reached Boris, who raised his nose to him and grunted.

"He's friendly," Veronica shivered.

We followed the old man, touring his tribal town. "You've landed in Ivoc," he clarified, looking back at us with icy blue eyes and raising his arms to the landscape as he walked. "Welcome to the Shinkai!" He laughed a little bit, plunging his walking stick into the snow beside every crunching step his fur boots took. Ornaments and beads rattled from atop the wooden stick with each motion. Murry thanked him for his guidance and introduced us all.

"Izaac," the man replied, as he raised his staff to passersby calmly. They all watched us with wary expressions as we strode, but since we were led by Izaac, their qualms seemed to fade. Igloos with fuming smokeshafts framed the path. We entered one of them.

A girl was tending to a humble fire inside the dwelling. Her white-blond hair was chopped messily just beneath her ears, and she possessed the same pale complexion and frosty eyes as the old man. She broke up sticks and fed them to the flames, shooting up alertly when Izaac appeared.

"Amber, could you heat some water please?"

She nodded and immediately placed snow into a pot.

Boris grunted; he was too large to fit through the cramped opening. Veronica kissed his snout and instructed him to wait outside. He snorted and looked around, shifting himself into a seated position.

Izaac removed his cape and hat. He ran a hand over his scalp to slick back his hair, but the strands were already frozen into form. He smiled at us, sat down, and accepted a steaming cup from Amber. He whispered a thank you, then blew the fumes from the drink and turned to us cheerily.

"When I heard you all approaching I thought you were my nephew." He laughed and took a sip.

"Lee isn't back yet?" Amber voiced, distributing more piping drinks.

Izaac shook his head and swallowed. "Haven't seen him since sunup."

Amber looked worried.

Izaac wiped his mouth and leaned close to her. "Don't fret. Your brother likes to take the long route, but he knows his way around."

I examined the rippling drink in my hands, vapors pluming from the cup and fogging my lenses. I wiped away the haze with my sleeve, then took a sip. The drink was mostly hot water with an occasional leafy flake. I swallowed and released a hot breath as the beverage warmed my insides.

Izaac returned his focus to us. "I s'pose you all like to take the long route too! You're a long way from home."

"What gave us away?" Murry joked.

Izaac laughed. "Fact that you ain't covered right." He pointed to Boris with his walking stick, " 'Cept him, he's got the right idea! Ha ha!"

Boris snorted.

The old man reached across the igloo with his staff and lifted the lid of a wooden crate. "Help yourselves."

We dug through the box and retrieved our own furry, winter garments.

"Part of it's bromgul, but the rest is gryrra ram," Izaac said. "Nothin' fancy like you'll find in the villages, but they're warm."

We thanked him fervently. I worked the provisional brown tunic off my body, the damp sleeves clinging to my forearms, then pulled on the new garb. I immediately felt my skin thawing in its warmth. I eased.

"Now tell me," Izaac implored. "What is it that brings you here?"

Murry admitted, "It's quite a story."

"I like stories." Izaac straightened up. "I'm a bit of a storyteller myself."

Murry folded his hands, searching for words, then agreed and relayed a condensed version of how we arrived and what our mission was. He punctuated the anecdote with a question: "I wouldn't suppose you'd know where to find this crystal?"

"Oh, yeah," Izaac nodded. "The Great Cave." He made a whimsical motion with his hands. "*Where a poor man goes to become rich.*"

"Is this place real?"

"Yes, yes. I've heard of it... Well, I've heard enough stories about it. Never been far 'nough from the tribe to confirm it." Izaac uttered a partial laugh, then recognized the seriousness in Murry's face and said, "I *have* heard of it. More than once."

"From who?"

"The one's who came back."

Came back? I pondered.

"It's there," Izaac went on with certainty. "Arduuk attests to its existence."

With that, Murry unfurled the map over the snow. "Where is it located?"

"Shiok Mor." Izaac shuffled closer and distinguished the valley on the parchment.

I asked him who Arduuk was, and Izaac looked taken aback. A disbelieving smile formed on his wrinkled face.

"Who's...?" He looked around the igloo disbelievingly. "Who's Arduuk?" He laughed. "My oh my! He's the Elemental of Frost!"

When I asked him what an Elemental was, his expression froze again. "You really ain't from anywhere, huh?" He shook his head, raising an apologetic hand. "Not that you ain't from *no*where, I mean."

Andy squinted at the man's hastened speech. Murry rotated to elucidate. "An Elemental is the designated protector of a land. Areok eventually became the Elemental of Ravac, for instance."

Izaac agreed with Murry's explanation. "And you know who Areok is, right?"

I nodded.

"Heh, alright. Fair 'nough. He is one'a yours after all." He patted his neice's shoulder. "Least the boy's done some research, hm?" He coughed and pointed to the Great Cave's location on the map again.

Murry nodded, and Andy and Veronica peered over the wizard's shoulder as he scaled the distance and determined our route.

"You should know, though," Izaac warned, pausing to scrounge the gentlest words. "It's been long since anyone's made a successful trip."

"Why's that?" Veronica asked.

Izaac shrugged, searching the ground. "I don't know." He let out a solemn laugh. "If they'd make it back to tell me I'd know."

Tenseness thickened the air. Murry cleared his throat, leaning forward. "Those who *have* returned—"

"Yeah?"

"What did they describe?"

The crackling flames of the fire pit smoldered, and Izaac's irises glinted as they followed the refracted light patterns in his ice walls. He finally spoke as he recalled, "A cave that hollows a mountain." He leaned, the flickering fire shadowing his face. "And deep inside, a crystal ceiling."

Murry rolled the map, and we all stood with him. Izaac seemed initially wary, but he eventually submitted to our resolve and got to his feet as well, lifting his hat and fur cape from their hangers. He capped his head and adorned his neck with the white pelt, then turned back to us.

He raised a finger to say more, when a new voice called, "*Uncle?*"

Izaac stopped, excused himself, then ducked out the passageway.

He emerged from the igloo and rejoiced, "Lee!"

A thrilled smile spread over the boy's face as he slid a hooked spear through a sling on his back. He dropped the lead of his drag sled and hugged Izaac, "Hi, Uncle." He bore indicative icy features, but was much taller, and appeared older than us.

Izaac stepped back, gesturing to the animal on his drag sled. "Would you look at that catch!" The body of a pinniped resembling an elephant seal with dermal plating lay on the platform.

Amber ran from the igloo to greet her brother. She wrapped her arms around him and he laughed, "Hey, sis."

"Where'd you hook it?" Izaac asked him.

"I went the long way to Irada."

"Not surprised."

Boris stood, blowing cloudy breaths from his nose and shaking away a dusting of flakes that lightened his russet fur. Lee's mouth released a few stunned half-words, before his finger raised to the minotaur and he vocalized, "What's—?"

"I don't know, but he's friendly," Izaac said.

Boris snorted to him as he plodded behind us. After we introduced ourselves and our mission, we noticed Zyvin wasn't at our sides. We looked around confusedly, before Andy and I checked the igloo. He was still inside.

"Zyvin, you coming?" Andy asked.

"Nah," he replied.

"Why not?"

"Whaddaya mean *why not*? You heard 'im! Somethin's keeping folk from comin' back."

"Dude, we'll be fine if we—"

"*You* will. The Aevæs *knows* I won't!"

Scooter appeared and chirruped on my shoulder. Zyvin raised his lip at the cephalopod, then buried his chin in his sheets and stared into the icy wall. "I ain't goin'."

Andy urged him, "We gotta get the crystal."

He scowled, "*You* do. I ain't goin'."

Andy and I lingered there for a moment, looking to each other with apprehension, then backed out the exit.

"He isn't coming," I reported.

Veronica's brow furrowed.

Izaac replied, "Well, he's welcome to stay here until you return." Lee asked us where we were heading, and Izaac answered on our behalf, "Shiok Mor."

"That's far," he said.

"You'll need hovers," Izaac told us, combing his strawy beard. "That's the only way to get there. We have some in the longhouse you can—"

Andy stopped him, "Whoa, whoa, wait wait wait. Did you say *hovers*?"

"Yeah."

Andy made wings with his arms. "You mean like—hover*ing*? Like *flying*?"

Inside the longhouse, Izaac tore away a sheet concealing one of the vehicles. It was simply designed, comprised of only one large disk secured in a sealed, wooden frame, with a steering mechanism mounted over a podium.

"*Ho-ho-ho!*" Andy uttered excitedly. He jumped onto the platform and gripped the handlebars, starting to make the anticipated propulsion sounds on his own. In the panel between the grips I spotted an empty, circular cavity.

Izaac retrieved a glassy, white stone and wiped it clean. "*Here we are.*" He set the rock inside the compartment, and the craft hummed and shot up a couple feet, before floating to a stable height.

"Whoa! *Ha ha ha!*" Andy exulted. "This is the best!"

Murry exhaled contentedly. He turned to his left. "Thank you." He shook Izaac's hand. "You've been refreshingly gracious."

The old man beamed, rested his staff against his inner shoulder, and added a second hand to the clasp. "It's who we are!"

I peered beneath the floating vehicle, stupefied, as Andy continued to make ecstatic noises.

"How does it work?" I asked.

"Hm? Oh, magnet!" Izaac said, tapping the disk-shaped platform with is staff. "One big one."

"But how does the magnet—?" I pointed to the stone spinning in between the handlebars. "How does *that* make it work?"

143

Andy let out another laugh as he bent his knees and bobbed in midair.

"Beats me," Izaac shrugged. "It's Xeevian."

Murry seemed to understand.

"All I know is it's made for Frost. It repels a specific mineral under the ice, some widespread deposit—apparently."

I was still baffled, but I accepted the answer.

We each climbed aboard our rides, springing into the air when the white stones activated the magnetic disks. A wheelless, wagon-shaped structure with the same magnetic underside was attached to the backend of Veronica's hover, into which Boris was guided. She waited until he was settled to place the stone and lift off.

I stared into the spinning rock in the center of my helm, watching the inside flash sporadically.

"Now when you want to return, spin the stone in the opposite direction," Izaac instructed. "That'll take you right back."

We hovered within the confines of the longhouse, swaying with the slightest of movements. Izaac looked us over, then nodded and reopened the hefty doors of the entranceway, letting in the spiraling snowstorm. I fidgeted with the controls. The handlebars were stiff and practically immovable. Izaac noticed my trouble.

"No steering," he called over the combined loudness of winds and hums. "Just lean to make 'em move!"

I shifted my weight to the right, and the craft moved with me. "*Whoa,*" I wobbled.

"Ready?"

I stabilized, then shook my head. "I think we need a moment to practice—"

"*Woo-hoo!*" Andy cheered as he rocketed into the blizzard.

Veronica went shortly after him, followed by Murry. Scooter chirped on my shoulder as I gawked into the turbulent whiteout. *Oh, man.* I swallowed, threw my weight forward, then vanished into the flurry.

"Good luck!" Izaac hollered after us.

My perception eventually adjusted to my speed as I barreled through the white. Falling flakes transformed into streaks as I accelerated, and excitement surged through me.

"*Woo-hoo!*"

"That's the spirit, Marvin!" Andy swerved to my right. "We *own* the snow!"

"You guys are idiots," Veronica informed us.

We laughed, blasting across the frozen terrain, and banking left around the steep rock face of a plateau when Murry signaled. The truest indication of our speed presented itself when our advancement became more treacherous. Stone jags protruding from the snow were suddenly visible, forcing us to slow and carefully maneuver around them. I let out a puff of air, glancing back at the fading dangers. I then stared onward at an open stretch of snow.

Murry examined the mountain ranges framing our flight, then called, "Keep straight here, this should lead to the valley!"

Andy hovered beside me. "Race ya!"

I shook my head at the suggestion, looking away.

Andy shrugged. "Whatever, man."

But once his focus trailed, I threw my weight forward and sped off. Andy let out a surprised laugh and raced after me.

Veronica sighed. She and Murry piloted their crafts close behind, as Andy and I raced through the snowy whirlwinds, neck-n-neck, toward the valley of Shiok Mor.

The Great Cave

Valley of
Shiok Mor

White Serpent River

FROST

Ivoc

13

The Great Cave

"**D**ude, I totally beat you," Andy declared, hopping off his inactive hover.

"No way!" I countered.

Andy looked to the group for support. "Veronica, what do you—"

"I'm not getting involved," she stopped him, removing the spinning white rock from its enclosure and slipping it into a pouch on her belt.

Andy shoved his hands in his pockets, nodding with certainty. "She's on my side." He winked at her, and a snowball crumbled against his face.

I tugged my shoe free from an icy impression and trudged ahead. Andy took a few leaping steps to my side as he tousled the flakes from his hair. The hovers were aligned in front of a sloping ridge that blocked incoming winds.

Veronica directed our attention toward the setup, verifying that we knew where to reclaim them. "Everyone know where to go?"

Andy saluted her. "*Snow* problem!"

He crouched as another snowball whizzed overhead. A huge smile fixed on his face. Still low to the ground, he loped for the fallen projectile, reshaped it, and threw it back, hitting Veronica's leg.

Before we knew it, an all-out war ensued. Veronica jumped high to evade a snowball flying for her feet. She successfully avoided it and chucked one of her own as she landed.

"Marv, you're on my side!" Andy called to me as he arched his back to dodge the attack.

"Don't you dare, Marvin," Veronica warned.

"I'm neutral," I insisted.

A snowball suddenly curved toward me.

"*Ohp!* Watch out!" Andy yelled.

I flinched at the incoming object, and a white ring of Ka surrounded it, stopping its approach in midair.

"Sorry, dude," Andy said. "Misfire."

The hovering, icy ball rotated only a few inches from my face. I looked to the ground, and energy shined over the billowing piles at my feet, permeating the upper layer and sweeping up newly-fallen flakes to swirl them into a sphere. It levitated to shoulder-height, and I repeated the process until I framed myself with a floating ring of ammunition.

"Whoa, whoa, hang on," Andy persuaded. "Let's be reasonable."

I launched all of them at once, and the rapid bombardment threw Andy off his feet.

"*Wahg!*"

Murry followed the map in his hands, focus uncompromised as he carefully stepped around Andy's snow-laden figure. He knelt by a slope and swept away the surface layer. "Looks like ice." He motioned for us to travel around the perimeter of the frozen river.

Boris followed Veronica as she walked after the wizard, turning to Andy and commenting, "I think Marvin won that game."

Andy chuckled as I helped him up, and we flowed back into the group.

"Sorry about that," I said.

"All good," he replied, knocking the remnant snow-impacts from his coat, his grin adhered. "You're getting pretty good at that."

I thanked him.

"I'm serious," he persisted. "You're basically a superhero now."

I shook my head and laughed, as we rounded the frozen river.

Jovial exchanges within the group sputtered to a hush as we stopped before the massive entranceway of the Great Cave. We stared silently into the opening. The high ceiling was toothed by dripstones and stalactitic icicles, and although the ingress was enormous, the deep passageway was too shadowed to see into.

Murry held the map out before him. "Certainly fits the description." He checked the parchment once more, then furled the paper, drew his wand, and ventured inside.

We followed him into the howling cave, patting snow from our bodies as we entered. The ominous echoes of winds and drips intensified through the hollowed passage the deeper we treaded. I raised my wand, whispered, "*Inferna*," and a small flame sparked from the instrument like a match.

Fire danced atop the wand as I inspected the walls, placing my mittened hand against the frozen surface. The tone of the rock was invisible beneath dense layers of dark blue ice. I stepped back, the leathery palm of my mitten peeling off the frozen wall, when a tapping sound resonated.

"You hear that?" I whispered. The group halted. I angled my ear at the noise, waiting.

A stream of liquid fell from above, soaking the side of my shoe. Dripping stalactites, I assumed. But, as I lifted my foot, lines of the gooey substance trailed persistently, stretching to the floor. I frowned.

What the?

My lit wand illuminated my upward glance, the orange glow sliding over the glassy walls as I searched. Then, in a recessed cavity, two reflective ovals gleamed. I sucked in a startled breath, drawing the attention of my friends and igniting the ferocity of the animal. It launched from its hole with a shrill cry, shooting in between us and sticking to the adjacent wall. I spun around, my flaming wand outstretched to expose its figure.

A horrid, blue-skinned creature adjusted its orientation on the wall with sharp nails. The long central claw of each foot chipped into the ice as it moved. Its head rotated, spying us with red, fragmented eyes and uttering clicks. The creature was jawless. A constant flow of saliva from a backward-facing maw seeped through the spaces of the four outer fangs that tipped its cranium. Its limbs flexed, and spines rattled with hostility, before it lunged again, throat shrieking and skin flaps puffing with air as it glided for me.

I panicked. Flame plumed from my wand, and the animal's charred body fell. We gathered around the fuming mass. A muscle contraction made one of the claws twitch. I jumped back and flamed the body two more times.

"Gee Marv, is it dead?" Andy asked.

I took a breath to calm myself. "What was that thing?" I asked.

More tapping sounded from above. Our faces drained with terror when clacking calls filled the air, overlapping. I raised my glowing wand above us, as the ceiling writhed with movement.

"Dire bats," Murry breathed.

A swarm of atrocities swooped for us, shrieking and clawing. Their outstretched flight poses limited their reach, but promoted fearsome speeds. Boris roared and swatted them away. Veronica dropped to avoid a strike, then shot down her gliding assailant. It garbled a wail and spun past me, as I flamed another incoming attacker. Andy tucked his head a few times as the bats zoomed by. He grunted with frustration, then raised his sword for protection, swinging and beheading one of the monsters in midflight.

"*Ugh!*" Andy sounded as the head bounced past him.

"This way!" Murry announced, leading us into a deeper tunnel.

We darted inside and pressed our backs against the cave walls, waiting for the irate swarm to pass. Claws and wingflaps cycloned by, heaving gusts into the rocky archway. Veronica held her breath and turned from the opening, as breezes flipped her hair. The wafts were laced with putrid, sulfuric scents. I shielded my face and held in a gag as the odor swirled through the tunnel and swept over us.

The screeches faded, and the flyaway strands of Veronica's hair floated back to her shoulders. We stayed silent for a while as the last of the shrieks echoed and dispelled.

Andy stepped away from his hiding spot, commenting, "Always exciting." His voice bounced off the high ceiling. Boris grunted from farther down the hall, redirecting our focus to a widening, steepened pass. I took two steps down the slope and nearly fell. I wobbled, and Veronica grabbed my shoulder to stabilize me. I nodded to her appreciatively, then worked my way to the landing. The floor below was illuminated by a jumbled light source streaming in from another, deeper passage.

I skidded to the more leveled area and stepped into a new tunnel with the rest of the group, running my hand across the icy wall as I walked. The angular light patterns seemed to rotate around me as I passed through. I stilled my breathing as I observed them, a frigid wind whirling over me.

"Whoa," Andy voiced up ahead. "Check this out."

As I breeched the exit, the cavernous howls turned into softer whistles, and the tunnel opened into a large chamber. I followed Andy's upward gaze and released a cloud of breath, "*Wow.*"

The entire ceiling was encased in sparkling, light blue gems.

"Alright," Andy said, swinging his arms in front of him. He picked up a hunk of ice and hurled it at the crystals, "*Huh!*"

The frozen ball piffed apart without any effect.

Veronica sighed and drew her crossbow, firing an arrow at the ceiling. Several large chunks detached and slid over the iced floor in all directions. The bow folded in, and she holstered the weapon.

"Well, I loosened it," Andy stated.

I walked to the center of the chamber, my footsteps cracking web-like fractures into the layer of ice that coated the snowy floor. I reached for one of the crystals, but my mittened fingers only brushed the corner and sent it sliding backward. It hit the base of a massive snow mound and spun to a stop.

Scooter appeared on my shoulder, observing my awkward progress. He chirruped at me, and I took a long stride toward the gem, testing the ground before putting my weight on it. I crunched through the frozen surface and sunk halfway into the snow, and when I took another step, my left foot buried all the way to my ankle. I let out a frustrated shiver, as snow clutched my skin.

I wrapped my hand over the crystal and raised it. The team rejoiced quietly. I held the crystal to my eye, turning it slightly to watch the inner prisms glint with light. I smiled.

That's two, I thought. From behind me, a sound rumbled, and when my friends became aware of it, their cheers ceased. The crystal's sheen was disrupted, and in its reflective surface I spotted movement.

I turned to witness the giant mound of snow heaving to life. My eyes traveled over the form, adjusting, distinguishing it from the snowy environment. The top part of it shifted, a shadowy crease forming in the mound, the outline of a muscle. And as I squinted, I could make out long white hairs coating the object, rising and falling.

It breathed.

The beast stood upright, lengthy white fur swaying as he rose. Ape-like arms hung at his sides, his short fingers spreading to brandish black daggers for claws. He rotated toward the clamor which disrupted his slumber, growing taller still, until the points of his long, dark horns were inches from the crystal ceiling. His face was centered in a woolly mane. Breath steamed from his flat nose, as his eyelids peeled to reveal glowing, red circles. They shined on us, as a rolling, leonine growl entered the air.

I edged backward, gripping the crystal to my chest. The cave beast snarled, then bent his fingers as his fatigued muscles flexed. An underbitten jaw fell open to release a deep, quaking roar that triggered my will to escape. But, my quickened, backward steps guided my right foot into the deep depression I had made, and I toppled into the snow.

"*Ugh!*" I grunted, opening my eyes in time to see a massive arm swing for me. I let in a terrified gasp and rolled to my stomach, the huge hand slamming into the ground at my right. Black claws scraped up icy fragments as I uttered half-shouts and scrambled to my knees.

Andy dashed to my side and grabbed my arm. "C'mon, c'mon!"

I got to my feet and ran, passing through the archway. We swerved through the curved tunnel and darted for the incline. Boris snorted, his flat hooves slipping against the icy slope. Veronica grabbed his arm and pulled. He skidded, clawed for the wall, and climbed up. Stable on the level ground, he huffed.

Andy staggered for traction himself, until Boris grabbed him by the collar and lifted him the rest of the way up the hill. I ascended shortly after, jostled when the cave beast's growl rattled the halls.

The monstrosity's hand reached into the tunnel. I raised my palm to the walls, attempting to push over a damaged ice pillar with my Ka, but the howling call of the enraged titan compromised my focus. The Ka instead manifested a diamond-shaped flare that blasted from my palm, irradiating the column and crumbling debris over the opening. The cave beast growled, unable to progress.

I tilted my head and jogged off with the others. *That'll work.*

Our footsteps reverberated off the concave walls, transforming into horrifying, sonorous echoes. The noises attacked us.

"Go, go," Andy panted.

Another tone pounded through the cave, the resonance of stone structures collapsing. The towering beast staggered through a wider passage, his horns crushing dripstones and shattering icicles as he traveled. He caught sight of us and growled again, sprinting at full speed.

"Run!"

We cleared the exit and fazed into the whiteness, wind sweeping our backs to accelerate the escape. I sucked in cold breaths with every motion, chilling my lungs and numbing the sensations of my fear-stricken body. An explosion of rock and snow went off behind me, as the cave beast wrecked the archway.

In unison, we threw our bodies sideways, hiding against the frame of the cave's ingress as the behemoth's wild speed carried him through the cloud of destruction and into the blizzard. He grumbled and cantered to a stop once he realized his prey had vanished.

Veronica placed her hand on my back, pushing me onward. Our group hugged the wall and trudged away, sights locked on the enormous silhouette as we snuck. The luminous, red circles searched the paths in front of him, then suddenly shined backward and fixed on us, as the violent winds muffled his throaty growl.

Veronica tore the crossbow from her quiver and fired an arrow. The beast wailed as the projectile stuck in his forehead. We scrambled for the hovers as he clawed his face.

I shoved the Frost crystal into my coat pocket as I ran, our vehicles coming more into focus with each passing second. *Almost there...* I told myself. Scooter shrieked and clasped my head. A giant hand swatted me off my feet. I screamed and soared sideways, tumbling to a stop some distance away, face down in the snow.

The hexapoid stumbled dizzily atop the back of my neck, then pulled at my ears and chirped for me to rise. I put my elbow on the ground and groaned, trying to stand. Snow stuck to my lenses. I reached to wipe them off, but a light blue tentacle curled from above and cleared the ice away for me. I panted and patted Scooter's shell, then gripped my painful abdomen and stood, staring through my streaked vision at the approaching fiend.

As I readied my wand, Murry stepped through the snowstorm and shocked the cave beast with a bolt of electricity.

"Zyros!" he shouted.

I gaped at the powerful display, then stepped forward, repeating the magic word and mimicking the rigid movement Murry had made. My muscles contracted, locking up. At first, I wondered if I had performed the spell correctly, but the doubt disappeared as quickly as it arrived when a blue bolt surged from my wand.

Jagged, lightning-like energy coursed through the air. The spell was less honed than Murry's; the central current waved and wriggled, branching with arcs. But the beam managed to reach the creature's stomach, and the combined power jolted our adversary. As the monster's jaw unclenched, buzzing sparks traveled over his enamel and escaped through his pointed canines. He raised his head, lip curling to bear fangs. He stamped forward. Boris clubbed his ankle, but he pushed past the attack and lunged for Murry and me.

At that moment, a shadowy, human figure became visible on a ledge over the Great Cave. As I peered at the form, it leapt down, disappearing into a cloud of blue mist.

The vapors swept in front of the rampaging monster before they assimilated and solidified into an armored warrior, who blasted freezing gusts from his hand to halt the charge. When the cave beast recovered, it swiped at him once more. Again, the warrior vanished, black claws passing through the cloud of fog before he reshaped. I blinked in astonishment at the fight, and in an instant I realized who had come to our aid.

The Elemental reached to his side. A sword of ice formed, beginning as a handle and hilt-guard and stretching outward, as if he pulled it from an invisible sheath. Sharp snaps sounded as its fractals grooved a blade, which he then slashed at the cave beast's incoming blow. The monster snarled. He levitated sideways, Ka shining over his white armor as he guided the predator away from us. When the infuriated cave beast issued a downward strike that fractured the ice of the frozen river, Arduuk refroze the water with a frigid whirlwind, and the monster's wrist was trapped.

The brute grumbled and tried to pull himself free, as Arduuk lowered to the ground in front of us. "That should keep him restrained." He stepped toward us, shaking his head at the brutish beast. "Rowdy, cave-dwelling yahlgors..." he muttered as he removed his helmet. "Quick to fury and slow to thought."

He had a dark complexion. His reflective, jet black hair was pulled back into a ponytail, and his beard, brows, and sideburns were angularly and intricately trimmed. He looked to us with dark brown eyes, then asked if we were harmed.

Murry stepped forward and bowed. "Had you not appeared we may have been," he said. "Thank you, Elemental."

Arduuk bowed in response. "Few are willing to brave these parts."

"We travel by necessity."

"You travel with favor."

Murry smiled genially at his compliment.

"Yes," Arduuk asserted. "Whatever it is, I sense your journey here is of great significance."

Murry conversed briefly with the warrior, gesturing to Andy and me as he relayed our circumstances. His words were carefully selected, and his brow was slanted with sincerity and respect. He laughed occasionally when he expressed the scope of our odyssey.

Arduuk nodded as he spoke. He stopped for a moment, his long, black hair blowing behind him as his gaze penetrated the spirals of snowy wind.

His eyes flashed, then returned to us. "I wish you well on your journey," he said simply. After searching each of our faces, he smiled, then began to walk. "Keep your wits. My brethren will guide you." He secured his helmet. "*Solaos rheatte*, travelers."

Murry bowed and returned the salutation, "Solaos rheatte."

Once Arduuk composed himself, he exchanged a parting nod and clasped his hands. The Elemental glowed, transformed into a cloud of blue mist, and then disappeared into the snowstorm.

14
Return to Ivoc

*A*fter staring into the flurry for a long while, we finally broke our lingering trances and brought ourselves to move again.

"Let's get out of here," Andy sighed. "I'm getting tired of almost being eaten."

"What makes you think that yahlgor wanted to eat *you*?" Veronica asked.

Andy opened his arms. "Look at me!" He slapped his chest. "I'm delicious!"

Veronica watched him skeptically, then climbed aboard her hover. I stood atop mine as well, lifting off the ground and shifting into a balanced float while the white stone rotated. I halted its spin, feeling a slight resistance and a buzzing jolt, then worked my fingers around the ovate rock and spun it counterclockwise. The craft jostled.

"*Whoa.*" I took hold of the handle bars to steady myself while the wooden frame groaned and swung around. The handles were even less functional than before, as the craft rigidly turned without influence, then flew forward on its own.

Ice flung around the magnetic platform, pelting my knees. I tried to keep my breathing steady as I watched incoming snowflakes flitter and curve around me like insects. The crafts piloted automatically, blasting across the frozen land in a v-shaped formation. It was as though they had tracked our movements to the valley and retraced them for the return trip. I touched my pocket, feeling that the crystal was still there. Relief washed over me. I relaxed my grip on the handles and turned to watch a herd of mammoth-like creatures march in the distance.

The fur on their faces was gray, while the rest of their coat was a faded, dark blue. Protective, spiky growths protruded from their foreheads and shoulder blades. Three pairs of sturdy legs helped the behemoths cross the icy plain, and dual trunks raised at us as we passed, trumpeting. One of the leading animals plunged his trunk between fissured ice sheets. He searched, sweeping the water below for fish, while keeping his second snout elevated to breathe. I wanted to observe them longer, but the hover carried me out of sight, and the weather simultaneously worsened to obscure my vision.

A forceful wind wrestled with us, making progression nearly unmanageable. I struggled to keep my balance as the craft teetered, creaking in the powerful gusts. The return trip was proving to be more perilous than our initial journey. I tried to lean forward and fly into the gale, but the force of the gusts was unyielding. At one point I couldn't tell if I was moving forward or backward. One white blur of obscurity stretched before me, and only the immediate snowflakes whipping past my lenses and the hazy outlines of my friends were distinguishable.

I occasionally glanced back to confirm the correct amount of silhouettes were flying in our formation. As I searched, one of the entities drew closer to my right side. Andy emerged from the haze of white and entered my small circle of visibility. He hollered something over the blusters.

"What?" I shouted.

He started to repeat his statement, "I said—" The front end of his hover struck an obtruding rock. I called at him, as his craft wobbled and slammed into the ground, dislodging the glowing stone from its cavity and launching Andy from his ride.

I immediately removed my hover's power source and the weighty transport dropped down, tunneling into the snow. With the excess momentum, I jumped from my sliding platform and plodded to find my friend. I heard the others deactivate their vehicles and let them fall behind my tracks.

I soon located Andy and rushed to his side, shouting through the wind, "Are you okay?"

"*Mrf...*" he grumbled in response, his head buried in snow.

I let out a relieved breath when he placed his palm down to raise himself. I grabbed his other hand and helped him to his feet.

Murry pushed through the blizzard after us, shielding his face from an onslaught of frigid air with the sleeve of his violet cloak. He brushed away the clumps of ice clinging to his furry, Shinkai vest and placed his hands on our shoulders, verifying we were safe. Veronica appeared behind him. She held up the discarded stone from Andy's hover in her right hand. I was astonished that she was able to pinpoint and recover the glassy, white rock.

157

Andy grunted as he reached for the item. "Thanks." He slipped it in his pocket.

Veronica looked him over, her blue eyes shining through the snowy whirlwinds. She hugged him. "Stop it."

"Stop what?"

"Stop... falling off of things."

Andy laughed. "I'll try."

Veronica watched him a while longer, trying to forge a grin, then stepped back to her vehicle.

Touching down seemed to undo the automatic feature of the hovers; when I spun the rock left, my craft whirred and turned in the direction of the valley, and I had to quickly reverse the rotation to regain control. Everyone mumbled disheartened groans, and Andy looked like he felt guilty of the setback.

Hoping the whiteout would subside soon, we made the decision to pilot our crafts anyway. But we quickly discovered the conditions were too extreme to fly in, and when the storm intensified, Murry instructed us to set down again.

Nighttime winds began to twist, and the above stratus faded into a dark, dusky hue. We powered down and parked our vehicles in a crescent-shape. In the center of which, Murry motioned us into a circle.

"Stay close!"

We followed his instruction without delay, clustering together in a tight ring, shivering. Boris joined us last. He stomped into position, put his back to the storm, and shielded us from incoming winds.

Murry spoke to me, "Marvin, focus your Ka. Try to create a dome around us, if you can."

"Okay," I breathed, cupping my hands. Energy charged, channeled down my arms and through my fingertips, and permeated my woven mittens to shine in the frigid atmosphere. I could sense loose particles of effulgence being drawn into the bubble. Their glow brightened softly, like lightning bugs, before becoming one with the spheroid shape. My numbed face grimaced as I attempted to concentrate the energy. The bubble's shine dimmed, resembling the scattered reflections of light rays through water. But it wouldn't stay.

My arms dropped, and the circle dissipated. Murry took the spell book from his rucksack and searched the text. Low mutterings sputtered from his mouth, before raising in volume to audible words.

"That's alright, that's alright," he said quickly, flipping through pages. "Let's see here..."

Aggravated, I tore my mittens off and reached forward again, reshaping the sphere. It wavered in the blustery atmosphere. Its form was as erratic as the weather.

A stray current of wind spiraled over Boris' shoulder armor and blew me off center. The Ka flickered. As I refocused, another powerful gust curved over Boris' shielding frame to attack me, this one delivering a clump of ice to the back of my head.

My eyes flashed white, and the energy instantly turned into a perfect sphere. I threw my arms open and the field passed through our bodies and expanded into a dome.

Like reflex, Murry whipped his wand at the ceiling of Ka, shouting, "Esyryn!"

Blue magic coursed upward, adhering to the interior of the dome and freezing into a layer of ice. The rippling current swept up stray snowflakes within the dome and converted them into luminous specks of light that circled around the main beam and enhanced the effect. The ice cracked as it spread downward, encasing us, and Murry finished the structure with a seal around the bottom.

Murry grunted as he eased down, with his spell book and we all followed suit. I slid along the wall until I settled into a sit, then lay my head against the icy masonry and observed patterns in the ceiling. The sweeps of wind were so thick with frost that they cast shadows through our translucent shelter. Locating an incantation, Murry set down the text, then leveled his left hand. A sphere of Ka rose from his palm, levitating and pulsing with light. He moved his free hand overtop, fingers flittering as if charming the energy.

He leaned forward and whispered into the glow, "*Solaos inverum: Inferna rhearan, rheum.*"

The Ka fluxed, infused with a new property that altered its coloration. The radiant sphere became sunset orange, then separated into several smaller specks of brilliance that flew about our shelter sentiently, each of them changing course to fly into us. One fazed through my neck, forcing inhalation. I instantly reached for my clavicle and felt a spot of hot energy radiating beneath my skin. And from then on, every breath I took was thickened with heat.

My friends' features were set aglow by the circles of warmth shining in their throats. We breathed deeply, and as we did so the spheres flared with luminance. Scooter scampered by delightedly, his shell glowing from the spell. He looked like a mobile light bulb.

I pulled my foot in to clear a path for him. As my knee raised, the crystal shifted in my coat pocket. My fingers instinctively traveled there to retrieve it, and when I held it before the group, our spirits were recharged.

The crystal traveled around the circular shelter. I handed it to Andy, and he cradled the rock like a baby.

"Aw," he crooned, "he has my eyes."

"And your brains," Veronica jested, stare not trailing as she transferred the prize to Murry.

"You all should be very proud of yourselves," the wizard said as he wrapped the crystal in cloth and placed it in his rucksack.

"Yep," Andy crossed his legs and leaned back. "I *was* pretty awesome out there."

Veronica rolled her eyes.

He shrugged at her, "What?" He flexed his arms. "Fearless warrior, baby!"

A fissure split in the wall beside him and he jumped. Veronica smiled and shook her head. I laughed.

Murry lifted his wand to reseal the crack with an icy beam. He repeated the spell in a few other areas to ensure we were fully fortified, then tucked away his instrument. I yawned, grabbing my Captain Galloway book from its compartment in my backpack and finding my page. My eyes glided tiredly over the words, sentences illuminated by a dull glow from the magic sphere in my neck. I lay my head against the thin wall of ice, separated from wild, tempestuous currents by those few inches. The flows rumbled through the wall, losing ferocity as they reached my ear. And as I breathed, the circle in my throat flushed with soothing warmth, and I was lulled to sleep.

Chilled breezes pierced our clement refuge. Lingering flits of mystic warmth regressed, and the foreign air nipped at my thawed features until the sensation bugged me from rest.

I sat up, seeing an exit-hole had been singed through our icy shelter. I ducked out of the provisional dwelling and stepped over a toppled, semicircular section of the dome. I approached the others, who were already preparing for flight.

"Hey! I was just about to wake you," Andy patted my back. "Through with your beauty sleep?"

I yawned, then helped him brush the snow from his hover.

"You're a ball of fire," Veronica noted as she lifted off the ground and flew around us. "C'mon, bozos!"

Andy looked at me and shook his head as she passed by. "I shouldn't have taught her that word."

With the weather calmed, we boarded our hovers and blasted over the frozen plain with ease. We were able to retrace our flight when familiar topographic features came into focus. We navigated the maze of rocky jags and banked around the base of the plateau, and before long, columns of smoke came into view.

We parked the hovers in the longhouse and searched the tribe for Izaac's igloo. I trekked ahead, trusting the instinctive steps my feet made and realizing later that the group was following my lead. I would have admitted that I was unsure of the direction, but the sound of voices entered my ears, and I tracked the noise into one of the dwellings. Izaac was telling a story.

"So then, the most *enormous* wuhlborough came chargin' up, swingin' her trunks..." Izaac used his arms to imitate the motions of the animal. He started mimicking the trumpet sound as well, which made Amber laugh and Zyvin's eyes narrow in languor.

He shot alert when Andy announced, "We're back!"

Izaac's ragged blankets rolled down his shoulders. He opened his arms to our return and climbed to his feet. "You've made it! Have you found your crystal?"

Murry patted his rucksack. "Yes. And your directions were invaluable."

"Well, let's see it!"

Murry retrieved the crystal. He held it out, unwrapping the treasure and cradling it in the brown cloth. It shined, light rays seemingly drawn to the inner prisms to contribute to its enrapturing sparkle.

Izaac uttered a stunned breath. "May I?"

Murry allowed him to hold it.

The old man turned the object with both hands, shaking his head with amazement. "This is..." He laughed disbelievingly. "This is quite impressive." He held it up. "Back in the day, these were the things to have. These were the sparks of conflicts!" He carefully returned it to Murry's hands. "You keep that safe."

We said our goodbyes, then left the Shinkai and headed for the shoreline. Izaac insisted that we keep the coats, so we felt confident our subsequent voyage would be comfortable. Zyvin trudged along quietly behind our tracks. Andy called back at him, asking how he felt, but he didn't answer.

Veronica stopped, a frown forming.

"What is it?" I asked her.

She walked past me, studying the waves. As I observed her, a worried feeling crept over my skin, and faster than my brain could label the problem, my gaze started scouring the shoreline.

The boat was gone.

15
Snowbound

"**I** thought you tied it down!" Veronica screamed.

"I did!" Andy shot back.

"Then where is it?" Veronica crossed her arms, glowering at the empty shore, before returning her furious stare to him.

Andy shook his head, flustered, "I... I..."

"Where is it?!"

"I don't know!"

Veronica stomped away, infuriated. She pinched the inner corners of her eyes and breathed deeply through her nose to make herself calm. "Alright," she whispered, circling around. "What did you tie it to?" Her hushed tone was even more menacing than her yell.

Andy jittered, searching his memory, then recalled, "A stick."

"A _stick_? What stick?"

"There was a stick!"

Veronica groaned.

Andy pointed past her. "There! It looked like that." A thin, black twig protruded from the snow. Murry examined it, glancing down the shoreline at a row of like branches. He took hold of the frozen piece of wood, and it glided from its icy crevice without resistance. Veronica's eyes flared.

"This is..." Murry sighed. "This is a territory marker."

Veronica took an angry breath. Andy rotated toward her, raising an index finger as if to offer a new point. But before his mouth could construct an explanation, Veronica's face twisted in outrage, and she stormed off, roaring. Andy dropped his arm and released a hopeless sigh.

Veronica rifled through a bag that was slung over Boris' shoulder, and chucked Andy's sword at his feet. "Try not to lose that too!"

"Veronica, I'm sorry!" Andy yelled after her. She ignored him, walking around the minotaur to distance herself. Boris watched her pass, puffing clouds of steam from his nostrils.

Andy's sight drifted to the snow, his eyes wrought with worry. He shook his head as he murmured to me, "Dude, I didn't... I wasn't..."

I shrugged, trying to configure consoling words, but before I was able to, Zyvin interrupted our tense pause, grumbling, "*Unbelievable.*"

Andy's eyes went wild and face went red. "Excuse me?!" He clamored through the piles of snow to confront him. "So how was your *sleepover*, huh? Were you *warm*?!"

Zyvin raised his lip and looked past him, as Andy got closer and louder.

The vein in Andy's neck throbbed as he unloaded his fury. "Did Izaac read you a bedtime story? And tuck you in? And give you food? While the rest of your team was *freezing* in the—"

"*Team?*" Zyvin stopped him. "I ain't part'a no team!"

Andy's features stretched in bafflement. "Whaddaya think this *is*? A free ride?!"

Zyvin prodded his finger into Andy's chest. "*Y'all* agreed to take me home."

"Yeah, but if you *travel* with us, then you *have* to contribute!"

"That's why I stayed behind!"

Andy clenched his hair. "*That's* what I'm talking about!"

Zyvin winced, recovering from the shrillness in Andy's shouts, then sneered, pointing to his blind eye. "You see this?" he questioned. "I ain't seen right for *too long* now. How'm I s'pose to do what you all do? How could *I* have worked those flying things?" He raised his spindly hand to intercept snowflakes. "Look at this! I ain't built for this." He opened his bony arms to the land. "I ain't built for any of this!"

Andy shook his head, dissatisfied with the excuse.

"I got a family you know." Zyvin's nostrils flared. "I got two kids who don't know where I gone, n' a wife who thinks I'm good as dead!"

Andy's mouth shifted, eyes still locked with his.

"*That's* all that matters to me. My family. I gotta stay alive for them somehow."

Andy looked to the snow, kicking a ball of ice. "You think you're the only one?"

The two stood silently for a long time. The argument seemed to have ended. Andy picked up his sword, starting to walk away, then turned around and pointed to Zyvin with the blade. "Hey, listen, I—"

Zyvin's eyes widened. He grabbed for his knife. "Is that it, then? You wanna fight me now?!"

"What?"

"Pullin' a weapon on an elder?"

"I was *gonna* apologize!"

"Where I come from, that's a threat!"

"Get over it, dude!"

Veronica reappeared at Andy's side. Her weapon's bow snapped open. "Back *off!*"

"What's this?"

"*This* is a threat!"

Zyvin snapped back with a yammering accusation not audible over the howl of wind, and Andy retorted, "You're seriously just wasting our time, now!"

"Coming from the boy who let our boat float off!" Zyvin growled, spit escaping through the gaps in his gritted teeth.

Murry stepped in between the ruckus and forced his wand down, sending a rush of wind over the arguers' bodies and halting the commotion. "That's enough!"

The bickering ceased. Andy adjusted his hair, "Geez Murry, light a match or something." He laughed partially, and Veronica shoved him to pay attention.

The wizard paced, trying to foster cohesion. "If we keep fighting, we'll never get anywhere. We'll have to think as a team if we want to move on." Andy crossed his arms and smiled at Zyvin, as if the mention of the word *team* placed Murry on his side. Zyvin pointed a blaming finger at him and rattled off a list of grievances. Again, the conversation deteriorated into chaos.

I watched my friends battle with words, their voices fusing into incomprehensible shouts. As the volume rose, my focus turned inward, toward the fragments of thought circling in my mind. I tried to focus on them, sequence them into options. And as I pondered, my legs started to carry me back to the Shinkai.

The others were taken aback by my sudden urgency, but as I speedwalked, they followed, through the maze of igloos. It was as if my body knew something that my mind had yet to define, and as I neared Izaac's dwelling, my pace quickened again.

Izaac's eyes grew wide as we ducked through the small entranceway.

"You're back," he voiced, puzzled by our return. I divulged everything, and his wrinkled face sank in sympathy.

Murry asked, "Do you have any boats in your tribe? We'd be willing to pay." Izaac stared past him, and Amber seemed fretful as she waited for her uncle to speak.

Izaac swallowed. His eyelids rolled shut, before he shook his head and uttered, "No."

We stood frozen in the igloo, unable to respond. The old man tried to offer more of an answer. "We..." he placed his hand on his chest. "We don't leave here." He cleared his throat. "We don't... we aren't seafarers, I mean."

When Lee stepped through the doorway, our conversation paused. He backed in, keeping a puzzled stare on Boris, who was waiting outside, then turned and saw us. He dropped a couple bags against the wall, then said, "I thought you all left."

"Their boat's gone," Izaac said. "They're stuck here."

Lee lowered into a seat and observed us a moment, then looked to the ground in thought.

Amber tapped her uncle's arm, "Aren't the Murkoi fishers?"

"Yeah," Izaac voiced.

"How would we get there?" I asked.

Izaac uttered a short laugh. "Keep goin' north till yer goin' south." The old man shook his head. "It's too dangerous. Too far. I don't even think the hovers'll do ya much good."

"What about the Ice Pirates?" Lee asked.

Izaac stiffened.

"Who're they?" I asked.

"They're seafarers," Lee explained, starting to smile. "I saw 'em pull ashore once in the harbor."

"Are they friendly?" Veronica asked.

"Depends on who you ask."

"They're criminals!" Izaac interjected, frowning. "And they ain't helpin' our situation with the Geltynites either."

"They're the *only* people in the region who leave and *come back.*"

"Yeah, but they ain't lookin' for a ride, they're lookin' for a boat."

"At this point we're not too picky," Andy said.

Veronica stood with her arms crossed. "Especially since Andy's the kiss of death when it comes to efficiency."

"I tied it to the stick!" he tried to defend himself. "It floated away!"

Veronica mumbled, "*Should've tied you to the stick, then you'd float away.*"

"Don't start this again," Murry told them, trying to refocus the conversation. "Which harbor?"

Izaac stammered, then started to protest, "I don't think you'd want to get involved with them." He swallowed. "Even if you *do* find them, they wouldn't agree to transport you."

"Sure they would," Lee said, rubbing his fingers together. "They'll do anything for a handful of siv."

Izaac sighed, then revealed, "They're to the west, in Hammon Shou."

Lee confirmed, "They just landed. If you hurry, you may be able to catch them."

Izaac pointed to the exit, "Just follow the mainland's coast a few megaspans that way and you'll find it."

We thanked them and exited the igloo. Izaac staggered to his feet, redonning his hat and pelt cape as he followed us outside.

"Take the hovers," he said, making a twisting motion with his wrist. "You can send them back like you did before. Whether you reach the pirates or not, the harbor village is the safest place for you to stay."

We thanked him again, hurrying to retrieve the hovers from the longhouse.

We all climbed aboard our rides, placing the white rocks to activate them and spring into the air. Zyvin shuddered at the loud hums. Although a spare vehicle was available, he held firm to his previous claim that he was unable to pilot it.

The group exchanged shrugs.

In formation, our hovers levitated over the trail bisecting the tribe, Zyvin bouncing around the space he shared with Boris in the rickety wagon-like tow. Although the platform was large, the majority of the room was taken up by the minotaur, who sat much calmer in comparison. Zyvin cringed and gripped the uprights as Veronica made a tight turn, and Izaac waved to us as we passed.

"Be safe!"

The Fractured Peaks

Valley of
Shiok Mor

FROST

White Serpent River

Hammon Shou
Harbor Village

Ivoc

While snowfall was constant along the coastline, the twirling flecks were far more bearable than the frigid, northerly conditions. We soared westward with ease, and before long, the outline of buildings came into focus. I made a tight turn, the repelling force below my hover launching pellets of ice as I rotated and set down. Andy landed beside me, followed by Murry and Veronica. Zyvin made a grumbling sound as he dizzily lifted himself over the railing and flopped into the snow.

"Is this Hammon Shou?" Andy asked.

Murry dismounted his hover, looking for clues and leading us through the village. Lines of buildings constructed from dark, splitting planks framed a central pathway through the town. Oval-shaped signs bearing unfamiliar lettering swung rigidly on rusted chains over the entrances of the shops, creaking as they moved. A chicken-sized bird with white, furry plumes and blue flesh squawked at us with an indigo beak before shuffling by. Besides the fowl, there were no other beings or townspeople milling about.

We maintained stride, and the street ended with a long pier that was just as desolate. A waterlogged rope hung from one of the beams, stiffened by freeze.

"Let's hope we aren't too late," Murry said.

Andy and I ambled toward the building closest to the dock. As we drew nearer, I could hear voices beyond the entrance. Conversations.

"Maybe we can ask for directions inside," I suggested. I pushed open the splintered, saloon-style doors and stepped into the dim building. The wide space was occupied by circular tables, around which hungry villagers were seated, some human, some humanoid.

"Hey-hey! It's a restaurant!" Andy announced. "Let's get some grub!"

"First thing's first," Veronica whispered. "Figure out where we are."

A pot of hot liquid was placed on the table beside us. The crimson-scaled customer eyed the dish eagerly, licking his sharp teeth and gripping a utensil in each claw, as the lid was removed. Within the steaming vat of stew squirmed a coil of shelled annelids.

Andy's expression sank. "Yeah, let's skip lunch."

The interior atmosphere was warmed by clouds of steam rising off piping-hot meals, and thickened with stray fumes from a nearby cooking area behind the main arrangement.

Andy took a big whiff. "*Ah.* Smells just like the school cafeteria, eh Marv?"

He wasn't wrong actually. I noted the eerily similar scents, then pointed to the center of the shop, where a large, humanoid bartender was working.

"Let's ask him."

His head looked like an octopus. A gelatinous mantle inflated as he breathed, and a beard of tentacles covered his mouth, if he even had one. The being was covered in orangish, dermatoid scales, with small thorns sprouting on his cranium and forearms. He wore muted clothes, with a splattered apron strung over his gut, and in his webbed, three-fingered hands he scrubbed a glass with a white cloth.

"Hey, there!" Andy greeted.

The bartender's yellow, billiard ball-like eyes rolled from atop their stalks to view him. His cranium quavered and filled with air.

"So, we're new to these parts and were wondering if you could clue us in on a few things."

The bartender's eyelids rolled shut, making a viscous click. His mantle deflated as he let out a breath, blowing his tentacles forward. He looked the other way and continued to wipe his glass.

"Hey!" Andy called.

"He might not be able to speak," I said.

Andy frowned. "Hello?"

The monster didn't turn.

Andy waved his arms. "*Hello-o?*"

He still didn't react.

"...Bonjour?"

The bartender made a mad, gurgling sound, scrubbing the glass harder.

Andy shrugged. "Ooday ooyay peaksay igpay atinlay?"

I started, "Maybe we should ask someone else—"

"DO—YOU—UN—DER—STAND—ME?"

The glass shattered and the monster slammed his fists onto the counter, rattling tankards and dishes. "*WHAT?!* Whaddaya want?!"

We jumped at the sudden outburst. Andy spoke, "You can talk?"

" 'Course I can!"

"Why didn't you answer me?"

"I was ignorin' ya! Ya yammerin' *twit!*" He rubbed his tired eyes, as bulbous sacks on his temples throbbed. "Just like a *human!* With yer need ta *converse* and whatnot!"

I immediately apologized, "Sorry, we didn't mean to offend you... Mister..."

The monster placed his elbow on the counter, sneering, "The name's Bozko, *human.*"

"Who you callin' human?" Andy questioned.

I stared at him strangely, then returned my attention to the bartender. "Right, Bozko, we were just trying to figure out where we are."

Bozko blinked drowsily. "Yer in a tavern, kid."

Andy snapped, "We know *that!* He's asking what town we're in!"

"Well, he should'a been more specific!"

"You're right," I said to the bartender. "I apologize."

Andy started, "Marvin, don't apologize to—"

"*Shut it!*" Zyvin whispered. Veronica rolled her eyes and walked away from us.

Bozko ran his fingers down his face, unraveling tentacles. "Yer in Hammon Shou," he groaned.

"Great, thank you," I said. He picked up the white cloth, and I raised my index finger, "Wa-wait, I—"

He glowered at me.

"I have one more question."

He sighed and dropped the cloth. "Go 'head, kid. I'll cooperate."

Before I could ask, Scooter clambered up to my shoulder and Andy knelt slightly to make eye contact him. "Look Scooter, your big brother is going to tell us something!"

Bozko's tentacles writhed. "I have half a mind ta throw you out!"

Andy chuckled, "You have half a mind alright."

"That's it!" he hollered.

"No, wait!" I said. "We're—"

"*Out!*" he roared.

A massive humanoid with dark green scales and four muscular arms burst through the kitchen door, gritting his underbitten jaw and slamming a fist into his upper-left palm.

"Get 'em outta here!" Bozko shouted. The monster picked up Andy and me by our collars.

"Whoa!" Andy shouted as his feet lifted up.

Bozko pointed to Zyvin. "*You!* You're out too!"

Zyvin stammered, then gulped when the monster's lower left hand wrapped around his throat.

"You, wizard! You know these humans?"

"Well, yes but—"

The bouncer placed his hand on Murry's shoulder, gripping his vest.

"Minotaur!" Bozko called.

Boris roared mightily in response.

The bartender tapped his fingers on the counter. "*Ehm...* you can stay." He pointed to Veronica last. "You, girl!"

She turned around, sighing.

He angled his head at the rest of us and asked, "You with them?"

She shook her head. "Never seen 'em before."

The monstrous bouncer tossed us out of the tavern. Andy and I faceplanted in the snow, while Murry and Zyvin were shoved out afterward. The humanoid growled and clapped two of his four hands together, before returning to his post.

Scooter clasped the back of my head, chirping. I raised myself partially and rotated to look at Andy through my snow-coated lenses. He smiled uneasily at me, and I let my head fall again.

We sat on the front steps, waiting anxiously for Veronica to return. Zyvin watched Andy bitterly for a long time, rocking on the creaking plank.

Andy caught his stare, locking eyes with him before finally asking, "What?"

Zyvin chewed and squinted at him. He replied, "You have a habit of dooming us."

"It wasn't my fault." Andy turned to me. "Right Marv?"

I opened my mouth to reply, then paused, trying to form an answer. "Well..."

Thankfully, Veronica exited the tavern before I could respond.

"We're in the right place," she reported, as Boris ducked out the doorway behind her. The minotaur turned his horns sideways to fit through, huffing. Veronica knelt by Murry, as he unrolled the map. She went on, "Apparently Bozko supplies the pirates with food rations for longer trips." She pointed to a location just west of us. "He says their ship was docked on the far end of town this morning."

Andy looked at her in disbelief. "How'd you get him to tell you?"

"I was polite," Veronica said, letting out a half-laugh and heading back toward the hovers. "You should try it sometime. Your people skills are about as tactful as a bloat-snouted squealer on Empress Day." She giggled and walked off.

Andy squinted in confusion as she left. "I feel like I'd be offended if I knew what that was."

I shrugged, equally baffled.

Veronica activated her hover without mounting it, and Andy groaned when he realized we had to walk again. We spun the glowing rocks counterclockwise, and the vehicles hummed, lifted off the ground, and returned to the Shinkai without pilots.

"How far is it?" Andy asked.

"It's walkable," Veronica responded. She and Murry took the lead. I watched as the hovering crafts disappeared into the hazy, white fog, then turned back to follow the group.

Hammon Shou was much larger than I originally thought. The village was an expansive grid. Rows upon rows of shacks and shops passed by on our right, while piers extended from the streets into the frozen water on our left. A frigid breeze knocked my hood back and pelted my exposed face with fragments of ice. I put my head down and leaned into the chilly force. The sky dimmed a few shades, and the wind chilled to a temperature indicative of arctic nightfall. I couldn't determine whether the days felt longer or shorter. I started to wonder if I had slept through half the day or if the day was half as long. Either way, Frost possessed an abnormal length of daylight—one to which I was not accustomed, and hoped I would never have to be.

174

The heavy fog parted like curtains to reveal the frame of a massive pirate ship. A loud order sounded from one of the shadowed bodies onboard, as a line of crew members carried crates up a lowered gangway and into the vessel.

Murry cleared his throat and raised his hand to grab the attention of the figure in charge. "Excuse me!"

The last of the crates passed by the captain, and he turned his attention to our approaching group.

"Yes, hello!" Murry hollered successfully, as we stopped at the base of the bridge-like structure.

The captain strolled down the creaking gangway to confront us. He was clad in layers of heavy, wintry garb. Most of his attire was a faded, gray-blue color with notes of darker navy, but his belt and boots were dark brown, splotched by discoloration and water damage. A thick vest seemed puffed out by multiple undershirts, and his outermost adornment, a faded blue coat, swayed behind him with every ambling step. A leather belt secured a sheath for his sword, the metal details clattering. And in the same moment, another steely sound became audible. Pieces rotating, clanking. After a short search I realized the noise came from the pirate's arm. The right sleeve of his jacket was frayed and folded, revealing a mechanical forearm and hand. A three-digit claw rotated and clanked shut a couple times, and a few snide laughs slipped through the pirate's crooked grin. His frizzy beard and eyebrows were bluish gray, laden with tiny icicles and bits of rime clinging to the hairs.

His controlled stagger ended a few paces before us. He scanned our group with frosty, blue eyes and reached with his organic left hand to adjust the tricorn hat on his head.

"You lost?"

"Somewhat," Murry admitted.

The Ice Pirate leaned on his heels and tucked his left hand in his coat pocket, lifting his chin as he listened.

"Our boat," the wizard started, eyes shifting toward Andy, "has been misplaced."

"That so?" He pointed to us with his metal claw. "Bunch'a outlanders snowbound on Frost, eh?" He concluded his thought with a muffled, dry laugh.

"Yes," Murry went on. "We understand you all are... of the few individuals familiar with these waters."

"What else ye hear?"

"That your expertise may be helpful to us."

The captain nodded, staring past us.

"We were hoping—"

"Ye wanna hitch a ride, then." He snorted through his rubicund nose, cocking his head.

"We are willing to pay for the service, of course."

His eyebrows arched. "Perhaps we can strike a deal, eh?"

Murry retrieved a bag of coins from his rucksack. "How much would you request?"

"How much ya carryin'?"

Murry paused, gleaming into the sack of silvery-gold coins. "About... one-hundred siv."

The pirate unpocketed his left hand, folding his calloused fingertips. "Give it 'ere."

Murry traded. The captain cradled the bag in his palm, extracting one of the coins with his metal fingers. "Ravacan," he stated, peering through the square-shaped hole in the center of the piece. "The heavy kind." He chuckled delightedly and pulled the drawstring to reseal his payment. He glanced upward, as if reacting to noise. "Stay 'ere. Lemme check on something real quick."

He scaled the incline, disappearing onto the deck, as we stood waiting at the base of the gangway, whispering relieved thoughts to each other that our offer was accepted. But before we could board, the gangway retracted.

"Hey, wait!" I called.

"Hold up! We aren't on yet!" Andy followed.

The captain reappeared, leaning over the guardrail and laughing. "Sorry!" he shouted from his perch. "Turns out we're all booked!" He popped the bag of siv into his hat. "But thank ya for yer *generous* donation!"

We continued to call at him in vain, as the ship pulled away. I watched helplessly as our chances of escape slipped into the fog, and desolation closed in on my senses. I searched my mind frantically, taking shaky breaths of the frigid, evening air. I became still when I concluded that there was no other alternative. *That's the only way out*, I realized. My hands reached for the vessel.

The boat strained, every plank on its surface groaning with tension. I felt my friends' eyes land on me when white beams shined from the spaces in the wood and brought the galleon to a standstill. A startled hush fell on the group, and I paused, just as amazed, then refocused.

My veins throbbed, brow creased, and eyes glowed with Ka to clarify my view of the target. A quaking energy seemed to pulse upward from my shoes, through my chest and into my arms to enrich my muscles with vigor. My knees were locked immovably as I began to pull. I lost track of my movements, but in a matter of seconds the backend of the immense vessel ground ashore. The ship groaned. Immediately, the gangway dropped.

The captain stormed back down, muttering curses. He waved his arms at us. "Whaddaya think yer doin'?!"

We were silent.

Murry slipped his hands into the sleeves of his cloak. "We had a deal," he stated, straightening up.

The captain cursed again and pushed past us to inspect the damages. "I just had 'er painted..."

My first thought was to apologize, but instead my arms lifted and Ka tugged on the ship again. The vessel screeched.

"Stop! Stop!" the captain roared.

I locked eyes with him. "I'll drag this ship back to Bozko's tavern if I have to."

The pirate inspected me for a long while, and his wrinkled features slowly curled into a grin. Laughs escaped his gap-toothed smile as he eyed each of our group's faces, before returning to mine.

"Ya know what? I like yer style, kid." His chuckles wound down, and his grin shifted to one side. "The name's Captain Cyrus!" The point of his cap dipped, half-hiding his face. "Welcome to the crew, *matees*."

16
The Ice Pirates

The captain brought us aboard his ship, puffing out his chest and nodding casually to the scrambling mobs of crew members as he strode. We neared a skinny, wild-eyed one, who stood shaken from the incident, trying to shape words. His pupils darted in between us and his captain. Cyrus calmly made a circular motion with his fist and, after a moment of hesitance, the old man bolted for a rotating crank-lever to draw the gangway.

It clunked shut behind us, standing vertical in line with the aft, as we proceeded across the deck and into the cacophony of confused shouts and hollers.

Captain Cyrus smiled back at us in spite of the clamor. "Didn't catch yer names."

Murry bowed his head. "Murry Marko."

"I'm Marvin."

"Andy!"

"Veronica Blaire." She nodded to her pet. "And that's Boris."

The minotaur snorted and Scooter chimed in with a chirp as well, before Zyvin grumbled his name last.

"Pleasure!" the pirate laughed. He looked ahead again, maintaining his pace for a few more steps, then asked, "Where is it yer headed?"

"Puerri Island," Murry explained, pointing to its location on his outheld map. "And then perhaps the closest port on Veindai."

"Ah, huh..." the pirate mumbled, squinting as he ran his fingers over the continents and labels. At first I thought he was inspecting the course, but instead he was feeling the wrinkles, fold marks, and frays in the parchment. He grinned. "This's what a good map looks like."

Our discussion was interrupted, when a pudgy man wearing a gray, woolen coat came rocketing across the planks of the upper deck. He redirected his squeaking strides down a set of stairs, missing a few as he flightily descended the sodden, wood staircase.

When he located of the captain, he caught himself on the guardrail, heaving breaths. His frenzied, rubicund features were nearly the same hue as his crimson bandana.

"Sah!" he called from above.

Cyrus tried to calm him down and wave him back to the helm. "Everythin's fine. Let 'er go, Lou."

"*Sah!* Wot happened?"

"Some boy be Ka-willin' our boat back aground, thas'all."

"Ka-willy... *wha?* I thought we'd hit a rogue breaker!"

"Nah, we're fine. Just got us some guests now! Set course for Puerri Island."

"Ain't that in the Vox Sea?"

"Aye... Well, it's the Veindaian Gulf to be precise, but they's all one now..." He shook his head at his words. "Set the path! Go check that map o' yers, an' hurry!"

"Aye, sah!"

He ran off. Captain Cyrus rotated to face us again, gesturing to the man hurrying up to the flying deck.

"Lou Burbunii," he introduced. "First mate. Best navigator on the open water." He let out a short laugh. "Darn good musician too."

"So you can get us there?" I asked him.

"Aye!" the captain declared. He scratched at his icy beard, adding, "We can get ya ta Puerri alright. Not sure how *close* we can get ta Veindai in the gulf..." His eyes trailed off as he thought. "Might need ta lend ya an old dingy or somethin'." He grinned, pointing elsewhere, "Just picked up a nice one, in fact! Found it earlier few spans east o' here. No one was usin' it..."

We went silent.

His frosty eyes examined our expressions, then a wry smile cracked on his face. "I'm foolin'! *Ha-har!*" He stomped his foot in laughter, as we released our tense breaths. Andy recognized the gag and let out a few laughs of his own, but then caught sight of the rest of our faces and punctuated himself with a cough.

"Never dull, never dull," the pirate reveled. "But, yeah. We'll get ya there." He wiped a tear away with his knuckle. "Lucky it's on our route, otherwise I'd never agree." He studied our looks, seeming to recognize a hint of apprehension, then assured us, "Don' worry! Yer with the Ice Pirates now." He raised his arms, wiggling his fingers and clamping his claw a couple times. "Yer in good *hand*."

He walked off with a laugh. Andy and Veronica appeared on either side of me, watching him leave.

"Maybe we should've considered other options," Veronica said.

Andy glanced at her with a disagreeing grin. "No way! These guys are cool."

Two pirates ambled by us, one of them snorting. He coughed, then hacked a greenish ball of snot across the length of the deck and into a small, metal bucket. The two of them raised their arms victoriously and cheered. Veronica looked at Andy, unconvinced, then dropped her bag of supplies. We set down the rest of our things, and wandered across the length of the ship to lean over the railing and watch the swells.

Enkartai's full moons gleamed brightly, piercing the overcast and conjuring a tide to initiate our voyage. The aft end returned fully to the water, and pirates leaned over the guardrails to check the hull, before being motioned to their stations by Captain Cyrus. Thick clouds parted as the mainsail unfurled, and as if drawn to the moons' luring shine, the creaking ship lurched forward, crashing through a misty wave and into the half-frozen ocean.

I stretched over the railing with Andy and Veronica, watching the reflective patterns wriggle and glint off the ocean's surface as we sailed. The chilled, salty air delivered invigorating scents to my nostrils, clearing my mind and refining my senses. Although I knew the temperature was still below freezing, as we departed I somehow felt warmer. I couldn't tell whether the buzzing sensation was actual or anticipatory, but as a whirlwind swept over me I smiled, knowing that any micro-current of wind would propel us closer toward our destination.

Calming waves sloshed against the hull. Andy leaned over the rail, grinning at Veronica.

"Pretty nice way to travel," he said.

She glanced at him, the heels of her hands pressing down on the barrier as she rocked. The corner of her mouth tugged to give a response, but she stopped herself and slid to her elbows, looking out over the water instead.

Andy nodded to his surroundings, his cheeks puffing with air. "*Pretty* romantic."

Veronica sighed and walked away from him.

Andy shrugged to me, and we exchanged quiet laughs.

A group of voices began to hum. Andy and I turned around, seeing three or so pirates tugging ropes to hoist a second sail. As they worked they sang:

We'll go off from the har-bor,
Hoist up the mast,
On an adven-ture
That shall not be our last!
We're the Ice Pirates;
We've done it all before!
Seeking high adventure...
From shore to shore!

Captain Cyrus appeared at our sides, chuckling internally and tucking his thumb and metal digit on the loops of his leather belt. He nodded at Andy and me. "Like a good shanty? Lou wrote this'un." He pointed. "This's my favorite line comin' up 'ere."

Our captain's Michael Cy-rus,
He's a jolly good man.
Seeking siv and trea-sure
On every wave he can!
Captain o' us scallywags
Knows 'xactly what we stand for!
Seeking high adventure...
From shore to shore!

The captain laughed heartily and clapped his hand against his metal forearm with delight, before wandering to the bow. The crew stomped and banged their fists against the nearest wooden platforms and surfaces in rhythm with the song, before starting up again and continuing for a few more verses.

Veronica leaned against the wall of the flying deck unenthusiastically, and her brow scrunched at Andy when he started to clap along. He glanced at her with a toothy grin.

"I like it!" he attested.

Right when a lull began to form, Lou burst from a doorway, wielding an instrument.

"*Ey!* He's brought out the ovaloo!" a bearded pirate exclaimed.

The first mate's eyes squinted seriously. He shook his right arm to loosen his joints, snapped his fingers above his head three times, then fiercely plucked the strings of his guitar-looking instrument, generating wild cheers from the crew.

The wooden ovaloo was finished with a dark, oaky color. The hollowed, elliptical body was secured to a lengthy, stringed neck. At the top of which, a spout-shaped structure protruded. At the moment I tried to figure its purpose, Lou blew into it, and my question was answered. The ovaloo was a half-string, half-wind instrument.

When he puffed air into the mouthpiece, the tune was flute-like, and when he plucked the strings simultaneously, the vibrations were bent into new sounds. Lou played inside a circle of shipmates. His pudgy fingers darted between staggered buttons and chords, and the audience clapped faster and faster to compliment the quickening beat. The one-man band leaned back then bent forward, playing with amplified vigor, until he reached maximum speed and gave the ovaloo a strong, final strum. The crowd cheered and launched into the closing verse of their song.

After the performance had simmered into casual conversations and occasional hums, Andy and I ventured across the deck. The ship was constructed from dark wooden planks, and the trim and polished accents were of an even darker hue. I glanced upward, following the swaying ropes and towering mastheads toward the tallest point of the ship, where a flag flapped in the wind. The image was only visible upon entering rays of moonlight, before becoming shaded again. I squinted to view it, as a breeze blew the flag into the light, revealing its fearsome design. The upper-half of a skull made of ice was centered on the black fabric. Sharp icicles extended off its cranium and teeth, and its eye sockets were illustrated to resemble a frown.

I kept my gaze fixed on the striking image as I walked. I couldn't believe I was aboard such an immense vessel, the type of which I had only been exposed to in the illustrations of history books. A grumbling sound caught me off-guard, breaking my stride and disrupting my thoughts.

The pathway of a massive humanoid holding a barrel was impeded when I unknowingly stepped in front of him. The fluidic grains of the container swilled as he made a few fidgety steps, only to be cut off again when I mistakenly mirrored his actions. Luminescent spots on his cranium fluxed as he let out a frustrated growl from behind dormant, green tendrils draping his mouth. I quickly apologized and altered my course. He squinted cynically at me with yellow eyes before huffing and lugging the barrel to the aft end of the ship.

I scratched the back of my head, allowing myself to recover for a moment, as Andy let out a laugh and slapped my back. "We've got a way with people huh, Marv?"

I finished a long exhalation and nodded in agreement, then continued toward the bow of the ship, where Captain Cyrus looked out over the ocean. His eyes remained fixated, as Andy and I milled. I leaned over the guardrail, seeing a sheet of ice had drifted toward us. The front end of the ship was sharp and plow-like, and easily cleaved through the slab without compromising speed. Captain Cyrus chuckled internally, standing tall as the ice sheets grinded apart, separating and welcoming us into a clear straight of ocean.

We joined him, watching the bright rays of moonlight reflect off the dark tides, as though the stars of a perfect night sky had been liquefied.

"Your ship is awesome," Andy said.

"Aye," Captain Cyrus agreed with him, running his hand over the top of the guardrail tenderly. "We call 'er *the Leviathan.*" He grinned. "Named after the vicious sea titan, said ta dwell in the chasms of the Vox Sea."

Andy and I hushed, as the captain turned to us. "Indigenous peoples call it the Kraicore," he explained. "*Kraicore,* directly translated, means *Death Snake.*" He set his arms on the railing, eyeing us a while longer before switching his stare to the tides. "They say she's colossal. A relic o' the ancient world."

"Is it real?" I asked him.

His eyebrows arched.

"I mean, have you seen it?"

He laughed, "If I seen 'er I wouldn't be here talkin' to ya."

My eyes drifted and fixed on the polished figurehead mounted on the bow: a sea serpent's face, carved with simplistic wooden features. The figure had swirling decorations in place of scales, a set of predatory teeth lining its horrid, grisly smile, and two huge, haunting ovals for eyes. I swallowed nervously.

"It's said the Kraicore could smell the tiniest drop o' blood from a thousand spans away." The captain started to chuckle. "*That's* why we call our ship the Leviathan. We can smell *treasure* from a thousand spans away! *Ya-har!*"

The crew halted their duties to echo his cheer.

My gaze had yet to stray from the figurehead when Captain Cyrus turned to us again. He seemed to notice my concern. He added, "It's an old Naga tale," to remedy my dread.

The detail was unfamiliar and his assertion was unconvincing, but I decided to accept it.

He watched us a while longer, then stepped away from the bow and motioned for us to follow him. "Lemme show ya to yer room."

He guided us across the deck, toward the ladders that descended into the ship's hull. Zyvin watched us approach. He leaned, half-sitting on the guardrail near the base of the flying deck, fingers tapping and foot rising and falling as he rocked silently. His eyes darted between us and the floor. He looked sick. As we passed by, he finally peeled away from his seat and drifted to our sides.

Murry caught sight of us, shut his spell book, and straightened up as we neared him and Veronica. Boris knelt by Veronica, shutting his eyes as she rubbed his snout and massaged his face. A pirate squinted at her unusual pet, lip raising in bewilderment.

"Tha's incredible!" he announced.

She looked at him, still running fingers through her pet's fur.

"I ain't never seen a beastie like 'im!"

"That's because there *isn't* anything else like him."

Boris snorted, watching her softly with his brown eyes before pushing off the floor and rising to his full height. The pirate gawked at him with greater astonishment. As we joined them, Veronica picked up our scattered belongings and equipment and distributed them. I slung my backpack over one arm and Andy reclaimed his sword. He touched the point to the floor and sighed, as the crew member's astonished expression faded.

"Ye got a sheath fer that?" the short pirate asked.

"A what?" he asked.

"Gotta keep a sword sheathed!" the pirate contested. "Keep it safe, keep it at reach."

Andy glanced at his weapon.

"Keep it covered too! Give folk the wrong 'mpression otherwise."

Zyvin's tired eyelids rolled shut, as he briefly locked stares with Andy.

The short man rotated and displayed the sword latched on his belt. "See?"

Cyrus spoke, "Well, if yer gonna keep blabbin' about it, find the boy a sheath, eh?"

"Aye, sah!"

The captain uttered breathy laughs, shaking his head as the pirate promptly descended the ladders leading into the lower decks. He signaled for us to follow him, before ambling down the flight of steps and guiding us deep into the galleon.

A couple levels down, the captain located a larger cabin against an inner wall, half-hidden behind the ladders. He took hold of the door hinge in his mechanical grip.

"Here we are," he said, glancing back at us. "This oughtta fit all o' ya." He worked the stiff handle down and wrestled the door open, but the room was already occupied.

Cyrus stopped at the sight of a gaunt pirate, sitting on one of the lower bunks with a sandwich in his hands.

"Charlie!" the captain roared. "What're ya doin' in the spare quarters?!"

The skinny man's eyes widened in shock, his mouth frozen open as red sauce dripped from the bread. "Nothing, sah—"

"Ya've got that right!" He pointed behind him with his thumb. "Go on, get movin'."

"But sah, this is where *I'm* staying."

"How in the Aevæs' Light was that arranged? Git out!"

Murry raised his finger to compromise. "Captain, we'd be more than willing to—"

"Ye hear that Charlie? Ya've upset the poor man!"

"This is *my* room!"

"Not anymore it ain't! We've got ourselves some guests."

Charlie let out an irritated groan, searching the splits in the ceiling for answers, as sauce streamed down his left hand. The captain prepared to shout again, when the man cried, "Fine then!

185

I'll be out!" He stood, then hobbled toward a crate and gathered up some fruit.

"*Oh-hoh-oh*, no ya don't! That food's fer the guests, now!"

"But sah, I'm '*ungry!*"

"Then go nibble on the guardrail!"

The bone-thin pirate muttered something angrily, dropping the fruits and heading for the door, but Cyrus stood in his way, holding out his hand and folding his fingers twice. Charlie stood dumbfounded, dissecting the expression, then sneered and hostilely relinquished the sandwich.

Charlie stormed off, as Captain Cyrus shook his head. "I'm sorry 'bout that, Charlie can be a bit *demandin'* from time to time." He popped the soggy bread into a trash-barrel. "Hope the room's big 'nough for ya. It's the finest we can offer."

"It's fine, thank you," Murry said simply.

The stout pirate returned to his captain's side with a sheath in his hands. "Found one!" He gave it to Andy, and Andy turned the item over in his hands, inspecting the thickly-stitched exterior and the patina on the gold brim.

"Cool!" he said. "Thanks, dude!"

The pirate nodded and hurried back up the ladders.

Captain Cyrus chuckled, as Andy secured the sheath onto his waist. "Enjoy yer stay!" He bowed, then shut our door for us and stepped off, his footsteps trailing as he scaled the steps to the main deck.

We unloaded our shoulders and backs, placing our belongings along the base of the wall. I set my book bag beside Murry's rucksack, taking my Captain Galloway book from the main compartment and tucking it under my arm, before stepping around to inspect our room. The walls of the cabin were constructed from the same knotted, amber-hued material as the rest of the ship, while the flooring seemed to have been sealed and resealed with darker colors. Although the floorboards had little give, they made slight snapping sounds as I treaded toward the bunks along the farthest wall.

Andy climbed up to the top, while I lay on the bottom.

"Oh, yeah." Andy stretched out, starting to laugh. "We're in the lap of luxury now!"

The thin mattresses were cradled in tarps that hung below their square frames like hammocks. Scooter curled up on my chest as I squirmed into a comfortable position and rested my head on an actual pillow. I released a long breath as I relaxed.

Andy's arm appeared over the edge of the top bunk for a second while he reoriented himself, tucking his hands behind his head and clearing his throat. He laughed again.

"Hey Marv?"

"Yeah?"

"What do you think our moms are thinking right now?"

I pondered his question. A slew of worried thoughts accrued, but before I could offer any guesses, Andy impersonated his mother's voice with an exaggerated, shrill tone:

"Andrew Bailey! What are you doing? Didn't I tell you not to go into alternate universes?!" Veronica and I started to laugh along with him, as he continued making rambling sounds with his fake voice.

Veronica hopped onto the first step of a ladder, bypassing the rest and sitting atop a second set of bunks. Zyvin stopped in front of an odd slab of wood that was fastened to the wall. He flipped the metal latch and a less comfortable-looking, hinged platform flipped down, secured to the wall with a pair of ropes. He sighed, and before anyone could comment, he adjusted its uneven padding and announced, "This one's mine."

Boris huffed as he lowered himself onto the floor beside the exit, while Murry took the final bunk. I flipped through the pages of my Captain Galloway book, finding my spot and reading for a few more chapters while calming currents rolled against the Leviathan's hull, swelling our cabin's creaking walls with each rush of water. It took me a while to realize that our cabin was actually below the ocean's surface. I placed the back of my hand against the wall, feeling chilled air rise off the boards. My hammock swayed in unison with the flowing sounds, and as the somnolent rhythms took hold of my senses, I succumbed to sleep.

Zyvin's eyelids peeled open, watching the remnant light rays from outside lanterns fade entirely. He stared upward for a long while at the slats in the ceiling, waiting. Only the occasional footstep unsettled the upper boards and made him restart his interval of delay. The manmade noises were spaced farther and farther apart, until the squeaks were too distant to distinguish from the ship's own sounds. He sat up.

Strands of damaged, grayed hair rolled to either side of his face, swaying into his line of sight. He brushed them back, irritated. He hated looking at them—seeing the effects of his imprisonment. For a long time he stayed seated on the uncomfortable plank, listening to the room settle and its occupants rest. He hadn't realized how tightly his bony fingers gripped the edge until the sensation in his fingertips started to drain. He pried his hands from the board and stood, taking a few wary steps across the room.

The sound of every movement seemed amplified. The snapping of floorboards, the drag of his clothing. A sudden, raucous snore made him stop abruptly, and caused the wooden pendants of his necklace to clatter together. He caught them with his right hand, standing rigid. The wizard's chest rose again to take in another loud snore, and then fell as he let out a long, quieter exhale.

Zyvin released his own lungful, shutting his eyes for a moment. His hand still clamped around his pendants, he felt the ridges and grooves in the jewelry's old carvings. With his thumb, he located the triangular nose and curved canines of the wooden wolf symbol, the centermost and largest of his three totems. He held on to the pieces a while longer, tracing the swirling, stylized features, then released them and completed his quiet advancement across the room.

He lowered himself, setting down a sore knee and shifting his weight until he eased. He rolled up his sleeves, uncovering his thin, pale skin, then steadied his hands out in front of him. He bent his fingers to pump heat through his frigid joints, and then carefully lifted the flap of Murry's rucksack, navigating its contents until he found one of the two cloth-covered crystals.

He held the weighty rock below his chin, unraveling the thick, brown fabric. Although the green gem's glow was soft, he still shielded its luminance with his body so its light wouldn't reach the eyes of his slumbering roommates. He balanced the crystal in the folds of the rucksack, and took his knife from his belt. He slid off the decorative sheath and held the blade out in front of him.

It was his father's knife. He turned it slowly. Stray glimmers of green light shined off the blade's reflective surface and glided into the engraving along the top of the blade. A family motto, lettered in the alphabet of the old language: *Ahl ejhum ain grador -- ihl chien'ain tradah.* Its translation echoed from his memories: *To defend honor, where no honor exists.* Zyvin's fingers tightened around the ivory handle. He held it backward in his fist, shutting his eyes and steadying his shaky breaths, before reaching for the gem.

His fingertips slid over the slick surface of the stone, finding an existing fracture in one of its angles. He plunged his knife into the separation, twisting and cleaving it apart, then caught the piece as it detached. He held the fragment to his eye, examining its size and shape. Once he determined it was the appropriate dimensions, he rewrapped the gem and repeated the process with the Frost crystal. The light blue stone was larger than the first, but somehow lighter. Its shine was brighter as well, illuminating the faces of the others. Veronica stirred.

Zyvin stopped working. He blocked the light with his body, waiting to ensure she wouldn't wake up. She rotated to her side, still asleep, and Zyvin sighed in anguish. Part of him hoped we would be caught. Or at least that one of the travelers would wake and question him. He could explain away his actions and postpone them for another night. But they remained asleep, and he returned to his project.

The second fracture chipped off its source and tumbled into his hand. Zyvin's face curled in distress as he put away his knife, returned the contents of the rucksack, and then quickly stepped for the door. His haste made the floorboards crack louder than before, and the minotaur's head tossed, his wet nostrils flaring and releasing a guttural snort. Zyvin stayed frozen in the center of the cabin, holding the crystal pieces tightly to his chest as the body of the massive animal settled once more.

Zyvin shuddered. His task wasn't complete yet.

He swallowed his fear, snuck past the enormous minotaur, and escaped into the hallway. Concealed in the corner behind diagonal beams, he knelt to the floor and unclenched his hand. In his palm, the two crystal pieces clung together.

Flits of green and blue energy irradiated within their prisms, sparked, and traveled between stones, exchanging luminosities.

Zyvin grunted and pried them apart, separating the wild reaction. Translucent ripples pulsed between the two, and the miniature shockwave nearly tossed him off balance, as the energies snapped back into their original enclosures. He threw his arms sideways, and a plasmatic, teal current arced from the crystal in his right hand and rolled over the wooden floor, leaving a dark, crescent-shaped steak on the boards.

Zyvin gawked at the aftermath. It appeared charred and discolored, but upon closer scrutiny, he reconsidered. He ran his hand over the damage. It wasn't burned. There was no residual heat from the blast, and the wood grain of the floorboards was gone, replaced by glittering minerals within platy fragments of dark gray material. The current had transfigured the matter entirely.

As he stared, wide-eyed at the effect of the crystals' power, a faint echo sounded. His eyes darted down the hall, toward the direction he thought it came, but the next noise reverberated from the opposite side. He chased it with his eyes. They circled him.

As he backed into the shade of the corner he felt them grow in intensity. Every hissing whisper and pounding note. The noises were inescapable. His eyes darted in every direction, desperately seeking the source, until he realized that they were resonating within his own consciousness.

The sounds collided, fusing into a harsh, articulate tone that urged him to complete the task.

It was him.

You may proceed, Shamaul voiced.

Zyvin swallowed dryly, rasping, "Yes," then uncurled his fingers, revealing the flaring green gem in his left palm. His arm throbbed. The sensation of a cold, foreign substance pumping through his blood, the web of veins in his forearm ran black. When the dark mixture reached the base of his hand's heel, Zyvin felt his muscles seize. The crystal rotated on its own, flashing with intensity and drawing his horrified gaze. The diamond-shaped fragment steadied like the arrow of a compass, then stood upright on its point and sank into his flesh.

Zyvin muffled a cry, biting on his uncompromised fist as the item buried half-way into his skin, sparking, before it twisted and disappeared completely into his hand. The skin closed. Zyvin dropped the second crystal to grab his wrist as he tried to bend his stiffened fingers. When the gem hit the ground, a whir of violent hisses coiled around him.

The second one! they demanded, the layered voices blending into the sonorous boom of Shamaul.

Zyvin shivered. His right hand fumbled across the boards to retrieve the precious gem that had settled in the flaky debris of the floor's abrasion. He panted and shook off the filth, then dropped the piece into his left palm, where the crystal sank, this time remaining on its side.

His face twisted and a short cry escaped his throat as a searing pain shot through him. Sickening snaps and pops sounded from his palm as the jagged fragment plied between tendons and bone, before finally settling within his muscle and dematerializing. The Frost crystal's matter tumbled, shimmered, and assimilated, then fazed through the armored palm of Shamaul's left hand to become solid again in the Dark Lands' atmosphere. His massive, metal-clad fingers closed around the bottom point of the gem, halting its ascent. The Dark Warlock raised the rare treasure to his serpentine eyes for examination, then reached for his scepter.

He released his hold on the gem and it floated in an aura of black Ka toward the head of his speared weapon. It clicked into the second of five diamond-shaped cavities cut into the semicircular blade. It buzzed in the presence of the Ravacan crystal secured overtop it, and the energies spilled and cycled through the central sphere of the scepter. Inside, their star-like particles collected, merged, and fluxed in a cloud of blue smoke. Shamaul observed it, a hissing breath slipping between his teeth and steaming against the inside of his silver mask.

That's all, right? Zyvin's pained voice echoed between the warlock's thoughts.

Shamaul's slit pupils strayed from his prize.

We're done now... No more?

Shamaul sat forward in his throne, reaching.

The air thinned, as Zyvin sucked in a futile breath, his body tensing.

There remain unfulfilled duties, Shamaul's sinister voice returned.

Zyvin stammered, disregarding the volume of his protest, "Bu... But you told me that I'd—" He grunted. His joints locked.

When you reach Puerri Island you will eliminate the Realmhoppers.

Zyvin's body numbed. He panted. "I... No—"

Tightness turned to pain. He gaped at his limbs in horror as they began to fade, and the freezing air slipped through his intangible form.

I placed you there. I can bring you back.

The walls rumbled, and a deafening vibration pounded through him as his surroundings pulsated between the safety of the hull and the specter of the Dark Lands.

"Alright!" he choked.

It required great focus to keep you whole. To tempt me now is unwise.

The unyielding tremor battered his psyche, as the hallway warped.

"*Alrightalrighalright!*" Zyvin screamed through airless lungs.

Shamaul released his hold on him, and he collapsed on the floor, heaving. The frail man reached forward, trying to crawl and lift himself, as his senses recovered. He cringed as the whirring noises trailed, and the dark sensations settled unnervingly in his gut. He lay there blearily, then raised his aching head from the floor, as a parting image flickered in his mind: his family encaged, his two children clinging to their exhausted mother's shackled arms.

Zyvin's right eye welled with tears as he stared into the distance helplessly, watching the foggy picture waver and haze.

I doubt you'll require further motivation.

Zyvin shuddered, "No."

The Dark Warlock rose from his throne, balancing a silvery, spherical stone in his left hand. His venomous eyes fixed on the image that it projected on its surface. Between the cloudy swirls, dark floorboards were visible. The picture wobbled as a hand appeared in the lower right to push off the ground.

"I will be watching," Shamaul spoke.

The image on the stone went dark when Zyvin's eyelid rolled shut, covering the second optirock secured in his left eye socket.

A few of Zyvin's anguished breaths echoed in the warlock's mind, before he allowed them to dissipate and scatter. He watched the optirock a moment longer, and then closed his armored fingers around it, strode across the chamber, and stepped onto the balcony to look out over his demesne. A particular fluctuation drew his attention skyward. Behind a thick ceiling of murky clouds, a nearly innocuous energy gathered. He focused on it, waiting for it to conjure again.

While the warlock stared, his goblin subordinate hobbled to the right of him, sniffing the air and stretching his head in an attempt to follow his gaze.

"What are you thinking, Sire?"

He didn't respond.

Gumble swallowed thickly, looking away. Through the spaces of the railing he spotted a pack of terrorwolves snarling at one another while tugging at remnant meat that clung to the ribcage of an indistinguishable carcass. When the last morsel was torn, the ravenous animals turned on the one who had claimed it. They snarled and stormed into the dead forest to battle over the bloody mouthful, leaving the bones to sit forever in the infertile, gray soil.

Gumble smirked, then turned alertly when his ruler spoke.

"It is almost time," Shamaul observed. "The Realms will experience a new era of darkness."

17
Leviathan's Sail

Calmer waves clipped the hull, bowed our walls, and tilted our cabin. The craft groaned groggily, as its panels strained and resettled. The very rhythms that had lulled me to rest, and instilled my dreams with maritime images of combers and shores, were steadily nudging me back into wakefulness. My eyelashes stuck together as my eyelids peeled back. My hand traveled gawkily up to my face, rubbed away the byproduct of sleep, and then located my crooked lenses and repositioned them on my nose.

My arm dropped back to my side as I took in a partial yawn and shifted. For a while I wavered whether or not to initiate my day, but as my mind reactivated and senses keened, the clamor of crew members scrambling topside became audible through the boards of the ceiling, and I gathered enough energy to move.

As I scooped Scooter from my chest, his blue tentacles emerged partway from his shell's aperture, and his large eyes blinked at me from within the carapace. He chirruped drowsily, then refurled himself and disappeared into his spiral home, as I placed him gingerly inside my coat's fur-lined pocket.

I stepped across the cabin and pushed open the stubborn door to see Captain Cyrus standing at the far end of the hallway, kicking at a scuff on the floor. He frowned at it, muttering something to himself in confusion. When Charlie entered, the captain stopped him, pointing at the discolored boards.

"Charlie, you do this?"

"What? No sah, I—"

"Thought so. Clean it up."

"Bu—but I..."

Charlie groaned futilely, as the captain patted his shoulder and walked off.

Cyrus grinned and nodded to me. "Ey, there! How was the room?"

I gave him a thumbs-up. "Good."

"Great!" Andy added through a loud, satisfied yawn. He emerged from the room stiffly, propping himself against the side wall. He tossed and caught a fruit he'd found from the food crate a couple times, before raising the exotic edible to his teeth.

Cyrus interjected, "Best save yer appetite for the feast."

I blinked. "*Feast?*"

The captain chuckled, before ascending the ladders. "Aye. Only the finest!" he announced. He kept on talking as he climbed, his voice trailing off.

Andy nudged me with his elbow. "This is the best!" he exclaimed, returning to the room and popping the fruit back into the crate.

Our activity stirred Veronica from rest. She yawned and stretched, then slid from her bunk, bypassing the ladder and landing beside me.

"What's going on?" she asked.

"Food!" Andy answered exuberantly. She was about to reply, when Andy wrapped his arms around her. "We get to eat, Veronica! We get to *eat!*" He buried his head in her shoulder and pretended to cry. She sighed.

Soon, a collection of voices congregated above us, signifying the feast was underway. We readied ourselves to join them, gathering by the door, when we noticed Zyvin was staying behind. He was curled up on his bedplank with his back facing us.

"You coming?" Andy asked him.

He remained silent, his tired eyes not straying from the wall. Andy exchanged confused looks with us, before repeating his question. Zyvin's eyelids rolled shut as he took in a shaky breath through his nose and finally shook his head to decline the invitation. He seemed sleep deprived.

"Are you okay?" Veronica asked.

"Fine," he grumbled.

"Do you need anything?"

"Nah... nah I'm fine. Jus' not feelin' up to it is all."

"Are you coming down with something?"

Zyvin shook his head.

"Seasick?"

"Homesick."

We lingered there for a few moments, until Zyvin waved us away and urged us to enjoy our meals without him. We expressed our condolences, left the cabin, then scaled the ladders and followed the raucousness into the dining room of the middle deck.

Metal tankards clanged together, their frothy contents spilling over the sides before being chugged down the gullets of rejoicing crew members, as onlookers applauded. A pair of like-dressed pirates finished their drinks, slamming down empty containers and shouting in triumph. Their names were Grall and Groddy, we learned. Twins. They turned to the short pirate, Herm, to referee who had finished their drink the fastest. He thought for a moment, then declared Grall the victor, and Groddy immediately demanded a rematch.

Andy clapped his hands and wiped away tears, still chuckling from a joke he had told, along with an audience of enraptured crew members. He grabbed at an ache in his side as he tottered in his chair and struggled to catch his breath.

"O-okay!" he gathered himself, clearing his throat. "I got another one!"

The entire table hushed in anticipation, chairs creaking as listeners leaned in.

"What do you get when you cross a *minotaur* with the *wind*?"

"*Oi!*" Lou called from across the room. "Wot *do* you get when you cross a minotaur wit da wind?"

"*Dairy Air!*"

The room exploded with laughter. Boris snorted. The entire cabin shook as the pirates stomped their boots and hammered their fists against the table.

"I love this boy!" Cyrus roared, grabbing Andy's shoulder and shaking him.

"*Guess there's a first for everything,*" Veronica murmured, smiling and looking away.

Pots of edibles circled the table, each guest piling more and more food onto their plate before passing them along, like Thanksgiving dinner. I didn't pay any attention to the contents of the containers before spooning portions onto my plate. Before I knew it, a heaping allotment of seafood—unusual fish, crustaceans, shucked shellfish, seasoned seaweed-like greens— along with colorful citruses and steaming bread, tantalized my nostrils with a unique blend of beguiling aromas, and activated my appetite.

With a two-pronged fork I tried to peel a hunk of meat from the cheek of a steamed fish head. The white meat flaked, separating whenever I attempted to spear it with the awkward utensil. I eventually changed tactics and picked it up with my hands. I popped the delicate slabs into my mouth and allowed the buttery meat to break apart on its own, and a warm layer of oceanic flavor spread across my tongue. I shut my eyes and reveled in the saltiness for a while, then reached for a wooden cup, filled with fizzing, purple liquid. I took a sip and allowed the tanginess to cleanse my taste buds. My abdomen buzzed. I set the drink down and constructed my next bite: A halved roll, topped with a creamy spread, topped with another hunk of cheek meat. As I chewed it, the medley congealed into a single texture, and a mixture of flavors enveloped my mouth. All foreign to my pallet. All delicious. I let out a gratified breath and reached for more. As I confirmed the deliciousness of each item I started spooning servings onto an empty plate beside me. Captain Cyrus caught sight of my project, tilting his head slightly at the behavior, before he was drawn back into conversation.

My attention traveled down the length of the table, as a pirate stood from his seat to adjust a light on the wall. The cylindrical, lantern-like fixture was filled with shimmering liquid. When the pirate twisted the bottom, air was introduced to the solution. The bubbles floated upward, jumbling a layer of sparkling sediment and brightening the amber glow. He rushed back to his chair alongside fellow crewmembers to watch intently as Boris tore the last chunk of meat from a massive, roasted limb, then dropped the clean bone into the pile of scraps before him. He released a puff of air from his flaring nostrils, snorting with contentment. The Ice Pirates exchanged awe-struck comments.

"His appetite's as big as he is!" one pirate proclaimed.

A bluish tongue emerged from Boris' mouth to lick at his two protruding fangs, then traveled up to moisten his nose. With mouths agape, the Ice Pirates delivered more and more food to the minotaur, then watched with fascination as he finished every portion. Veronica leaned on her pet lovingly.

Scooter chirped in rapture as he scampered across the table, nibbling on leftovers. He vacuumed up crumbs and gnawed on the remnant meat from discarded fish bones, before circling to where my right hand rested on the table. His cool tentacles wrapped around my wrist as he hoisted himself upward and crossed my arm like a bridge to my shoulder. One pirate was especially amused by his antics.

"Would ya look at 'im!" he hooted, coughing between laughs. "He's like a wee li'l lusca!" He took another sip of his beverage before laying his head down on the table and falling asleep. Beside him, Charlie grumbled in anger. I sat forward in my seat to see that his right hand was trapped beneath the unconscious pirate's cranium. He grabbed his wrist and tugged repeatedly, as the napping man smacked his gums. Charlie growled.

Captain Cyrus squinted at him skeptically.

"He won't move," Charlie declared. "I'm caught!"

The captain lifted his metal-plated forearm onto the table with a *clunk*. Charlie gawked at it. He swallowed tensely and locked stares with his captain for a few moments, before looking away and returning to his dilemma. He carefully lifted the man's head and slid his hand out from underneath. He rubbed his bony fingers, and then quietly reached for a roll.

Murry sat back in his chair, patting his stomach. Captain Cyrus raised his cup to him, chuckling before taking a swig.

"So, ya've told us *where* yer headed, but ye haven't mentioned *why*." Cyrus dried his mouth with his sleeve, then sat forward. "Yer quite a ways from home."

"*Oh*, yeah," Andy said between chews.

"What brings a band o' Ravacans this far north?"

"Necessity," Murry replied simply, sipping his steaming beverage.

"Seems you took a bit of a detour, then. Hammon Shou ain't exactly *on the way* to Puerri now, is it?"

"We're on a mission!" Andy declared.

"A mission!" Lou echoed enthusiastically.

Andy swallowed his mouthful. "There are these five crystals, right?"

Cyrus' stare went blank.

"We have to collect them all so we can—"

"*The Orb*..." the captain voiced.

Andy laughed, "Yeah!"

Veronica tried to grab Andy's attention with her eyes, but he remained focused on his meal. He took a massive bite of a dripping drumstick, as the pirates started to murmur to one other. Horror pulsed through us. The merry conversations had dissolved into whispers. Captain Cyrus studied our faces carefully, then switched to Charlie when the gaunt pirate leaned in to ask, "How many have ya got so far?"

"Two," Andy answered immediately, simulating their size with his hands. "And they're *big*—!"

Veronica kicked him.

"*Ow!*"

They shared a silent argument, as Charlie sat back in his chair, chewing pensively as his eyes locked on the centerpiece of the table: a hefty, metallic container, crafted in the likeness of a cauldron hoisted by mermaid-like beings. Along the exterior, swirling designs imitated rolling waves. His eyes traced the patterns, before settling on the contents of the bowl. Burgundy liquid bubbled inside, with five small, dark eyeballs bobbing on its surface. His tongue moistened his upper lip hungrily, and his hand wandered across the table to claim it.

CLANK!

The dining room hushed as Captain Cyrus' mechanical hand clamped around the pirate's wrist. "Don'tcha be touchin' that fish eye soup, Charlie!"

Charlie squirmed. "*Why?*"

The captain's lip curled. He released him. Charlie covered his wrist, scowling back in perplexity, then went for another item.

"Ya know..." Cyrus sniffed the air. "I think I fancy the smell o' that'n as well."

Charlie slammed his hands down, pushed himself away from the table, and stormed off. Heads rotated as he plodded out the exit and slammed the door. We waited a few tense seconds, as the examining stares of the dining room returned to our faces. I swallowed hard, trying to decode their expressions, before Captain Cyrus broke the silence:

"Mr. Marko!"

Murry's eyebrows rose alertly.

"I wanted ta thank ye again for yer substantial contribution to the Leviathan." He raised his cup to the wizard. His crew seemed to ease.

Murry lifted his drink in return and nodded respectfully.

"Yer part o' the crew, now," the captain nodded with certainty. "The Ice Pirates'll ensure your safe arrival." He turned to the rest, shouting, "Won't we?"

"Aye!" The sea farers resounded.

"We's in the comp'ny of adventurers!" one announced.

Lou stood, puffing out his chest heroically. "Like Alzerus Rufroy!"

I silently released a lungful of fear, as the festivities resumed. Grall and Groddy spoke to us:

"You should call yerselves the *Adventurers Five!*"

"There's six o' them, ya gudgeon!"

"Who's the sixth one, then? The hexapoid?"

"Nah, there was another—where's he at?"

Murry explained that Zyvin wasn't feeling well.

Cyrus made a toast. "To yer friend's health, then."

The crew pumped their vessels. "*Ya-har!*"

Lou stood. "To *adventcha!*"

"*Ya-har!*"

The slumbering pirate snorted and shot awake. "To *siv* and *treasure!*"

"*Ya-har!*"

Cyrus raised his finger, cup held high. "And," he added, "to the safe and fruitful travels of our new hearties."

"*Ya-har!*" The last cheer resonated the greatest, transitioning into vociferous laughter that seemed to rattle the walls. After a moment, it became clear that the jostling came from winds outside as well.

"Got some good gales out there," Herm commented.

Cyrus agreed, and the dining room emptied soon after. I transferred the remainder of my massive serving to the unused plate beside me.

Andy chuckled, "You're still hungry?"

I told him it was for Zyvin.

Captain Cyrus nodded in approval, ladling some fish eye soup into a spare bowl. He handed it to me. "For whatever's ailin' yer friend." I thanked him, then carried the extra meal into the hall and followed the others back to our cabin.

Veronica twisted and tugged the doorknob. The swollen door squeaked against its jamb as it flew open. Zyvin raised his head at the noise, as we all filed in. I delivered the food to a crate by Zyvin's bed. He examined it carefully for a long while, then nodded to me thankfully. He opened his mouth to say something, when Veronica voiced, "That was way too close."

Andy nodded, pushing through the entrance. "Yeah, they should really recut this door."

"You know what I'm talking about."

Andy looked taken aback.

Veronica clarified, "*Why* would you mention the crystals?"

"I..." Andy's eyes widened as he searched for words. "I dunno. They asked. What's the matter?"

"They're *pirates*. You just told a roomful of *professional thieves* that we're carrying two of the most valuable ores on the planet!"

Andy blinked. "...*Yeah?*"

"That's not good!"

"Veronica, your voice carries," Murry warned her.

She reined in her volume, then leaned in to whisper, "You could've jeopardized our stay here."

Andy let out a laugh. "They're on *our* side, though."

"We don't *know* them. We don't know what they're thinking."

"They seem pretty cool to me."

Three knocks turned our attentions to the doorway. I spun around last to see Captain Cyrus standing in the ingress. My stomach twisted. *Did he hear the conversation?*

He stepped into our cabin. The floorboards snapped with each heavy footstep through our silent room. He smiled.

"How's 'e doin'?" he asked.

Zyvin's throat bobbed nervously as the captain approached and knelt to observe him.

Cyrus squinted at him prudently, asking, "Dizzy? Fatigued? Confused?"

"Little," Zyvin voiced.

"Head pain? Eye pain?"

"It ain't medical."

Cyrus laughed, then lifted himself off the ground. "Yer gonna be fine. Yer in good company it seems." He wandered toward the exit, then stopped himself, digging something out of his pocket. "One more thing." He retrieved a small, cloth pouch— Murry's siv. He tossed it to the wizard. "We don't take from our own." Captain Cyrus grinned, then scaled the ladders.

Murry felt the weight of the bag. "It's heavier," he said, unraveling the string tie and peering inside. Atop the pile of silvery-gold pieces sat two ornate, golden coins, with small gems and nautical designs bedizening their borders. Murry lifted of the weighty doubloons, his mouth trying to shape words.

"*Whoa*," I breathed.

"They're like hockey pucks!" Andy said.

Murry returned them to the bag, still speechless. We stood silent for a while, until Andy and Veronica's stares drifted toward one another.

Andy smiled impishly at her. "Told ya."

FROST

Hammon Shou
Harbor Village

Bujin Ocean

The Vox Sea

18
Changing Tides

The icy gales thawed and overcast parted to reveal a vibrant, rosy sunrise framed by golden, feather-thin trails of cloud. Our fifth day on the water had carried us through the threshold of the Vox Sea, and into a calm, tropical clemency that demanded less of our wintry provisions. I abandoned my Shinkai furs in the cabin and stepped out onto the deck, basking in the sunrays for a moment as I breeched the exit. I shut my eyes as the light glinted through my lenses and blanketed my features in warmth, instilling my body with energy and my thoughts with optimism. I sucked in an invigorating, salty breeze, then smiled as my feet began to carry me across the planks.

A powerful swell rushed against the starboard hull, and the Leviathan uttered a rolling growl as it strained, swayed, and reoriented. My calves tightened and foot placement adjusted automatically as I completed my advancement across the ship to join with Andy and Veronica. They leaned on the banister, giggling while exchanging words. I reached the guardrail next to them and set my elbows down to look out over the sea. I grinned at the sparkling waves, then turned at the sound of excited whispers.

I traced my friends' enthusiastic sights toward a pod of creatures arcing from the ripples of the ship's wake. I had seen these animals before. Majestic, dolphin-like mammals with translucent skin and glowing, colorful innards leapt from the water. Their multihued systems fascinated me. Each time a central, blue organ throbbed, beads of yellow light were pumped through a matrix of veins to deliver brightness and color to the surface of the body. Blues, violets, greens, and reds all flashed along their flesh. Yellow light flared in their foreheads in synchronicity with their echoey clicks. From behind us, I heard passing pirates refer to these creatures as *skimmers*.

In mid-leap, the leader of the pod rotated, revealing a pair of what I originally thought were tendrils, but upon closer inspection I noticed that the slender structures possessed features of their own—eyes, gills, and fins. On the underbelly of each skimmer, lamprey-like fish had latched on, and with time, it seemed, their mouths had fused entirely to their hosts, their skin had become see-through, and the same luminescent quality had mingled with their blood and decorated their interiors.

The Vox Sea teemed with life. From above, a flock of squawking waterfowl with feathers of equally colorful hues swooped after a cloud of fleeing crustaceans, diving, disappearing, and resurging from the water with beakfuls of squirming, gray bodies. One of the pursuing skimmers clicked at the intrusive animals and leapt at them, spinning in midair and flinging droplets of water at the birds to scatter their formation. Veronica's eyes flashed with amazement at the inspiring acrobatics.

I smiled when I came to the realization that this part of the world was new to Veronica as well. The leading skimmer clicked victoriously and leapt again, higher this time.

"*Whoa-ho-ho!*" Her face lit up, as the creature completed two more rotations and splashed back into the water.

Andy shrugged. "I can do that."

Veronica shoved him playfully.

As we observed the marvels, a strumming sound took our attention back to the deck. Lou strolled by, playing a casual tune on his ovaloo. When he caught sight of our group he waved, then redirected his steps to meet us.

"There's our guests!" he beamed. We grinned back at him and exchanged pleasantries, before he added, "Cap'n says 'e wants to speak with one o' you; discuss your departure an' all."

Andy dithered and scratched the back of his head. I could tell he wanted to stay back with Veronica, so I volunteered to go. A grin tugged at his mouth when I nodded to him and stepped away, while the first mate imparted the directions to Captain Cyrus' quarters.

As I made my exit I made sure to glance behind me, catching sight of Andy and Veronica as they drifted back to the railing to return to their view. After a couple seconds of delay, Andy's hand traveled around her, before settling hesitantly on her waist. He paused a moment, standing rigid as if braced for some type of negative response. But to his surprise, she accepted the gesture, and after a moment, relaxed further and leaned on him.

He peeked over her rested head and shot an excited expression my way. I replied with a thumbs-up, laughing quietly, and then continued my trek across the deck.

Returning from an exploration, Scooter scampered on the railing of the flying bridge, trailing me. I caught sight of the scurrying cephalopod and held my arm out to intercept him as he leapt. He chirruped happily and hitched a ride on my shoulder as I walked. When I moved against a current of bodies, I felt compelled to excuse myself, but each of the pirates beat me to it:

"Comin' by."

"Pardon us."

"At yer flank, Marvy."

Even the green humanoid, Lugg, gurgled a salutation to me, and then made a large, semicircular detour to accommodate.

I finally found Captain Cyrus' quarters at the aft end of the ship. As I knocked, the door swung open, revealing the captain hard at work at his desk. In his left hand, Cyrus twisted the handle of a metallic tool to tighten the bolts on his plated forearm.

As I entered the room, a floorboard squeaked, drawing his attention. He smiled, nodded to me, then raised his arm to inspect his handiwork. His mechanical wrist swiveled swiftly, as his three metal digits clamped together twice.

"Better," he chuckled in approval, spinning his claw back to its original orientation before waving me inside. "Marvin! Come on in!"

He swept away a pile of screws and metal parts from his desk, uncovering a map of the world. I strolled through the small room, glimpsing at the few nautical portraits and curios tacked to the dark, splitting walls. The captain raised his chin to me as I approached. The frost that once clung to his beard and eyebrows had melted, his thawed hairs frizzing in the tropic air. I looked over his shoulder at the map, as he pointed to the Vox Sea.

"This's us," he said. He tapped our location with his calloused index finger, then dragged it to the left, into the Veindaian Gulf. "This's Puerri Island." He rotated in his chair to look at me seriously. "The gulf is fulla these warped, rocky peaks," he explained, shaking his head. "The Leviathan's too big to traverse 'em."

I nodded as he talked, examining the giant, worn map spread across the entirety of his desk. The canvas was pinned at each corner to the tabletop, with navigational instruments strewn over the surface. The material was a deep, tarnished tan, with notes and coordinates scribbled in the borders and around coastlines. My eyes glided across the labels and lettering, and into the centermost section of the Vox Sea, where a large section was either missing or amended—patched by a square piece of parchment of a lighter, cream-colored material. I followed the meridians leftward from the patch and into the Veindaian Gulf, where a cluster of tooth-shaped structures were inked, along with the diminutive island labeled *Puerri*.

Captain Cyrus cleared his throat to continue, "I imagine we'll have ta drop ya off close as we can—loan ya a lifeboat."

I nodded again and locked eyes with him, waiting for him to say more. His eyebrows arching quizzically, I tried to decode the purpose of his stare, until I realized he was treating me as the representative of my group, and was awaiting my opinion of the plan.

"Oh," I voiced. "Sounds good."

The captain chuckled, as my sight trailed and settled on a polished, wooden case on the pirate's desk, inside of which a compass swiveled on its gimbal. My eyes followed the direction of the tool's trembling, red needle and found an old picture edged by a metal frame: an image of a regal-looking pirate standing valiantly, his hand rested on the shoulder of a young man to his left. I squinted at it, trying to determine whether the sepia-toned image was a drawing or in fact some type of photograph.

Captain Cyrus reached for the picture, referring to it as a *casting*.

"I hated standin' still fer this." He pointed to the pirate. "Captain Stephen Moor," he said cheerily. "The first Ice Pirate!"

I nodded in fascination.

He gestured to the boy at his side. " 'N that's me!"

"Really?"

He chuckled lightheartedly. "Aye!" He covered up the boy's right forearm with his thumb. "See?"

I laughed with him, as he lifted the frame. The young Michael Cyrus had long, shaggy hair like Andy's, and stood with a stance akin to the captain's. Stephen Moor's brow was arched with certitude, his chest was pushed out, and a slight smile was visible beneath his long, swooping mustache. He was dressed in multiple, padded layers that embellished his brawn. In addition, his outermost accessory, a long, dark coat, was shouldered with elaborate, fringed epaulettes, and his hat was adorned with an immense, white feather. To his right, another, gaunter young man stood half-hidden behind the captain.

"Spent many a season on that ship," Cyrus reminisced. He was about to say more, when a chained pendant untangled from the frame's stand and clattered onto the desk with a metallic *ting*. I gaped at the new object: a blue jewel housed in a decorative, golden ornament. The metal was bent into swirling designs that curved inward to form needle-thin points on which the shimmering, azure stone was balanced.

Captain Cyrus picked it up. "Been lookin' fer that."

I asked him if it was a crystal, and he answered, "Nah. Just as rare, but not what yer after." He turned it in his left hand, feeling the angles and clearing the dust. "This's a talisman," he went on, his fingers closing around it. "A healing stone. If you're injured, you hold it in yer fist." He demonstrated. "The jewel turns to dust, n' the minerals heal any wound."

"Like magic?"

"Aye, but more potent. It'll fix more'n just the surface stuff, y'see." He added that ancient civilizations had ground the jewels into powder and consumed them to cure ailments. He handed the talisman to me. Before I had a chance to object, he insisted, "Yer gonna keep that. You'll need it."

I examined the treasure as light rays streamed through an open window and irradiated the particles inside. As I rotated the gem, the sunbeams revealed a marvelous display of living minerals, tumbling and twirling within their enclosure—like coryphées in the spotlight.

The reflected shine gleamed brightly against my lenses, coaxing an astonished breath from my lungs. Scooter chirped elatedly, equally amazed by the beauty of the talisman. As my fingers traveled around its metallic perimeter, I discovered multiple circular frames secured on one of two axes. The jewel was centered in some type of gyroscope.

Fascinated, my second hand lifted to study the sides, as Captain Cyrus spoke, "Y'alls are good people."

I looked up at him.

"Ye've made quite an impression here." He nodded with certainty. "I know fer a fact the crew'll be sore to see ya—"

CRASH!

A sudden, sonorous tone broke the calm and tilted the ship: a thunderous explosion, followed by waves breaking and boards creaking. The Leviathan roared and reared, as loose screws and metal parts went rattling sideways into the slats of the floorboards and the captain's compass swung wildly on its gimbal. My legs locked as the floor inclined. Cyrus' chair lifted onto its back legs, and I grabbed his wrist, just as the ship slammed back to the ocean. The captain jettisoned from his seat, stability regained. He growled to himself and stormed from his quarters, as I followed close behind.

Cyrus marched onto the main deck, me at his heels, quickly navigating a swarm of frazzled, shouting pirates. My short breaths quickened as the air become sour, coating my insides with moisture and dread. A damp breeze laced with unknown horrors wisped over my face and slipped into my nostrils. The foul scent made me cough, rattled my mind and unnerved my thoughts. I suddenly feared for my friends and pushed through the crowds more frantically, until Andy and Veronica emerged from the chaos.

I clamored to their sides, shouting, "What's happening?!"

"I dunno!" Andy answered, as Murry, Boris, and Zyvin circled around us.

Cyrus pressed onward toward the front of the ship, roaring over the cacophony, "What's goin' on here?!"

"Sah!" Lou hollered from the bow. "South Frost Invadas!"

In the distance, a massive ship emerged from a curtain of fog, lined with armored bodies and fuming cannons.

We were under attack.

19
Battle At Sea

On the bow of the encroaching vessel, a fearsome figure stood tall and vigilant, his hands clasped behind him. Like his counterparts, he was clad in a suit of heavy, all-white armor, distinguished as the superior only by a tattered strip of crimson fabric draped over his left shoulder. The commander glowered at us, his features concealed entirely by a white helmet. The headpiece was cast in the likeness of a stylized, leonine predator; faint outlines framed the sinister eyes and muzzle, and twisted downward into a wicked, fang-lined smile.

The ship was similar in size to the Leviathan, but was constructed from a lighter-colored material. The planks of the galleon were clearly wooden, however their grain possessed a strangely reflective, silvery quality that was mimicked by the metal banding and trim reinforcing the hull. The trim was embossed with elaborate swirls and arabesques that funneled into the figurehead on the bow—a strange-looking creature with the face of a lion and a mane of coiled tentacles. Its crew all seemed to halt their duties to gather around the guardrail and stare us down, chests heaving and clawed gloves curling maliciously at their sides.

"Geltynites," Captain Cyrus sneered.

"And their draggin' their foul weather with 'em!" Herm added.

A dark, roiling nimbus trailed the enemy ship, sparking and thundering, currents occasionally escaping from the webs of energy and coursing over the waves, shooting up steam and thickening the foggy veil.

Cyrus turned to his first mate. "Where were we hit?"

"Starboard hull. Just clipped us," Lou reported, shaking his head. "No major damage."

"Maybe it was a warning shot?" Garl suggested.

"T'ain't no warning—they know who we are!" Groddy shot back.

The hissing mist constricted our bodies, as the clouds thundered again. Boris roared at the storm, and Veronica touched his elbow to calm him.

"*Dude...*" Andy whispered to me. I turned to him, but before he could conjure a sentence, Lou asked the captain for an order, and all eyes were drawn to him. Captain Cyrus' stare remained fixed on our group, his jaw sliding pensively.

"Sah?" Lou asked.

He sucked in a breath, then said, "Do not engage. Fly the Moonflag."

"The noncombat?"

"Aye."

"Right, then—I'll go dust it off."

Lou disappeared, and the deck went silent. After a moment, the squeaking of pulleys was audible, dragging anxious gazes skyward. The peaceful banner was hoisted, topping the mast with a pristine, blue flag, centered with the white silhouettes of Enkartai's twin moons. I swallowed hard and released a long, chilled breath, then checked the faces of my teammates.

Andy and Veronica watched the flag, while Boris peered over our heads at the Geltynites across the water. Murry's eyes searched the floorboards, his brow furrowed in thought. His hand steadied near his hip, covering the compartment on his cloak that holstered his wand. When his eyes rose to me, I felt myself mirroring his action. My hand traveled to my side pocket, locating the distinctive carvings of the wand's handle. I had nearly forgotten it was there.

Zyvin's gaunt face drained of color at the sight of the Moonflag that fluttered atop the mast. His throat bobbed. He clutched his sheathed hunting knife close to his chest and began muttering a rhyme. As the Geltynite ship drew nearer, his voice became more audible:

"*Merciful one, abundant with valor, enrich us with Ka, to raze all dishonor.*" He repeated it over and over, tightening his grip and quickening his recitation each time, until the opposing vessel lined up with our own and his voice shuddered with trepidation and tripped over words. "Merciful one, enrich us with Ka—!"

"*Hush up!*" Cyrus whispered to him.

He continued to mouth the lyric, as the massive ship approached, its occupants huffing and snarling to one another in inhuman utterances. They seemed enraged, but their leader stared forward, not issuing any commands.

No orders were barked. No cannons were fired. The vessel pressed onward into the hazy fog and passed us by. Zyvin's face dropped as he let out a long breath of relief. In unison, the Leviathan's crew did the same. Resettled, they all began patting shoulders and releasing reassured laughs. I started to join the quiet celebration, but stopped when I noticed Captain Cyrus' expression.

His brow remained tightly furrowed, his upper lip curled into a sneer. His faded boot flexed as he tapped his foot, almost innocuously. He was counting. The more moments that passed, the angrier he became, and when his foot rested, I heard Lou's coarse throat let out a cry:

"They're comin' about!"

Cannons boomed, and the Leviathan rattled upon impact, as the Geltynite vessel rotated and attacked us from behind. Captain Cyrus tore the cutlass from his belt, the blade roaring as it scraped against the rim of its sheath.

"Man the stern chasers!" he shouted. "Hoist the Frozen Skull!"

I staggered and shielded my face from a backblast of splintered debris. The Moonflag had disappeared, and from the clouds of airborne wreckage, the original tattered banner was drawn upward in its place. I clenched my ringing ears as I coughed, then reached for my wand.

Chained harpoons pierced the Leviathan and reeled back, swinging the ship sideways as a wave of Geltynite crewmen leapt from their ship like animals, latching onto the hull and clawing their way up to the main deck.

"They're boarding!" Lou cried.

"They want our loot!" Garl yelled.

"They want our heads!" Groddy attested.

"Whatever they want, they can't have it!" Cyrus exclaimed, turning to his crew. "Scrape these worthless salt-suckers off my ship!"

The pirates roared in unison, pumping their blades in the air and storming into the fray, while their captain cried after them, "And don't feel tempted to make their deaths sufferable!"

I ducked down as a massive, curved sword passed over my head and lodged in a beam. While the outraged monster tugged at the handle, I brandished my wand.

Through a spray of disorienting rain I shouted, "*Zyros!*" and a strange, jolting sensation arced over my nerves. It seized my muscles, while a swirl of electricity conglobated in the charged atmosphere. It swept up loose ions and sparked uncontrollably, then exploded and irradiated the Geltynite's armor, coursing in between the spaces of his metal plating and making him stagger away.

The beast's body contracted violently. His clawed fingers bent inward and head shot back as he roared at the frothing sky, his outcry cut short when Boris' club bludgeoned his stomach and sent him soaring off of the deck. The minotaur huffed, then turned and batted away other attackers.

Refocused, I faced a new adversary and flung another electric spell. This time the ray remained intact, and its current arced off the Geltynite's armor and onto a second member of the horde. When the blue energy discharged, they both spun backward, and I let out an impressed laugh. As the sky thundered, my spells became more powerful and precise, enriched with a new energy, as if the storm itself channeled through my wand.

I observed the same phenomenon happen with Murry. With a sweeping movement he summoned a vortex of wind that curved into the bodies of two Geltynites, hoisting them up. They tumbled gracelessly into the sky before being dropped to the hungry waves below. Distracted, I backed into someone and spun around in shock, then eased when I locked eyes with Andy.

" 'Sup, dude?" he laughed.

I cocked my head to the side and caught my breath, as we reassumed stances to ward off attackers. "Oh, y'know," I answered in between pants. "Everyone and their brother want us dead."

"Glad we're keeping it consistent."

"Uh-huh."

Across the deck, Veronica deflected a swinging blade with her extended multiweapon. In a propeller-like motion her staff dislodged the sword from her opponent's grasp and battered his face, her final rotation striking at the right angle to remove his helmet. The monster turned, his enraged, wolfish features exposed. He caught Veronica's returning blow, and uttered a low growl. She tugged on her immovable staff, then switched tactics and pressed a button on the handle to launch the compromised segment out of the beast's fist. The speared end stuck in the side of a crate. Her confused adversary grumbled in bafflement, before the chained segment retracted, and the wooden box it towed slammed right into the back of his head and splintered apart.

The knocked-out beast landed at our feet, his unmasked face lying sideways against the floorboards. I tilted my head as I examined him. The Geltynite possessed qualities from myriad predators. His face was square, but wolf-like. His rough, tan skin was covered in brown fur that flowed from an angular peak on his forehead to his jawline, where a significant underbite forced sharp, lower canines to protrude and press against his upper lip beneath a flat, leaf-shaped nose.

I started to study the markings on his armor, when my eyes rose automatically and stomach twisted in dread. "Watch out!"

A Geltynite's claws narrowly missed their target and plunged into a barrel. Zyvin tripped backwards into a stack of supplies. Ruby liquid gushed from the pierced container. The monster freed himself, his metal-clad talons making a loud scraping sound that petrified his opponent, as he heaved snarling breaths and pursued him.

Zyvin's voice trembled as he gawkily staggered to his feet, an avalanche of sundries toppling around him. Frantically, he grabbed whatever he could find and chucked them at the monster. The Geltynite roared in aggravation and shielded himself from the bombardment. Each new item *tinged* as it bounced off his helmet and rattled his balance. In frustration, the Geltynite tore off his mask and roared, only to be hammered in the back of the head by Lou's ovaloo.

Delirious, the aggressor wobbled, flipped over the guardrail, and then splashed into the water. Lou laughed and took Zyvin's hand to help him up.

"Good work!"

Zyvin looked sick as he steadied himself, then stumbled to our sides. The first mate leaned over the railing to survey the swells, and as he squinted, his pensive stare sank in terror, and he called for his captain.

Concerned onlookers crowded the rail, and we followed to copy their gazes. I could hear gasps and murmurs, but amidst the swaying throng I could barely make out the source of the upset. Then, a cluster of bodies parted, and I could see them.

Captain Cyrus waded through the ruckus. "What is it, Lou?"

"Sah!" Lou hollered. "Sharkpeople!"

The beasts stormed at the boat in a voracious craze. A formation of countless black fins cleaved the churning surface, slicing through waves and leaving froth in their wakes. The dorsal fin of the foremost creature swerved erratically, thrashing below, then resurging to leap from the water and reveal its hideous form. Rows upon rows of dagger-like teeth fortified its jaws, crimson gills flexing as they gnashed. It had the head of a great white with humanoid limbs, webbed fingers ended with flesh-tearing claws, fin-like feet, and a long, spear-shaped tail that corkscrewed behind it—impelling midair twists and turns before splashing back beneath the currents to pursue the bodies of Geltynites that had fallen overboard. We watched in terror as the sharkpeople swarmed, and clouds of blood plumed upward like fire, dying the murky depths and partially concealing their grisly fate.

Captain Cyrus sneered at the tumbling mass of gluttonous creatures, then looked to his sides at his fear-frozen crew.

Baffled by their idleness, he shouted, "Well? What're ya standin' around for? Give 'em something to eat!"

Spinning, the captain's metal claw clamped around the torso of an inbound Geltynite. It whirred mechanically as he lifted the marauder, then chucked him off the ship. Cyrus rotated his shoulder and huffed, redrawing his cutlass and marching off. His silent crewmen examined one another's expressions, then scrambled apart.

There was danger in every direction. Above, the tempestuous clouds crawled with electricity, arcing and thundering, singeing the masts and charring the ship. All around, the scraping of metal and clanging of blades rang out between lightning strikes. And below, the clicking screeches of ravenous creatures called insatiably for more. Rain pelted my vision and numbed my body. Sounds demanded my attention in all angles. I could hardly focus on any one thing. My senses became overwhelmed, and my spells were suddenly messy—launched at my attackers more from reflex than focus. And as I grappled with my capacity to perceive the frenzy I failed to notice the inclining floor. Scooter chirped in my ear and I looked up in time to brace myself, as a loose crate came sliding into me.

My lungs emptied and spell short-circuited. My drenched sneakers finding zero grip in the deluge, I collapsed and the weighty cargo swept me across the length of the deck and slammed me into the railing. I sucked in a painful, wheezing breath and coughed, before my eyesight unhazed and hearing keened to behold the Geltynite ship impacting the Leviathan. Hull against hull, a resonant grinding rattled the two vessels. I struggled to push back against the crushing container, Scooter shifting on my shoulder and uttering urging squeaks. Ka glowed from the wood grain as I pressed, but diminished and flickered out. I grunted and changed strategies.

Sandwiched between the crate and the guardrail, I worked my way to the right, pulling myself along with the railing's uprights, but stopped when a battle landed in front of me. Captain Cyrus fell to the ground, weaponless, a sword's edge swinging for his neck.

He blocked the attack with his metal forearm, shouting as the inner mechanisms spasmed and sparked. Cyrus pulled off his attacker's helmet with his left hand, then pressed his sparking forearm against the creature's face. Electrocuted, the Geltynite let out a stuttering wail, before the captain reached for the collar of the beast's chest plate, set his boot on his gut, and flipped him overboard.

Captain Cyrus leaned over the rail as the fuming Geltynite fell to the shiver of sharkpeople.

"How do ye like that'n guppies? I even cooked it fer ya!"

The pirate let out a coughing laugh and wiped the blood from his face, as the angled ship jostled and crashed to the water to become level again. He rolled onto his stomach, spitting and rising to his knees.

Lou appeared at his side to help him the rest of the way. Cyrus raised his claw, its metal digits twitching and clamping uncontrollably. He shook his head and growled as he covered his malfunctioning arm, trying to restrict its movement.

"I have ta make some repairs," he told his first mate.

Lou nodded, drawing a dagger from his belt and surveying the chaotic fray to provide cover while his captain escaped.

"Outta the way, Charlie!" Cyrus ordered, shoving the pirate aside as he descended the ladders and disappeared into the lower deck. Charlie scowled at him before following Lou back into the battle.

I don't know why I didn't call to them. It might have been my dazedness, breathlessness, or inability to think straight, but only after the pirates left my small frame of visibility did my motivation to escape resurface. Reengaged, I levered my left arm over my chest and pressed with all my might to move the stubborn crate. I felt it inch forward. Scooter chirruped and I pushed again, and this time the container lurched and flew sideways, making me topple over on my stomach. I shook my head, and looked upward, expecting to see the person who had helped me. But instead, the world went black, as a Geltynite's armor-clad heel delivered a crushing blow to my forehead.

A jarring sound pounded my unattuned eardrums—something which I first interpreted as a rolling growl, but later reconsidered. When my vision returned, pulsing through the moonlit blur, the sight of dripping, chained harpoons dragging over the boards of the waterlogged deck became distinguishable as the source, with their unwieldy spears clunking and metal reels clicking loudly as they retracted. I drifted in between levels of consciousness, settling momentarily in an inactive, limbo-like state, before a fetid odor invaded my nostrils and my senses snapped back.

My eyes shot open to behold the face of a scowling, unmasked Geltynite in brutal clarity. His skin was notably paler than the rest. Scarred flesh striped the left side of his face below a grayed eye that looked to have sustained some damage as well, and a mane of silvery-white fur crested his head and jawline, framing his rancorous visage. Pulling back, I could see the red fabric on his shoulder plate that identified him as the leader, and before stepping away, the beast blew another horrible breath from his warty, bat-like nose.

I cringed as the awful-smelling gust swept over my face and disheveled my hair, and when I turned my head to escape the odor I discovered that my body was constricted in ropes that were secured around a post. I looked ahead to see all my friends and the Leviathan's crewmen tied to the bases of masts themselves.

Andy, Veronica, and I shared one pillar, with the rest of the group scattered in various locations. I turned to my sides, exchanging uneasy looks with them, then leaned and saw Murry across the way, tied to one of the other masts. He nodded to us to communicate his wellbeing.

Peering farther across the deck I could see that particular attention had been paid to Boris, who was bound in numerous crisscrossing ropes and extra-elaborate knotwork, with two nervous-looking Geltynites standing guard at either side of him. And on the opposite end of the ship, Zyvin was tied to the mizzenmast, completely cocooned in an absurd amount of rope that wrapped from his neck to his ankles.

"I'm tellin' ya—*Aack!*" he choked, as a pair of invaders tightened his bonds. The two of them growled and signaled to one another—the first one flipping the wooden pendants on Zyvin's necklace and the second one voicing approval.

I tensed when I turned back and saw the body of a dead Ice Pirate being flipped overboard, a gushing stab wound in his abdomen.

"*What happened?*" I whispered to Andy.

He opened his mouth to reply, when the pale Geltynite roared at his crewmen, harshening the muteness of the Ice Pirates and hastening the diligence of his invaders, who gathered up metal miscellanea from the Leviathan, loading them into crates and bringing them to their commander for review. They referred to their leader as Barmuth, and awaited his approval before climbing across a boarding plank and lugging the stolen cargo onto their vessel.

Many of the items they carried seemed mundane. While they managed to confiscate some things of utility—swords, daggers, cannonballs—the majority of their haul was comprised of simple items: tankards, plates, utensils, lanterns. Practically anything with a somewhat silvery hue was loaded up and shown to Barmuth, who removed his gloves to handle each item.

He felt their craftsmanship carefully, frequently bringing them close to his nose for further inspection. He sometimes growled at a scent he found detestable and threw the item aside before sending a crewman on his way.

He shook his head, recovering from one such smell, before his furious stare shifted to us.

"Again," he demanded. "Where is your captain?"

Lou lifted himself upward, as much as his restraints permitted. "Ye ain't gettin' no'in outta us!"

The commander's head swiveled toward his counterpart, who immediately took out a sword and lunged for the first mate.

I sucked in a terrified breath and held it, and a repelling force suddenly halted the strike, the point of the weapon stopping just inches from Lou's stomach. The Geltynite sneered and pressed, letting out a perplexed grumble, as the sword wobbled, then flashed white and was flung out of his hands. I exhaled.

The crewman was immediately shoved aside and chastised for what Barmuth interpreted as clumsiness.

"Enough!" he barked, cheeks puffing with air. "The one who relinquishes Cyrus will live."

"He's hidin' down in the lower deck," a voice revealed.

Stunned silence fell on the crew, and heads rotated toward the betrayer. Barmuth paced across the line of Ice Pirates and knelt to lock eyes with Charlie, his features cringing fiercely. "Where?"

Charlie licked at his chapped lips and swallowed, taking note of his crew members. "There's a false wall two levels down," he said, pausing again to acknowledge the venomous glares around him. He cleared his throat. "Looks like a stack of barrels. Behind that's a door. That's where 'e is."

One of the Geltynites returned from the ladders, confirming Charlie's claim of a secret door, and the Ice Pirates exploded in fury, spitting insults and writhing to get free.

"*You filthy rat!*" "*Mutiny!*" "*Traitor!*" they all protested, as Charlie was untied and set free, and the commander sent several of his crewmen into the lowermost deck of the galleon to apprehend the captain.

"Bring him to me!" Barmuth demanded. He stroked his knuckles, maintaining his hateful frown as he waited. He nodded to Charlie. "Thank you for your cooperation."

The pirate kicked away his ropes and rubbed at the red marks on his wrists, then smirked, "My pleasure."

Captain Cyrus rotated his compromised mechanical arm on the surface of his workbench. Loose parts clattered, his metal digits still fidgeting uncontrollably and scattering the pieces of his surrounding setup. He held down his arm and peered through the dull lighting at the extent of the damage, his face curling in disgust at the mangled metal plating and frayed, sparking cords.

"*Filthy, rotten vermin,*" he muttered.

He reached for a flat tool from a drawer and flipped over his arm, prying open an access hatch and inspecting the convoluted engineering inside. He carefully slipped the instrument in between his exposed circuitry and loosened a bolt, and the jittering fingers clamped together even faster than before. He tightened it again and they slowed. With his sleeve he dried his perspiring brow and sighed, turning alertly at the sound of heavy, unfamiliar footsteps.

Several sets of them descended the creaking ladders outside his refuge, and muffled, guttural voices could be heard intoning commands. He muttered a curse as he bit down on the handle of his tool and reached inside with his bare fingertips, locating a severed wire.

"*There ye are.*"

He licked at his gums, grimacing as he twisted the frayed ends around each other. And when the cord turned hot, the mechanisms whirred, reactivated, and he tore his hand away. Hearing the false wall roll sideways, he quickly latched his arm shut and wrapped up his project, as a force pounded from outside.

The door's hinges snapped, and the heavy structure toppled over as a militia of Geltynites burst through.

"Captain Cyrus!" one of them roared.

The pirate shook his head, laughter slipping through his sardonic, gap-toothed smile. His three metal fingers folded in and recessed into his mechanical arm.

"Yes, yes," the captain finally answered. He turned to face his aggressors, the sound of scraping metal piercing the air, as a long sword blade extended segment-by-segment from the end of his metal forearm. "And to whom do I owe the pleasure of killing today?"

A pair of Geltynites took Charlie by his elbows and aggressively ushered him toward the boarding plank, ignoring his stammering objections and nervous inquiries. They pulled him along, gesturing at an intricate setup of nauseating cuisine. On the deck of the South Frost ship, a small, square table had been made up for him, centered with a platter of undercooked organ meats.

"*Sick*," Andy commented under his breath.

Charlie gaped at the meal, then up at his enormous escorts, trembling in their presence while cringing at the ongoing eruption of insults coming from his former crewmates.

"Go forth!" one guide roared.

"Claim your spoils!" the other demanded.

Charlie recoiled. Even the invaders' praise was intimidating. He finally moved, taking a few fidgety steps toward the plank on his own, until Barmuth stopped him.

"Wait..." he breathed. The commander's yellowed fingernails dug into the pirate's shoulder as he halted his advancement. Barmuth sniffed the air, his head tilting in thought. "I recognize you..."

"What?" Charlie's eyes widened in shock. "N-no you—"

"Yes!" Barmuth smelled him again, becoming infuriated. "You were a member of that scoundrel Stephen Moore's crew!"

Charlie's features drained, as the invaders all snarled at him in fury and the Ice Pirates' backlash simmered. He let out a gasp when the fearsome commander hoisted him by the collar.

"No, no!" Charlie wailed, flailing. "It ain't true, I swear!"

"Liar!" Barmuth bellowed. He hurled him down. Charlie screamed as he plummeted between the two galleons and into the teeming sea, his terrified shrieks intensifying with the sound of tearing flesh.

When I turned away from the noise, I felt the restraints around my right shoulder loosen. My gaze rose to trace the sensation and I caught sight of Scooter, his saw-like teeth chittering softly as he chewed through the ropes. Veronica locked eyes with me. I turned back to Andy to confirm that he saw it as well, then worked my hand downward to locate the handle of my wand in my pocket. The coils started to tumble, and Veronica, Andy and I adjusted to steady them, making them appear as though they were still secured around us. While Scooter leapt to the next post to start freeing the second set of captives, the pirates encouraged him with their limited gestures and whispered croons.

I scanned the others, seeing that they were aware of the situation and onboard with whatever plan we were formulating. The only person who I couldn't lock eyes with was Zyvin, who was still staring at the area in the water where Charlie had been chucked, his expression frozen in terror. From his slightly elevated vantage he must have seen the entirety of the horrific act. In fear of being noticed I decided not to try to grab his attention.

Ropes continued to snap. In the distance, I could see Scooter leaping and eluding the gazes of the invaders as he traveled across the deck, finally arriving at Boris. The guards were too concerned with the minotaur's behavior to notice that the hexapoid was gnawing their once-sturdy roping down to threads, before scuttling away.

Barmuth's back remained turned to us, his hands clutching the banister, watching the water and heaving furious breaths. Veronica eyed an unchecked crateful of the pirate's confiscated swords.

"*Got a plan?*" Andy whispered to her.

She nodded. "*Yeah.*"

"*Should we have a code word?*"

"*No.*"

"*...I think we should have a code word.*"

"*Shut up.*"

My muscles tightened, preparing to throw off the pile of heavy cordage and fight our captors, when the sound of footsteps on creaking wood redirected my focus. Everyone's heads rose alertly to witness Captain Cyrus ascending the ladders, unattended, his coat and pants splattered with bloodstains.

While breaths of contentment collected amongst the Leviathan's crew, Barmuth's harsh expression became even more severe, his upper lip curling fiercely to reveal gritted fangs. Cyrus threw his arms sideways emphatically, laughing as he strolled across the deck to greet him.

"Barmuth! What an *enormous* displeasure!"

Barmuth uttered a growl.

"Just had a chat with yer li'l welcome party. Should'a told me you were comin', I'da cleaned up more!"

"You're coming with us."

"Ooh, I dunno. My schedule's a bit packed at the moment. So, I thanks ya fer the invitation, but I'll have ta *politefully* decline."

The captain extended his metal claw for a sarcastic handshake. The commander scoffed at the gesture. Barmuth reached forward, and his clawed, bear-like hand clutched Cyrus' metal one like a vice, holding him there for a brief, unnerving moment.

"It wasn't an invitation."

"Well," Cyrus gritted, "then I won't be so politeful."

A segmented sword emerged from Captain Cyrus' mechanical arm, spearing the Geltynite's palm.

Barmuth roared, as the captain twisted and ripped his transfixing weapon free through the side of the Geltynite's hand.

"Code word!" Andy yelled.

Veronica rolled her eyes.

We all puffed out our arms to break our restraints, and Veronica shot a chained spear from her multiweapon to harpoon the crate of cutlasses and reeled back, the box sliding over the drenched floorboards and skidding to a stop in front of the pirate crew. In an instant, the Ice Pirates were rearmed and the Geltynites were suddenly outnumbered.

Captain Cyrus' eyes lit up, just as astonished as Barmuth.

He grinned, exulting, "Hey, ain't this timely!" He slashed away an invader that attacked him from the side, and the wounded Barmuth seized his opportunity to retreat.

We all stepped over the mounds of tangled roping to fight off the invaders, pressing forward as a unit. As we advanced, I nudged Andy's elbow.

"Nice code word, man."

"Thanks, bro."

Veronica sighed, then reached for her crossbow, the limbs snapping as she loosed three arrows into the cluster of enemies.

The Geltynites shielded themselves. Many clambered over the guardrail and leapt back to their ship, bypassing the boarding plank.

"Fall back!" an order resounded from the enemy vessel.

The horde hastily obeyed, and those at the back of the crowd were prodded onward by the Ice Pirates.

"Go on!" "Git outta here!" the pirates scorned, exchanging some parting sword clashes and jabs.

A stomping sound reverberated from the left, as Boris stormed into the fray, his head ducked down and horns aimed at the fleeing invaders. The last remaining Geltynites were plowed over like bowling pins and flung off the edge of the ship, splashing into the waves as their vessel pulled off.

"Ya-har!" Captain Cyrus rejoiced. His crewmen echoed him with fervor.

Scooter had managed to chew through half of Zyvin's coils when we arrived at the mizzenmast. The cephalopod leapt onto my shoulder, and Andy hacked through the remaining amount with his sword. The rope unraveled and Zyvin fell, tripping over the heap and losing his footing. He staggered into Murry, who helped him regain his balance. I asked him if he was alright, and he nodded, still staring at the waves.

He shook a rope from his shoulder and it fell to the debris-laden floor, as Captain Cyrus strode by, inspecting the mess.

He shook his hand at the clutter and told Lou, "Have Charlie patch this place up."

Lou shook his head, "Charlie ain't wit us no more. 'E committed mutiny! Told the Geltynites where ye were!"

"That turncoat! Where's he hidin' now?"

"Bottom o' the ocean."

Cyrus raised an eyebrow.

"The Geltynites threw 'im overboard right afta they got wot they needed."

"Jus'..." Zyvin voiced, shaking his head in disbelief as he gaped into the distance. "Jus' got tore apart..."

Captain Cyrus sighed through his nose. He stepped to the guardrail, squinting into the fog. His eyes flashed, then he quickly doubled back. He muttered something to Lou, who nodded and took off down the ladders. I was about to ask what was happening, when the captain started to guide us across the deck.

"Time fer you to get goin'."

"What's the hurry?" Andy asked.

I started, "We can still help, if—"

"Ye've done plenty. Now get to yer island. Just keep headin' west."

Before we knew it he had guided us into an old lifeboat. Pulleys squeaked as he swiftly lowered us into the water, the two connections unhooking themselves as the craft achieved buoyancy. Captain Cyrus' ice-colored eyes locked with each of ours, gravely at first. Then, he cracked a laughing, gap-toothed grin, drew a sword, and sped off.

As our lifeboat floated away and the mist thinned, another South Frost ship appeared, maneuvering around the retreating, damaged one, its cannons rotating.

"*Oh, no,*" I whispered.

Captain Cyrus sliced at the air. "Keep 'em coming, ya scurvy felines!"

The cannons thundered, and a wave of spiraling ammunition launched at the Ice Pirates. We let out a short yell, and I felt my hands reach forward.

There was no sound of impact. It took me a moment to realize that the cannonballs had seemingly frozen in time, suspended in midair in auras of Ka. I could see a white shine reflect back at my eyes from the inner glass of my lenses. However, it didn't obscure my sight. In fact, it enhanced it.

Through the glow, my vision flew beyond me, arcing around the objects I had linked with. Behind the anomaly of floating ammunition, the Ice Pirates tilted their heads in fascination. And from the encroaching vessel the Geltynites looked even more taken aback, pulses of energy rising off of their awestruck bodies.

I couldn't believe what I was experiencing. My consciousness seemed independent from my physical form. I let out an astounded breath, hearing the distant echo of my own exhalation, as I felt the icy rain pelt against the surface of the objects. When they hit, the raindrops scattered miniature waves of Ka, contributing to the pulsating glow. The cannonballs all rotated in synchronicity, like model planets, before I heard another echoing breath, and sensed my arms make a backward, throwing motion.

My surroundings snapped into normalcy in time to witness the cannonballs fly backward, tearing apart the enemy vessel that had fired them. Boards snapped and splintered and water gushed into the open gashes. Roars of anger and distress erupted from the crew of Geltynites as their ship reared upward.

"Ha ha ha!" Captain Cyrus celebrated, raising his weapon in unison with his cheering crew. "Good shot, boy!"

Andy, Veronica, and Murry patted my back, all vocalizing their praise and amazement, especially Andy.

"Dude, that was incredible!" he declared, pushing his fingers through his wild hair and going on to rehash every component of the event with his reactions. Although I couldn't follow his words, I nodded in thanks and looked for a place to sit, feeling suddenly dizzy and exhausted.

I collapsed on a bench-like surface to the left of Zyvin, who hardly noticed my presence at all. He appeared similarly sapped and somewhat despondent. I sat there in a haze as my senses recovered, residual energy tingling on the edges of my nerves, as the sail of our small boat caught the wind and floated onward, and the Leviathan disappeared behind a curtain of mist.

20
Disseverance

Minerals tumbled and twirled within a whirlwind of mystic vapors, the small, flat squares reflecting a spectrum of colored light that fused in the likeness of the five travelers. They each slept in shifts, exchanging duties after periods of time to adjust the mainsail. Before long, Zyvin's tired eyelid rolled shut, and the image scattered. As the sediment dimmed and resettled along the bottom, the warlock's serpentine eye was mirrored on the surface of the darkened stone. Shamaul rotated the optirock slowly in his sharp, metal-clad fingertips, his stare fixing on the pictureless, gray clouds inside.

"I have found it!" Gumble rejoiced, holding a crystal cluster above his head. He waddled awkwardly beneath its weight before setting it down on the floor. His purple tongue hung below his accomplished smile as he awaited his master's approval.

Gaze not straying from the empty optirock, Shamaul voiced, "He is going to betray me."

Gumble swallowed dryly. He licked at a stream of mucus beneath his nose, then grunted as he hoisted the treasure to the center of the chamber where his master sat. The goblin panted and peered through the surface of his find. The prisms of the crystal were alive with black, smoke-like billows. Miniature explosions of dark crimson occasionally flared within them, like lightning hidden in cloud. Gumble lifted and dropped the crystal a few times, hoping the sound would draw the warlock's attention. After a few failed attempts he slammed the gem down harder, and a fragment detached, a streak of scarlet energy coursing over the broken edges as it steamed. The goblin went to retrieve the piece when a current of Ka swept it up and delivered it to the warlock's grasp.

He examined it carefully, then allowed the crystal to levitate upward and float into position beneath the other two, clicking into place in the third diamond-shaped cavity on the blade of his scepter. The Ravac and Frost crystals trembled, and the central sphere glowed brightly as new energy spilled into the fluctuating, mercurial mixture. Shamaul's fingers rested upon the glassy enclosure on his scepter. Gumble straightened up proudly. After reviewing the reaction a moment longer, the Dark Warlock rose from his throne and left, the torn edges of his cape flowing over the goblin's body as he exited his chamber and descended the staircase.

Gumble hacked and rubbed away an unpleasant itch on his nose. His mouth twitched slightly as he peered out a casement at the swirling clouds outside, then scrambled for the stairs.

Long arms swinging gawkily and knuckles occasionally pushing off the stone floor to propel his hobbling gait, the goblin frantically caught up with Shamaul.

"It's happening, isn't it?" he inquired as he and his ruler hastily passed through the halls. Another flight of stairs compromised his balance and he fell down the last few steps, before lifting himself achingly and hurrying again to his master's side, who stood at the end of a passageway lined with cells.

Gumble's three-toed feet caked with filth as they slapped against the cold, dank stones of the dungeon floor. He took a moment to snicker at the emaciated faces of the prisoners they had amassed. He looked through a couple barred doors, before he folded his hands and waddled beside the warlock, who stared ceaselessly through the one that confined the she-wolf.

The woman kept her head low, veiled behind frizzed, reddish brown hair, with her two children clutched in either of her shackled arms. Dried blood streaked her hands from when her metal bonds with inward-facing spikes prevented a transformation and kept her in her human form.

"Your half-bred husband has shown me nothing but weakness," Shamaul spoke.

Annella didn't respond. Her back continued to arch and fall as she breathed quietly and looked to the floor, covering Dariun and Mae's faces as well.

But the younger one peered, wide-eyed through her mother's fingers at the ruler of the wicked continent, as he concluded his statement, "I don't suspect he'll uphold our arrangement."

Shamaul turned away toward the exit of the dungeon with a pair of his guard-orks, but stopped when Mae pushed through her mother's hold to shout at him, "Your spirit is stained by cruelty!"

228

Annella's hand clamped around her daughter's mouth and pulled her back. The insult was borrowed, she knew—the same curse she herself had shot at the Naga woman who traded them.

Her breathing halted and mind seized when the metallic footsteps redirected, and Shamaul returned. Lowering himself to the girl's height, he locked eyes with her terrified expression, the brow of his silver mask appearing to frown.

"The term you are seeking is adaptability," he said to her coldly. "The distinguisher of the strong. The driving component of the natural order."

He rose up, his body making the sound of a tightening rope as he stood at his full, imposing height. Behind him, a frail old man hoisted himself to a seated position, pressing his face between the bars. Annella's gaze rose to see him, as his bushy eyebrows slanted in dismay, and dark eyes gleamed past everyone.

"No... no..." he uttered shakily at something unseen.

Shamaul turned, spear-tipped tendrils snaking from his sleeve.

Still staring into the distance, the man started to yell, "No! No, no, no!"

"Stop it, Hein!" Annella pleaded.

"No! N—"

Spears pierced his neck, and he crumbled on the floor. Mae let out a muffled scream from behind her mother's hand. The warlock's metal barbs retracted from Hein's body, and the rope-like coils that wielded them regressed into his sleeve. Shamaul observed the family a second time, Dariun frozen in shock and Mae thoroughly frightened, while their mother's brassy-hazel eyes burned into him.

He decoded the composition of her rage. When she exhaled, her nostrils flared and released short, rapid breaths, the veins in her neck throbbing. When she inhaled, her upper lip curled with hate. In the midst of his inspection, he recognized a particular muscle beneath her left eyelid twitch, and in the same instance an unusual, invisible energy pulsed off of her.

"Separate them," Shamaul ordered.

He stepped away, as orks invaded the cell and pried Dariun and Mae from Annella's arms. Annella's explosive screams amplified off the hard angles of her cell and echoed through the otherwise silent caverns of the dungeon. Her vocalization transformed into beastly roars, breaking, then turning back into pained, human wails.

Outside the castle, Gumble implored elaboration.

"Has the time come? Will you end our disseverance?" Gumble asked, his master turning slightly at his words, scepter spearing the ground as he walked. "End this... imprisonment?"

Shamaul glared through the smoky fog at the outline of the immense barrier in the distance, before clarifying, "To be imprisoned is to be locked away from one's element."

Gumble blinked in recognition.

"The only impact their keeping me here has made is my *incubation*."

A horde of creatures crawled, crept, and stomped from their dwellings, flowing into formation behind their ruler and marching toward the wall.

Shamaul concluded, "And when the barrier topples and the Orb is mine, the sunseekers will witness the extent of their folly."

Gumble grinned fiercely, releasing a wicked cackle that melded into the uproar of resonant growls and screeches, as the ocean of bodies swept over the land, craving destruction.

Bujin Ocean

VEINDAI

Puerri Island

The Vox Sea

21
Puerri Island

Zyvin balanced his necklace on the heel of his hand, pointing out the central wooden pendant.

"An' this'ere is the _wolf_," he explained to us. "My wife made it for me. The wolf is loyal and fiercely protective."

Veronica smiled at his description. "It's beautiful."

Zyvin thanked her.

"What is your wife like?"

"Loyal and fiercely protective," Zyvin answered, chuckling a little. He slipped the necklace back over his head and adjusted the orientation of the three totems, then leaned back on the edge of the lifeboat, resting his elbows on the brim as a swell of water rushed underneath us and swayed our tiny craft. Stinging, airborne saltwater swept over my skin, as our small boat sailed on, chasing the hints of morning that pierced the lingering murk.

Murry folded up the map and set it down on his lap, then smiled at Zyvin and mentioned, "I've heard Lycanthrone is a lovely place."

Zyvin nodded. "It is."

"What made you leave?"

Zyvin stared off, shaking his head. "I... Well, actually I never stayed long. I met Annella in Alva Durna. Stayed there mostly."

Murry stroked his beard, brow furrowing quizzically. "I'm not familiar."

"It's out in, ah..." He pointed in a nonspecific direction. "One of the..." His fingers ran over the creases in his forehead as he thought, seeming strained by his recollection. He sighed, pinching the area in between his eyes. "Don't worry 'bout it."

Andy lifted his arms. "Hold on a second!" he exclaimed. He leaned forward on his seat and pointed to Zyvin. "You can _shapeshift_?"

"Nah. I mean, not fully." He cleared his throat. "My daddy wasn't Lycanthian like my mom, so I could never go full-wolf, y'see? But Annella sure can, and my boy Dariun can." He scratched at his chin and examined the floor of the boat, smiling. "We ain't sure 'bout Mae yet, but she's a lot like me in every other way, so..." He let out a half-laugh, then shrugged. "I dunno. We'll jus' wait n' see."

Andy gaped back at him, still dumbfounded.

"What?"

"Why didn't you tell us that sooner?"

Zyvin shrugged. "Never thought it was anything outta the ordinary." He gestured to each of us. "Your world don't have shape-changers?"

Andy and I shook our heads, and Zyvin's eyes widened in genuine surprise. He took a bite from a piece of fruit and chewed it slowly, eyes shifting between us and the tides.

He looked like he felt uncomfortable, so I turned away, examining other sights. I found myself studying the warped shapes in the strange, rocky jags that protruded from this part of the sea, wondering what processes had formed them. I was about to point them out to break the tension. But before I could, the steaming fog descended entirely, and a small, solitary island was spotted in the distance.

"Is that it?" Veronica asked.

Map reopened, Murry stood up and announced, "That's the one!"

Andy rose stiffly from his seat. "Thank goodness," he stretched out. "I can hardly feel my butt."

Veronica kicked him.

"Ow!"

We laughed, and I turned to Zyvin, expecting to see excitement in his eyes. Instead, I watched him stare blankly ahead, taking in shaky breaths. Sensing my gaze, he turned to me, his right eye welling and his grayed, blind eye glittering in an unusual way. He managed to forge a grin before he turned back, his expression reverting as he faced the approaching landmass.

Despite how desperately Zyvin tried to focus he could not clear his mind, nor conceal the trepidation and terror that roiled within him. And when the lifeboat's bow ran ashore and the crew all filed out, his body became cold, and without any warning, the horrible hisses manifested again.

He froze, shivering as the ghastly noises overlapped, fused, and warped into voices that whispered his name.

He stayed there rigidly, not wanting to leave the lifeboat or join with the others.

"*Zyvin?*" one of the travelers asked. "*You okay?*"

He didn't look up to see who had lifted him and helped him aground. Whoever it was went on to comment on the small size of the island, to which the wizard agreed before stating how "island life must be quieter." He then looked to Zyvin for confirmation, who only found himself capable of nodding and muttering, "Sure."

The two Realmhoppers volunteered to escort him through the thicket to locate his home. Grayed hairs swayed before Zyvin's vision as he stared down at his feet, watching them rise and fall automatically at the heels of Marvin and Andy. The sticky, tropic air collected in his throat, and when he coughed, the hissing whispers seemed to disappear for a moment, freeing his thoughts.

"So, we're sure this island doesn't have legs, right?" Andy joked.

Marvin laughed softly, shaking his head and analyzing peculiar plant life as they wandered through the wooded terrain, while his friend glanced back at Zyvin.

"This isn't a *mobile home*, right Zy?"

Zyvin took a moment to process his words. "Uh," he voiced. "Nah, I... I don't... Nah."

"That's encouraging."

"How much farther now?" Marvin asked.

Zyvin's head throbbed in pain, and his bony fingertips wrapped around the ache. "Ahm..." he sounded.

"Geez, don't hurt yourself," Andy laughed. He nudged Marvin's arm. "C'mon, we'll find it."

Zyvin covered his face in shame. He was unnerved by how well the plan went, and how trusting they both were. The noises of crunching leaves and snapping branches blended into a whir. They echoed and dissipated, leaving only a single sound audible:

Keep going, something whispered.

"Keep going," Zyvin repeated.

The hisses intensified, as Marvin pointed down a twisting, narrow path. "This way?"

Yes.

"Yes."

Just through there.

"Just through there."

Zyvin's hand traveled to his waist, resting atop the handle of his father's hunting knife. His throat clenched when he felt the intricate carvings that decorated the ivory, and his heartbeat raced, sending miniature shockwaves through his body as the weapon slid out of its sheath.

The same pounding sensation was tangible across the plains of the Dark Lands, pulsating through the horde and the warlock's form as an onslaught of fists, clubs, horns, and tusks smashed into the barrier in an attempt to sever the magic-bound stone.

Shamaul lowered the optirock, halting his observation momentarily as another fluctuation carried his gaze skyward. The warlock's stare fixated on the spiraling storm, as the clouded ceiling writhed, less patterned than usual. His Ka fluxed at the presence of an exotic energy collecting in the air: a unique, untapped power that strayed far from its source in the cosmos.

Intoxicated by the phenomenon, he jabbed his scepter into the air and ordered his subjects onward. The creatures shrieked in compliance and flooded around him, trampling one another in the midst of their clamor and swelling against the base of the barrier with amplified force. A nearby ork pounded his bleeding fists into a separation over and over, seeing the thinning field of magic waver abnormally. Flesh torn and bones exposed, the wounded monster let out a raucous wail and slammed both of his damaged hands down a final time.

CRACK!

A booming tone resonated from the point of impact, and silence befell the savage throng. Shamaul stepped past the stilled mobs and reached forward, spiky, armored fingertips touching down on the main fissure of a matrix of cracks. From behind him, Gumble uttered ecstatic yowls, hopping in revelry.

"It's working!" the goblin applauded between bounces. "It's *working!*"

The blue sphere atop Shamaul's scepter shook with energy, and the surrounding blade shrilled as he plunged it into the

235

crevice. The monsters balked at the sound, waiting anxiously, as their master intoned a spell.

Blue energy flashed, running through the web of cracks and exploding, detaching chunks of rock and crumbling the section away, revealing glimmering streaks from the outside world. The mass reeled at the element, but lurched forward at the warlock's command, wildly clawing away rubble and debris. Their master turned away from the upheaval momentarily, lifting the optirock and watching the edge of a knife enter its field of visibility. Light glinted off the metal blade and rattled the sensitive minerals inside, before they circled and reconfigured into the shapes of the Realmhoppers' backs, as they traversed the dense, forested maze.

His snake-like eyes narrowed on the image, his impatience stirring winds that rattled airborne particles as he issued a mental command:

Proceed.

Zyvin shuddered, fingers losing sensation as they tightened around the handle.

"Which way?" Andy asked, he and Marvin coming to a stop at a fork in the path.

End them.

"Zyvin?"

Now.

The travelers turned around, flinching in terror and voicing gasps, as the knife swung down. Shamaul's stare rested on the flittering picture before he rotated, slipped the optirock back inside his cloak, and summoned a gargoyle. Peaking around a boulder, Gumble viewed the exchange curiously, and when the gargoyle flew off and his master stepped away, he hastily clambered across the rubble to follow him and learn what had happened.

The Dark Warlock waved away a crowd of creatures, who promptly disengaged the barrier to escape the searing glow that filtered through the quivering dome in fractured streaks. They withdrew from the light, releasing pops and grumbles as they blinked and shook their heads in an attempt to alleviate their spotted vision.

Shamaul reached, the weakened magic separating like water. He stepped through.

As the mystical dome flickered, the Dark Lands' clouds pumped out, becoming aggravated in the outside atmosphere and puffing into new, anomalous formations. Stepping across the graveled, barren plain, Shamaul observed the effect intently. The cluster of deformed clouds in the sky above the Dark Lands swelled like the pustules surrounding an infection, and on that side of the barrier the air was sickeningly uncontaminated.

Shamaul's inspection trailed, leading to a part in the twilight-colored canopy, through which bright sunlight gleamed. Lacking eyelids, the warlock raised his hand to partition the shine, and when his eyesight unblurred he saw steam rising off his armored glove.

"Sire?" Gumble spoke, drawing his attention backward. The goblin stood, partway emerged from the dome, and although he appeared clearly bothered by the light, his skin did not burn.

Shamaul growled. Either some part of the spell remained intact, or his understanding of it remained incomplete. The metal of his armor singed and bubbled, and smoke began to lift off the fabric of his cloak as well.

He clenched his fist and uttered an incantation: *"Shaliok, rheum beledohr."* Although he whispered the words, they resonated everywhere, and in reaction, the surrounding shadows bent, crawled over the land, and flowed onto his body, forming an aura of darkness that behaved like flames. As they enveloped him, they blocked the sunrays, and the burning ceased.

His goblin subordinate edged from the darkness.

"Sire?" he said again, swallowing with hesitation. "What happened?"

Shamaul looked to his right, noticing the rotting corpse of a massive, horned dragon that lay half-buried in the reddish gravel, its jawbone hanging open in a disturbing smile. Mostly bones remained, bleached white by the sun. Multi-legged annelids traveled in between crevices to gnaw on the peeling meat, and smaller ones devoured finer tissue in the joints and sockets.

One of them wriggled around the milky sphere that was once an eye, and the warlock's observation of the creature was cut short when Gumble repeated his question, adding, "What has become of your spy?"

Shamaul turned, his piercing, yellow eyes appearing even more fearsome through the dark aura, startling the goblin. The warlock said nothing, and yet Gumble nodded as though his question had been answered, and backed into the shade.

Annella tugged fiercely at her chains, strenuously trying to lever the rusted metal free from the uneven grit. The exertion made her wheeze, taking in the sour fumes of decay that already lingered so horribly in her lungs. When her arms hung limply, her hearing detected something outside. Beating wings. Clawed scratches on stone. Words. Her eyes darted down the hall, breaths shortening, as stomping footsteps halted and cranks rotated.

She sucked in a breath and pulled down on the chains over and over again, each pounding note stirring growls of aggravation from ork henchmen. And although she could hear them redirect their surveillance down the hallway she was barred in, she continued with her strategy.

Then, rebounding across the chambers of the castle, a terrified scream of Mae's struck Annella's ears. The sound turned into a ring. Her muscles locked. Her mind braced. Her pupils dilated to dots, and all her careful focus dissolved into fury.

Muscles expanded, adrenalin masking the pain of the shackles' spikes pressing through her skin. Fingers changed into claws, and enamel snapped and reconfigured into fangs. The guard-ork that threw open her cell door had little time to react when the she-wolf pulled down her chains—each ripping with it clusters of wall—and lunged free, her teeth sinking into his neck. The impact toppled him over, and the downed ork garbled a short cry, before the Lycanthian tore out his throat, and he sprawled on the floor.

Annella lifted herself, spitting out a mouthful of ink-colored blood, then located the guard's ring of keys through her pulsating vision. The bands fell from her wrists, clanging when they hit the ground. Her raw wounds stinging in the humid air, she staggered down the hallway in pursuit of her children.

Metal bars rang out as a heavy, cage door dropped, trapping Dariun and Mae as they tumbled into a pit. Dariun pushed off the slick ground, spying a pair of red eyes gleaming at them through a shallow passage, while a trap door slowly rose to set the predator free.

He locked eyes with his sister, holding her by her shoulders. "You have to change, okay?"

238

"I can't!"

"You have to!"

"I can't!" Mae protested, her voice breaking as her face streamed with tears.

The trap door clicked open, and devoid of options Dariun lifted her onto his back. "Hang on."

A fearsome boar charged at them, and Dariun dashed sideways. Blood-colored mist spilled out of his pores, hanging in the air, and when he leapt through the mystic cloud he emerged in wolf form. His sister clung tightly to his back, screaming as the boar chased them. The starving creature swerved when Dariun redirected, and—its hooves less nimble on the damp floor—slid and slammed headfirst into the stone wall. The boar shook its elongated cranium, its unhinging jaw hanging open and belting out a terrible, high-pitched squeal.

At that moment, a roar of terror erupted from the hallway, as an ork collapsed at his station outside. The cage door flew open, and a massive, red wolf leapt into the pit, tackled the emaciated boar, and clamped down on its neck, twisting its head sideways and killing it instantly.

Mae slid off of Dariun's back as he shrank back into his human shape, catching his mother's embrace as she transformed as well and wrapped her arms around her children.

Before she could console them, Mae asked, "What happened to Daddy?"

Annella paused, suddenly aware of her necklace's pendant pressing against her chest. She pulled back, then brought her children to their feet and guided them to the exit, whispering, "Come on."

My body went numb as I gaped at the hunting knife, its blade lodged in a tree trunk directly beside us. Zyvin clung limply to the handle as he slid down, knees pressing into the damp soil, weeping uncontrollably.

"I'm sorry... I'm sorry..." he repeated between breaths, his totems swinging and knocking into his chest with each exhalation. He tugged his knife free from the dense wood and fell over on his back, wincing and covering his face. "Oh, I couldn't do it! Aevæs save them; I couldn't do it!"

"What the heck is going on?!" Andy demanded. He leaned over him, awaiting reply.

Zyvin didn't respond. He shuddered and pulled himself up with the tree. He rested his head on the dark, scaly bark for a while, before he howled and pushed away from it, screaming at himself as he ran.

"Hey!" Andy yelled, as Zyvin zigzagged through the grove.

Andy took off after him, and I stayed behind, still paralyzed by shock and confusion. *What couldn't he do?* I wondered. My throat tightened, and I found myself staring blankly into the brush for a seemingly-endless moment, eyes trailing to the ground as I shook my head at impossible explanations.

I felt Scooter's tentacles shift on my shoulder, the brim of his shell touching down as he hid halfway inside it and chittered. Then, my mind reactivated and impelled me to run. I burst through the foliage and arrived at the shore in time to see Zyvin hunching over in the sand, still bawling and clawing at his hair, while Andy rallied Murry and Veronica and pointed at him, hollering accusations.

The group's equipment jostled as they ran, Veronica asking what happened.

"He attacked us!" Andy shouted.

"You don't understand!" Zyvin cried, spittle launching through the gaps in his teeth. "I never meant for this to happen!"

"What? Getting caught? You tried to kill us!"

"No!"

"I *saw* you!"

I hurried to their sides. Veronica spun to face me, starting to ask what I had seen, when Zyvin let out a pain-filled cry. Our jaws fell open as we watched him lever the point of his knife under the blind eye in his left socket. Veronica's face curled at the sight, and Andy let out a disgusted groan, "What're you—?!" It made a sickening pop as he plied it from his skull, and the discolored sphere rolled over the ground. He fumbled to retrieve it and held it up to us, imploring we look. As I squinted at the object I realized its silvery color wrapped around its entirety. It had no veins on its surface, and no connective tissues hanging off of it. And the longer I stared, the less organic it appeared.

"It's an optirock!" Zyvin sobbed. He chucked it into the sea, nearly tripping over his own feet. He caught himself and sniffed, then went on, "He's been watching you the whole time. He sent me to... I thought he jus' wanted the crystals, but he..." Tears streamed down the right side of his face. "He..."

"Who's *he*?" Veronica questioned.

Zyvin's head shot up, features draining to a ghostly hue. He stepped backward, raising his hands as if shielding himself. "Please—"

"Who sent you?"

Zyvin swallowed, then fretfully answered, "Shamaul."

The tension snapped. Andy shouted at him and ripped the sword from his sheath, and Veronica drew the crossbow from her quiver. The sides of the weapon folded out as she aimed, but Murry placed his hand overtop the rail and guided it down, deterring her with his eyes.

He could not stop Andy, however, who promptly side-stepped around them, his anger boiling into scathing sarcasm. "You're just *full* of surprises today, aren't you Zy?" He pointed his sword at him. "Remember Frost?" He sliced at the air. "This is a threat, right?!"

Zyvin curled up, uttering desperate whimpers, and with each sound he made I felt fearful energy lift off of him.

"Andy," I said.

Andy turned back to me wildly, his face burning red. "What, Marvin?"

"Just... wait a second."

He must have thought I was deranged. "Why?"

I shook my head, not entirely sure myself. "I dunno, I just... I don't think he's—"

"He's a traitor!"

Zyvin backed up into Boris' chest, whose voluble snort sent him scrambling back to the center of the ring. He dropped down to the gritty ground, pleading his case.

"I never wanted to, I swear!"

Andy threw his arms sideways. "Why'd you do it, then? What *else* are you keeping from us?"

Zyvin pressed the heels of his hands against his forehead, crying, "He has them."

"What?"

"Shamaul has my family."

We all paused. Zyvin seized the silence to reveal everything that he could. He told us about dungeons and terrifying monsters, being captured and traded, subjected to horrific spells, and something about the crystals. But, his sentences quickly turned frantic and disjointed, and most of his words were spoken too quickly for any of us to interpret. The last phrase he was able to communicate was "cosmic energy," before his lungs emptied with a sharp whistle and he fell over on the ground, heaving for air.

Andy looked taken aback. His sword dropped into the sand as he approached him. "Hey, are you—?"

Zyvin shot up, screaming, smoke pouring from his mouth. Andy fell to the ground in terror and shuffled backward, and I pulled him to his feet.

Zyvin lurched, holding a pain in his gut and coughing and retching at an endless flow of murky, black fog that spilled out his throat. I watched in horror and disbelief as his skin became transparent he started to fade away. He looked at his vanishing limbs and cried out hoarsely, "AAAHH!!!" With his fleeting amount of energy he shambled over the ground and reached for us. "HELP MEEE!!!"

Murry stepped forward, wand in hand, shouting, "Luminiera!"

A bright, white flash washed over Zyvin. Its brilliance seemed to evaporate the evil smoke, and when the clouds dissipated his body solidified, and he collapsed, face-first in the sand. Andy knelt to retrieve his sword, panting, and then silently crossed the shoreline, as the rest of us followed.

As we left, I heard Zyvin push himself off the ground, calling after us.

"Pleeease..." he wheezed.

I looked back, seeing him attempt to stand.

"He'll sense me here again... Don't let him..." He took a few steps on his knees before he fell over, lying in the hot grains exhaustedly.

We stood outside the lifeboat, exchanging troubled looks. The small craft creaked and tottered as the waves kicked up beneath it, making its triangular flag flap side-to-side from atop the swaying masthead. Veronica leaned on the brim, holding it stable and halting the action.

She nodded to Andy. "What do you think?"

Andy cupped the back of his head, muttering, "I can't think right now."

She glanced at Murry, who flipped his hood back and combed his shaky fingertips through his hair. He covered his head again, sighing as he stated, "He won't survive here."

I suddenly felt the group's stares shift to me. I intercepted them just as Andy said, "Your call," and I turned to Zyvin.

His body was sprawled out, the reaching tides swelling in from the right and nudging him slightly, though he remained stationary. On the horizon I could see an intimidating raincloud form. It thundered.

"We're onboard either way," Veronica whispered.

I sighed. I had no idea why the decision had fallen to me. I could hardly piece together exactly what had happened, or *how* it happened. But, examining my friends' expressions, I took in a slow, steadying breath, and delivered my thoughts.

22
Into the Mist

My racing heart served as a backbeat for the orchestra of roars and rumbles that sloshed against our boat's frame and boomed from the strata of the incoming storm. Blood pumping down my arms, the tingling, hypersensitive nerves in my fingertips detected every abnormality as I gripped the edges of the lifeboat's bow and we skipped across the choppy waves.

The sky exploded and Boris roared, his antsy hooves making the lifeboat sway even more, until Veronica petted his face and calmed him. The sound also startled Scooter, who darted across the craft, leaping and clambering, then disappearing into a bag of supplies at the back, where Zyvin lay tiredly.

His legs were curled up to his chest, and his hands were clinging tightly to a decorative flourish on the stern, his elbows and forehead knocking into the wood with every jostle. Earlier he had ripped a strip of fabric off his clothing and tied it around his eyeless left socket to protect it from saltwater and rain, although the rag had already saturated and become plastered with damp strings of gray hair running down his face and adhering to his chin.

Andy grabbed my shoulder for stability as he made his way to the front, stopping at the sight of a streak of lightning that glowed through the condensing haze, followed by another blast of thunder. The second strike made Scooter flee from the supply bag—as though the shelter had been compromised—and crawl up my leg to hide in my right pocket. Feeling his fretful shakes, I covered him with my hand, and when a third bolt went off and the rain started to fall, he retreated fully into his shell.

"Come on, no more rain!" Andy groaned, as renegade winds swept in to fling the downpour at us from every direction. I blocked a spray with my forearm, although more water launched at me from behind, drenching my back.

I couldn't believe any of it was happening. I expected we would return Zyvin home and take off for Veindai the next day.

Instead, we were absconding from an uninhabited island, Zyvin in tow, while trying to put sufficient distance between us and Shamaul's apparent range of mental influence over our passenger.

I kept glancing back at Zyvin to make sure he wasn't enveloped by the smoke-like substance, and Murry seemed to be on guard as well, his wand clutched by his side. As Puerri Island drifted off behind the thickening wall of obscurity, I lost all sense of our location. We had launched in the direction of the first rush of wind to fill our sail, and blasting across the tumultuous currents in a blanket of steam had fried my cognition. All I knew was that we had to be elsewhere.

After a long period of silence, we started to ease. But a sudden cry of terror made us spin around, seeing Zyvin stare off into the mist, face twisting in fear.

"No... no, no, no, it can't be!"

"What is it?" Veronica questioned.

Murry prepared his wand, but no smoke appeared, and Zyvin's body remained unchanged. He dropped from his seat and curled up on the floor, covering his head and crying:

"I'm sorry, I'm sorry!"

Andy and I clamored simultaneously: "Zyvin, you need to talk to us." "What is happening?"

"It's him!"

My heart skipped a beat. "What do you—?"

"He's here!"

A resonant howl trailed the shadow of a monstrous, winged beast as it whipped past us, disappearing in the fog. Zyvin clasped his ears and rocked, stammering incomprehensibly under his breath, as the monster's wings threw spirals of vapor over our bodies.

"Aeralisk!" Murry shouted, commanding a gust of wind into the sail and propelling us away from the unseen horror.

From the left, the figure reappeared fleetingly, screeching, the force of its wingbeats throwing us off kilter and sending us down another tunnel of fog. The mist seemed to rotate around us. We altered course several times, swerving in avoidance of the monstrosity. And in sync with our hastened retreat, the storm clouds above thundered like war drums. They impacted rhythmically, striking without fail, while the lightning recessed into its nimbus.

Rain pelted from above, fog steamed from below, and the storm twisted into something unnatural. The clouds drained of color, and Zyvin yowled as the nightmare returned.

Powerful gusts surged in from the right, and we yelled, the blasts of wind and rain nearly capsizing our tiny vessel as it spun around, facing backward. Murry cast more wind into the sail, but the boat went rigid.

"Guys!" Andy called, directing our attention to the black Ka that glowed from the boat's wood grain, holding us in place. Boris drew his club and roared at the sky, as the frightening creature tossed two wingfuls of air downward to steady into a hovering flap. The heaps of mist parted to reveal the monster.

There sat Shamaul, riding atop a terrifying, undead dragon. His skeletal steed's jaw swung open and ribcage expanded and closed, as though it still had lungs to fill with air. Its joints cracked as its wing bones curled in, cupped the wind, and pressed down, even though the webs of skin were riddled with holes.

Under natural circumstances, the badly-torn membrane would never provide lift. However, a frightening gas roiled inside, emptying through spaces in the bones and mingling with dark Ka that surrounded the creature and allowed it to levitate. From behind the smoky veil, the dragon's head threw sideways, spying us with dead, pearl-like eyes. Its nostrils fumed as the evil mixture in its ribcage bubbled up and spilled from its throat, popping and releasing ghastly wails.

We clutched our ears at the deafening sound. As it roared, flecks of black spiraled from its mouth like embers, flickering and extinguishing as they flew skyward. I felt this was the substance that influenced its movement and simulated the motions of life—screeching, flapping, breathing—drawing upon postmortem memories engrained somewhere deep in its being to reanimate the terror. The dragon was merely a vehicle for the warlock.

Shamaul's face was hidden behind his hood and silver mask. The headpiece possessed qualities that resembled the top half of a skull, with the exception of two pointed, fang-like shapes curving downward from the place where teeth would be. I knew that at one point this entity was Murry's son. I knew that at one point he must have been human, and for the most part his armored form bore human characteristics.

246

However, judging from the parts of his body that weren't concealed—his serpentine eyes and ram-like horns—I decided that whatever lied beneath was anything but.

He rose to his feet, balancing effortlessly atop his floating mount. His black armor clicked together as he straightened, and his ripped-up cape and shredded, black cloak flowed around him like the tattered war flag of a ruthless kingdom.

Yellow, snake-like eyes scanned us from behind a rippling, dark aura. They examined each of us coldly and exactly, shifting across the line, and then fixing on Zyvin. His armored finger rose to point at him, as the winds warped and shrieked.

"*Pleeeeease!*" Zyvin hollered, still on his knees, arms thrown open and tortured face streaming with tears. "Don't hurt them!"

Shamaul stared back without empathy.

"I *did* all I can! I obeyed your will, I betrayed my resolves! You *have* to pardon this, you have to!" He searched the warlock's stare futilely, cringing at his silence. "You have to—!"

"They are already dead."

Zyvin shuddered. "*What?*"

"I anticipated your betrayal."

Our concerned gazes glided onto Zyvin, whose neck throbbed and body shook with infrequent intakes of air, as Shamaul concluded his sentiment:

"I never intended for them to survive."

Zyvin's features tightened in agony as he doubled over and gripped his sides, as if holding a wound. "*No-ogh!*" he choked, his streaming tears indistinguishable from the rain.

Sympathies not able to escape my clamped throat, I reached out to touch his shoulder. His skin was ice cold. I tore my hand away as he screamed and threw his head back, his iris ablaze with golden fibers.

"You lied to me," he cried, his prominent jaw pushing out fangs.

The thundering clouds pulsed blue, silhouetting Shamaul's figure and intensifying Zyvin's rage.

"You lied to me!" he bellowed again, freeing his knife. Through his gritting canines he graveled words, tears rolling endlessly. "Ahl ejhum ain grador..."

Shamaul's head tilted.

"Ihl chien'ain tradah!"

247

Zyvin's legs pushed off, launching him with animalistic power. I gaped, bewildered and terrified as he soared, feeling a tightness form in my chest. His battle cry warped into a wolfish roar, but it garbled as he reached the warlock's height, cut short by several spear-tipped tendrils piercing his abdomen.

We shouted in unison, Murry and I launching spells and Veronica firing arrows, all of which exploded or splintered apart against a dome of Ka the warlock had conjured.

As his tendrils writhed from his sleeve, burrowed, and figure-eighted through Zyvin's body, Shamaul intoned, "Your ambition is foolish."

Zyvin stabbed the knife into Shamaul's ankle.

"*Grugh!*" The warlock buckled, nearly falling from his platform. Zyvin levered his blade from the space in the armored plating, but Shamaul regained stability and drove the spiked appendages deeper, as new ones snaked in.

Zyvin fought, slashing wildly at the tendrils as they slipped toward him. They spewed ink-like fluid when they severed, before they were replaced by another pair that hooked beneath his chin. The two pulled up while the rest pressed down. Shamaul's head lowered, a horrifying crack froze time, and we all watched helplessly behind the wriggling barricade, as Zyvin's head detached from his body.

The two parts of him seemed to tumble in slow motion. As they splashed down, Andy fell to his knees, and Veronica buried her face in Murry's chest. The wizard gaped at the atrocity as he shielded her head, his horrified pupils fidgeting from the image before landing on the warlock.

Shamaul returned to his seated position, studying each of us for segments of eternity. My chest filled with pain, and I realized I hadn't breathed. I took in trepidatious micro-breaths as Shamaul's glare swept over me and locked with Murry's.

Shamaul's hand rose to us and we gasped and backed, but in the midst of his motion the warlock's dark aura flickered out, and the rain sizzled and vaporized against his exposed, metal armor.

He rotated his outstretched hand in observation, then clenched his fist, reshaping the dark spell. An agitated breath hissed from beneath his mask, before his attention darted sideways, yellow eyes peering into the hazy horizon for several seconds. He let out a growl, his aura weakening again.

He turned to us and spoke, "It seems fate has conjured you a crueler end."

I looked to my left and saw Zyvin's head bobbing in the currents, a speared tendril still lodged in his neck. The severed appendage suddenly came to life, dragging the head behind it as it snaked and slithered up the prow and knotted itself around the flourish, as blood continued to pour into the sea. When I looked back, Shamaul had flown off, fading into the blur atop his abhorrent ride.

As Shamaul disappeared in the distance, a buildup of lightning jolted from above, scathing the water and producing a bright flash that deteriorated the warlock's lingering Ka, freeing our boat and allowing the surf to rock us again, pushing us violently side to side.

"What was that about fate?" Andy spoke over the sea as it became more raucous, his worried eyes darting to each of us, desperate for answers. "What'd he say?"

I shook my head and searched the sea, trying to think, then noticed the deep redness seeping into the water, spreading outward behind us and mingling with the ink-like substance in the traumatized waves. As the two bloods swirled and blended, a massive wave rolled, and in the distance I beheld the source of the torrent.

A gigantic, dark green fin flapped open, turning the water into foam as it surged after the mixture. I froze, as Captain Cyrus' story resurfaced in my memories:

A drop of blood... the voice recited. *A thousand spans away...*

23
Death Snake Chase

Beneath the rippling, murky surface, two massive, burgundy ovals ignited: the burning eyes of a primordial killer the modern world had yet to snuff out. Below them, the glint of monstrous teeth shone through plumes of agitated sediment, a crocodilian foot clawed, and even farther in the distance where visibility hazed, the point of a tail emerged to swipe the cloudbank. Rattling, salt-strewn squalls twisted through the quelling mist, whipping it formless. The course air battered my face, blurred my lenses, and scattered my thoughts, as it blared a haunting, siren-like howl that signaled the arrival of the Kraicore.

Every moment that passed brought her closer to the prow. Every part of my being pleaded for explanation. Every one of my senses strained, desperate to deliver some sliver of evidence that could rationalize the beast. But failed, when a horrific, pulse-pounding roar vibrated from below, and fermented my fear. The frightening sensation raced up my legs, locking every joint as it scaled my body and gathered in my solar plexus. Although our lifeboat had long since freed from the warlock's Ka, none of us rushed to the sail. We were all immobilized, gazes held captive by the incoming beast of legend, unable to fathom how life could allow such a depraved creature to prowl the world. And yet, there it was. It was as if *this* was how she hunted. Her mere presence could freeze any life form incapable of comprehending her existence.

The tempest writhed, sparked, and gushed, striking the Vox Sea with lightning and boiling the bloods that swilled and churned into the wicked mixture of ingredients that summoned the titan. And as she breeched the surface and roared again, a shrill outcry of Andy's shattered our trances:

"GOOOOO!!!"

"Aeralisk!" Murry and I shouted in near unison.

The sail swelled and our craft sprang to life, skipping over the waves and jostling our cargo. The sudden takeoff made Andy slide, slamming to the back with a grunt, before pulling himself upward to lay eyes on the dripping, dismembered tendril knotted to our boat. Tethered, Zyvin's head tossed and tumbled in the wake, leaving a trail of blood for the serpent to track. Andy pulled at the knot and it oozed, drenching his hands in thick, oily slime. Disgusted, he got to his feet, rubbed off the filth, and when a rogue wave clipped us he stumbled into me, compromising my focus for a moment and cutting out my spell.

The sudden, uneven inflow of wind made us bank left, heading straight for a pillar of rocks. Veronica levered the sail, Murry redirected the wind, and we swerved, barely escaping impact.

We released a cumulative breath, but recoiled at the sounds of the formation crumbling, followed by volatile, prehistoric roars. Chunks of stone splashed into the surf beside us to amplify my fear, and I immediately reactivated the spell. Upon shouting the command, I felt wind cyclone down my arm, sweeping up airborne droplets that glittered and vaporized in the presence of magic, then burst in the flow. I placed one foot forward and leaned, hoping the added pressure might strengthen the stream.

Don't look back, I told myself. *Don't look back.* Then, Scooter scurried up my torso and onto my shoulder. He shrieked, dragging my attention to the incoming serrations of teeth.

Never in my wildest nightmares could I have envisaged a more frightening monster. The Kraicore was a fearsome amalgamation of fish and reptile. Fragments of rocky buildup and dark bluish coral snapped off of her body as she surfaced and articulated, the last of which detaching mostly from her snout and spiky brows. Plated, green scales armored her body, which seemed to stretch on forever, and her massive, frilled tail thrashed in the distance, driving forward her house-sized cranium.

Her face possessed the blended qualities of a viperfish and a lizard: eyes unblinking, unfeeling domes, the color of blood; nostrils flaring up front; and gills flexing behind her cavernous maw, which hung open as she swam, bearing crimson gums fortified with jagged, overelaborate teeth—like those of a deep sea fish cast in the durable enamel of a predatory reptile.

Face to face with the ancient killer, the fossils of the carnivores I beheld in the museum suddenly paled in ferocity. And the longer I stared, the less powerful my spell became. Andy stumbled past me, zigzagging as the floor teetered and swayed, then tried again to untangle the tendril affixed to the back of our boat. He pulled at the knot in vain, as more blood dyed the frothing seawater that drained into the monster's gaping jaws, like a black hole with teeth.

Frustrated, Andy ultimately drew his sword and hacked through the tether, and Zyvin's head spun backward into the void. Though the blood trail vanished, the creature showed no intent of slowing, and in fact picked up speed, her open mouth making the sound of a wailing wind tunnel as she closed in.

Andy's chest pulled in tired breaths, his eyebrows slanting over his defeated gaze. As lower teeth impacted the back of our boat, I felt my heart pound, while my eyes darted in between the sail and the Death Snake's chasmal maw.

With no time to think I discharged the wind spell, then spun around and shouted, "Zyros!"

Only after the spheroid blast of electricity entered the mouth did I realize how insignificant it was, shrinking into a speck of light as it flew, illuminating the towering rib-like bones and undulating musculature like a flare plummeting into a pit. When it disappeared, the Kraicore's gills pulsated and lower jaw lifted, scraping the lifeboat's stern and inclining our craft. It smashed back to the waves with a boisterous crash, flinging loose bags of equipment overboard. I lost my footing and fell, wand escaping my grasp and flying into the titan's craw as well, along with several bags of supplies, a plethora of loose items and gear, and finally, my backpack.

The serpent dove below the surface, her long body arching under, tail spiraling. My fingertips traveled to my chest, confirming my father's dog tags were still secure around my neck. As I felt the metal pendants shielding my racing heart, a hand reached down to hoist me by the loop of my elbow.

Murry asked if I was alright, and I nodded. Looking me over, he saw that I had lost my wand, and his eyes filled with worry, then dread, as the water bubbled white. Andy peered over the edge and I followed him, seeing sets of fangs unlacing with a bellowing roar that boiled the sea.

Andy scrambled back from the edge. "Not good!"

Murry's pupils raced, diverting to the sky. He frowned, sucked a breath through his nostrils, and with the Aeralisk spell still flowing from his wand, reached his free palm toward a part in the clouds and incanted, "Solaos inverum!"

A great twist of wind curved from above to strengthen the gust and drive us away. Our tense sail strained and mast cracked slightly. We narrowly cleared the circle of foam before it exploded and sent the Kraicore soaring into the sky.

She surged, rearing high enough to bite the clouds, then twisted and plummeted sideways like a whale would. The resultant wave flung us into the air, and when our boat crashed down, the shock was enough to split our burdened sail in two.

The frayed sail flapping wildly, Veronica pulled back on a rope that tightened the stretched fabric—a last ditch effort to capture the gusting wind spell that maintained our pace. At that instant, Murry's wand behaved less like a firearm and more like a maestro's baton, conducting the mystic gales into the divided sail with sweeping, flourishing motions, and to my surprise, effectively distancing our lifeboat from the titan's rage.

"Great!" Andy rejoiced.

The Kraicore reoriented herself below the surface, set sights on our fleeing vessel, and caught up with us instantaneously.

"*Great*," Andy repeated, less enthused.

The Kraicore breached the water repeatedly, each time twisting to land on her side. As she turned in midair, she exposed her pale, fleshy underbelly—the one area that was not protected by scales and spikes—as it quavered for food. She landed with an enormous splash, and my grip tightened around the brim. My throat throbbed as I hollered for the others to hang on, and we all braced, as another wave curled underneath and threw us skyward.

Although my eyes were shut, I sensed the last droplets of water trickle from the boat's underside, and heard the Kraicore leap after us, followed by unsettling silence. When my eyelids finally peeled, my whole field of visibility was dominated by teeth. They clamped shut just feet from the craft, before the monster fell back to the sea—on her stomach this time—keeping her awful gaze locked upon her prey.

Watching her sink below the currents, my unfettered thoughts suddenly snapped back to question how we managed to stay airborne for so long. I glanced over at Veronica, who pulled back on the rope that stretched the torn sail open like wings, catching Murry's spell, while Boris snorted and dug his fingernails into the bow—particularly disquieted by the flight—and Andy wrapped his arms and legs around the base of the mast.

He stared at me in disbelief, and I traced his astonished gaze to my hands, then to the floor. The slats in the boards were set aglow, and a cushion of Ka cradled the craft, with feathered flits of energy rising off the sides. As soon as I became aware of the effect, my grip fidgeted, and the glow flickered slightly. We glided down, the sharp decent causing a rough landing in the irate waters. Boris stamped his right hoof down on the wobbling craft, his muscular bovine legs steadying the float, as his raucous huffs settled into more stable breaths.

"Good boy," Veronica crooned, as calmly as she could.

I stood up, staggering for balance and wheezing breaths, as the Death Snake's spines pierced the surface. I turned. Looking into the distance I spied the outlines of jagged rocks rising from the sea. Beyond them lay shallower waters and the Veindaian coastline, I knew. But making it through the labyrinth of spikes would be next to impossible. Then, my eyes flashed at an idea.

"We need to go around," Veronica said.

"Sail into them," I responded.

"What?"

"Sail into them. And slow the wind a little."

Murry raised an incredulous eyebrow, before Veronica shot back, "Marvin, they're unnavigable!"

"We don't *have* to navigate them."

They thought I was crazy. Their increasingly confused expressions examined me as I panted tiredly, Andy especially skeptical.

"He's lost it," he alleged.

"No, we can make it over," I explained, kneeling to grasp the edges of the boat again.

"Are you sure?"

I lifted my shoulders and voiced a pitchy, "*Yeah,*" not quite as confident-sounding as I intended, and Andy's head rolled with a groan.

"I'm sure," I attested, more firmly this time.

Andy turned to Murry, whose frazzled stare bounced between his and mine. I projected all of my certainty through my eyes, and after a brief, silent exchange, the wizard lifted his wand and tapered the wind.

Andy released a loud, reluctant whine and wrapped himself around the mast, as Boris snorted and tucked down, Veronica levered the sail, and Scooter's tentacles clasped tightly to my shoulder.

I adjusted my grip, searching for the lifeboat's Ka, which the rushing waves and pattering rain made difficult to locate. I kicked at the boards with my foot, trying to feel if the vibrations would scatter the unseen energy. I shook my head at the attempt.

It's there, I reminded myself.

Three sparks of lightning went off in the distance, as the Kraicore leapt and fell.

"Get ready!" I called.

A humongous wave surged under us.

"Now!"

Veronica pulled back on the rope, Murry inflated the sail with wind, and when we went airborne the small boat beamed with Ka, while the Kraicore jumped and gnashed at our gliding vessel.

Hovering just beyond reach and high above the dangers of the water, the strategy incurred infuriated bellows from our pursuer. She leapt, snapped, and fell, splashing onto her stomach and disappearing below to build speed, before resurging.

My muscles strained and arms shook wildly, an overflow of adrenaline pumping through my system. I shut my eyes to concentrate, blocking out all sound, focusing only on sustaining the field.

This has to work.

Something more potent than adrenaline raced through me, releasing my grasp on the craft and adjusting my stance. My eyes shot open, shining white, and my arms heaved sideways, throwing a perfect sphere of Ka around the boat.

I had never experienced anything like it. I was in tune with everything: detecting the slightest signature of Ka in every raindrop, every breeze. The Kraicore bathed in the same luminescent outlines, which traced her grizzly features. They fluxed as they neared our boat, flashing with radiance as the serpent's snout bashed the dome, propelling us higher. The jostled crew's shouts and hollers blended into an echoey whir, but from the discordance I extracted that we were nearing the spiky ridgeline.

It was critical that I hang on, but every jarring impact threatened to suck me out of the trance-like state and back into the chaos. The glittering outlines began to fade. Another strike. Pain burned through my muscles. Another. I fought off my bodily senses for as long as I could, releasing a scream that matched the volume of the titan's roar, as we passed over the jagged rocks and the Kraicore leapt after us.

An uneven splash. A mangled shriek. My arms finally gave out and dropped to my sides, the field of Ka spiraling out of formation and delivering the broken lifeboat back to the currents. The landing buckled my legs and I fell backward, my descent halted by hasty arms that rushed to catch and lower me to a lay. From my low angle, through my dizzied, glazing vision, I saw a massive, frilled tail thrash, attached to a skewered abdomen, and a fleshy underjaw hooked on a giant, rocky jag.

The Kraicore tossed and pulled, her swinging tail toppling smaller pillars of rock and throat bellowing roars between each throe, unable to detach herself from the spikes. Not a second later did the mast break in half, as the creaking boat bobbed in the micro-currents, drifting toward land, and my surroundings hazed out with the whispered praises of my teammates.

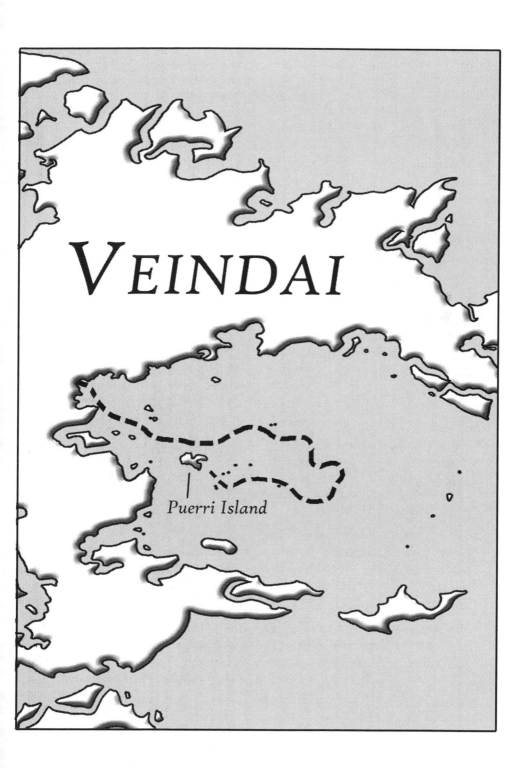

VEINDAI

Puerri Island

24
Landfall

Delicate strands of fog strayed from the burdensome murk, slithering across the sandy shore, weaving through trees and vines, and climbing up mountainsides to escape the wicked, whirling tempest that festered above the dying tides. The smoky overcast from which they fled mutated into horrible formations: a thick, gray shroud of obscurity that the light of Enkartai's twin moons could not pierce. The clouds instead filtered an abnormally-dim moonglow, the color of unpolished siv, which cast muted tones across the land. The stars were invisible as well, and even the forest's menagerie of bioluminescent creatures seemed absent that night.

But, within the shade of a sheltered ledge carved in the final summit of the Entohc range, a pair of flaming, orange-red eyes remained ablaze. The exhausted warrior to whom they belonged rolled over achingly, pausing once his keen vision spotted a band of five tugging their mangled boat ashore. He shot up, temporarily forgetting the pain in his limbs, as he watched a minotaur gingerly lift the body of an unconscious boy from the boat and carry him onto land. A smaller, shelled creature scurried after them, and another traveler, clad in orange, stumbled and flopped into the sand, causing a girl to trip over his sprawled-out body. She shouted something hoarse at him, to which the face-down boy made an apathetic gesture and a muffled response, before they both abandoned the argument and remained lying there tiredly.

The white-robed warrior leaned forward, examining the bustling forms more prudently, wondering if they were in fact the travelers he had been told of. An elderly man in violet wizard's robes hurried after the minotaur, rotating a rucksack from his back to his stomach to retrieve some supplies. The warrior's eyes flared at the sight of the wizard, sensing something oddly familial in his Ka. He lifted himself, but recoiled at the sound of whispering calls outside.

A waterfowl flapped by his cave, its echoing chatter bending into sounds unnervingly similar to those of his homeland. He recessed. Behind him, his windserpent, Kail, made a weary coo, her webbed talons reaching and clawing in dreamscape, as her broken leg curled up to her chest. The warrior hung his head and sighed.

"Patience, Grimmoch," he reminded himself, as he lay his head against his steed's tan scales, and her gentle breathing lulled him to rest.

My eyes peeled open to behold the morning sun. I squinted at the light, as cawing blurs soared overhead and a translucent, hole-ridden ceiling rippled above me in maritime breezes. My hand reached out automatically, setting down on the bent-up wire frames of my glasses and returning them to my face.

The world came into focus. Directly above, the tattered, split sail buffeted in the wind, sunlight spilling through the holes. When I worked my way into a sit, I realized the boat's damaged mast had been propped up as an improvised shelter, and along the shore other parts of the lifeboat had been scavenged as well. The bow of the craft jutted from the sand just a few feet away, which I presumed was a second shelter. In its shade sat Murry's rucksack—one of the few items to survive the attack—and since it contained the crystals, I took solace in its wellbeing.

The sparkling sand reflected the morning sun. The shore was aglow with golden tones and a warmth that matched its vibrancy, and instilled me with repose, despite the horrors we had just endured. One look at my friends and I could tell the same feeling had inhabited them as well.

Veronica set something down in the shade of the adjacent shelter, patting the sand from her hands. She stood, caught my stare, then waved to me. She stepped back to the water's edge, passing by Boris as he delivered two hefty armfuls of branches and logs to the growing pile of provisions. He snorted and returned to the forest to find more, with Scooter hitching a ride, climbing from his lower right cheek-horn to his upper right head-horn, and whistling gleefully from his high lookout.

In the center of camp, several curved, dense boards from what I assumed had been the stern were arranged into a circular frame to contain a roaring fire pit that Murry stoked. Andy emerged from the brush with uprooted ferns in hand. Murry took them and nodded in appreciation before stripping the dark green leaves from their stalks and adding them to a steaming concoction that bubbled within a blackened fruit husk. Murry seemed delighted by the aroma, but Andy seemed overwhelmed by it, and when he noticed I was awake he grinned and walked over.

"Hey buddy!" Andy slapped my shoulder and dropped beside me. "Welcome back!"

I rubbed an ache on my forehead and asked, "How long was I out?"

"Hoh, man..." Andy looked off and shook his head, cheeks puffing with air as he thought. He squinted as he turned back to me and approximated, "Few days?"

"What?!"

He started to laugh. "I'm just kidding, man."

I buried my head in my hands and let out a groan.

"You *were* out cold for most of the day, though. Murry said you were in something called a *Ka sleep*. He wanted us to watch you through the night and make sure you weren't glowing."

I peeked over my hands. "Why? What would that mean?"

"I dunno... you'd explode or something."

My eyes grew wide.

Andy started to laugh again and I let myself fall back on the sand as he wiped a tear from his eye. "I'm so sorry, dude!" he squeaked, reaching to pull me up.

"You're hilarious."

"I'm sorry," he repeated.

As he grabbed my hand and helped me up, I noticed he was wearing a wristband made of dark blue shells, and I asked him where he got it.

He rotated his hand to glance at it, grinned, then held it up proudly. "Veronica made it for me!"

"Oooooooh."

"I know! Plus, we're going on a hunting trip later."

"And it's just the two of you?"

Andy pushed his tongue into his cheek and nodded with delight.

"*Nice.* Sounds like a good first date."

"Oh, yeah," Andy said, continuing to nod as he popped the collar of his orange jacket and wiggled his eyebrows.

I laughed. "Just make sure you don't make that face, okay?"

Our chuckles cut short when Veronica strolled by with a sly glare. She watched us over her shoulder as she passed, half-smiling, then shook her head and walked off. Andy grinned and nudged me with his elbow, and our antics resumed.

As Andy got up and paced to mentally prepare himself for his date, I joined Murry by the campfire.

"Good morning," he greeted. "Feeling rested?"

"Sort of," I answered. "My head hurts a little."

Murry nodded, as if expecting the response, then handed me a cupful of steaming liquid.

"What is it?"

"Toffa tea," he proclaimed. "Made from the fronds of the Toffa fern."

I took a big whiff and hot, minty steam coated my nostrils.

"This tea will make you *strong*," Murry said, balling a fist to signify strength.

I took a sip, and the bold flavor coursed through me. It was like drinking a candy cane. "*Whoa-hoh!*" I coughed.

Murry cracked a wry grin, shrugging, "*And,* like most things that make you strong it doesn't taste all that pleasant."

As the tea's warmth spread through my body I felt the ache in my forehead melt away. Surprised by the effect, I took another sip, and Murry smiled.

Andy shuffled around behind me, murmuring to himself.

"You okay?" I asked.

He looked up. "Huh? Yeah, yeah I'm fine." He zipped up his jacket. "Zipped or unzipped?"

"I dunno... zipped?"

"I like it unzipped." He reopened the jacket and straightened out his T-shirt, then combed back his hair and took a deep breath. "*You got this...*"

"Are you nervous?"

"Me? *Pfft,* no."

I watched him skeptically. Taking another swig of tea, I chewed on fragments of fern leaf and a mild, herbaceous aftertaste soothed my throat.

Andy saw Veronica patrolling the shore. She intercepted his stare and smiled back at him softly.

He turned back to me. "Okay, I'm nervous."

"You seemed so confident a second ago."

"Yeah, but that was before."

"Before what?"

"Before I realized that everything I do and say *matters* now."

Veronica knelt by the water, picking up shells. Andy knelt by us, whispering, "What should I do?"

Murry poured another cup of tea. "When *I* was a boy, I'd show off my magic to impress the lassies." The wizard's eyes flashed in remembrance. "Once, I put on a small lightshow with the Luminiera spell. Oh! And another time I made a pot of flowers *dance* to impress a girl." He shook his head in revelry and chuckled at the memory.

Andy stared at him blankly, nodding. "Okay. Great. That doesn't help me at all."

I drank the last of my tea, then made a calming motion with my arms. "Just, *relax.*"

Andy stared at me for a long while, pointing. "Wait... are *you* telling *me* to relax?"

I shrugged, then nodded.

His attention shifted to Murry, who raised a second piping cup. "What's in that tea?" Without a moment to protest, Andy snatched the beverage from Murry and gulped it down. His face curled up. "*BLECH!*" he retched. He dropped the small wooden cup and wiped his tongue.

Veronica appeared. "Ready?"

Andy hunched over, sputtering coughs.

"Are... you okay?"

"Uh-huh," he wheezed, clasping his knees and coughing again. "I'm just, y'know... dying to spend time with you."

She grinned slyly, then grabbed his elbow and tugged him into the forest.

Murry retrieved the discarded cup, squinting inside and turning it upside down. The last amount of tea blipped from the rim. He sighed.

I chuckled, then said, "I can help you make more. What does this fern look like?"

Andy followed his guide into the dense forest, weaving around tree trunks and bushes and looking to Veronica frequently.

As he worked through a cluster of greenery he asked her, "So what exactly are we looking for?"

Before she could answer, she stopped abruptly and raised her hand. Andy nearly tripped over himself as he bounded to a stop. He stood with his arms outstretched, waiting. Having detected something he hadn't, Veronica lowered to the ground and glided behind a bush. Andy followed.

Parting leaves, the two beheld a small, feathered reptile that Veronica recognized as a variant of mouvel, a scavenger, gnawing and ripping mouthfuls of meat from the carcass of an ugly, swine-like quadruped. The mouvel cocked its spear-shaped head, attention darting around the clearing as it gnashed the bloody bits messily, before plunging back into the ribcage.

Veronica examined the scavenger's feast. The body was covered in thick blood, much of which streamed from a fresh bite mark on the bloated animal's neck. It had been inflicted by fangs from jaws far more powerful than a mouvel's, she knew, trying to picture the culprit. Perhaps a large cat of some kind.

She halted her speculation when Andy whispered, *"Hey, it's a mini furadon!"*

Veronica released an amused breath from her nose as she reached for an arrow from her quiver. "Yeah," she agreed. "Only this time *we're* the hunters."

She loaded her crossbow, taking the moment to inculcate her guest.

"Opportunity is the key to hunting," she told him. "When you find your target you have to keep still, and control your heartbeat."

The crossbow's string clicked as the ammo locked into place. Veronica looked up to see Andy staring back at her blankly. Her bright, periwinkle eyes sparkled and met with his light blue ones, which only deepened his trance and made him unaware of the smile forming on his face.

Veronica turned her head, allowing her hair to drape and conceal her blushing features. "Focus, Andy."

"Huh?" Andy blinked. "Oh. Yeah." He shook himself alert. "Keep still. Control your heart. Got it."

His embarrassment manifested as another impish grin, while Veronica eyed him cunningly. She took aim.

The mouvel dipped its head a few times to pick meat from the fallen creature's bones. Veronica steadied her breath, and Andy leaned in with apprehension. The arrow flew, but at the last moment the mouvel plunged back into its meal and the projectile whizzed overhead, sticking in a tree. The scavenger shot up again, green feathers bristling alertly as it let out a whooping call and skipped off.

"Dang it!" Veronica groaned. Her crossbow rotated a new arrow into its rail. The string clicked. A couple spans ahead of her, Veronica spied the escaping reptile hopping atop a log, fidgeting and hooting from its new vantage. "Maybe we can sneak up on it again," she suggested. She looked to Andy for his thoughts, but he was gone. She spun around, suddenly worried. "Andy?"

A frenzied squeal transferred Veronica's attention back to the mouvel as it fled into the brush, Andy hot on its tracks.

"YAAAAHH!!!" he hollered as he charged after it. Completely bewildered, Veronica packed up her gear and hurried after him.

Andy bounded over logs and under sloping branches in pursuit of the nimble creature.

"I gotcha... I gotcha," he uttered determinedly between pants. Strides ahead, the fast-footed reptile's head rotated on its swooping neck to examine its pursuer curiously. Andy squinted in confusion as the mouvel cocked its backwards head, watching him while still weaving around tree trunks with ease. Its beak-like jaw fell open and gurgled a shriek, a purple tongue spraying green saliva.

Andy winced, "Gross."

The mouvel's head swiveled forward as it hooted and leapt across a gully, a pair of orange wingflaps stretching between its legs and little arms to complete the vault. Determined, Andy ducked his head and charged on. He jumped.

The space between ledges slightly farther than he anticipated, Andy's attempt at duplicating the stunt was unsuccessful. A loud SPLAT drew Veronica to the scene. She stopped at the ledge and peered below to see Andy face-down in a pile of mud. He lifted his head, thick globs rolling down his face. He blew the clumps away from his lips to try and speak but ended up hacking instead, and winced when he saw Veronica crossing her arms, expecting to be chastised. But instead of reprimand, he heard giggling. He stared up at her again, parting a curtain of visibility in his mask of muck.

"Wow, you're quite the athlete," she joked.

He muffled a quip inaudible through the slime.

Veronica laughed again and reached into the gully to help him up, "C'mon mud-face. I'm not done with you yet."

My fingertips ran over the leather cover of Murry's book of spells.

"Since you lost your reading material," he said.

I initially tried to protest the gift. "I can't accept this."

"I've read it many times," Murry assured me. "There're many good spells in there. *Old* spells. It's important they reach the minds of young spellcasters like yourself."

I thanked him.

"Speaking of whom," he went on, reaching for his fresh cup of tea, "we'll also need to find you a new wand. A spellcaster without a wand is like an artist without a brush!"

I laughed. "How'd the tea turn out?"

He took a taste and smacked his gums. "Splendid," he said. He gestured to the woods. "This place... Veindai is known for its medicinal plants." Noticing the dwindling fire, he pointed to our stack of kindling. "Pass me another log, would you?"

I reached, and without even thinking about it, a log from the pile glowed white and nearly knocked me over when it launched into my arms.

Murry's eyes grew wide, his pupils straying to scan the locale. "This place is rich with Ka as well..."

"We're back!" Andy announced. In his fist he clenched the body of a bird-like reptile by its neck, and Veronica followed with two others.

"Ah-ha!" Murry applauded. "I see the hunt was successful."

"Yep," Andy said. "These mothballs didn't know what hit 'em!"

"Mouvels," Veronica corrected.

"What's all that?" I asked, pointing to Andy's white T-shirt, which was caked in dirt and dried mud.

He stared down at the mess. "Uh..."

"Camouflage," Veronica answered for him. She smiled at Andy as the two unloaded their kills for Murry to prepare.

Dusk fell quickly on the cove, but our campsite remained aglow. I chewed on my serving of legmeat before the gentle, thalassic rumblings of incoming waves pulled my attention to the Vox Sea.

The sparkling expanse of indigo currents reflected a deep crimson sunset, silhouetting a flock of waterfowl as they cawed and soared inland to roost. A smile dithered on my features as I observed the sloshing breaks and fizzing sea foam, slightly bothered that the very waters that birthed the Kraicore were garnering my admiration. I shook my head at the puzzling duality, wondering how something so beautiful could be so deadly.

Scooter chirruped and scurried up to my shoulder, joining my lookout as I pondered the waves. A gentle sea breeze flowed over us, calming my mind as I breathed it in. A mixture of smells collected in the atmosphere. The herbaceous scents of the forest clung to the moist air, which merged with the smoke from the fire and our freshly-cooked meal. It was a nice aroma, until it coupled with a much less aromatic smell: one that was stale and fetid. My face twisted at the stench, and I plugged my nose and scanned the area in search of the source. I then realized Andy had removed his shoes and socks.

"Well, would ya take a look at these calluses!" he exclaimed, inspecting his bare feet in the glow of the fire. He held a foot up to Veronica. "Look!"

"*Ugh!*" she shouted, shoving his ankle aside and covering her nose.

"What?"

"People are trying to eat! Keep your stinky feet to yourself."

"My feet don't stink!" he shot back, pretending to be offended. "That's just testosterone, baby!" He turned to Boris who sat beside him, tearing meat from a bone. He lifted his foot to Boris' nose. "*You* don't think my feet stink, right Boris?" Boris sneezed and Veronica broke out in laughter. A coat of dribbling mucus smattered his foot. "Aw, nasty!" Andy traipsed off to the shore and shuffled around in the tide to wash it off, as Boris continued to snack.

"That's what you get," Veronica teased as Andy returned.

"Yeah, yeah." He patted Boris' shoulder. "Good one."

Boris snorted.

We finished up our meal, Andy, Veronica, and I laying out on the sand, while Murry retired to his shelter and Boris curled up for a rest. The last traces of sunlight flickered out on the horizon, and a curtain of clouds opened to present us the stars.

"Beautiful," Veronica stated.

"Thanks." Andy flexed.

She shoved him and we laughed.

"What do you think's going to happen?" I asked.

Veronica sat up. "What do you mean?"

I shrugged. "Everything. How's this all going to turn out?"

Veronica thought a moment. "I dunno," she said. "But I think it'll be up to us."

"For crying out loud, are you two getting existential on me?" Andy interjected. He pointed to me. "We gotta get some more of that tea in you, Marvin."

I laughed, "Shut up."

25

The Dark Elemental

Night rolled over to dawn, and the group gathered around the unfurled map.

"We'll head west," Murry declared, dragging his finger along the proposed path and landing on a mountain range labelled *Entohc*. "Now, once we arrive here, we must—"

A blast of wind folded the parchment as a vast shadow swept over us. I shielded myself from the clouds of grit that shot up from the ground, and when they settled, I beheld the source.

A dragon-like creature snaked through the sky, partly shadowed by sunlight. The animal possessed two front legs but lacked back legs, and by some wonder of adaptation it could fly without wings. When she landed I could make out finer details: a long, serpentine body covered in tan scales, tail barbed with a bony, diamond-shaped osteoderm. Long, angular ears rotated and flicked at us, and double-eyelids moistened a pair of green, reptilian eyes. The creature's head shook and nostrils flared, huffing like a horse would, before her rider dismounted a worn, leather saddle and approached us.

The rider was clad in ragged robes that appeared to have been white at one point, but had long since been discolored by ash, dirt, and what looked like dried blood. His face was completely concealed, wrapped in strips of bandage-like fabric. But through the eyeholes torn in the cloth, a pair of orange-red eyes blazed like fire.

As he neared us, the rattles of weapons pulled from holsters and sheaths sounded behind me. As if operating under a shared thought everyone armed themselves in unison. My hand went to my waist to do the same, but I was immediately reminded I had no weapon to draw. I clenched my fists.

The stranger strode forward, showing us his hands. "Do not be alarmed."

"That's far enough!" Veronica said, aiming down the rail of her crossbow.

His arms lowered as he slowed to a stop in the sand, his dragon hopping to his side on one leg with the other one curled up to her chest. The warrior removed his still-sheathed weapon from his belt and threw it aside, clattering out of reach.

"My name is Grimmoch. I am an Elemental."

"From which land?" Murry inquired.

"The Dark Lands."

Our stances held firm.

"I am aware of the connotation, but you must trust me—"

"Sorry, we haven't had the best luck with people in masks," Andy said.

Grimmoch thought a while, his flaming eyes diverting to search the ground. He sighed, then returned, "If it will earn your trust, I will show my face. But please, do not run from me." He uncinched a knot and unraveled the fabric that veiled his appearance. As the last of the material slid away, his gruesome countenance was revealed.

His face was like a skull. Black musculature was visible between the spaces in his external skeleton. Thick, dagger-like teeth lined his jaws, and within the shade of his eye sockets, two flaming spheres watched our reaction.

Reading our astonishment he spoke, "Expecting a handsomer visage?" He let out a somber laugh, then sunk back, staring past us into the distance. "My face is not my own," he asserted. "It is the face of Shamaul's malice."

Veronica lowered her crossbow and stepped forward tentatively, sympathy softening her gaze as she studied his features.

"How did Shamaul do this to you?" she asked.

"Simple," Grimmoch responded. "I am his son."

Another wave of shock pulsed through us. The news should have launched a thousand questions, but we remained standing there, frozen, until Murry stepped past us.

Grimmoch noticed his approach and started to clarify, "I swear to you, I do not align myself with him—"

Murry hugged him.

"Grandson," he said.

Embers popped and sizzled as the fire pit reignited, drawing us into cross-legged sits to listen to Grimmoch's words. The Elemental rotated his wrist until the flames reached a height that he considered suitable, before he joined us by the warmth.

"I have taught myself new spells," he said. "I learned them from an old set of books in my father's..." His eyes strayed as he sighed and lowered to the ground. "...library."

"What sort of spells?" I asked.

"The ones which create light."

Beside the glow of the fire pit, diminutive flecks of sheen glittered between the threading of the Elemental's white robes. The platinum reflections activated my wonder. I couldn't tell whether they were an effect of the material or perhaps some type of enchantment. Tracing my stare, Grimmoch commented on them:

"These robes, they belonged to a paladin. One of the brave Ka wielders who constructed the Dark Lands barrier long ago, I wager."

He touched the frayed edge of the discolored, silken garb. For a brief moment, I sensed a flittering force ripple from the cloth.

"I will go to any length to buffer my father's influence." Grimmoch's eyes blazed between thoughts. "To keep the darkness away."

Grimmoch's dragon limped over, sliding into a lay beside Boris.

"What breed of dragon is she?" Veronica asked curiously.

Welcoming the change of topic, Grimmoch replied, "A windserpent. Her name is Kail."

Veronica rubbed the reptile's snout. Kail shut her eyes and cooed. A grin tugged at my features, watching the creature's dog-like amiability, then faded when I noticed she was coddling her left leg.

"Is she hurt?"

"Her leg is broken. We have been on the move so long, she has yet to heal properly." He lowered his head, a tiredness resurfacing. "I've tried all manner of healing spells and medicinal plants. I believe I have warded off infection, but I can tell she is still in pain."

I slid closer to the windserpent to examine her broken limb. Reaching into my pocket I retrieved the talisman Captain Cyrus had given me, the blue jewel twinkling as it twirled on its chain.

"What is that?" Veronica asked.

"A healing stone," Grimmoch breathed.

"Captain Cyrus gave it to me," I said. I looked to Kail, then to Grimmoch. "Would it be alright if—"

"Please."

Following Cyrus' instructions, I clenched the talisman in my fist, and the stone shimmered and released dust. The sparkling, blue grains slipped through my fingers, spiraling in the atmosphere. They landed on Kail's leg and seeped through her scales. Stirred from rest, the windserpent sprang up, ears twitching as she set weight on her foot. She was healed.

I turned the talisman over in my hand. The central gem had shrunken slightly; the golden axes on which it poised were more visible. Vitalized with a new energy, Kail let out a roar and took off, sweeping through the sky above us. Grimmoch watched his steed's acrobatics in revelry and expressed his gratitude.

We proceeded to exchange stories, Andy and I relaying how we arrived in Enkartai and Grimmoch detailing his escape from the Dark Lands. As Grimmoch talked I tried to determine his age. I figured he was a young adult, but slightly older than Andy and me. However, the diction he used conveyed a wisdom indicative of someone much older. The Elemental spoke at length about the state of the Dark Lands and the horrors within its walls. But mostly, he spoke of Shamaul:

"In his isolation, he has become obsessed with a cosmic energy—something which he first attributed to a particular lineup of stars, then later presumed to be from an extra-celestial entity. He believes traces of this energy would imbue him with the ability to break his curse and pierce the seal of the Dark Lands."

"Well, it worked," Andy interjected.

"What do you mean?"

"We saw him," Veronica said.

"He killed our friend," I voiced.

Grimmoch paused. "I am very sorry." He watched the rolling, noontide waves for a moment, then lifted his head and went on. "Whatever this power is, and wherever its origin lies,

Shamaul wishes to harness it. That is why he desires the Orb. He believes it can bring him there."

Tightness formed in my chest as Grimmoch's flaming eyes returned to us, flaring with urgency. "If you saw him, the barrier must have been destroyed. It is only a matter of time."

"Before what?" I asked.

"Before he assembles an Orb of his own, and you are trapped here."

The tightness rose up to my throat and knotted. "What do you mean 'trapped'?"

"The Orb is anomalous. I do not fully understand it." The Elemental examined us seriously. "But what I do know is that the reaction between the crystals—" He interlaced his fingers. "The force which draws them together—It is strongest the longer they have been separated. It takes cycles for this energy to return. Without it, a new Orb cannot be formed."

Andy started, "So... what you're saying is—"

"If Shamaul constructs the Orb before you, you will be confined here for a long time."

Andy and I exchanged troubled looks.

"He must not succeed," Grimmoch reiterated.

"*No pressure*," Andy murmured.

Murry stood. "Then we should hurry." He rallied us along. "If we leave now we can make it to the mountains—"

"Those mountains have been mined," Grimmoch interjected. "You must go to Xeev City."

"Xeev City..." Murry opened his map to search for it.

"Yes. The Ka Master Orin will direct you to your next crystal. I would fly you there myself, but Kail cannot carry all of you," Grimmoch said, mainly referring to Boris. As his windserpent touched down, Grimmoch mounted her saddle. "I have business there as well. I will inform the council of your arrival," he promised.

We said our goodbyes, and before he took flight the Elemental told us, "Follow the copse of trees that bear green fruit; they will guide you there." Then, he flicked the reins and took off.

I found myself staring at the water again. The sun was nestled in a bed of golden clouds. Its shine sparkled atop the crests of waves, which reflected the warm colors and released soothing rumbles. Between the calming sounds, however, a slideshow of dreadful images flashed in my mind:

Shamaul's face. Zyvin's body.

I clenched. But just as our footprints were swept off by the tide, so was my trepidation, and I was left with a peacefulness to which I was unaccustomed.

It was a disturbing calm at first. I almost felt as though I *had* to worry, as though it was unnatural, and inappropriate for me not to. And with the news that our window of time was narrowing it seemed only fitting. Yet, I was serene. As fast as the stress threatened to take over it was subdued.

It was a necessary calm, I realized. Veronica and Andy appeared on either side of me.

"Ready to go, man?" Andy asked.

I started to nod, when Murry called from behind us, "One moment!"

The wizard lifted a stone that he had been carving. We parted as he stepped to the water's edge and planted it in the sand, and then stepped back with him to observe it. There was a single word carved in it, scribed in an archaic, unfamiliar alphabet.

Andy asked him, "What does it say?" and I wondered the same, until my gaze drifted below the word to an illustration of a wolf's face, and the question was answered.

It said: "Zyvin."

26

Kardaac Forest, Veindai

The tree trunks twisted and branches wove around each other into helix-shapes. The green fruit they bore resembled papayas and their glossy, diamond-shaped leaves began to rattle whenever unseen forest creatures would scamper through the ceiling of verdure, snapping off and spiraling to the ground like tiny propellers. They were infused with scents akin to citrus blossoms which seemed to attract the likes of all jungle dweller.

A small bird maneuvered amid the downfall of spinning leaves, hovering just a few inches above me. It looked just like a hummingbird save for its four wings, blue feathers, and extra plumage decorating its tail. I found myself staring at the bird for a long while, until Andy, noticing my fascination, interposed, "Are you thinking about Alison?"

His question took me off-guard. "No," I lied.

His eyebrows arched skeptically.

"Maybe," I admitted.

"Knew it."

I stifled a laugh. "What gave it away?"

"*Please.* Your eyes were practically turning into hearts."

"Right."

"Hey, when you're friends with a guy who's as stuck in his head as you are, you learn to read minds." He slapped my arm jokingly.

"Who's Alison?" Veronica chimed in.

"A girl Marv's into." He pointed at me. "I *swear* if you don't ask her to prom—"

"I'm working on it!"

"Uh-huh."

"*You* don't have a date to prom yet, either."

"Hey, hey whoa! Don't turn this around on me."

"You know, I hear the 'Acy Sisters are available..."

Andy's face dropped. "You're joking, right?"

I laughed.

"What's an 'Acy?" Veronica asked him.

"A babbling creature that never shuts up."

"Oh, sounds like a perfect match!" she teased.

Andy slipped his hands in his pockets and shrugged. "*Eh.* Not what I'm looking for."

"Yeah?" Veronica's stare steadied on him. "What qualities are you looking for?"

"Oh, y'know... Smart. Pretty. Good with a crossbow."

She shoved him.

Andy chuckled, ducking under tall, ferny fronds that dripped moisture from their spade-shaped leaves. "I feel like I'm walking through your apartment, Marv," he joked.

Veronica and Murry looked confused. I explained, "My mom has an indoor garden."

"It's more like an orchard," Andy said. "And she has these bayberry candles that she keeps lit year-round—"

"Okay, well what about your dad's Celtic collection?" I teased. "That chandelier with shamrocks hanging from it... what did he call it again?"

"Don't go there, Wessel—"

"A sham-delier?"

"Alright, alright. Truce!" Andy laughed.

We continued through the arboreal tunnel, the path winding and narrowing as we ventured, with new variations of flora and fauna emerging before my eyes. A viridescent insect flew past my face to nestle in the whitish petals of a flowering shrub. Its wings flittered as it fidgeted, then zipped off when the leaves shook suddenly.

The shrub uprooted itself on four insectoid legs. I gawked at it in disbelief, at first thinking the limbs actually belonged to the plant. I then noticed a pair of ovate, yellow eyes gleaming underneath. Secured to the flat, brown shell of a crustacean, the plant was carried to a more sunlit patch of land. The creature's tiny graspers emerged to pick several berry-like growths from the plant on its back before burying itself once again.

Amazing, I thought.

Every turn produced something I had never seen before, and I was excited to see what wonders lay ahead of us in the next clearing. Andy, however, was less enthralled by the wildlife.

"Grah!" he grumbled, swatting repeatedly at a dragonfly-like bug that buzzed about his face. "It wants my blood!"

"Stop swatting at it and it won't bother you," Veronica said.

Andy dropped his arms, still tense. The bug disappeared.

"Told you."

He panted, "I guess you're—"

The bug landed on him.

"Agh!" Andy shook it off and drew his sword, swinging at his tiny opponent. He slashed at the air. Veronica shouted at him and Murry attempted to dissuade his hysteric reaction, until Andy's blade cleaved into a tree trunk. The impact disturbed the surrounding foliage, and in the blink of an eye, a black blur sprang from the leaves with a rancorous snarl.

"Whoa!" Andy fell on his back, while his sword remained lodged in the bark and a beast landed before him, clawing dirt as it skidded to a halt and roared. A predator resembling a panther, jowls curling to bear fangs while a barbed, scorpion-like tail swayed behind it and poised, dripping venom.

Veronica hoisted Andy by his jacket collar, pulling him into our circle. Murry identified the cat as a *manticore* just as another pair leapt from the undergrowth. The wizard drew his wand, Boris his club, and Veronica aimed her crossbow at the ambush of predators that surrounded us, growling and clawing. One of the manticores eyed me hungrily and licked its chops. Needless to say, my interest in the wildlife had tapered off at that point.

Boris lifted his head and issued a challenging roar, and the manticores lunged. But before any strike landed, a violescent streak of electricity zigzagged through the wood, pinballing between assailants. Purple energy trailed a silver blur, which became distinguishable as a humanoid figure when breaking stride to deliver blows. Momentum carried his armored fists and knees into the bodies of our attackers with immense force, sending the manticores spiraling limply into the forest.

Within seconds, the fight was won, and the speedster stopped before us. He had a tall, slender torso and long limbs, all metal-clad. Purple energy that illuminated the spaces in his silver armor faded as he stepped forward at normal speed and assumed a strong, valorous stance. He observed us from behind a thin, dark visor that bisected his headpiece: a nearly-featureless, chrome helmet that crested backward in the shape of a shark fin.

Our stares shifted to one another, exchanging identical awestruck expressions. Andy finally broke the silence and addressed the newcomer:

"Uh, thank you?"

The warrior nodded, "Certainly," his voice crackling with an electric vuzz. "The Ka Master Orin has sent me to retrieve you."

We gave him our names and he introduced himself as Zax, the Elemental of Veindai. He gestured in the direction he came from and told us we'd be guests in a building called the *Spire*. The cadence in his speech suggested it was a place of great opulence and prestige.

But amid his explanation, I felt a tightness form in my throat. An unwarranted sense of dread that pulled my attention deep into the forest.

"You okay, Mav?" I heard Andy ask.

The feeling subsided. I shook my head. "Yeah, I'm—"

A loud crack sounded from the left. I snapped a section of branch off a low-slung tree and spun around, a bolt of lightning firing from the improvised wand into the body of a manticore in mid-leap, claws inches from Murry.

The fried cat flew sideways, and the wizard turned to me in shock. I gaped down the length of the steaming twig, chest heaving breaths and heart pounding. The rhythm skipped when something sharp dug into my shoulder, releasing my grip and collapsing my legs.

"Marvin!" someone yelled. Andy tore his sword from the tree and chopped through the tail of another manticore that had lain hidden in the brush behind me, the barb remaining stuck in my flesh. Boris roared and bludgeoned the feline with his club, killing it instantly, while I fell over on the ground.

Venom pumped into my blood until the severed barb fell out, and a scramble of bodies flowed around me in a haze of cloudy light. My vision blurred, and hearing could only detect the fizzing of blood in my burning shoulder-wound. The group deferred to Zax, the violet smudge I distinguished as Murry especially adamant. The figure approached. Silver hands reached for me and the last sensations I felt were those of being lifted and carried, and a flurry of wind. Then, my surroundings faded entirely, and I blacked out.

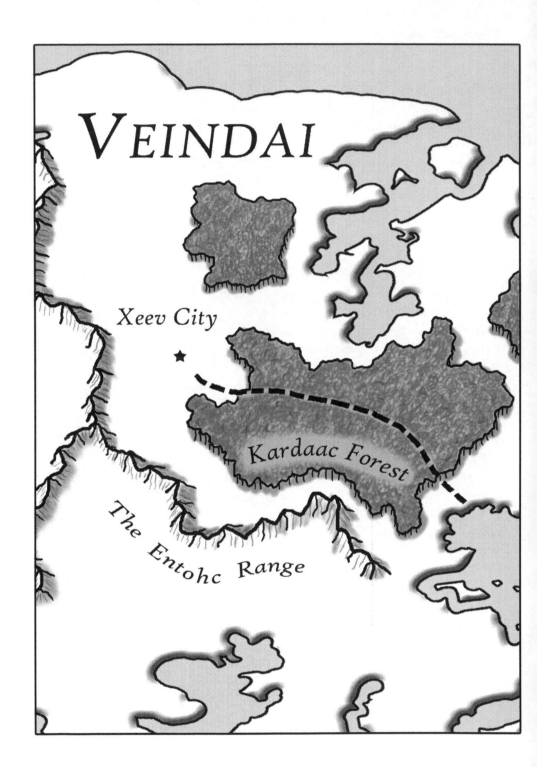

VEINDAI

Xeev City

Kardaac Forest

The Entohc Range

27
<u>Xeev City</u>

Somewhere between consciousness and delusion I felt myself floating. Or at least some part of me. I was initially unaware of how I arrived there: drifting through this dreamscape like leaves falling on water, converging on a central current to be swept off into the vastness.

What happened to me? Am I dying? Although this place had no walls or surfaces, everything echoed. *Where am I?* My own thoughts bounced back at me, sometimes in unfamiliar voices.

I had no idea how long I stayed there. This place had no time. But as a rush of ethereal breezes flowed over me, some of my worldly senses started to reactivate. Light flashed and softened to golden beams; somewhere in the distance my skin felt their warmth. And as if drawn to that sensation, I seeped back to reality.

My eyelids parted. Brightness overwhelmed my dizzied vision. I squinted and blinked away the sting as my surroundings came into clarity and I beheld a twirling blue charm. The talisman hung above me, pendant spinning on its gold chain, tangling, then spinning again in the opposite direction. A high ceiling stretched beyond it, affixed to stone walls of a warm, summery coloration. Flits of gold in the masonry reflected sunglow that spilled in from open windows behind me, which invited floral aromas to fill the small space as well, stirring me to fuller wakefulness.

As my head tilted in curiosity, I felt a plush material displace beneath it. A pillow. I was lying in an actual bed. My limbs went still with shock. *Had I returned to Earth somehow?*

My speculation cut short when something flicked my right ear.

"*Weird,*" someone voiced.

I rotated as much as I could.

"Hello?" I rasped.

No one. I turned back, then tensed up when a girl appeared on my left, peering over me.

She was a teenager, about my age. She was slightly shorter than me, with a snowy complexion and ocean blue, shoulder-length hair that parted around pointed ears and flowed lightly with the slightest of movements. Her bright eyes widened with jubilation as she watched me, her pupils tiny dots encased in sky blue irises.

"I heard you have a *giant* gash," she said. A disturbingly-excited grin spread across her face. "Can I see it?"

"Lael!" another new voice shouted.

She bounced backward in surprise.

"What are you—? Leave our patient alone!" A tall man with a considerably receded hairline and serious eyebrows took her by the elbow and pulled her from the room, as a woman stepped around them.

"Oh Guhlfrumn, she's just curious." She lowered to my bedside. "Please pardon my brother," she implored, her pretty face aglow with sincerity.

Guhlfrumn returned, muttering, "That girl is troublesome, Nietta."

"You and I got into a fair amount of trouble when we were her age."

"Indeed!" an older gentleman with a white-blue beard declared as he entered from the left. "I can attest; I bore witness to it!"

Guhlfrumn rolled his eyes and Nietta giggled. She touched my hand. "How are you feeling, young one?"

"I'm okay," I said, still very confused. They all possessed varying shades of blue hair that grew past their shoulders, pointed ears, and were dressed in long, flowing robes with golden decorations embroidered on the sleeves and trim.

No, I definitely hadn't returned to Earth, I determined.

"You remember your name, son?" the old man asked as he helped me into a seated position.

"Marvin Wessel."

"Good, good." He donned a pair of gold-rimmed spectacles that had multiple lenses attached to swiveling pins, each one slightly smaller and more convex than the last. "Now then," he said, the lenses all flipping down at once to magnify his sight. "Let's have a look at that shoulder, eh?"

I caught sight of Lael peeking around the doorway, trying to remain hidden as they pulled my collar down over my shoulder and unraveled a bandage, revealing pristine, unwounded flesh. Lael looked supremely disappointed.

Detecting her presence, Guhlfrumn shot a stern glare her way, and she promptly disappeared.

"Verdon, he's cured!" Nietta praised.

"Yes, but there was little for me to do," he admitted as he removed and folded his spectacles, then tapped the healing stone above my head. "This was on him when he arrived."

"How very fortuitous."

"Arrived where?" I finally asked them.

Their conversation halted, the three of them silent and puzzled as if the answer was obvious.

After a moment, Nietta leaned forward in her seat, grinning gently at me. "You are in Xeev City. Elemental Zax delivered you from the forest."

"You were stung by a manticore!" Verdon said, a little too zealously, before returning the talisman to my hands and folding my fingers over it. He pointed. "And it's a good thing you had *this* with you, because otherwise, hoh! You'd be—"

Nietta nudged him.

"Eh... *ahem*. No matter, though. Here." He placed Murry's spell book on my lap. I picked it up and looked it over.

Nietta went on, "You and your friends are our honored guests."

My head lifted immediately at the mention of my friends. "Where are they?"

Guhlfrumn and Nietta escorted me out of the infirmary and into an active street, where the group was milling about. When they caught sight of me they hurried over.

"Hey!" Andy rejoiced as he fake-tackled me. I exchanged hellos with all of them, intercepting a high-five from Andy as Veronica hugged me and Murry squeezed my shoulder. Boris raised his head and greeted me with a hearty snort, as Scooter leapt from his horn and adhered himself to my face. The cephalopod chirruped with glee and scampered over to my shoulder, his tentacles settling over the spot where my wound had been.

I petted his shell. "Good to see you too."

The reunion invoked a half-smile from Guhlfrumn before he composed himself and stepped away with his sister, allowing us to continue.

"How are you feeling?" Veronica asked.

"Good," I said, untangling the talisman's chain. "Thanks to this."

"Keep it safe," Murry advised. "You may need it again."

"Yeah, you've been spending a lot of time unconscious," Andy added.

I nodded, "Point taken," and slipped the chain around my neck and tucked it under my shirt, the metallic pendant clinking against my father's dog tags.

"Right this way!" Nietta called. She led us down the busy street, Guhlfrumn gesturing to the surrounding stately buildings and towering statues of lordly figures that lined the roads:

"Much of what you see before you is artifacts, lifted from the ruins of our former home."

"Like a museum?" I asked.

"A memorial," Nietta said. "An effort to resurrect the soul of our fair Eramir."

Guhlfrumn presented his hand to a staggeringly tall, needle-shaped structure in the distance. "The rest of the city is adapted from this new environment. A product of Eramiri ingenuity, and the ambition of Orin the Ka Master."

That was the second time I had heard that name.

"Who's Orin?" I asked.

Guhlfrumn's forehead wrinkled in stupefaction. "Who is Orin? Why, he's—"

"The weird old guy at the top of the Spire!" a voice interjected from above. Our sights lifted to see Lael lounging atop Boris' shoulder armor. The minotaur seemed to just now notice her. He snorted at his passenger charily, as the girl went on, "He's a real shut-in, doesn't get out too much."

"*Good gracious.*" Guhlfrumn rubbed his eyes. "Do you *not* have exams to study for?"

Lael shrugged. "*Eh.* They're going over stuff I already know today. Ka fields, transplacement..." She wiggled into her seat, her leg swinging languidly from her perch. "They should just let me graduate already."

Guhlfrumn muttered, "*Perhaps if you attended...*"

Boris flicked his ear as Lael proceeded to poke at him. "What *is* this thing?"

Veronica's lip curled.

Nietta intervened, "You mustn't bother our guests now, darling. They're weary."

Lael's eyes flicked right, intercepting Veronica's death stare. She returned to her original seated position, straightening up as if to slide off the minotaur's shoulder.

"I'm weary too," she contested, and then vanished in a puff of blue smoke.

My mind braced. *What the...?*

Suddenly, she reappeared in my arms. "Stress is a terrible thing, you know. Haven't *you* ever been in a stressful situation?"

I stared at her in disbelief for a moment, before garnering enough sense to talk. When my voice finally unlocked, I answered her, "Quite a few as of late."

"I knew *you'd* understand." She peered up at me unblinkingly, then grinned broadly. "I think we're connected..."

I glanced over her at Andy, whose finger made a swirling motion beside his head as he mouthed the word: *Psycho.*

The girl continued to stare at me for an uncomfortable length of time.

I started, "Well—"

"Sh!" she pressed her finger against my mouth. "I don't like goodbyes." She released my lips, then grinned again. "See ya soon, round-ear."

The girl disappeared into thin air. I let my arms drop to my sides, glancing over at my friends.

"That was odd."

"That was Lael," Guhlfrumn said.

"What sort of magic was that?" Murry inquired.

Nietta corrected, "Not magic. Ka."

"She's a talented girl," Guhlfrumn added. "Much too distracted to hone her gifts, however."

Nietta waved away Guhlfrumn's pessimism. "She'll have her entire adult life to worry about that." She stepped ahead. "Keep true, travelers! We're halfway there."

My sneakers clopped over the sand-colored, hexagonal stones which patterned the winding roadway. Every step brought me deeper into the amazing city and enhanced my sense of awe.

Equally rapt, Scooter chirruped and scurried from shoulder to shoulder, marveling at the surrounding wonders.

Flowering vines climbed up the bases of buildings, the stone bricks of which glittered like gold when struck with sunlight from the right angle. City folk emerged from balconies to air their linens and tend to elevated gardens. A pair of scarlet birds with blue and white chests trilled a song as they somersaulted around each other, like jets at an airshow, diving and weaving around giant arches which supported an advanced system of aqueducts that gushed with fresh mountain water.

A clanging bell caught my ear and I sidestepped from the path of a wooden carriage drawn by what looked like an oversized ram. The animal uttered a low, grunting bleat, and Boris returned a snort to it as the animal stomped by, bells ringing with every jostle of its cargo, impelling children to race from their homes, exchanging gold coins for sweets.

The Spire seemed to grow taller and taller the closer we came. Before long, we had arrived at the grounds of the edifice, and found ourselves immersed in the city's marketplace. It was the inverse of Alzo Village's bazaar. Rather than vying for patronage, the vendors sat back in their huts while lines of people amassed to survey their goods. Andy's eyes caught something in the distance and he spun around.

"Murry! Can I borrow some money?"

"Hm? For what—?"

"Pleasepleasepleasepleaseplease!"

Murry took out a sack of coins and picked out a few. "Good gracious, what is so urgent that—"

Andy grabbed the siv, "Awesome, thanks!" and took off into a small tent. Murry straightened out his cloak and composed himself, as our guides turned around, just steps from the Spire's entranceway. Murry cleared his throat.

"It appears we'll be taking a slight detour."

We entered a burgundy tent stocked with a large variety of sundries and unwittingly walked in on an argument.

"What?! Outrageous!" Andy balked.

A short, elderly vendor with thinning blue hair and a hunching stature slammed his fist on the table, shouting, "It'll be five siv pieces or no deal!"

"I won't pay any more than one for both of them!"

"That's robbery!"

"Fine, then!" Andy slapped two coins on the counter. "Two. But that's my final offer!"

"You know *nothing* of commerce!"

Guhlfrumn stepped in. "Mr. Fleeson, what's the matter here?"

"Him!" He pointed at Andy. "This round-ear's tryin'a tell me how to run *my* business!"

"This young man is an honored guest of Orin."

"Yeah, so suck it!" Andy chimed.

"He don't seem so honorable to me!"

"I apologize for the inconvenience, Mr. Fleeson, I—"

"Apologies! That's all your li'l committee's good fer, ain't it?"

"I'll have you know the council works very hard daily to ensure the security and maintenance of—"

"Political ballyhoo, that's all I hear!"

Pretty soon they broke into an argument of their own, and Andy backed away, scratching his head.

"What were you trying to buy anyway?" Veronica whispered.

Before he could reply, Nietta reached into a small pouch and dropped several coins onto the counter. "Will this cover it, Mr. Fleeson?"

The old man's jaw shifted pensively. He scooped up the money and counted out the difference, then nodded and exchanged the handful for a sack of items. Andy reached inside and pulled out his first purchase, a necklace with a sharp, fang pendant.

"Yes!" he laughed gleefully. He looped it over his head and showed it off to me and Veronica. "Eh? Pretty cool, right?"

Veronica rolled her eyes.

I examined the fang on the end of the knotted string and asked, "What type of tooth is that?"

Andy turned it in his fingers and shrugged. "Dunno."

"It's manticore," Mr. Fleeson said.

The group went silent, stares shifting awkwardly between me and the shop owner, who looked completely dumbfounded by our reactions.

"What now?" he asked.

Andy removed the necklace and returned it to the vendor's hands. "Too soon."

The old man boiled with rage and began to ramble incoherently, while Nietta and Guhlfrumn attempted to quell his outburst.

"*Oh, dear,*" Murry muttered, backstepping.

"We should probably go before he kills us," Veronica advised candidly.

I nodded and followed the crowd. Andy hugged his remaining purchase to his chest as if shielding it as he headed for the exit. Boris snorted and rotated toward the opening as well, his horns ripping the cloth ceiling as he moved, leaving behind a gaping hole. Mr. Fleeson gawped at the damage and stammered, his face becoming bright crimson. Nietta sighed and reached into her coin pouch again.

While amends were being made inside the tent, we convened outside. Veronica folded her arms and stood before Andy:

"Have you ever made a positive first impression?"

Andy shifted the sack in his arms, still simmering. "Well, he said he was gonna charge me extra because it was going out of season."

"What was?"

Andy reached into the bag and pulled out a jar filled with royal blue flower petals, then offered it to Veronica. Her eyes widened, arms unlocking as she took the jar with both hands and peered through the glass.

"That's the stuff you put in your hair, right—?"

She hugged him.

Nietta stepped outside, her features shaping a grin when she beheld the embrace. Guhlfrumn appeared soon after, muttering to himself.

"*Well that was a headache and a half...*" He pushed through the sagging doorway, his voice harshening when he addressed us. "I hope you're quite content with—"

Nietta nudged him with her elbow. His eyes rose, and his stern expression softened. Veronica released Andy, turning the jar over in her hands to further inspect the contents.

Guhlfrumn blew a sigh through his nostrils, then spoke, "Come along, now."

Each level of the Spire seemed to serve a different purpose. Large arching openings invited oceans of city folk to flow through to the main level, which felt mall-like with a vast array of shops and services open to the public. In the center of the mosaicked floor stood a tall, marble-colored statue of a bearded man, draped in robes and donned with jewelry. His left hand gripped a staff while his right one presented a crystal, and along the circular base was an inscription engraved in another alphabet.

When I asked Guhlfrumn what the inscription was and whose likeness the statue commemorated, he explained that the lettering belonged to the alphabet of an old language called *Trymbadorian*. He answered my second question by translating the epitaph, reciting, "*Jhemoore, most venerable, the last Ka Master before the collapse*," then spoke at length about how much of Jhemoore's original vision for the Eramiri people had endured over time.

Listening to Guhlfrumn's historic narration, we climbed a staircase that spiraled along the wall of the Spire, and from my elevated vantage I spied an elaborate mosaic of colored glass that stretched across the structure and shaped a map of the world. As I admired the artwork I reflected on our journey thus far, and although they were labelled in the fanciful, calligraphic alphabet I couldn't read, I recognized each landmass from our own map— Ravac, Frost, Veindai, Meisio, the Dark Lands—but in the midst of my inspection I came across an unfamiliar landmass: a teardrop-shaped microcontinent between Ravac and Veindai in the exact center of the map, the place I had known to be the Vox Sea.

But how? I wondered. The land was decorated the most opulently, stylized with golden rays around its coastline, and a ribbon about its southern shore that framed its name. I frowned, pondering, *Could that be Eramir? How could an entire continent vanish?*

My mind swirled with questions I didn't know how to ask, and before long the map had slipped from view and we arrived at the second level, where Eramiri were scribing and rescribing leather-bound documents and scrolls to be filed away in a sort of archival library that Guhlfrumn ardently deemed "all the world's knowledge," which Nietta quickly amended, "So far."

The next floor's occupants were just as busy, tinkering with odd-looking contraptions and gadgets, and in a distant chamber I could see a group of engineers working on something big concealed in a white tarp. A component of the project jutted out between the folds in the fabric: something I thought resembled the wing of an aircraft, but possessed the texture of stone. The most explanation I could gather from our guides was that it had belonged to Zax at one point, and we quickly carried onward.

As the circumference of the building began to narrow, we ascended levels more quickly, passing through spaces dedicated to studying, dining, and diplomatic discussions, along with off-branching outdoor walkways and balconies devoted to gardening and contemplation. Floors upon floors of living accommodations followed, my muscles burning with every step. Grunts of exhaustion sounded from the group as well, though our guides pressed on, unfazed.

"Are we there yet?" Andy wheezed.

"Very soon," Nietta answered.

When the space constricted to a solitary tower, lanternlight compensated for dwindling windows and illuminated portraits of Eramiri regality. Based on the paintings I began to conjecture what the Ka Master might look like. I imagined a tall, bearded figure with a wise countenance and a kingly visage, much like the statue I beheld on the ground level.

We filed into a dim, semicircular landing that barely accommodated our party. Nietta knocked twice on a small wooden door.

"Enter."

The door creaked open. Inside, the uppermost section of the Spire: a saucer-shaped ceiling topped the large, circular room, bisected by windows and edged with a widow's walk that overlooked the cityscape. A few overflowing bookcases sat against the walls, the floors stacked with additional volumes, scattered trinkets, and tools. And across from us, someone sat at a curved desk, vigorously scribbling on a sheet of parchment.

Guhlfrumn stepped forward. "Your guests have arrived."

Orin's head lifted, white, wispy hairs rising above the back of his chair. He swiveled to face us.

He couldn't have been more than three feet tall, with features similar to those of a bullfrog. Bushy eyebrows arched thoughtfully above yellow, ovoid eyes with rounded, cross-shaped pupils. His skin was bluish green and moist like an amphibian's, and the pudgy fingers of his tridactyl hands were webbed. Whisker-like hairs bunched together into a long, sloping moustache that stretched from the corners of his mouth to his waistline, around which a rope-belt cinched his beige robes. Tiny, pointed ears perked atop his head, the only feature of his that was remotely Eramiri.

Motioned onward by Nietta, we approached the Ka Master, who straightened up as we neared, fleshy neck puffing with air as his slit nostrils took a breath. We stopped before him, Andy and me at the forefront with Veronica, Murry, and Boris lined up at our backs. We stood for a few moments, no one saying a word.

Orin arched an eyebrow.

I exchanged glances with Andy, then extended my hand. "It's an honor to meet you, sir."

His nostril's flared and pupils dilated. He hacked and coughed.

I retracted. "Is something wrong?"

"*Blimey!*" he sputtered. "Great Aevæs!"

"What?"

"You!" He waved his three-fingered hand at us, shielding his nose with the other. "All o' you! Coming in here smelling like Aquimaar swamp gas. *Fuff!*"

We looked down in unison to inspect our dirty, discolored clothes. Andy smelled his pits.

Orin went on, "Where'd you manage to find all o' that filth?!"

"Uh..." Andy scratched the back of his head. "A bunch of places?"

"Out!"

The door slammed behind us.

"*First impressions...*" Veronica crooned as she pressed her back against the wall and slid into a sit beside Andy and me.

"Not our strongest quality," I said.

"I don't smell it!" Andy attested.

Guhlfrumn and Nietta joined us in the hall shortly after. Guhlfrumn sighed and shook his head, pinching the space between his eyes.

"What did he say?" Murry asked.

"He said... you have 'offended' his nostrils," Guhlfrumn recounted.

"Harsh," Andy said.

"He insists you not speak to him again until you are clean," Nietta added. She and her brother returned to the stairs. "If you would follow us to the main level—"

"The main level?!" Andy bawled. "After we climbed *all* the way up here we have to go back *down* again?"

Guhlfrumn tried to explain, "We apologize for the inconvenience; Orin is... very particular—"

Nietta interjected, "The bathhouse is located on the lowermost level of the building, you see—"

"Waitwaitwaitwait," Andy raised his hands. "Bathhouse?"

"Yes."

"You mean... with running water?"

"Yes, of course."

Andy stood up. "Lead the way."

28
A Moment's Rest

Clutching the handgrip of a sliding panel on the wall above me, I tugged right, releasing a cool waterfall that cascaded through a lattice grate and stripped away layers of residuum from the many stops of our lengthy journey. I knew the most trying parts of our adventure were still to come; the looming specter of Shamaul still clawed at my subconscious. But just as my body was rid of impurities, so was my mind, and the rushing waters carried off my timorous thoughts.

My hand traveled along the smooth tile wall to locate a chain pull-lever with a wooden handle. Pulling down, I heard a whoosh of flame from someplace unseen, and steam filled the stall. I huffed a couple times, shaken alive by the sudden change in temperature, water just below scalding, then scrubbed my body with a handful of leaves that I was told would seep cleansing oils.

Feeling renewed, I drew the curtain and stepped outside. Plumes of vapor trailed me to thicken the haze of my blurry vision. I wiped away droplets of water that clung to my eyelashes, felt around for the cubbyhole in which I stored my glasses, and once they returned to my face I beheld an Eramiri woman standing in front of me. I went rigid and covered myself, although the dense fog already concealed my lower half. She just smiled, presented me with a towel and provisional linens, and then walked off, carrying my collared shirt and khaki slacks with her. I gulped as I watched my only set of clothes disappear, then stepped into the leg holes of the braies.

I ran into Andy in the center of the bathhouse, clad in the same unusual undergarments.

He chuckled, "We look like we lost half our costume for the renaissance fair."

I agreed, pulling at the poofy, white fabric. "They're not the most flattering pants in the world."

"Looking good, boys," Veronica called from a massage table.

Andy struck a body builder's pose for her and she laughed. He nodded to me. "Let's roll."

The two of us strutted toward the center of the bathhouse, discovering a row of circular tubs recessed into the floor, piping steam. We came across one that was unoccupied and hopped in.

"*Ahhh.*" Andy tucked his hands behind his head. "This is the life, huh, Marv?"

"Absolutely." I rested my elbows on the brim and sank into my seat as a red-robed Eramiri passed, dropping a handful of pearls in the tub that fizzed when they hit the water and formed an aromatic layer of foam. We thanked her as she departed.

While we lounged, I peered through separations in the fog at our teammates. Veronica lay on a table as a masseuse kneaded her shoulders; to the left of her, Murry seemed to have gotten a similar treatment before he fell fast asleep; and across the chamber Boris received the best treatment by far, a team of four Eramiri lathering his fur coat, with two others waxing his horns and thoroughly scrubbing his hooves. The minotaur's nostrils grunted and his eyes blinked drowsily as fingers ran over his brow and massaged his crown.

Scooter scampered over to me, enlivened tentacles slipping over the slick floor as he slid to a stop by my right elbow. The hexapoid chirped and made a few circles, as if to show off his newly polished shell. I petted him.

"So what do you think?" Andy asked, his tone suddenly more serious.

"About what?"

He lifted his chin to the bathhouse's concave dome ceiling, inside of which a mural depicted green mountainsides and shining purple crystals.

I rested my head on the back of my seat. "I was trying not to, honestly."

"The crystals grow on mountains, right? Mountains aren't as bad as snow monsters."

"I don't..." I searched the currents, then shook my head. "I don't know."

"As far as I know they've all been mined," someone new chimed in. We turned right and saw Lael bathing beside us, splashing water over her arms. "All the ones that're easy to get to anyway. Only Orin knows where the rest are; you should ask him."

"That's what we're trying to do," I explained. "He said he wouldn't talk to us unless we were clean, though."

"Where'd you come from?" Andy interjected.

Lael looked off. "Well, my dad's from the Tzatir and my mom—"

"I mean just now."

She shrugged. "I don't know what you're talking about. I've been here the whole time."

"Your hair is dry," I noted.

She dunked herself. "No it's not."

Andy and I exchanged glances.

Lael went on, teasing, "Unlike the two of you, I naturally smell good. I just like the water." Her knee lifted from the foam. "It clears my mind, helps me think." She flashed a grin at me. "Helps me focus on what I want."

I laughed nervously and whispered to Andy through a fake smile, "*This is getting uncomfortable.*"

"*Getting?*"

Lael's foamy leg stretched skyward before she rested it on her other knee. Andy turned around.

I let out a nervous laugh as I talked to the back of his head, "*I could use your help here.*"

"*No can do.*"

"*Why not?*"

"*I gotta maintain eye contact with Veronica to prove my loyalty.*"

"He's right," Veronica called.

"*Just change the subject or something.*"

My eyes returned to Lael, who seemed to take pleasure in my discomfort.

"Are you alright?" she asked, her leg dipping back under. "You look bothered."

"Hm? Oh, no no, I'm fine." I quickly thought of a neutral topic. "Uh... these underpants they make us wear are pretty strange."

"Oh, yeah," Lael leaned forward. "I hate how they always bunch up in the water."

I nodded along. "Mm-hm, yep."

"That's why I never wear them."

Andy and I stood up at the same time:

"*Ooookay.*"

"Time to get out."

"Yeah, I'm getting pruny."

"See ya later."

We exchanged awkward goodbyes with Lael and shuffled away, leaving her giggling to herself.

Sphira, I read. *The combustion spell. Capable of collapsing small structures.* I turned the page. Accompanying the description was an illustration of a spellcaster, knees bent slightly, wrist making a whirling motion as denoted by an arrow looping around his wand.

When I looked up from Murry's spell book I saw throngs of Eramiri moving silently and resolutely about the library, robes flowing behind them like ornate curtains as they found their stations, either for studying or scribing. Many of them occupied the table where I was sitting, unrolled parchment scrolls, and began to ink. When my desk began to overcrowd I decided I should find a new spot.

Flattening the wrinkles in the robes I had been allotted and checking the pocket in which Scooter was napping, I strode to the other side of the archive, passing by stacks upon shelves upon cases of literature. The unique blend of aromas that all old books have, the mysterious, oaky fragrance, the smell of impending discovery, hung in the air. I felt very at home here. In a small way, this familiar activity connected me to Earthly matters, even if the content of my reading involved magic words and spellcasting.

My feet carried me onto a balcony, the view of which was comprised of rooftops, treetops, and the stars. Serenaded by a nocturnal chorus of trills and chirps, I lowered into a chilled, metal chair and cracked my book again, studying the new spells.

"You are a Realmhopper," a crackling voice conveyed.

My attention was drawn out of the words and toward the Elemental standing beside me, gazing out upon the city. I hadn't even realized he was there.

"Realmhopper?"

Zax continued, "Circumstances plucked you from your Realm, deposited you in another."

I nodded.

"We are alike."

I shut the book as the hero removed his helmet. Metal latches on the back of his headpiece hissing as they detached, revealing his face. Although I had encountered countless unusual spectacles on my adventure, his countenance was the most otherworldly. His dermatoid scales were the color of tarnished gold. Moonlight refracted through the epidermis as he rotated. When he faced me, I realized his helmet mirrored the shape of his cranium, sharp and sloping like the top of a crescent. A single, ring-shaped optic receptor flared with a purple, gaseous substance as it floated to view me from within its large, ellipsoid socket. Below it, a pair of mandibles plucked at mouth-cords like a harpist—which, when gill-like structures on the sides of his neck flexed, produced his voice:

"It was a beautiful place, my Realm. Upon hearing stories of its prosperity, Orin named his city after it."

"That's amazing," I said.

"I advised against it. At the peak of its excellence it was swallowed by Czerrek the World Eater, a tyrannical being not unlike Shamaul."

My throat locked up at his recollection.

Zax gripped the railing, gaze sweeping over the city again. "Frailty is an unfortunate consequence of beauty. The world is like a precious gem. There are those driven to defend it. To safeguard its glory for all time." His head shot sideways, seeming to hear something I couldn't. "Others are driven to envy by it, swept up in a mad scramble for acquisition. To conquer it." His optic ring sparked. "To destroy it."

Zax's helmet returned to his face. "You are a defender," he affirmed. "Trust in Orin. He will aid you in your quest."

With that, the spaces in his silver armor glowed bright purple, and in a flash of the same hue he dashed over the balcony and disappeared from sight.

A rush of wind flowed over me, and I returned indoors. Losing my place in the spell book, I flipped to a random page, one which was bent-up and folded over on itself. I straightened out the paper and started to read, *Touric Enavelir...*

"There you are!" Andy appeared on my left, also wrapped in Eramiri robes. "Figured you'd be in the library."

"What's going on?"

"Orin's ready to talk to us apparently." He headed for the exit. "C'mon, let's go."

Andy took off and I followed, my pace slowing almost instantly as my eyes trailed to return to the words of the spell book.

Touric Enavelir, I read. *Arcane spell. Recited when banishing evil spirits.* My eyes scanned over a pair of illustrations that showed a figure raising a staff high in the air, then thrusting it sideways, emanating light rays. *Only known to have been performed by Ka Masters.*

"Come on!" Andy called.

Committing the magic words to memory, I shut the book and hastened my steps.

Our footsteps resonated through the cramped staircase and vacant hallway, the soft, orange glow of lanterns guiding our ascent. The door to Orin's quarters creaked open, and we waited in the ingress for Guhlfrumn to make our presence known. He leaned over the back of Orin's chair, whispering something that made the Ka Master pause his scribblings and motion for us to enter. Guhlfrumn repeated the gesture and we walked inside.

Orin kept his eyes on his work as we assembled behind him. "What'll it be, then?"

I deferred to my friends, who seemed to be waiting for me to say the first words.

I addressed him, "We're from Earth."

Orin's ears perked.

"Andy and I are. We're Realmhoppers."

Andy's brow scrunched at my use of the new term, but Orin swiveled to face us, engaged. "Yes, I am familiar with your kind—Zax, Areok—" He pulled at his long mustache. "What is your mission here?"

"Uh..." I looked at Andy, then back to Orin. "We're just trying to go home."

"Ah. *First-time* Realmhoppers I gather."

We nodded.

The Ka Master chuckled to himself, shaking his head. "Oh, yes. I've heard this story before." He rotated back around, opening a desk drawer stuffed with materials. "So you're after the Orb, then... the crystals?"

"We heard you know where to find them."

"*Mm-hm.*" He shoveled handfuls of crumpled-up paper from the drawer and scattered them along his desk, digging deeper. "*Le'see here...*"

"We have two of them already," Andy entered the discussion. He went on, trying to testify our merit, "We've been through it all—coliseums, creepy caves, sea monsters. We're seasoned warriors."

Orin lifted an eyebrow at him.

"So... y'know," Andy coughed, clapping his hands together. "We're prepared for whatever you throw at us."

"Here." He tossed a purple crystal to him.

Our jaws fell open. Andy turned the gem over in his hands, gawking at it in disbelief.

"Wait, that's it?!" he exclaimed.

Orin swept all the loose paper back into his drawer and shut it. "Yep." The Ka Master returned to his work.

Murry, Veronica, Andy, and I huddled around the crystal, watching sparks of power go off in its prisms. Andy looked up from the prize, still in shock.

"Seriously?!"

Orin glanced up from his writing briefly. "Hm? If that's too easy I can have you tidy up the place for it." He looked around the roomful of half-finished inventions and crumpled paper, then reconsidered. "Nah. For that much work you'd deserve a whole cluster o' crystals! I could never afford it." He waved us away. "Hop along, now."

As we headed for the exit, Orin pulled Guhlfrumn aside and exchanged words with him. The councilman cleared his throat, then navigated to the front of our group.

"Right this way."

Light danced through the prisms of the crystal, enlivening flecks of purple energy that charged, irradiated, arced, and reoriented, like the buildup of an electrical storm viewed through a kaleidoscope. I rotated the diamond-shaped stone in my hand, a white sheen running over the surface as lanternlight struck it from a different angle.

"How did this happen?" Andy said, more to himself than anyone else as he paced around the room he and I were assigned. "I don't believe it."

"I'm looking right at it and I don't believe it." Scooter climbed from my stomach to my shoulder as I sat up in my bed. "I don't believe I'm sitting in an actual bed right now."

"Yeah! That too!" Andy patted the plush mattress. "Or this!" He grabbed the lapels of his orange jacket, which he had changed back into. "They cleaned it! I don't even think it looked this good when I bought it."

I looked down at the threads of my green collared shirt; they too seemed more vibrant than ever before.

"You're right," I replied.

Andy continued to pace, his laps becoming shorter as he ran his hand back through his hair, frazzled. "I mean... I just—" He took a breath to compose himself. "First the bathhouse, now the crystal... they're spoiling us!"

I laughed.

"Seriously! I feel like, I'm just *waiting* for something to pop out at me."

"You rang?" Lael said.

Andy nearly hopped out of his skin when he caught sight of Lael reclined in our open window. "*Oh, geez,*" he muttered.

"So you guys got a place in the Spire, huh?" She took a stroll around our room. "Pretty nice. I'm not even allowed to be up here."

"You're really starting to scare me," I told her.

She smiled as though I had paid her a compliment. "Good," she said, warping just inches from my face. "You *should* be scared. *Whah!*" She crouched and threw her hands sideways, Ka opening every drawer and cabinet in the room.

A grin crept across her lips, awaiting reaction. I looked around, acknowledging the open drawers and dressers, then snapped my fingers and reclosed them all in a white flash.

Lael's arms went limp and mouth agape. Andy and I left the room nonchalantly:

"We should probably get this crystal to Murry so he can wrap it up with the others."

"Yeah, that's a good call."

"But... but..." Lael stammered, still awestruck.

We entered Murry's room, finding the wizard had redonned his cleaned, purple cloak. He stood before a floor mirror, wand in hand.

"Hey Murr, can we put the crystal away in the rucksack?" Andy asked him.

"One moment," he replied. He angled himself, his wand wavering, then rotated to a new position.

"So, are you taking up modeling or...?"

His eyes raised at Andy, then returned to the mirror. "I was going to duplicate a new wand for Marvin; his was lost at sea." Once he found the right angle, he shouted, "Renora!" and flung a yellow beam at the mirror. It reflected off the sleek surface back at him, but instead of engulfing the wand, the light swept over his entire body, and in the blink of an eye there were two Murrys standing in the room.

"What the—?" Andy hollered.

"That, was unintentional."

The duplicate Murry's head darted around the room like a frenzied bird's, eyes wild and unfocused.

"*Renora... Renora...*" it whispered over and over.

Guhlfrumn walked in, mouth parting to address us. But when he laid eyes on the disturbing spectacle he fidgeted and backed away.

"What are we going to do about this?" Andy questioned hysterically.

"Remain calm," Murry assured us. "It's only a shade, it'll fade away soon."

Right on cue, the copy became transparent, still uttering the word "*Renora*" as it disappeared.

Murry cleared his throat. "See?"

"That was creepy," Andy said.

"I've actually read it's a legitimate strategy for some spellcasters, as a sort of ruse to confuse opponents."

"He's right," Lael said, who was sitting on a crate in the corner of the room now. "You can never make a *permanent* copy of a living thing. But if you focus your Ka you can keep your shade

299

from disappearing for a while—even control its actions." She kicked her feet, proudly edifying us. "My teacher said it's like a physical shadow. The technique is called *semblance*. Watch."

Lael shut her eyes, clenched her fists, and gritted her teeth.

Murry started, "That's perfectly alright, dear, there's really no need for a demonstration—"

"Almost got it!" she grunted.

Guhlfrumnn reentered, hesitant at first. He glanced around the room for anomalies, then sighed in relief and reported, "The Ka Master would like to invite you all to the dining room for a lavish meal."

Veronica and Boris appeared in the hallway.

"Count us in," she said. She leaned against the wall, her hair tumbling over her shoulders, with blue petals lacing her tresses. A smile tugged at Andy's mouth as the two made eye contact.

"Excellent. I'll pass the message along."

A prolonged, strained squeal reached Guhlfrumn's ears and made him look around the doorframe, finding Lael clenched up on the box. He groaned and took her hand to escort her from the room, imploring that the rest of us meet in the dining room at our earliest convenience.

Murry looked down at his wand, then to the mirror. He shrugged. "Perhaps we'll just purchase you a new wand," he told me.

"Good plan," Andy commented. "No more of that freaky semblance stuff."

Lael's head peaked in between us. "Think he bought it?"

Andy shrieked.

29
A Lavish Meal

Lavish was an understatement to describe the food Guhlfrumn had alluded to. Rolls swathed in a buttery glaze; sweet, fruity tarts smothered in hot, tangy sauce made from wild berries; a chartreuse whip with flakes of pine green that smelled of mint and syrup; dark brown meatballs that oozed fatty juices, peppered with bright red spice; salads tossed with extraterrestrial-looking curled greens and spiraled sprouts, dressed with a piquant, auburn zest; and the centerpiece: a humongous roast from an unknown animal with marbled, crimson meat flaking off a round bone, rubbed with fresh spices and herb, its steam pumping out a hearty, gamey aroma. And that was just the first round.

I stared, awestruck at the mouthwatering expanse of food that decorated the elongated table, overwhelmed by the choices and unsure where to begin. But, as the aromas flooded in my nostrils and battled for supremacy, one scent stood out among the other combatants, and I chose my victor.

A slab from the roast gushed with juice as the prongs of my fork sank into it and delivered it to my plate. I passed the platter along to Andy, who had already begun assembling his sampler. He added a hunk of roast to the mix.

"I'm in Heaven."

Boris seemed equally content, putting away enormous quantities of food from nearly every platter. A pair of servers eventually designated themselves to exclusively cater to him, replenishing his plate and even feeding him directly by hand. The minotaur's blue tongue emerged to lap up remnant crumbs from his snout before a server's red cloth tidied up his lips and chin, and he uttered a gratified snort.

Scooter, too, was enjoying the meal; this time he was not merely the recipient of leftovers. Instead, he had his very own plate made especially for him, food cut into smaller portions more suited to accommodate his mouth, and he vacuumed up every helping unstoppably.

Veronica sliced into a rare piece of roast and popped a chunk in her mouth, her eyes rolling back in revelry. Murry, Andy, and I shared her enthusiasm for the dish. The meat was tender beyond belief, practically melting into meat-flavored butter as I chewed. And when I swallowed, its gamey, lamb-like aftertaste set my taste buds abuzz and incited my fork to spear more.

Guhlfrumn and Nietta joined us as well, with Orin sitting at the head of the table. A server presented the Ka Master with a bowl of broth.

"Excellent, thank you," he said. He blew away the steam and sipped from it. He smacked his gums with delight, then spoke to us, "How is it that you found yourselves here?" He leaned in. "How is it you discovered the Orb?"

Andy swallowed a mouthful and began, "We were on a field trip."

"A trip to a field?" Nietta said.

"No, not necessarily," I clarified. "It's a trip meant for educational purposes."

Andy tilted his wrist. "Debatable."

"*Anyway*, we found it in a museum."

"It was locked away in this dusty old room."

"But the door just swung open for us."

Orin, Guhlfrumn, and Nietta all sat forward in their seats, transfixed by our recollection.

"Then, when we touched it, *boom!*" Andy threw his arms open. "White light everywhere!"

"We woke up in a forest."

"That's where *I* found you," Veronica pointed.

"Yeah!" Andy said. "Like, right when we arrive we almost get eaten by this big turkey—"

"Furadon."

"Right. But luckily she was around."

"You owe me," Veronica joked.

We laughed, continuing to recap the tale. By this time, even the servers had halted their rounds to listen in on the conversation.

"I remembered the legend of Areok the Gold Knight, saw the parallels in their stories," Murry said. "I felt I could help them, felt I could..." His voice trailed off, rasping. He took a sip of hot tea. "...perhaps, make a positive change."

"You did," I told him.

He chuckled softly. "But," he went on, "what I didn't expect was how much *they'd* help *me*." He smiled at all of us, eyes misting. "I am privileged and honored to know these young people."

"Murry, you're choking me up!" Andy exclaimed. He pointed at the rest of us. "We have to group hug after this!"

We went on to share stories about Inuento Isle, Frost, the Ice Pirates, and the Kraicore.

"You truly *are* seasoned warriors," Orin said.

"How long do you plan on staying with us?" Nietta asked.

"Unfortunately, time isn't on our side," Murry replied. "We'll be on our way first thing in the morning."

"Well..." Andy looked down at his plate of food, swallowing. "*One* more day couldn't hurt, right?"

"One more day could compromise your mission," someone voiced.

Grimmoch entered the dining room. His tattered, stained robes had either been rejuvenated or replaced by pristine ones, embroidered with golden, interlacing designs around the trim. A long cape flowed fluidly behind him, the edges glinting with the same elaborate filigree. Once he lowered into an empty chair I noticed a symbol had been painted on his forehead. The icon involved a horseshoe-shape framing a single dot, which was crowned by three lines that resembled sunrays. I would later learn the symbol was called the *Eye of the Aevæs*. The rune glimmered with golden minerals as he nodded.

"Shamaul plots to assemble the Orb himself. I've just received word from Zax that he encountered gargoyles in the mountains."

"They're looking for the crystals," Veronica said.

"The mountains are picked clean. If those filchin' skyrats come across the slightest speck, I'd be surprised." Orin drank up the last of his broth. "Shamaul has an outdated perception of the world, on account of his imprisonment. Based on the story you shared I assume he thinks you're Kraicore bait by now." He sopped up the remnant stew with a halved roll. "Sure, he thinks it's smooth waters ahead..." He waggled his small fist in the air. "But there's a storm comin' for him."

"I *knew* there was something weird going on," Lael said from a branch outside the window.

Guhlfrumn became livid. "Young lady, this is a private gathering. You are not permitted—"

"Ah, Lael, come in," Orin said. He pushed out a chair with his Ka and she warped inside to seat herself. "I had asked her to help tend to our guests—keep watch over them."

Guhlfrumn looked flabbergasted. "R-Really?"

"*She's a little too good at her job,*" Andy whispered to me.

"Yep!" Lael straightened up proudly, pointing to Guhlfrumn. "That makes *me* your boss!"

"*Ehm...* no it doesn't, dear," Orin said. "As promised, though..." He clapped his hands, and the servers brought out platters for each of us, lifting the lids simultaneously to reveal a decadent-looking dessert.

"Schu-faun!" Orin called it. "Made from the milk of greatrams and berries picked from the northern glades. Enjoy!"

The dessert we were presented with was indulgent: dense, creamy whip served inside a shell spun from russet, sugary pastry and topped with dark red berry syrup. As the mixture bathed my taste buds in heavenly sweetness, full berries emerged from the suspension, popping into a gush of tang when I chewed. I tore a crisp piece of pastry from the shell and used it to scoop up more of the filling, the flavors harmonizing even more exquisitely with each bite.

Everyone promptly polished off their plates, and the dinner adjourned. Guhlfrumn and Nietta excused themselves from the table first, thanking Orin for the invitation before retiring for the night. I placed my hand on the table so Scooter could climb up my arm. He did so sluggishly, stomach full of food, and made a tired chitter as he settled down in his usual spot. When I looked up I saw that Andy, Veronica, and Murry had circled up in the center of the room.

Andy opened his arms to me, calling, "Get over here, Marv! I wasn't joking about the group hug thing y'know!"

I heeded the call and we all clumped together and hugged. Boris stomped in behind us last, his massive arms wrapping around the entire group as he squeezed, snorting affectionately. Everyone grunted. Veronica laughed.

"*So much love,*" Andy squeaked.

Boris released us and we all began to file out, but before I made it to the exit, Orin called my name. Since Scooter was drifting off to sleep, I handed him to Andy and said I'd catch up, then returned to the Ka Master.

Lael was whispering something to him as I approached. He nodded in thanks and exchanged goodbyes before she looked at me knowingly and vanished. I approached Orin and knelt to his height as he smiled.

"You're a brave lot," he nodded. "More'n any travelers I've encountered since the time of Areok."

I thanked him for the compliment.

He nodded again, squinting in thought, then tilted his neck to the side as a signal for me to follow him.

I trailed, as he ambled from the room and onto an outdoor walkway, where nocturnal insects awaited to herald our arrival to the nighttime milieu. There, Orin's astute stare rose to meet mine, his yellow eyes shining luminously through the darkness.

"So, I understand you're a Ka wielder..."

30

The Ka Master

The glow of moonbeetles speckled the night, their tiny bodies igniting with a unique, blue luminance as they hovered closer, inspecting me curiously before floating off like candles in the fog. The forest adopted supernatural tones beneath Enkartai's twin moons and, although the city's populace was already fast asleep, this winding pathway was alive with starlit splendor.

"You spoke a bit about accidents before," Orin said.

It took a second for his words to reach me; I was too deeply entranced by the breadth of bioluminescent creatures and nightblooming flora to absorb his statement.

I finally broke free. "What was that?"

"Your story. How you and your companion found yourselves here. Found the Orb."

"Oh, yeah," I rejoined. "It all sort of happened by accident."

"Most things do," Orin stated. "That's why I tend to think quite highly of happenstance."

We pushed through the brush, continuing along a placid stream that rippled softly and reflected starlight.

"What do you mean?"

"We're here, aren't we?" he chuckled.

I still didn't grasp his meaning.

When he sensed my confusion he expounded, "So many things had to have gone right and wrong for us to be here, talking, on this night. How carefully planned those accidents must have been. How perfectly timed those coincidences."

He hopped along the stones of the streambank, not breaking stride. "Only once you've reached your destination and embraced your destiny can you look back upon the trail, and see the purpose of every twist you encountered along the way."

He passed freely under a low branch that I had to duck for.

"That's when it all becomes clear," he told me.

Greenery parted to behold a circular clearing edged with rocks and flowering shrubbery. What looked like a long-extinguished fire pit lay dormant in the center of the ring, and my assumption was proven accurate when the frog-like teacher levitated a bundle of new logs atop the smoldered, gray ash. He opened his webbed hand, a sphere of white Ka forming above his palm.

He whispered into the light, "*Inferna.*"

The energy turned red and conflagrated. He chucked the fireball into the wood, a loud *fwoosh* sounding as it caught, then sat cross-legged by the warm, orange glow and invited me to sit.

I joined him. Expecting more sage words to be exchanged I sat patiently, warming my hands by the blaze, but for a long while Orin just stared quietly ahead, the dancing flames reflecting off his bluish green scales and casting shadows down his wise features.

When he finally spoke, his words were methodical and precise, "Tomorrow I will bring you to Meisio. The penultimate crystal you seek resides there, in a volcanic region known as Vulcra. The Elemental Erah knows those parts better than anyone else. I will task Grimmoch with locating her to help you."

"Thank you," I said.

Orin nodded. "Beyond that," he went on, "the Dark Lands will present you with your greatest challenge. Within its borders, in a ravaged battlefield left frozen in time, stands a structure of my own design, called the Mesalon."

In the soil, Orin drew its likeness with the point of a twig: five curved beams intersecting in the form of a dome with diamond-shaped cutouts inside each one.

"It was created to safely combine the energies of the five crystals." His yellow eyes lifted to mine. "This is the same structure Areok used to return to Earth."

I swallowed dryly, listening to every word.

He scratched at the ground with the twig, his tone dropping to a more severe cadence as he continued, "Your adversary will be merciless when you find him. Shamaul will not relinquish the final crystal willingly."

A new picture formed in the soil: an image of warriors with swords drawn, and an imposing figure atop a hill. Swept up in the white glow of Ka, the illustrations began to move on their own, doing battle with the enemy.

"I have no doubt that destruction is a component of creation. That loss is a component of gain," Orin said, as the image in the ground was swept away by stray breezes. "But this is a mission that mustn't be failed. Every step you take across our world will be the influence of our historians. No detail overlooked, no angle uninterpreted. You, Marvin, were meant to be here."

My chest tightened and throat knotted at the deluge of praises I wasn't sure how to accept.

Orin mused, his eyes searching the patterns in the flames. "I can sense it," he asserted. "Your destiny is reaching out to you."

"How do you know?" I asked.

"I don't. You do."

"What do you mean?"

"It's there in your Ka. Your noble path—right there, outlined for you. To decipher this message is the vocation of all heroes."

I laughed at his assertion. "I wouldn't call myself a hero—"

"I wouldn't call myself a Ka Master!" Orin quickly rebutted. "But that's the title that comes with the job, now, isn't it? Tell me..." He hopped up on a rock to reach my height. "If the winds of destiny are blowing, you lift your sails, correct?" He leaned in, awaiting my answer.

I tensed up at his sudden intensity. "I guess so?"

Orin's face scrunched. "You are defiantly modest, aren't you?"

He descended from the stone and strolled to the outer edge of the clearing, his webbed hands clasped at his back as he stared at the stars. Then, he turned to me, eyes aglow, and recited words that would be emblazoned in my mind forever:

"All the world is elements," he spoke. "Elements in their righteousness and depravity..."

Water, weather, land, fire. Orin gestured grandly to the facets of the nighttime jungle which contained traces of the elements he spoke about: the stream, the sky, the ground, our fire pit. With fervor, the Ka Master elucidated me on the inherent dichotomy of each element's properties—their capacity for use and misuse—and I absorbed every word of it.

"Indeed, these attributes have spilled into other worlds, invisible to our own. Separate, and yet connected. All the worlds are elements. And we, we are the greatest elements of all, because we can choose our own power. Directed by light or deceived by shadows. The path you take is up to you."

"How will I know which path is right to choose?" I felt myself say.

Orin smiled. "Your path has already chosen *you*," he explained. "It is the noble, virtuous path that chooses us all. All you must do, is decide to follow it."

With that, the master raised himself, stretching, and made his way from the clearing. I asked him why he was leaving so soon, and he said the outing was never meant for him, but for me to discover *Omni-Ka*. Naturally, my follow up question was for a definition of the new term, to which he chuckled.

"Your power," he clarified. "Omni-Ka is a state of connectedness with all of the Ka signatures around you. It imbues you with strength, heightens your foresight, enhances perception..." Orin was already gone from the clearing, continuing to call out the list as he returned to the trail. "Imparts experience... wisdom! It's the staple of any good Ka Master. I find it's best to meditate beforehand..."

His voice became fainter and fainter as he departed, and I was left sitting there, alone in the middle of a forest.

This is an unconventional teaching method, I thought.

I had so many questions that I wanted to ask regarding Omni-Ka, but since the last bit of audible advice Orin gave me was to meditate, I decided it was the best course of action I could take to uncover the answers.

Seconds changed to minutes, minutes to hours. I felt like a rock in a stream as time flowed over me. A dewy film formed on my skin and condensation dripped from my glasses as the night went on. I became hyperaware of my own breathing as well. In and out. Long, shallow breaths. My consciousness drifted, and images began to cycle through my mind: raucous classmates on the school bus, laughter and shouts, Alison, a wooden door creaking open for me, an immense white flash, Alison again.

Although my eyes were closed that whole time, the environment shined through in different ways. As my heartbeat sent shockwaves through my body, Ka lifted off my skin in unison, tracing the trees and the stream and the trail and the Spire, inside of which I sensed Andy, Veronica, Murry, Boris, and Scooter resting, their content breaths rising in harmony with the calm, quiescent energy of a city asleep.

A sudden flux of Ka indicated life close by, and my eyes shot open to behold it: the hummingbird-like creature I had seen before, its feathers glowing bright blue. It cocked its head as it viewed me, then hovered to a shrub at my left that bore flowers which matched its plumage. As its slender, black, needle-shaped beak drank the nectar, the glow of its feathers intensified, and the flower petals tumbled to the base of the plant to enrich the soil with nutrients necessary to produce future blooms.

An entire flock of them gathered. *Glowbirds,* I somehow knew they were called. They drank up the nectar to attain their radiance, then grouped together and circled me. The tiny birds picked up speed, cycloning about my body as the world pulsed with dreamlike, golden light. When the ethereal flock broke formation, I remained fixed on the first of the creatures to catch my eye; how I managed to distinguish it from the others was beyond explanation. It ventured skyward, through a separation in the rustling forest canopy, before vanishing from sight, leaving behind a view of the stars.

A grin spread across my face as I observed the celestial wonders twinkling above, and in that moment I heard the voices of doubt and worry submit to those of gallantry. They faded to mere echoes in the vastness that held no credence, I realized.

These floating themes, vying to be sequenced into thought, could not achieve fullness within the beams of contentment warming my heart. And whether an effect of my sudden tiredness or some other power, the stars of the night sky appeared to shape a constellation in the likeness of a proud man's smile. I wiped a stream of tears from my cheeks, a feeling of sweet somnolence washing over me, lifting me to my feet, and carrying me back to the path.

31
<u>*Departure*</u>

Morning's warmth and gentle breezes lured me from rest. My arms and legs stretched out amid a soft, pillowy envelopment. Bedding. I hardly remembered returning to my room last night. Rolling onto my back I nearly succumbed to its silken embrace, but as suntones shone through my closed eyelids and mild winds buffeted my hair, my reluctant muscles reactivated.

One hand traveled to search for my glasses while the other opened the sheets. *Today we leave for Meisio,* I reminded myself, knowing the longer I lingered there the harder it would be to abandon Xeev City's luxury. So, with my glasses redonned I sat up to start the day, only to find myself nose-to-nose with Lael.

"Morning, round-ear!" she beamed.

The shock subsided quickly when a yawn surfaced and escaped my lips. "Good morning," I greeted her groggily. I pulled my legs in and rotated to get out of bed.

Her face squinched. "That's it?" She hopped up to follow me as I rubbed my eyes and found the mirror. "I was hoping you'd scream or something."

"Sorry to disappoint." I wiped the sleep from my eyes and adjusted my hair. As Lael peeked over my shoulder, I noticed her brow slanting in the reflection.

"Are you leaving?"

I nodded. "Have to."

Her gaze strayed to the floor, her sandaled foot drawing an invisible circle-shape on the boards.

Sensing her woe, my throat knotted. I swallowed hard and returned to the mirror to flatten a stubborn curl that kept popping up. I changed the subject:

"Do you know where everyone else is?"

"They're down in the range. Waiting for you I think." She strolled to the window and leaned. "Yep, I think they're still there."

I had no idea where this place was.

"Can you take me there?" I asked. I immediately regretted my choice of words when a devilish grin stretched across her face.

"You got it!"

"Oh, wait, hold on—*OOF!*"

She tackled me. In a wild spin of blue vapors we tumbled across negative space, blasted through a tunnel of energy, and reappeared outside in a cloud of the same blue fog. We landed in a heap.

"*Weehoo!*" Lael hooted. "I'm so glad that worked, I've never taken anyone with me before!"

I wobbled to my feet. Dizzy, I reached to touch my head and discovered all of my hair was standing on end.

"Oh, wow..." Lael said. She licked her hand and flattened the curl I was brushing down moments ago, leaving the rest afrizz. She grimaced at the chaotic do, giggling awkwardly.

Andy saw me and walked up. His sword was sheathed in a new leather scabbard that fastened to a harness on his back, and layered shoulder padding of a similar material lay overtop his jacket.

"Hey dude—*Whoa.*" He pointed at my hair and chuckled. "You've got a serious case of bedhead goin' on there."

"Yeah, well..." I gestured toward Lael as an excuse for my condition, but she had already disappeared. I sighed and abandoned the explanation. "Yeah."

Andy threw his arm over my shoulder and brought me into the range. When my head stopped spinning I was able to get a gauge of the place: an outdoor training area for fighting, swordsmanship, and archery, with stations dedicated to each of the practices.

Across the way, Veronica aimed her crossbow at a set of round targets, landing bullseyes every time with a fresh sheaf of projectiles tipped with deadly metal arrowheads. Boris was outfitted with new gear as well: a sheened pair of sturdy, silver pauldrons replaced his dinged shoulder armor, and a large belt of the same metal adorned his waist. Although others were using the space to practice fighting, the minotaur felt more content snacking on handfuls of hay from the bales that marked its perimeter. Scooter joined him in repose, trilling a song from atop his right head-horn.

Murry crossed the dusty ground to greet us, his chest and shoulders now protected by leather padding and spaulders overtop his violet wizard's robes. Before two words were exchanged he excitedly presented me with a rectangular wooden box.

"Have a look at this."

I opened it, and lying inside: a brand new wand.

"It's the best of the best," Murry attested as I picked up the instrument by its spiraled handgrip. The wand must have been fashioned from a segment of tree branch. Above the grooved handle, five thin laterals were curved into a globe-shape that acted like a hilt-guard. Beyond it, the finer ends were twisted tightly around one another into the form of the wand, the entirety of which had been dipped in some type of metallic finish that fortified it—a significant coating, as I determined from its slightly weightier handfeel.

"This must've been expensive," I said.

"Oh, don't worry about that. With the siv the Ice Pirates gifted us it was nearly an even trade!"

I held the elegant tool before me and turned it, the sunlight glinting off swirling woodgrains that were still visible in the chrome-like metal. At the same time, I felt a swell of energy rise off of it. The wand seemed to project a power all its own.

"This is amazing," I smiled, turning to Murry. "Thank you."

His face welled with fulfillment. "Just wait until you give it a go! Here—" He led me before a target. "Try it out!"

Veronica strayed from her practice as she joined Murry and Andy behind me to observe the demonstration. I aimed at the wooden target, the wand already fluxing with power as I brought to mind the spell, and shouted the command:

"*Sphira!*"

Bright blue energy concentrated in the globe and flashed through the spaces in the coils before casting an explosive wave of magic. It burst into an indigo cloud upon impact and decimated the target to splinters. A succession of *oohs* and *whoas* sounded behind me as the smoking pieces returned to earth, scattering over the ground. I was just as amazed.

"Well done, well done m'boy!" Murry shook me by the shoulders, more excited than I'd ever seen him. "Would ya look at that! There's no trace of it! Ho-ho!"

One of the chunks of wood tumbled, finding its way beside Guhlfrumn's foot. The councilman folded his arms and eyed us sternly. We froze in his presence.

"*Ehm*, apologies for the damages, councilman," Murry spoke for us.

Nietta stepped around her brother. "Not to worry!" she assured us. "That's what targets are meant for, right?" She leaned in, blocking the side of her mouth secretively. "*We've been meaning to replace this equipment anyhow.*" She waved for us to follow. "Right this way!" she sang. "The Ka Master's sent for you to board his personal transport vessel. You'll be departing soon."

"Better leave before there's another explosion," Andy commented in my ear as Guhlfrumn contained his ire and joined his sister. The rest of us flowed into formation.

Everyone was allowed to keep the new equipment they procured from the range, and before I left I received my own padded vest to bring with me. As we followed Guhlfrumn and Nietta I discovered a set of leather loops near the hemming of the waistline that were perfect for holstering my new wand.

The rustling and clanking of our new armor and gear incited stares of wonder and curiosity from city folk as we marched at the heels of the councilors. Some of them even bowed to us as we passed. When I realized they looked upon us as true heroes, a swell of confidence enraptured me, so much so I hardly registered that we were ascending the Spire once more. Surely if we were departing by boat there would be no need to scale the edifice again. But, as we stepped through the invention room and onto an outdoor platform my questions were answered, and my inquisitiveness dissolved into awe.

A flying machine. The hull of the vessel was akin to that of a Viking longship, but in place of oars a set of fin-shaped canvas paddlers rotated by way of gears and pulleys. At the stern, a strange-looking, gyroscopic contraption was secured, centered with a distinctive purple gem: a Veindaian crystal.

Is that its power source? I wondered. It was at least one of them, I determined, as hot steam puffed from chambers skirting the base of a tall, balloon-like structure. It resembled a zeppelin, skeletoned with the same sturdy boards that comprised the hull and married to the body via rigid metal uprights. The entire structure was elegant, painted with deep crimson and cobalt tones.

"*No way*," Veronica, Andy, and I all seemed to say at the same time.

Orin waved at us from inside. "All aboard!" he called from the helm, dropping a small gangplank for us to enter. "Meisio awaits!"

Andy shook his head in disbelief. "What time period are we in?" he muttered, mostly to himself, to which Orin replied, "The future! This is my brainchild, travelers. One day these beauties will speckle the sky."

The interior was just as impressive: rows of embroidered seating that bore the same flashy color scheme, a steering mechanism that resembled a ship's wheel, along with several pulls and levers that controlled other functions.

I lowered into my seat, blown away by the technology that looked like it was ripped from da Vinci's sketchbook. Andy and Murry followed, with Boris entering behind them, snorting with precaution as his large hooves navigated the ribbed floorboards with Veronica's guidance.

Beside the vessel—which Orin called a karv—I caught sight of Grimmoch prepping his dragon for takeoff. The windserpent whinnied and cooed as a pristine saddle was secured to her back. Grimmoch fastened the last buckle and mounted, gripping the reins.

"All set?" Orin asked him.

Grimmoch affirmed. "I have detected Erah."

"Where?"

He gestured to the east. "Si'Uarda. In a small town outside the Vulcran chasm."

"Let's hope she stays there."

Grimmoch turned slightly, focused, listening. "She senses me." He returned from his introspection, assuring, "I will remain linked with her."

A sudden gust of wind drew my attention outside where Zax stood at attention next to Nietta and Guhlfrumn. Orin addressed the three of them: "The city's in your hands while I'm gone." He pointed at Nietta. "No overspending."

Nietta agreed.

He pointed at Guhlfrumn. "No *underspending*."

Guhlfrumn sighed.

He nodded to Zax. "Keep us safe."

The Elemental saluted.

As Orin went on to flip switches and pull levers, Andy interposed, "So, is this thing like a prototype or something?"

"That's right!" Orin said proudly. "Never been tested."

"Oh, lovely."

"Tallyho!"

Air whooshed into the upper chamber as Orin heaved a pull-chain while the gyroscope spun wildly from the stern. Within moments we were airborne. Scooter scampered across the floor to spiral up my leg and clasp to my arm as the entire structure rattled and levitated, puttering as it rotated toward the eastern sky.

The Spire narrowed as we ascended beside it, passing floor after floor. I stood to watch it go by, and on the windowsill of the room Andy and I had stayed in sat Lael, leg swinging as she lounged. She waved to us.

"There's your admirer," Veronica nudged me.

"At least she's fully clothed this time," Andy commented.

Lael smiled and ducked inside the room.

Andy went on, "That girl is crazy, Marv."

"I heard that," Lael appeared behind him.

"Gah!" Andy shouted in surprise and spun around. She was gone.

In a puff of blue, Lael reappeared in front of me, poking my nose, "Boop!" and warped off again.

As the karv levitated to breach the cloudbank we saw Lael standing atop the Spire on the saucer-shaped roof of Orin's study.

Andy watched her with trepidation and turned to Orin at the controls. "Faster, please."

Lael waved to us jubilantly, I raised my hand to return the salutation, and Grimmoch soared to our side on dragonback as we all took off on our flight toward the rising, golden sun.

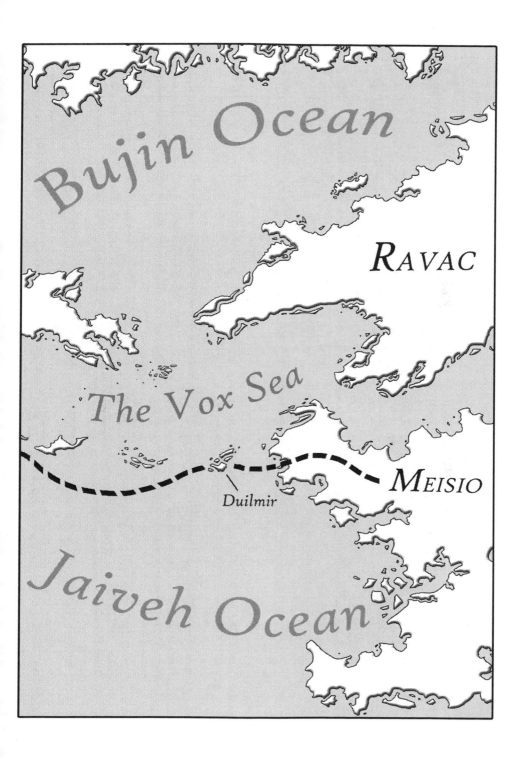

Bujin Ocean

RAVAC

The Vox Sea

Duilmir

MEISIO

Jaiveh Ocean

32

Si'Uarda Desert, Meisio

"**Y**ou have it. Just hang on, now..."

Grimmoch's direction came steady and stentorian over the gusts of the incoming airstream, but despite his reassurance Andy and Veronica expressed second thoughts:

"This is insane!"

"I can't _believe_ I let you two talk me into this!"

"Hey, don't forget this was _Marvin's_ idea!"

"Are you sure about this, Marvin?"

"Yeah, why not?"

Andy and Veronica looked incredulous, as though they could list a thousand reasons.

I laughed, "When'll we get another chance to do this?"

The two exchanged glances.

Andy shrugged. "He's got a point, you know."

Veronica sighed and held on.

Snaking through the zephyrs, Kail's emerald stare fixed on her master from where he stood on the karv's interior. Her sharp ears swiveled, awaiting command.

"Ready?" Grimmoch asked us.

The three of us rose and fell atop the windserpent's back.

"Uh..." Andy checked his harnesses and straps. "I guess so."

Veronica tightened her grip on Andy. "Ready."

I locked my fingers around the reins. "Let's go!"

"_Se'pha!_"

As soon as the directive struck Kail's ears, we were off, moving at velocities fierce enough to turn gaseous particles of cloud into stinging pellets against my skin. The cumulous ceiling opened into a tunnel as we blasted through, the wind blaring like trumpets as we emerged to a pristine sky.

Once our hollers had subsided to quiet awe, we were able to take in the majesty that surrounded us: a heavenly expanse painted rose and gold by sunkissed cirrus brushstrokes.

Kail porpoised at a more peaceful pace at this height, one which the karv had yet to reach. Unlike the lower strata, the winds at this altitude were gentle, angelic breaths, the sources of which must have been equally aghast at our presence there.

I couldn't fight the smile forming on my face, and my friends shared in my reverence.

"This was a good idea," Veronica admitted.

Andy agreed. But before long, Kail's head shook like a raring horse. Huffing and clawing, her webbed feet cupped with air in a galloping motion as she flew higher. The saddle seemed to expand beneath me as her scaly chest inflated, then shrank again when she roared, crested, and dove back into the cloud.

"I take it back!" Veronica shrieked.

We plummeted straight down like a rollercoaster, our screams fading against the roar of wind and the dragon's call, until our reptilian ride pulled up and leveled, and our cries changed into laughter.

The windserpent snaked back to the karv's flank, slowing abruptly. We were battered and frazzled, but plastered with goofy expressions and hair that was permanently blown back. We laughed with one another in our delusion.

"You really did a number on them, girl," Grimmoch noted.

Kail cooed.

With Grimmoch's assistance, the three of us made the tricky midair transition from dragonback to karv deck with relative ease, much to the relief of Murry.

"*Thank the Aevæs,*" he murmured as he guided us back into our seats.

Boris snorted at Veronica's return, and Scooter leapt from the wizard's shoulder back onto mine, cheeping ecstatically. Orin glanced over his shoulder from his position at the helm, pretending that he had just noticed our arrival.

"Oh, you're back?" he said in feigned surprise. "I was beginning to think my karv was losing its appeal."

For a moment I couldn't tell whether he was joking or actually peeved, but when Kail's midair twists and aerobatics incurred cheers of delight from Veronica and Andy, a grin tugged at his mouth.

Grimmoch vouched, "A voyage of this length could turn even the most stoic passenger restive, Orin."

"Speak for yourself! Not counting the stop on Duilmir I've been piloting this whole time."

"Say no more!" Andy got up. "I can take over from here."

The Ka Master squinted at him until he sat down again.

Murry coughed to quell the awkwardness. "*Let's see, now...*" He took out the map, tracing the line of our two-day travel over the wavy patterns that represented the Jaiveh Ocean, landing on the island called Duilmir, then continuing onward across the worn, seasoned canvass.

As he examined our flightpath I looked back upon our previous destinations and the obstacles we faced there. When my eyes landed on Inuento Isle my muscles tensed up, feeling the phantom pains of the Morogma swatting me across the coliseum. They fluxed across my skin, changing into a buzz. For whatever reason the sensation only made me smile more.

I'm different now, I told myself.

Feeling watched I turned to Andy, who seemed disturbed by my constant grinning. He pointed at the balloon's chambers directly above.

"Maybe you shouldn't sit right under the vent, Marv."

I didn't have a chance to explain myself before Orin announced that we were landing, and a spiral of sand chittered over the karv. Burying partway in a dune as we landed, the gangplank dropped and we filed out onto the dry, scorching landscape. In the distance, the image of a western-style town rippled through the heat.

"She expects you," Grimmoch said.

I wanted to ask him how his visions worked—what it was like to blend his thoughts with someone else's—but opted for information more pertinent to our mission instead. I asked which building we should search, and he closed his eyes to focus, then described the surroundings he saw, deeming it "some kind of eatery."

"Find Erah," Orin instructed us, pulling levers to shut down the whirring vehicle. "We'll be right here if you run into any trouble."

"Who, us?" Andy asked. He laughed a little, but his levity quickly faded into seriousness when no one laughed along. "Yeah, that's probably a good idea."

Boris took the longest to adjust to the sandy terrain, his hooves sinking deeply with every stroppy step. But he eventually found his stride, plodding along at our backs as we trekked into the dilapidated town. Only several of the buildings we came across seemed viable, the majority having been chipped apart into skeletal remains. It wasn't hard to find the one we were meant to explore: a saloon—one of the few buildings to still have its roof and all its walls—stood jam-packed with patrons in the middle of this desert town.

I glanced back at Grimmoch, who stood guard beside the karv while Kail rolled around like a cheerful dog in the sand dunes and Orin busily cleared grains from the inner workings of the craft. I locked eyes with the Elemental. His vision of Erah's whereabouts involved a setting just like the saloon, and when he offered me a reassuring nod, I swallowed my fright, filled my chest with an empowering breath, and marched onward at the lead.

Out front, hitching posts secured several large, gray-scaled reptiles harnessed to sled-like caravans. One of the creatures cocked its head at us, croaked, and licked its eyeball as we passed. I made a circular diversion to avoid the animal before heading for the entrance, outside of which loitered a pair of bulky figures bedecked with weapons. Each was bald, muscular, and wore ragged, tan clothes and dark-tinged goggles. In addition, their cracked, blistered skin was smeared with gray ash, making them resemble their reptilian steeds.

Peering at our aircraft in the distance, the two shared a muttering conversation that halted with our arrival, arms crossing and lips curling to reveal rotting, crossbitten teeth. They retracted just as quickly when Boris issued a warning grunt. The musclebound brutes shrank in the presence of the enormous minotaur's shadow, then begrudgingly stepped aside to allow us to pass.

Veronica whispered praise and petted him, "*Good work*," and Boris snorted affectionately, as the group pressed through swinging doors to enter the saloon. The inside was just as faded and rundown as the exterior, although it did provide a welcome respite from the relentless sun.

As we stepped to the center, we were eyed down by droves of thieves and gangsters dressed akin to the ones outside. They ripped mouthfuls of overcooked meat from charred bones and chugged down fizzing guzzles of green liquid to wash it down, much of which splattered over the sides and streamed down their faces until a forearm would rise to wipe it clear, leaving behind gruesome grins.

"Not the friendliest of establishments, is it?" Murry stated.

"Let's find Erah and get out," Veronica posed.

We split up. Finding seats at the long bar that wrapped around the back wall of the space, Andy and I sat, trying to scan the crowds of bodies from afar.

A hulking bartender interrupted our inspection, "What'll ya have?"

"Nothing, thanks," I replied.

"*Hmmm...*" Andy pondered as he swiveled around, staring up at a poorly-written menu tacked above us. "What's the special for today?"

"Igna'kontra will run ya twenty-five siv."

"*Houf!* That's steep. What about water?"

"Rainwater's fifty."

"For water?!"

"It's a desert, kid!"

After we were denied service, I caught sight of a woman sitting on the far left of the room. She was dressed in red lace and ribbons with jewels bedizening her hair. She wasn't exactly dressed for combat, but since we hadn't seen any other women, we approached her.

"Excuse me," I tapped her shoulder to get her attention. "I think you might be waiting for us."

"You two the boys I'm waiting for? Figured you'd be older." She eyed us with disgust. "Yer practically babes."

"We prefer the term *prodigies*," Andy said.

"We're new to the whole Realmhopping thing," I clarified.

"Whatever." She took a big swig of foaming liquid. "Two-hundred siv."

"Wait, what?"

"No siv no deal."

"You're *charging* us?"

She frowned, nodding.

My throat knotted. "Is your name Erah?" I asked her.

She scoffed. "Sure, if that's what you'd like it to be."

Andy and I snapped into realization just as Veronica's arms hooked around us.

"Not her, geniuses!" She swiftly ushered us over to the other side of the room while the lady in scarlet gave us an irritated look and flagged a second drink.

"Probably should have led with the name," Andy reflected.

"Probably."

"You *think?*" Veronica shepherded us into a secluded area. "Try not to cause any more trouble."

I agreed and apologized. Andy took offense.

"This place is a madhouse! *You* try finding someone in here!"

Veronica looked to her right. "What about her?"

Andy shot up disbelievingly. "Who?"

She pointed. "Her."

"Where?"

"*There!*"

Within the shade of an alcove across the restaurant, a dark-haired woman sat with her back facing us, nearly invisible through the dim lighting.

"Oh... good eye," Andy said.

Veronica sighed.

It was a fair deduction. She was dressed for combat, clad in all-black materials save for her shoulder spaulders, gauntlets, belt, and boots, all of which were cast from durable-looking segments of golden metal, shaped into flourishing yet functional layers of armor that both adorned and fortified her body. At her side, a long scabbard hung on her belt. Whatever weapon it sheathed must have been deadly.

We made our approach, this time accompanied by Veronica. Closer up, I saw the woman's braided dark hair contained streaks of crimson. Wrapping her locks, a trident-shaped circlet of matching gold finish crowned her forehead, and beads hanging from either side hooked to a black mesh veil that concealed the bottom half of her face. The most I could tell from her exposed features was that she had a warm, suntanned complexion and intense eyes that were smoldering hazel.

Her metal-clad fingertips drummed a half-full cup of water beside a plate of food that had been picked clean long enough for flies to amass about the remnants. She shooed them away more politely than she did us.

"Is your name Erah?"

"*Sh!*" she responded.

A waiter shuffled past us, replacing the woman's empty plate with a new one, upon which lay the roasted head of a boar-like animal. I winced at the gruesome serving, but the woman hardly paid it any mind, thanking the server without turning around.

Andy looked annoyed by the interlude. "Look, we're trying to find someone, so if you could just—"

She lifted her hand to wave us back, still not taking her eyes off something across the room.

Andy threw his arms up in resignation and left.

I stayed. Something about her exuded power. When her eyes flashed my way I felt compelled to wait, and when I lowered into a seat beside Veronica, she traded her focus again.

From this spot I could see what she was so intent on. Tracing her stare I found the same men we had encountered outside speaking quietly by the bar. Tuning out the ruckus, I managed to pick up a part of their conversation:

"Not exactly hidin' was 'e?"

"Nah. Picked 'im up right outside Incirrus. Lured 'im out when they took the girl."

The woman's fingers wrapped around a silver knife leftover from her meal, digging into the tabletop as the bulkier of the two took a sloppy sip from a tankard and went on, "Yep, they's off to Reikar now."

The lankier one shook his head and sneered at the floor. "Incirrus crew gets all the good bounties..."

Andy reappeared with a slip of parchment in hand. "Yeah, I think that's her," he told me.

"How do you know?"

He pointed to an illustration of a woman's face and said, "She has the same eyes."

Beneath the picture was the word *Erah* followed by a number with multiple zeroes. I locked up when I found out she was wanted, along with everyone else, apparently.

"Well, I'll be..." a dark voice grated. Andy looked horrified when he saw an ash-smeared thug stand from the table beside ours, the blade of his scimitar scraping free from its sheath. The sound was echoed by countless other metallic hisses as the rest of the saloon caught on, including the two gangsters. They tore out their daggers, as the lanky one grinned, "Looks like our luck just turned around, eh?"

Within seconds, she was surrounded.

Veronica scowled at Andy, "Do you remember that conversation we had earlier?" He didn't have a chance to reply when Murry appeared behind us with Boris to try and usher us someplace safer, but the densening crowd became unnavigable.

"If it ain't the pyromancer herself!" one of the menacing brutes exclaimed.

"Gracin' us with a visit!" another mocked.

The crowd chortled.

Swords drawn around her, she unhooked her veil, revealing a dangerously beautiful countenance which matched that of the wanted poster.

"*There* she is," the instigating brute crept forward, sniggering fiendishly. "Huntmaster's lookin' fer ya, Erah..." He picked up her unfinished glass of water and gulped it down, smacking his chapped lips. "Elemental or not yer worth a small fortune." He chucked the glass over his shoulder. As it shattered, he produced a copy of the wanted poster from his vest, setting it on her table and pointing to the hefty sum below her name. "See that?"

Without warning, her table knife pierced the man's hand, nailing the page to his palm. "*AAHG!!!*" he wailed, holding his wrist as blood spurted out and seeped over the reward.

"Sorry, can't read it," she answered.

He staggered back, then lunged forward dizzily. "You... you filthy, rotten wyvern-wench—*Oof!*" A kick to his abdomen sent him flopping onto the pile of broken glass. He let out a shrill scream, a puddle of red amassing beneath him before he fainted from shock.

Erah grabbed the attention of a stunned-looking server and pointed to the boar's head on her table. "I'll be taking this to go."

The server tossed her a knit bag then fled, as the rest of the crowd balked at the short work she had made of her musclebound assailant. The Elemental rose from her seat. A long, thin scarf flowed behind her like a swallowtail flag, as she paced in the breezes that slipped through the spaces in the uneven wallboards.

"Anyone not looking to fight should leave now," she warned.

Non-huntsmen, including the woman in scarlet, the servers, and several others heeded the command. Even the bartender took to shelter from his own establishment, sighing as if this happened regularly. Veronica, Murry, Andy, and I exchanged glances, then drew our weapons.

The crowd exploded, literally. The first surge of attackers were met with a fireball thrown from Erah's hands, the shockwave of which sent burning bodies sprawling past us. She then unsheathed a fierce, silver sabre and ducked beneath the smoke to swipe at the ankles of those who charged next, toppling them onto a growing pile of vanquished huntsmen.

A great twist of wind cast from Murry's wand turned a line of attackers head-over-heels and dropped them in a heap. I fired the Sphira spell at several others, while Andy clashed swords and Veronica issued blows with her multiweapon.

"You see this, Andy?" Veronica called over the fray. "This would constitute trouble!"

"I get it, I suck!" Andy replied.

With a twirl of her multiweapon Veronica swatted the scimitar from a huntsman's hands, then whapped him in the face. He stumbled backward, covering a bright red, diagonal mark, then gritted his rotting teeth and sprang, only to be clubbed by Boris, who sent him flying through the ceiling.

I shielded my face as boards splintered and tumbled from above, dust pluming. A whorl of gritty wind flew in when another enemy was clubbed through the wall, the sandy squall disorienting a section of the gang before they too were rammed by the unstoppable minotaur.

Eventually we cleared a path to Erah, circling up with her between our parries and spellcasts. We grabbed her attention just as she slashed away her current threat.

"What are you doing?" she questioned.

"Uh... helping you?" Andy said.

She directed us outside, following close behind whilst summoning a fire that coursed down her blade and set the remaining attackers fleeing or ablaze.

What was left of the roof crackled with flame and collapsed, smoke rising in the wreckage as screaming huntsman ran to the sand to roll the flames off their bodies.

"Thanks a lot, kid, I liked that place," Erah commented to Andy as we marched at her side.

Orin and Grimmoch ran up.

"Blimey! What in the Aevæs' name happened in there?" Orin clamored.

"Things got a little heated," Andy remarked.

Veronica punched him.

"*Ow!*"

"Huntsmen," Erah reported. "Apparently I made Reikar's list."

Orin buried his face and groaned, apologizing profusely for her situation.

She rested her hand on her sheathed sabre's pommel. "Don't stress over it," she grinned. "Today's one of the calmer days I've had in a while."

The bulky huntsman from earlier, now covered head-to-toe in soot, waved his scimitar and charged her woozily, slurring the cry, "*Fer tha Huntmaster!*"

A bolt of Ka knocked him flat, unconscious. Orin smoothed his moustache.

Grimmoch took her shoulder. "How big was the bounty?"

"Huge," she said proudly.

"I would take that as a compliment."

The two laughed. Orin still seemed bothered, rubbing his webbed fingers across his forehead.

Murry caught sight of something and interjected, "Oh, um, Ka Master?"

"Hm?"

He pointed, directing attention to the lankier of the two huntsmen we first encountered, who was sprinting toward the unoccupied karv and calling to his unconscious cohort:

"Charvy! Get up, Charvy, I got it!" He scrambled up the sand dune, repeating, "I got it, I got it!"

Orin sighed. He moved a finger. The air hummed, and the man suddenly went flying, shrieking, "*AIEEEEEE!!!*" as he jetted, followed by a big puff of sand rising from impact a great distance away.

"Anyway," Orin rejoined. "If you're still up to the task, we have room in the karv."

"Of course I am, but I can't let you fly us to Vulcra."

Orin frowned. "That's absurd, why shouldn't I—?"

"The Ch'valiac have resurfaced."

Orin's scales went pale. "Reptons?"

Erah nodded. "Just yesterday a rocflyer went down trying to deliver supplies to us. You fly anywhere near their territory and their catapults will ground you."

The Ka Master was still shaken. "Reptons... you'll need an army!"

The Elemental cocked a grin. "I have one."

Orin still looked unsure, but Erah contended, "I have no intent on bringing your friends into a warzone. They'll be safer taking the hidden passages."

"You sure you can manage all that?"

"It's my duty."

Ultimately, though warily, the Ka Master agreed, and all of our supplies were transferred from the karv to a sleigh hitched to one of the big lizards that Erah referred to as a *sandstrider*. Grimmoch mounted Kail, and Orin reactivated his aircraft with the parting message:

"Grimmoch and I will gather the other Elementals."

I tilted my head in confusion, and as though he sensed what I was about to ask, Orin punctuated, "You will not be facing Shamaul alone."

"One crystal at a time," Erah said, lifting the final bag onto the sleigh. "For now, you're with me."

We traded guides, waving as the karv lifted off and Grimmoch flicked Kail's reins, disappearing against a bright gleam of sun. We all piled into the caravan. Boris huffed perplexedly as he was guided onto yet another unfamiliar method of travel, taking up the majority of the rearmost seating alongside Andy and Veronica.

"Okay, I have *zero* legroom," Andy said.

"Suck it up," Veronica replied.

Erah strung up the leads around the reptile's cranium. "Atta girl," she soothed the animal as she stroked her scaly head and took her seat up front. The sandstrider resembled a giant monitor lizard. Her head swiveled and neck puffed with air, uttering eager croaks.

"What's her name?" I asked Erah.

"I don't know," she replied. "She isn't mine."

Just then, the huntsman Charvy woke up from his delirium, grumbling and holding his head, then shooting to his feet when he saw us.

"Theivin' rogues!"

Erah quickly flicked the leads, and our shouting pursuer vanished in the heatwaves as the sandstrider shuffled and shot off across the desert plain.

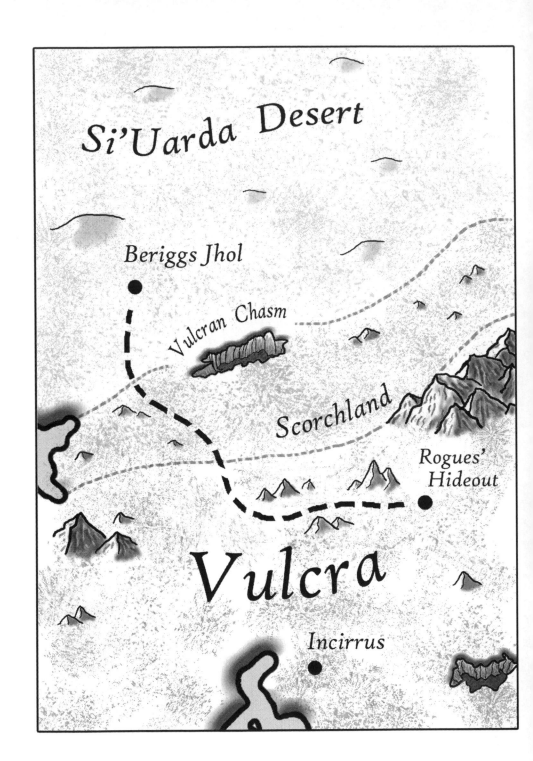

33

The Vulcran Rogues

Sweat beaded my forehead as sunrays beat down. But as fast as the droplets formed they were whisked away by the gritty breezes that battered my stinging features. We went through canteens fast. I poured out half my share onto a bundle of tarp to make a reservoir for Scooter to splash around in and moisten his skin. And as he twirled his tentacles the water drops misted and cooled my tightening flesh.

Our caravan joggled and bounced when its sub runners sliced through sand dunes. The sandstrider's unyielding endurance carried us from the dry plains to an even more barren scorchland. Although I had noticed the rapid transition on Murry's map earlier I was still alarmed by how fast the environment transformed. The sand changed to cragged, red stone; the clouds became smokestacks; the dry air fumed with sulfur; and all at once the bleeding sky seemed to catch fire.

Here on the region called Vulcra everything burned. Embers hovered in, still aglow like fireflies from some faroff eruption, only to spiral and extinguish when our heavy cart blasted through, barely skirting a menacing lava flow as we funneled into a valley where big, sail-backed lizards with indigo scales chewed on quartzy stone. They were docile for the most part, lounging lethargically on steaming rocks and hooting as we passed. The most trouble they caused came from a pair of males with the highest sails doing battle for supremacy. The webbing in their spines trembled and lit up when they hacked balls of compressed, flaming stone at one another.

I was sure that the sleigh's sparking runners would light up like a match, or that our wooden caravan would turn into kindling at the slightest provocation, but with expert tact Erah mastered the reins, the sandstrider swerved without issue, and we barreled on through the narrow pass.

I felt something rubber press against the back of my head and I turned around to see Andy was resting his sneakered feet on my headrest.

"Sorry Marv, gotta stretch," he said.

Aware of our antsiness, Erah called back, "Almost there."

Rock formations framing the pass seemed to warp inward in the shape of a ribcage, eventually constricting into a serpentine channel the farther we ventured. Murry shook his head, flipping over parchment.

"I can't find this pathway on the map."

"That's why we're taking it," Erah answered.

"Yep," I felt Andy cross one foot over the other. "Nothing wrong with taking the scenic route."

THUNK!

"*Ouch!* What gives?"

"Who, me?" Veronica asked.

"Yeah, you hit me."

"How could I hit you? I can't even reach you," Veronica retorted, as Boris snorted from his spot in between them.

"I dunno. You've got your ways."

THUNK!

"*Ow!*"

A rock pelted Andy's shoulder, hurled from someplace high above us. While Andy held his arm, I traced the trajectory toward a crag in the rocky overhangs. There, a pair of dull, red eyes spied us.

"*What the?*" I uttered.

Veronica went for her crossbow, but surprisingly Erah stilled her, pulled to a stop, and dismounted the caravan. One hand rested on her sword while the other retrieved a knit bag from the sleigh. She headed for the middle of the basin just as a hundred tiny bodies spilled from the crevasses.

"Uh... Erah?" Andy called.

She raised a hand without response, as a tribe of miniature creatures flooded around her, some of them no taller than two feet. Some bounded on their knuckles as they ran while others waddled in with spears brandished at the Elemental, spewing aggressive curses at her in a gravelly dialect. Animal bones armored their limbs and torsos, making them look like walking skeletons. They all wore the halved skulls of condor-like birds with hooked, black beaks. Through the eye sockets their grim, red stare gleamed fiercely. And although their skeletal armor hid most of their body, patches of scaly skin led me to believe they were reptilian.

Are those Reptons? I wondered, still very confused. I decided against it when Erah addressed them diplomatically, even using a few terms they seemed to understand, before reaching into her knit bag and retrieving the boar's head. She chucked it to them and they swarmed the skull.

Whatever species of scavenger bird donated its bones to this tribe must have also imparted its appetite. They crazily and voraciously ripped off bits of tissue to chew on as the Elemental returned to her seat.

"What are those?" I asked.

"Cravlings," Erah said, gathering the reins. "Carnivores. Very territorial."

They gnawed on stringy tendons and fought with one another over the eyeballs.

"What ghastly little creatures," Murry remarked.

"They keep out worse," Erah replied.

The cravlings made short work of the offering, meat juices splattered over their small bodies. The skull, picked clean, was hoisted by what I presumed was the alpha, who pumped it in the air and chanted his gratitude as we took off again.

The narrow pass drained into a cavernous opening through which the sandstrider slowed to a canter. Howling sounds rebounded and jumbled as we descended, disorienting my sense of location until Erah ignited a fireball in her palm to brighten our travel.

The deeper we went, the mistier it became. Scooter scurried from shoulder to shoulder to spy at enormous flowstones and stalactites, chasing the echoes of dripping water that rippled the glassy surface of underground pools. Eventually, the sandstrider came to a halt before a dead end, and we dismounted the sleigh.

Trying to pose his concerns politely, Murry cleared his throat and mentioned, "I believe we may have taken a wrong turn."

But, Erah shook her head and contended, "This is it." She strode before the back wall, proclaiming, "It's me. Come on out."

I nearly jumped out of my skin when a figure peeled from the wall.

"Honestly, Erah, send a messenger bird next time."

Another one lifted from a surface behind me. "Aye that, firelass. We were 'bout tae tear ye apart!"

The Elemental laughed jovially as a giant, musclebound man with a significant gut, and a short, frazzle-haired woman stepped into her fireglow. Both were coated head-to-toe in camouflage paint that matched the rocktone identically. The woman, who Erah introduced as Katyra Frinch, bowed gallantly to us.

"Any friend o' Erah's is royalty to us!"

The man, who Erah called Narwiel, responded, "An' if we're with royalty, they deserve a royal feast! I'll 'ave Garmut stir up more o' that famous stew o' his."

"I'm surprised you're back so fast, Erah," Katyra said.

"I'm surprised you have Narwiel on watch. Not exactly known for his stealth, is he?

"Ah, he's doin' plenty fine!"

"Aye that! Frinchy's showin' me the ropes. 'Sides, I've been told I resemble a boulder." Narwiel drummed his rotund stomach and laughed heartily. "Scared the pants offa this'n! Ha ha!" He practically knocked me to the ground when he slapped my shoulder.

Katyra picked up a rock and went to the wall, becoming almost invisible again with her back turned. Then, with a resonant, coded knock, a section of stone sunk in and rolled aside, exposing a secret passageway.

Hitched to a stalagmite, our sandstrider lapped up water rapaciously from a pool as we unloaded our belongings from the sleigh and followed Erah's companions through the torchlit tunnel. Our footsteps echoed all around, waning when the rumbling stone door grinded shut behind us and the creak of another introduced a bright, homey light and the silhouette of a woman.

"The Elemental returns," the figure declared to the room beyond, from which cheers of delight rallied and hands appeared to welcome us all inside.

The space appeared to have been converted from a recessed cave. The walls were uneven, dark stone decked with myriad weapons—axes, swords, crossbows, polearms—that framed either side of a frayed, crimson flag that stretched along the back wall. The banner was centered with a simple, black insignia shaped to resemble the silhouette of a giant bird with wings outstretched in flight. It looked like a heraldic eagle with an elongated neck and tail.

Throughout the quaint hideout milled a ragtag band of warriors, all of whom were experts in their fields. Erah introduced us to each of them. Ushering us inside was Aeralyn Terris, an archer. She was a tall, pale woman with coal-colored eyes and long, black braids plaited with gold. A long-range bow was strung at her back beside a quiver of countless arrows with feathery fletchings of varying, vibrant hues.

An iron cauldron licked by the orange flames of a crackling hearth was tended to by a stout man named Garmut Ayels, a skilled close combat fighter and saboteur. He had a dark complexion and muscular arms adorned with segmented metal bracers. His seasons of experience on the battlefield were manifested in the crisscrossing scars on his face and chest, the powdery white mutton chops that framed his square jaw, and the cracked, patinaed battle axe that hung on his belt.

Reemerging from an antechamber was the woman we met earlier, Katyra Frinch, a specialist in stealth and reconnaissance. Now smocked in a leather tunic and rid of her camouflage paint, I could see that she had long, pointed ears sprouting out from her wild, auburn hair, an orangish complexion, and bright green eyes. The spritely lady was child-like in size and disposition, zipping about the hideout to make levity with her comrades.

One of whom, nicknamed Fuze, remained impassive during her antics as he funneled black powder into a round, metal casing. He was their demolitions expert, and much to the chagrin of Katyra, talked rarely. He wore dark-tinted goggles not unlike those of the huntsmen we fought earlier, with strips of pale cloth wrapping his arms and face in a mummy-like pattern. For a while I conjectured what they were for; they were too thin to offer much protection. I wondered if his skin had been burned, and when he lifted his project for inspection and a section unraveled, I realized he had no skin at all. Rather, scales of a tannish hue fleshed him, none of which looked to have sustained any damage. He rotated the metal sphere in a four-fingered hand, face-fabric parting for a pointed tooth-lined mouth to huff fog onto the surface that he then wiped clean and shined.

My field of visibility was suddenly overwhelmed by bristled, gray-and-brown fur. I was taken aback when a large wolf named Fenra circled the floor, the beloved pet of Narwiel Bon Drafus.

Narwiel, like Katyra, had shed his camouflage and went to retrieve a steaming pot of stew from Garmut to compliment his tankard of fizzling drink.

He was a fighter whose weapon of choice was a massive, long-handled war hammer. His hair was jet black, eyes similarly dark, with an olive complexion and an outfit comprised of dark red tones and platy iron armor. Only in the newfound brightness of the room did I get a sense of Narwiel's startling height. He was a giant, with brawn and stature approaching those of Boris, who he took to immediately.

"Would ya take a look at this'n!" he rejoiced, approaching the minotaur in wonderment. "I can actually look someone in the eyes fer a change! Ha!" The jolly man patted his fur and brought him to a bench that squeaked beneath their combined weight. "Tell me beastie, what's yer story?"

Boris huffed and flicked his ear.

Narwiel guffawed, as if hearing the punchline to a joke. "A card he is, this'n! Garmut, feed this starvin' critter!"

Boris received a bowl of stew. Narwiel lifted his in one palm, toasting, "To yer travels, beastie. An' many new ones!" Narwiel awaited addition from Boris. When the minotaur snorted, Narwiel completed the toast by tapping Boris' vessel with his, laughing, and downing his serving in one chug. Boris sniffed the contents of the bowl before his blue tongue licked the broth.

Fenra the wolf sniffed the minotaur's leg, then rounded to her owner, her long, bushy tail swaying as she eyed the food. The canine was prehistoric in size, dwarfing almost everyone else in the hideout. But, for someone of Narwiel's proportions, she was the perfect lapdog. She licked her chops and made a whine, instantly drawing Narwiel's notice, who melted at the sound.

"Don't tell me ye've gone unfed me darlin' bonnie creature." He buried his head in her fur, planting kisses on her muzzle and hollering, "*Garmut!* Ma poor puppy's dyin' o' hunger!"

336

"I'm dyin' of cookin'!" Garmut grumbled as he carried the cauldron at his side. Now drained of broth, he fished out a meaty bone and gave it to Fenra, who chewed on it ravenously.

"They say yer part terrorwolf, but yer all sweetheart ain't ye?" Narwiel crooned. He kissed her again and her tail wagged.

The next batch of broth was put on the fire, filling the small space with a rich steam. When prepared, we were all invited to pull tables together and share the dish, which Garmut referred to as *mugree*, whilst exchanging stories of adventure.

"*Another* spot o' mugree, Narwiel?"

"O'course! I'm but a growin' scout, Garmut."

"Y'ain't no scout. N' you've grown plenty."

Despite their heated words, the argument was clearly feigned, and another heaping helping was ladled into Narwiel's bowl.

"Ye've a heart o' pure gold, Garmut."

"You've a stomach o' iron, Narwiel."

Katyra interposed, still fidgety with excitement over Andy's and my account of arriving in Enkartai. "So you two are Realmhoppers! Just like Areok! Have you met him? What's he like?"

"We hadn't heard of him until we got here," I said.

"Really? He's a legend! Areok the Earther! The Gold Knight! I wondered when he'd return."

"He ain't returning," Fuze said, tearing bread with his sharp teeth.

"Oh, come now, he's got to come back someday." Katyra looked to us, wide-eyed with enthusiasm. "When you return to Earth, you must send him my best! If you come across him, that is."

"We'll tell him you said hi," Andy replied.

"We have to return to Earth first," I added.

"For that, you'll need the crystal." Erah went to a barrel, retrieving a tightly-rolled piece of parchment. "I know of a place where these stones grow, far enough from Repton territory to avoid any unnecessary trouble."

"I'll believe it when I see it," Veronica said, mostly to Andy.

"*What?*" Andy asked. "I don't mess up *all* the time."

Veronica shrugged. "You have your ways."

Andy was about to snap a comeback, but Murry interjected, "Contain yourselves," then asked the Elemental, "Where is this place?"

She unfurled a map of her own over the table and pointed. "Here. In the heart of Titansmaw. Tomorrow I'll bring you there."

"But Erah," Garmut interjected. "What about the plan?"

Erah's eyes strayed.

Her teammate went on, "The Vulcran Rogues are to converge on the Repton's canyon. All o' the factions have united with us. They'll expect to see their Elemental leadin' them."

Erah ruminated, then noted, "Grimmoch tells me that Shamaul has acquired three of the crystals himself."

The room went silent.

"If the Orb's power falls to him our entire world will be threatened." She folded her hands and shut her eyes. "But my first allegiance is to Meisio." She took a long breath, before her hazel eyes reignited. "I will fight alongside you, I swear. But I cannot return from Titansmaw before the battle begins. You will have to lead them, Garmut."

"Me?"

Erah nodded. "You've been fighting longer than I've been alive. I know no one more capable."

Garmut bowed to accept the responsibility.

Erah continued, addressing us, "I'll bring you there before dawn. Hopefully we can avoid any Repton camps."

Katyra proposed, "If you take the gulches you should go unnoticed."

Aeralyn affirmed, "I've taken those trails before. I know a fast route."

Erah appointed her navigator, as Narwiel rustled Fenra's ears. " 'Tis a bold undertakin', me firelass." He patted the war hammer that he rested against the table. "I'll be sure tae knock a few extra Repton skulls in yer absence!"

Erah grinned. "Make 'em wish they hadn't crawled out from their holes."

"Or captured our people!" Katyra piped.

Fists pumped. "Yeah!"

Narwiel lifted a tankard. "For Vulcra!"

They gave a cheer and drank.

338

Andy reviewed the plan, tracing the shapes of the map. "So if we stick to these... wiggly things we're good, right?"

Aeralyn agreed, "Should be."

Andy nodded along, looking to Erah next. "And once we get to Titansmaw, we just..." He made a snatching motion. "Grab the crystals and skedaddle. In and out."

"That's the plan," Erah said.

Andy let out a lungful. "Alright," he said, becoming more confident. "Sounds easy enough."

34

Titansmaw

"**Y**ou didn't say Titansmaw was a volcano!"

Andy's yell reverberated through the gaping cavity as he, Veronica, Erah, and I strafed along a narrow ledge that grooved the interior and corkscrewed deep into the crater's core.

"Think of it less like a volcano and more like a vertical cave," Erah suggested.

"Not really an improvement!" he shrilled.

"Stop yelling!" Veronica shouted, just as loud.

"Well, forgive me for not being onboard with burning alive!"

"This place is a fossil," Erah countered. "It's completely inactive. There hasn't been lava for cycles."

"Oh, yeah? Then what's that?"

A ruby-hued luminance glowed from deep within, cascading light along the banded walls in the pattern of fire. The Elemental identified it:

"That's what you're after. That's crystal light."

I made a shrug between careful sidesteps. "That's good news I guess." Pebbles loosened beneath my shuffling sneakers, plummeting into the black hole. Andy and I watched them fall.

"Right." He pressed his back against the wall as we resynced our footsteps with the group. " 'Cause falling into a never-ending abyss is way better."

From her higher vantage, Aeralyn called down reports of the battle's prelude. From what I gathered, we were making decent time. Combat had yet to commence, Reptons had yet to catch wind of the incursion, and the many factions of the Vulcran Rogues were amassing to claim the most optimal grounds. Erah seemed satisfied with the update. She hurried ahead with renewed vigor, making the transition from narrow ledge to rocky platform and turning back to ensure we made it across safely as well.

Murry, who had elected to stay behind with Aeralyn and Boris, called down words of encouragement. They echoed and fractured apart against the uneven tunnel, transforming into whirs by the time they reached my ears. Nonetheless, the meaning pounded through, and I made the dismount to safety. Boris, whose oversized hooves had prevented him from descending alongside us, made huffs and grunts to echo the support of the others, and Scooter chirruped from his lookout atop the minotaur's head-horns.

The four of them shrank into mere dots as we tunneled downward into the howling chasm, guided onward by the glow of distant crystals. Unnerving animal sounds trailed us as we descended: the clicks, warbles, trills, and blares of unidentifiable cavelife. Anything could have been watching us.

Andy held his sword. "I don't like this."

"We're almost there," Erah promised.

A few more tricky hops and strafes led us to a more spacious walkway where the framing wall glittered with roseate minerals. I ran my fingers across the coarse sediment, searching for a more promising deposit to excavate, but instead came across something smooth and metallic.

I lifted my wand, whispering, "*Luminiera*," for a brighter inspection. Before me was a large, round door, recessed into the stone, fitted with inlaid gears and bordered by elaborate, draconic decorations cast in bronze. I marveled at the misplaced architecture.

"What is this?"

Erah approached it, her gold-clad fingertips touching down upon the filigreed metal. Her eyebrows danced in scrutiny, then slanted into a focused frown when she pressed her palm against the door's central, sun-shaped mechanism.

"I thought this was a myth," she finally spoke. She twisted the dial. The rotation uncovered grated vents that puffed hot steam, but puttered out. The door remained shut. She tried again. The steam wheezed. Nothing.

The dial clunked back to its original orientation as Erah released it and stepped away, whispering her frustration. Andy peered over the ledge of the platform, similarly disparaged when he spied a crystal cluster some distance below our walkway.

"Please tell me that isn't our only option..."

Twisting from the unusual door's ornamentation were several bronze dragon-figures that vortexed the sun-shaped handle. Each possessed trumpet-shaped mouths, hollow bodies, and tails that funneled into an overelaborate knotwork of tubing around the doorframe. The Elemental tilted her head as she studied the patterns, then stepped forward.

"Maybe not."

She turned the dial once again. This time she summoned a fire that flowed down her arm and spilled into the gaping mouths of the hungry dragon-forms, which set the tubing aglow and whistling with heat, before the archaic apparatuses sputtered to life, reanimated dormant gears, and opened the door.

Steam rose off the door's searing surface as it swung open, unveiling a room so packed with crystals that we bathed in shimmering, red light.

"No way," Veronica breathed as she entered. Erah went next and I followed, while Andy appointed himself watch outside. He shaded his eyes to exaggerate his vigilance, while the rest of us crossed the threshold. Inside, nearly every inch of the room from the floor to the ceiling was filled with crystals, the majority of which culminated in a single cavity where a solitary sword's blade was buried in a massive cluster of the stones.

As Veronica and I marveled over the unusual weapon, Erah's hand covered one of the diamond-shaped points of a crystal stack. Her arm muscles tensed as heat glowed in her palm and enflamed a gem. The crystal's inner energy spun madly into a piercing white color, then flashed when the piece cracked and detached. Once removed from the greater mass, the gemstone possessed an even grander luminance, especially along the fractured edge, where illumined energy glowed on the jags like droplets of magma. Erah held on to it for us while it cooled and approached the sword, equally transfixed as Veronica and me.

"Bombar's sword," she said.

I looked to her as she stepped past me. "Who?"

"Bombar the Brazen," Erah said. "A fabled hero of Vulcra who forged his sword in the molten gullets of three different volcanoes."

"Why would he do that?" Veronica asked.

Erah shrugged. "Most think his brazenness had an influence on it—hence the title. Others think his method may have infused the blade with mystic properties." Erah traced the notching in the handle and pommel ornament. "The Sword of the Sun..."

The weapon resembled a medieval broadsword. Its design was fairly simple: octagonal pommel, sleek handle with a burgundy wrap, an angular crossguard, and a grooved, burnished blade which possessed semi-rounded cutting edges and a diamantine point. The weapon was made from lustrous, brass-colored metal. Though partway imbedded in the crystal, I could tell from the sword's ricasso that the blade too possessed an atypical, bronzy finish. I wondered whether the color was imparted by the gemstones, or a metal uncommon to smithing.

With her free hand Erah grasped the handle, adding, "Bombar was a believer in spirits having multiple embodiments. It's said before his death he enchanted his sword so that only he, or someone of kindred spirit could lift it again."

The Elemental gave the weapon a valiant pull. The housing stone made a low hum that vibrated into a ring the harder she strained. Flames rolled over her muscles when she made a second attempt, externalizing her fiery exertion. But still, the blade remained lodged. She released her grip.

"Not budging."

I tugged on the handle myself, trying to determine what could keep the sword so rigid. There looked to be sufficient space in between the blade and its crystal casing. *Maybe it's an optical illusion*, I considered. Perhaps refracted light made the sword *look* as though it was floating there, and the blade was actually sealed in place.

Satisfied with the gem's cooler temperature, Erah offered the crystal to me. It was still warm. Fiery light burned inside of it, compacted into a white-hot sphere that spasmed and bounced, almost sentiently, like an insect trying to escape enclosure. *One more to go*, I thought. I slipped the erratic stone into a spacious compartment on my vest, then went to Andy.

"Did you get it?" he asked. "What was that room like?"

"Yep," I patted the pouch, then motioned behind me. "It was pretty cool. Have a look."

Andy and I traded duties. I stood watch outside while he voiced his awe and stepped around the chamber. Soon after, Veronica followed Erah to my side in mid conversation:

"Maybe there is something to that legend," Veronica said.

"Maybe. If that's the case, then perhaps it's a good thing I couldn't lift it."

Veronica looked confused. "What do you mean?"

"Well, I wouldn't really consider myself his successor," Erah replied. "While I admire the stories of Bombar the Brazen I recognize how different we are as warriors. Taking on the Dragon King unaided, *riding* untamable beasts—his undertakings were borderline senseless."

Andy reappeared behind us. "Guys, check it out!"

The three of us turned to see him swinging the legendary sword effortlessly, slashing an x-shape in the air and laughing.

"Someone just left this thing lying around!"

Erah was speechless.

"*Of course,*" Veronica murmured.

A distant rumble drew my attention. "What was that?"

Erah snapped out of her trance as another one pulsed, vibrating beneath our feet.

"The battle may have started," she reasoned. "We should get moving."

When Andy learned his newfound weapon was legendary, his chest swelled with confidence, and he swaggered on ahead of us, twirling it like a cane. His conduct incurred eye-rolls from Veronica and constant reminders from Erah that the weapon was a prized artifact. This only embellished his antics.

We retraced our steps, finding ourselves on a walkway framed by statues of knightly warriors.

"This place must have really been dormant for a while," I said, noting the age of the abandoned carvings.

Andy agreed, "Yeah, they turned it into an art exhibit."

Erah cringed when he tapped his sword against the figures, intervening to lower his blade.

"It was a stronghold once," she clarified. "Many heroes were forged here."

"These guys are looking pretty rough," Andy said, face-to-face with the figures. He came across one in particular, a sculpture of something nonhuman with a grisly set of overlapped fangs. He squinted at in in revulsion. "This one's just plain creepy."

When he prodded it, a claw shot out, locking around his throat and hoisting him in the air.

It wasn't a statue.

"Repton!" Erah cried. She tore her sword free, but before she could land a single strike Andy squirmed and swung his new weapon upward, slicing below the creature's elbow and severing its forearm. It shrieked and held a steaming wound, as Andy dropped down and scrambled to our sides, frantically prying a dismembered claw from his neck.

The Repton made a gurgling snarl as it lowered into a prowling pose, menacing teeth flashing when his jaws gaped. This creature was made for killing. Faded green scales in the pattern of cracked stone covered his body, and if those didn't offer enough protection, he also possessed some type of armor. When flames coursed down Erah's sabre I saw that patches of gold metal had been melted over certain parts of his hide, most notably on the dagger-like claws of his remaining hand and the spines running down his neck and back.

A long tail arched behind him like a poising snake, baring a diamond-shaped barb that had also received a golden coating. It steadied over his shoulder beside a face that harkened to those of the prehistoric killers we beheld in the museum. And as the beast's crocodilian smile crept open, a thick, red tongue lapped up streams of stringy saliva that epitomized carnivorous hunger.

I bounded backward as the Repton took a swing, metal-tipped claws clashing with Erah's blade, sparking. The Elemental ordered us to stay behind her, and we hastily heeded as the beast took another swipe, this time with his tail. Erah's leg buckled with the heavy impact, but her sabre still managed to block the next attack and slice at an unarmored section of torso. The bloodied monster disregarded it, perhaps too consumed by wrath to notice the fatal gash, and pressed forward with undying ferocity.

I drew my wand, Veronica her crossbow. But Erah, sensing our intentions, demanded we stay back. The cramped space began to shake and take damages. Statues tumbled and columns fell as the Repton swung madly at the Elemental. Three claws landed, tearing black fabric from her arm and grazing flesh. Erah grunted. Her blade, now burning red in compliance with her rage, issued a searing upward cut that removed the beast's remaining arm, leaving a sever more jagged than the former. A powerful back kick sent him skull-first into a statue, going limp as it crumbled and buried him.

The flames on her blade extinguished with her steadying breaths. The steaming metal hissed as it slid into its scabbard, while Andy, Veronica, and I all gathered around the vanquished creature alongside her.

"They're not supposed to be here," Erah huffed. She treaded past the fallen monster, navigating chunks of broken statue. "What are they doing here?"

I knelt over the felled Repton, examining its gruesome features. "They aren't after the crystals too, are they?"

"No," Erah answered. "They have a fixation with gold, but not crystals." She turned her back, lifting her gaze to the circle of sky above us. "Something isn't right."

In a flash, the monster reawakened, snapping its undead jaws at us and shrilling a terrible noise that rattled the space. The shock knocked me to the floor and shook me to another state, activating something deep within.

The world pulsed with light, its occupants wading through the gold-hued brightness in slow motion. An arrow was suspended in midair, the string of Veronica's crossbow vibrating and rippling energy into the airspace through which Andy's sword slashed, its blade aglow with a unique, mystic effulgence. Erah was in mid spin, hand going for her sabre. And I was floored while a diamond-shaped barb thrusted toward me.

A transparent ghost of the Repton's tail moved in what I interpreted as normal speed, fazing into the center of my gut, with a slower-moving physical form trailing its apparition. Before it could land I rolled away from the striking path, shot to my feet, and blinked.

The Repton's barb struck the floor. Andy lobbed it off. Veronica's arrow stuck in its neck. Erah slashed at it from behind. I pushed my hand forward, and a shockwave of Ka blasted the beast from the platform. It soared backward, screeching, then fractured apart a lone crystal cluster on the opposite wall far below us and tumbled into the basin like a rag doll.

I backed from the edge, letting my heartrate slow and turning to Erah to catch her contemplative stare. Andy asked if we could leave, but Veronica brought the group's attention to two more Reptons at the bottom of the volcano. The crystal fragments had plummeted alongside the body of their defeated brethren, gaining luminance in their fractured state to expose a skulking pair of creatures who were wrangling an ostrich-sized, reptilian bird. When its long, serpentine neck reared it was nearly the same height as its captors. It had black feathers, a toothy beak, and wings that were tipped with hooked talons. I realized it was the same bird that was illustrated on the Vulcran Rogue's armorial markings and flag. The poor creature let out a desperate yelp when a chain tugged at its fleshy neck, then flapped its dragon-like wings when it was prodded from behind.

"What is that thing?" Andy asked.

"It looks like a furadon," Veronica said.

"It's a basilisk." Erah knelt slightly to watch, trying to stay hidden although the Repton pair had already become well aware of our presence. Their shadows stretched in the glow of the crystals while trampling scattered eggshells and dried nesting material and pushing the creature toward a tunnel that it was almost too tall for.

"It's huge," I said.

"It's only a chick," Erah replied, prompting us to follow her as she hurriedly scaled the platforms. "We have to get out of here before—"

The volcano shook. Wind roared through the opening in heavy squalls, nearly jostling us from our awkward footholds.

"Keep going!" Erah commanded, pushing against the whirlwind toward a sheltered ledge obtruding from the midlevel. As we neared it I could hear the hollers of Murry and Aeralyn echoing above through the bluster. But again they faded when a piercing, distressed wail rattled the walls from the inside, belted from the throat of the youngling and intensifying the fury of the gales.

Erah grabbed my arm, I grabbed Andy's, and he grabbed Veronica's, as we strafed and clambered for the sheltered nook before it was too late.

Then, the mother arrived.

35
The Basilisk

Rock stacks tumbled and shuddered the walls as a monstrous set of stone-piercing talons hooked over the brim of Titansmaw. Black grit and ash-strewn squalls battered us with storm-like force, heaved from the heavy beating of chiropteran wings. They surpassed the volcano's vent in span when the nightmarish bird stretched, threw back its long neck, and belted a trumpeting screech.

I made it to safety behind a semi-sheltered ledge alongside the others, just in time to watch the terrifying face of the basilisk emerge from a cloud of agitated ash and snake through the depths. The mother's head was matted in jet black feathers that flared into a frilled crown. Her thick beak was the color of textured brass, lined with the dagger-like teeth of a tyrannosaur. Most peculiarly, a blood-red tongue fletched with thorny growths made a scratching sound as it dragged along the roof of her beak and flicked, releasing sparks.

The basilisk reached our level. Through the spaces of an arch-shaped flowstone that divided us, I saw the wire-thin pupil of a serpentine eye shift.

"_Don't move,_" Erah whispered.

Acrid breaths blew from the giant's nostrils, pumping the small space full of noxious odors. It was so vile and thick, I could almost see the wicked gas spilling from her toothy beak. I held my breath and winced, the horrible odors assaulting my tearing eyes. Erah scrunched her scarf over her mouth. Veronica turned her head away. Andy stifled a gag. The creature scanned our level for an eternal few seconds, before shuffles in the basin and a wail from her chick made her snake-like neck swoop even deeper.

I risked a look over the edge to see the chick being pulled forcibly through the small tunnel just as the mother arrived to face an unfortunate Repton left out in the open. She screeched, a flick of her thorny tongue ignited her volatile breath, and a wave of fire scorched the dry brushwood of her nest and burned the intruder alive.

I retreated to the sheltered space to escape the heatwave. Shadowed reptilian and bat-like cavelife, now exposed by firelight and stirred by the wild inferno, went scrambling, leaping, and gliding to flee the enraged mother's wrath.

"This place is getting way too popular!" Andy yelled over the firestorm.

We moved on to the next platform. I could hear Andy yelling out his list of grievances amid the roar of fire and wingbeats of cave dwellers:

"*No* chance of burning..."

A wave of fire roared by.

"*Completely* abandoned..."

Cave dwellers shrieked and flapped past us.

"You've got your crystal. *And* a sword!" Erah contended.

"She has a point," I panted, rounding to the next ledge and sidling for an alcove. "It could be worse."

"Get back!" Veronica yelled.

The four of us dodged an avalanche of boulders that tumbled from above.

"You were saying?" Andy shouted.

Rocks snapped from their formations when the basilisk tossed, wings and tail throwing, as her beak wailed laments and pumped more fire into the crater. Though we were half-hidden behind a stony barricade, the heat was unbearable. My cooking skin felt like it was peeling off. Sweat evaporated and steamed over my lenses as my gaze strained skyward, where the foggy silhouettes of our teammates were just barely visible.

Shouts of terror emitted from the apparitions. Murry and Aeralyn, likely believing the basilisk was trying to attack us, began firing spells and arrows at the bird's haunch in an attempt to draw her attention.

It worked. Almost immediately the monster changed targets, rearing from the blazing gullet of Titansmaw and going after them instead. Spellcasts and arrows whizzed through the air high above me, where the basilisk opened her wings, puffed her chest, and flicked her sparking tongue.

My mind braced. *Oh, no...*

As fast as my feet could carry me I bounded up platforms and shimmied over ledges, a blend of adrenaline and intuition guiding my frenzied footsteps. I arrived at the peak and dropped to my knees to dodge a huge, swinging tail, then looked up in time to see fire spew from the animal's mouth. *Am I too late?*

Just then, hands wrapped around my shoulders and lifted me to my feet. It was Murry. I was about to voice my relief, when he instructed, "Be still. She senses movement."

The fire breath cut out, seemingly aimed at nothing. I tilted my head, trying to understand what had happened, when Aeralyn rose from behind a boulder a short distance away. An arrow of hers shot past the giant's face, who breathed fire at it before lowering into a patrolling skulk once again.

"We need to get out of here," I told Murry. Veronica, Erah, and Andy bounded up behind us in a mad scramble.

"Made it," Andy panted.

The basilisk swiveled at the clamor, but another arrow whizzed by. Her pupils quivered at it, tongue flicked, and flaming breath disintegrated the projectile in midflight.

We became statues. The fearsome bird's head snaked low, looking over her perch at where she last detected movement. Her tail swung over our heads, threatening to swat us from the peak should it stray any lower.

While the bird's back was turned, Aeralyn snuck from her hiding spot.

She spoke to Erah in a muted tone, tapping the Rogues' avian insignia painted on her shoulder armor. "There's our mascot, huh? Told you we should've gone with a roc. Far more docile birds..."

"But *we* aren't docile, are we? What's the status on the battle?"

Aeralyn's throat bobbed.

Reading dismay, Erah snuck toward the edge, disregarding the terror beside her and Aeralyn's cautionary words. Erah's face turned white. Whatever she saw made her back up rigidly.

"No..."

Aeralyn kept her voice low while confirming, "We had the advantage at first but then they poured from their holes like vermin. I've never seen so many."

Erah was still, but unable to prevent her rage from manifesting red flames on her body. They rolled over her shoulders as her fists clenched. The basilisk cocked her head at the activity. Aeralyn quickly fired an arrow sideways and the bird torched it.

"Keep it together, Erah. We need you."

Erah's burning hazel eyes shifted.

"We need a plan," Veronica chimed in.

"If we move we're done for," Murry noted, watching the patrolling monster across from us. Scooter hid partway in his shell and chittered atop Boris' head-horns. I looked to the basilisk, studying her patterns. Another arrow kept her occupied. Her thorny tongue flinted hot sparks which bust into a fiery current when her fleshy throat pumped its fumes. Her flickering pupils then shrank into slits again and she resumed her patrol, never straying from the peak.

Aeralyn preloaded her bow. "I'm running low."

Murry waved his wand, duplicating one of the remaining shafts in her quiver. She looked amazed by the magic, then nodded to him in thanks. I formulated a plan.

"I think we can sneak by if we move slowly," I said. "We keep her distracted with the arrows and slip away."

Veronica was onboard. She loaded her crossbow, volunteering to shoot as well, and Murry readied his wand to replenish their supply when needed.

Everyone agreed and we moved as a unit. Projectiles arced in to distract the beast. One step, arrow, another step, arrow. The process kept the basilisk's back to us as we inched closer to the side of the volcano. But before we could escape, a sizable shadow jetted past me and disappeared into Titansmaw. I blinked. No one else seemed to notice the anomaly.

Am I seeing things? I wondered.

Whatever it was seemed to have spooked the cave dwellers inside, because a cloud of shrieking creatures erupted from the vent soon afterwards. Squirming bodies and erratic wings. One veered from its flock, ramming into my stomach and knocking me flat.

An animal with the abdomen of an overgrown beetle and the wings of a bat gurgled and clicked as it continued to flap incessantly, keeping me pinned. My friends broke formation to help. Eventually, we managed to pry the animal off and chuck it away, but my relief faded when I locked eyes with the basilisk. They gleamed through the cloud of creatures, a sinister, serpentine stare.

In that moment the shape of the basilisk, transfused with darkness by smoke and swarm, filtered into the likeness of Shamaul. I seized. Andy and Veronica hoisted me to my feet, just as the bird's head reared back, chest puffing.

"New plan..." Veronica said.

The bird's tongue flicked.

"Run!"

We scrambled apart, as a section of Titansmaw burst into flames. We skidded down the slope in different groups. Andy ended up by my side.

"It was a solid idea," he told me.

We landed on the ridge that spiraled Titansmaw's exterior and continued our sprint.

"It was," I said. The basilisk flapped and circled the volcano. "But it'd be unlike us for things to go smoothly."

A section of walkway crumbled as the bird's tail swatted it. We switched paths. A couple rotations below us, the majority of the group was being pursued. Between pants, Andy talked to me.

"I think I have another idea."

I skidded down a slope beside him, landing on a walkway directly above Veronica, Murry, and Boris. "Yeah? What is it?"

The basilisk swooped toward them, screeching and flapping. They darted in the other direction.

I repeated, "What's your idea, Andy?"

"Well, it's more like half an idea." He picked up a handful of ashy gravel and heaved the rocky particles past the bird's line of sight. She immediately turned to pursue the chunks while our friends escaped around the bend. Andy nodded. "Okay. It's up to two-thirds now."

We ran, always staying at least one level above our friends and their pursuer. Suddenly, the basilisk reversed flightpaths and touched down on a lateral rock formation in front of Veronica, Murry, and Boris. Her wings spread open threateningly. Turning fast, Boris' hoof became lodged in a crag. He snorted, trying to pull free, while Veronica ran to him and Murry doubled back to help. The basilisk's jaw unhinged. Andy and I stopped in our tracks.

Andy's voice shook with nerves.   "Oh yeah, this is happening."

"What is?"

The blade of Andy's new weapon flashed as he sheathed it in his scabbard, then shoved several handfuls of gravel into the pockets of his orange jacket.

"What're you—?"

He leapt.

The basilisk shook and reeled wildly when Andy landed on her back. Boris was pulled free just moments after, as Veronica shouted at Andy, "What are you doing?!"

Andy could only yell and hold on for dear life to the creature's neck as she swung her head and flailed violently. She let up momentarily, screeching. Andy threw gravel past her eyes and she flicked her tongue at the movement, sparking flames.

"Run!" Andy warbled. "I got this—*Whoa!*"

The basilisk began to flap.

"Andy, jump!" Veronica called.

I bypassed the walkway and shuffled down the steep cliff to Veronica's side, drawing my wand as Erah and Aeralyn followed the commotion around the bend as well. As my feet touched down, the basilisk took off, with Andy still on her back.

Veronica yelled out his name one more time, but the beast was already airborne. With two fistfuls of black feathers and his legs firmly clamped around the base of her neck, Andy was flown skyward.

Veronica stared wide-eyed in shock, unable to speak. I stood at her side, equally dumbstruck, as I watched my friend soar into the distance.

"What in the name of Ka is he doing?!" Erah screamed.

Andy and his ride disappeared into the smoky overcast that hung above a dismal battlefield. There ahead of us, a legion of monsters pressed against the dwindling army of the Vulcran Rogues and their allies. They were outnumbered by innumerable masses that flowed endlessly from a canyon. Reptons hoisted catapults up wooden ramps, and more reinforcements seemed to emerge from every crack and crevasse in the earth.

Fire ignited on Erah's blade, ready to slay every one of her enemies, no matter the odds. But before she had a chance, a resonant roar thundered from above.

Everyone, even the Reptons, lifted their heads at the sound. The nimbus exploded as the basilisk dove through, speeding toward the enemy force. Andy was still on her back, and while the distance between us was great, I was able to trace every move he made. His left hand gripped the creature's plumage. The other reached into his jacket pocket to retrieve a fistful of gravel. At the nadir of their flight, Andy chucked the grit in front of his steed's eyes. Her pupils flickered, her thorny tongue flicked, and the Reptons disintegrated.

Like a massive flamethrower, she scorched them. The firewave made a deafening sound akin to an eruption, razing the field and leaving behind charred bodies and blackened ground. The Vulcran Rogues pumped their weapons and cheered—the odds abruptly tipped in their favor by their own mascot—and charged headlong at their retreating foe.

Aeralyn made a cheer too.

Boris snorted and Scooter chirped.

Murry slid his hood back and ran shaky fingers through his gray hair. "Unbelievable."

"He's okay," I voiced, relieved.

I could hear Andy whoop gleefully as the basilisk banked and made another pass.

"He's really okay."

Erah shook her head. "That sword was meant for him." She treaded on, but a new sound made her halt. Stares returned to the volcano's vent. There, a shadowy figure burst free, emitting sibilant howls.

A gargoyle. I knew I wasn't seeing things this time.

Unlike the one we encountered in Frost, no dark spell flickered on his body, and his skin didn't steam in the absence of it. Despite this, the minion of Shamaul looked aggrieved: dark gray scales crisscrossed with scars, beady yellow eyes sunken with fatigue. On frayed wings, the creature careened through the fire-tinged sky, clutching a red crystal in his hands. Without warning, another one screamed from the crater and fought with him over the treasure. The newcomer tore the rock from his comrade's claws. It cackled. As a reward, two arrows zipped high and pierced both wings simultaneously.

The gargoyle plummeted, crystal slipping from his grasp into a dark crevasse. The body spiraled and disappeared into a battlefield where warriors and warbeasts trampled overtop it.

The remaining minion's scarred, starved body and drained, bony limbs hung exhaustedly beneath slow-beating wings. His scornful stare was blank and seething with hatred.

Aeralyn lowered her bow to reload. "Nice shot."

Veronica grinned. "You too." But by the time more ammo rotated onto her crossbow's rail, the gargoyle had disappeared into the smoky haze, abandoning his mission.

My fists clenched at my sides, as I stared into the whorls of dark, coiling smoke and sent a message to the warlock through my thoughts:

You won't win.

Below us, triumph was nearly secured for the Rogues. Only a fraction of the Repton army was left standing. And the Vulcrans, chasing victory, mounted their advance without restraint. Far in the distance, I saw the basilisk swoop low on a clear section of plain. There, Andy dropped quickly to the ground, unbeknownst to the enormous, feathered animal. The great bird screeched, made a few bounds and hops, then took off toward the canyon— presumably to recover her stolen chick—and left her rider to chuckle to himself and fall over in the dust.

Murry cleared his throat. "Well then..." He redonned his purple hood, gripping the strap of his rucksack as he followed the Elemental's lead down the face of Titansmaw. "Let's go collect that boy."

The sharp, black claws of the sandstrider sparked like flint against the rough, stone terrain, as did the metal sub runners of the sleigh. Our wooden caravan's boards bowed and rattled with growing intensity when sudden swerves and fishtails caused cargo to slide around, producing a noise like a fitful percussionist. We skidded to a halt so Aeralyn could dismount and join Narwiel on the battlefield.

The jovial warrior looked like he was having a great time, ravishing every moment as he walloped another Repton with his war hammer. He issued a blow with every marching stomp, sending enemies sprawling. Aeralyn sniped a few foes as she entered, and Narwiel smiled broadly at her.

"D'ye see it? D'ye see what came from the sky?"

"Saw the whole thing." An attacking Repton garbled a cry when her arrow buried in its scales. "Had a stellar view of it too!"

Narwiel let out a booming laugh. "T'was a thing o' beauty!"

The Repton Aeralyn felled attempted to stand. Noticing this, Narwiel whistled, and from behind a boulder a gray blur sprang. Fenra pounced on the creature. Her vice-like jaws clamped down on the Repton's neck, growls sputtering between the red bubbles of a gushing neck wound. I cringed at the brutal cracking sound as the giant wolf shook him dead, before trotting to her master's praise.

Narwiel cuddled her. "Oh, ain't ye a cutie!"

Her tail wagged.

My fingers locked around the outer edge of our ride when it suddenly jolted forward again, weaving through fighting masses and crossing paths with a massive, rhinoceros-like warbeast ridden by Katyra, who cheered jubilantly as the monstrous juggernaut's forked horn plowed through a crowd of Reptons. The warbeast stampeded ahead at full-speed, spurred on when two Repton catapults—likely tampered with by Fuze—collapsed in a fiery explosion, and a heralding call of Garmut rang through the air:

"For Vulcra!"

The battle cry was answered by an outburst of cheers that drowned out the next explosion, this time caused by the mother basilisk, who swooped into the Repton canyon and flamed the outpost in pursuit of her offspring.

Andy waved to us and jogged over when we cleared the battlefield and neared him. The sandstrider made a croak and slowed to a canter when Erah pulled back on the reins. I extended my hand over the side and Andy took hold. The caravan gained speed once Andy was hoisted aboard and seated.

Erah flicked the reins, shaking her head. "I can't believe you're alive, kid," she admitted.

"I'm gonna kill you," Veronica said.

"Good to see you too," Andy replied. He patted soot from his arms and face, a goofy expression still glued to his features. He nudged me. "That was awesome, right?"

"No!" Veronica interjected. "You almost died!"

Andy tucked his arms behind his head. "I think the words you're looking for are: *'Thank you for saving me, you stud!'*"

She shoved his head.

Andy chuckled. "It was a good idea! Tell her it was a good idea, Marv."

I smiled and shrugged. "The first two-thirds of it were solid."

"Har-dee-har."

Andy's eyes floated backward, swept up by the scalding intensity of Veronica's stare. She chewed on the side of her lip, subduing her grin into a sneer. Andy squinted, trying to dissect her expression. "I can't tell if you want to punch me or hug me."

Her smile broke free. She did both.

Rumbles, explosions, and cheers faded behind us, and a pair of valiant, avian screeches punctuated the distant cacophony. Erah steered us through an abandoned harbor town called *Incirrus*—I spied its name from the map Murry had unfurled.

Erah pulled to a stop, detouring. She disembarked the caravan for a moment to investigate an empty shack. *Skabrand's Smithing*, the signage advertised. In the newfound calm, Andy and Veronica had quelled to quiet chatting and soft laughter. Boris earned a few chuckles when he leaned into a forehead massage provided by Veronica, making a comical, contented huff that blew her and Andy's hair back. Scooter scurried around the cargo area, scuttling and climbing over the bags of provisions and packages of food we brought with us from Xeev City. After a marathon around the sleigh, he landed on my shoulder.

I petted Scooter's shell as I quietly watched Erah drag her hand along an empty workbench. She took a few sullen steps around the desolate space until she came across something: a solitary token sitting in the center of a table. She held it to her eye. It was a gray, spherical stone, alive with swirls of glittering minerals inside. An optirock. After a moment, she held it close to her heart, then stored it in a pouch on her belt and returned to her seat. A tear streaked her cheek, which she promptly cleared, then flicked the reins.

A short pier made of dark, trodden boards creaked as we transported our belongings onto the lone vessel that bobbed beside it: a new-looking sloop decorated with cherry planks and bright blue panels, finished with a resilient gloss, and bolted with brassy fasteners. Two pairs of tall metal torches of the same brass color stood at attention on either end of the hull. The inverted cones that topped each one were stuffed with a flammable material, blackened from multiple past lightings. As choppy waves rocked the hull, a set of lofty masts swayed, atop which red flags flapped in the salty, sulfuric breezes and bore the symbol of the Vulcran Rogues.

When Boris stomped to the edge of the pier to unload his haul, a short man came running toward us, waving his hands to dissuade further action.

"Nonononono!" he called, bounding to a stop before us. He had similar features to Katyra; short in stature with orangish flesh and pointed ears. His beady, green eyes widened in worry behind round specs, and his auburn beard flapped as he talked. "This is Madam Kaladonna's personal sloop; I cannot allow you to—"

"Tell her I said it was okay," Erah entered, carrying the last of our bags to the boat.

The old man balked. "Elemental Erah..." He made an awkward bow. "I-I... well, I don't... uh, what is...?" He couldn't find the words.

Meanwhile all of us had settled into seats on the boat.

"Just hold on a moment, please, what is happening here? I've been hearing explosions and such all day and Incirrus is a ghost town and..." He stopped when Erah looked at him in puzzlement.

"The battle, Mert. The coup on the canyon."

"Goodness, that was today?!"

Andy leaned to me. "Someone didn't get the memo."

Mert's frantic eyes searched the pier. "Well firespouts, I didn't hear a peep about this! Did we win?"

Erah smiled gently at the old man. "Yes."

"Well that's a relief I s'pose. Hey, hold on now—!"

Erah was unlooping the moor line. "Hm?"

"This is Kaladonna's favorite boat. What kind of dockmaster would I be if I let you take it on my watch? She'll have my head!"

Erah knelt to his height and held his shoulders. "You were in the shelters with the rest of the town."

"No I wasn't... I was here the whole time."

Erah's eyebrows arched at him.

"Oh, I see."

"I'll write Kal a letter explaining everything. You get someplace safe and relax."

"Alright... but if I go missin' you'll know why!"

After the old man shuffled off, Murry said to Erah, "We hope this isn't an inconvenience."

She shook her head. "Not at all. Kal owes me anyway."

We each thanked the Elemental for all her help.

Erah smiled, "Of course," then grasped the stern of our boat and bowed her head. She whispered an incantation that summoned mystic steam. It coursed through the spaces in the planks, spiraled up the four brass staves of the torches, and ignited them with blue flame. Erah grinned at the flickering effect, which danced in the reflection of her pupils and brightened her features.

When she wished us all well I asked if she would come with us, and she politely declined, saying, "I have someone I need to find." She took my hand in hers, looking into my eyes as she would an old friend. "You'll be fine. You've done this before."

The sail seemed to open on its own, and out of nowhere a favorable wind swelled the cloth and launched the boat into the ocean.

Erah turned. Her left hand traveled to check the optirock she had collected. Her right hand drew her sabre. Fire rolled over her blade, and distance wiped each of us from the other's view. Vanishing in the steam, with only the light of four azure flames for guidance, our enchanted vessel splashed and pivoted, cresting the dark currents that would carry us into the unknown.

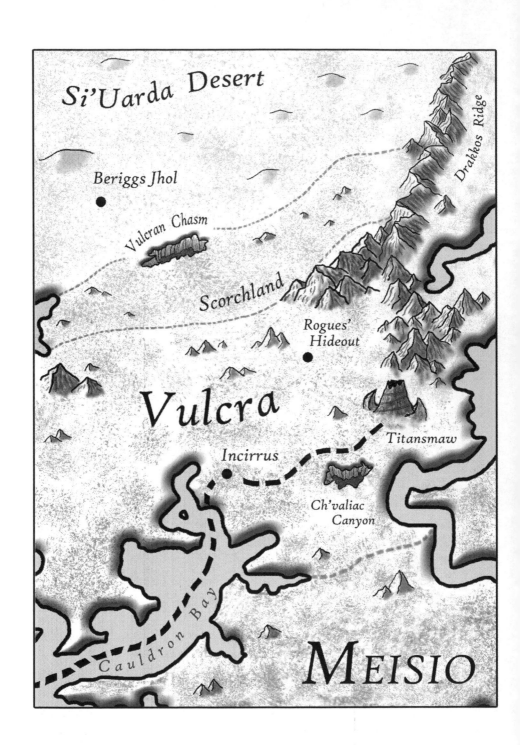

36
Desiderium

Misting waves sloshed the hull, trailed by whistling ocean breezes. The tones harmonized like the breaths of a slumbering giant, and our wooden sloop swayed in the soporific waters; tilting, creaking, cradling. Leaning over the brim, I was restless, observing a vibrant school of five shimmering fish that swam beside our boat. I made elliptical motions with my fingers, particles of Ka rippling the liquid surface and enlivening their formation.

They disbanded when I suddenly ceased my conduction, attention pulled skyward when the calls of spearbirds hummed from somewhere high above the clouds. Massive shadows crawled across the darkening canopy. Had I not encountered these behemoths earlier in our journey I might have been frightened. Before long, they too vanished, leaving our craft solitary in the dusking expanse.

It had been at least a day, perhaps two, since we took off from Meisio, but our distance from land and the somnolent rhythms of the Jaiveh Ocean offered me no respite. My mind was wide awake, churning with questions of what challenges our ultimate destination would bring. _Where do we go when we get there? Where are the crystals?_ The maps at Murry's disposal held no answers, only dark and ghastly shapes that raised more questions. And the only person who may have been able to shed light on them was Zyvin. I shuddered. _What about the monsters inside? What about Shamaul?_ I stopped myself, not bearing to think anymore.

A welcome distraction came when Scooter sang atop the masthead, chirring a sound I had never heard from him before. It was a singular noise—something between a bird's song and a wildcat's yowl—and it was the only sound uttered between any of us.

Everyone was quiet, glued to their own personal diversions to pass time. Across from me, Veronica was cleaning her multiweapon, dragging a cloth along the staff several times before moving on to her crossbow. Beside her, Boris was snacking on mouthfuls of bread that we had brought with us from Veindai. At the stern, Murry was sitting meditatively, his head bowed, eyes shut, and hands folded inside the sleeves of his cloak. And at the front, Andy was stretched out in a lounging pose, admiring the sheen of his new sword.

I rested my elbows on the boat's brim and contemplated. We had explored an entire world, seen impossible sights, fought unwinnable battles. And we were still here. Yet, the closer we came to the final part of our journey the more anxious I felt.

Why? I couldn't stand the feeling. The dread knotting in my throat; the hesitance locking my muscles; the droning, ceaseless worrying. I thought that mindset was gone for good. I never wanted to feel that way again. Though the outside world was completely silent, the voices of fret and concern were deafening. I suppressed them for a moment, asking myself, *Why am I feeling this way?* I should have felt unstoppable. In Enkartai I had learned magic and Ka, made incredible friendships, and felt more courageous than I ever had before. I froze, realizing the truth.

I didn't want to leave.

I scanned the faces of Veronica, Murry, Boris, and Scooter, my mind now becoming even quieter than my surroundings. *If we succeed, I may never see them again.* I swallowed hard, faces from Earth now flooding my memory. My mom, relatives, Alison. *If we don't succeed, I may never see any of them again either.*

I leaned back, searching for answers in the gray clouds that mackled the nighttime sky. Before they could offer resolution, Andy started making a popping sound with his mouth, trying to alleviate his boredom. He made one last pop as I turned my head to him, and he laughed.

"Sorry, man." He crossed one foot over the other. "It's tense in here."

I agreed, sitting up.

Andy laughed again. "I bet ol' Shammy has no clue we're coming." He twirled his sword.

I let out an amused breath and smiled a little. Andy's optimism was infectious.

He went on, pretending to approach the Dark Lands wall and knock. "Hey neighbor! Just wondering if you could spare a cup of sugar. Also, give us all your crystals."

"That'll go over well," Veronica commented.

Andy cracked a confident grin and shrugged. "Yeah, well, I'm not too concerned about politeness ever since the whole, y'know, *feeding* us to a giant sea serpent debacle."

I shook my head at his banter, asking, "How do you do that?"

Andy settled back in his seat. "Do what?"

"Stay positive," I clarified.

The point of his sword touched down on the boards. He rotated it as he gathered his thoughts. "I'm not always," he admitted. "I mean, I've freaked out plenty of times—you've seen that." He looked up at me. "I'm freaking out right now."

Veronica crossed her arms. "Really?"

He sheathed his sword and nodded. "I'm terrified." He was abnormally serious.

I shook my head at the notion, then said, "A couple days ago I saw you jump on a basilisk."

"Well yeah, that was nothing," he joked. Veronica shoved him as he cracked a grin. "I did it 'cause I had to. Doesn't mean I didn't freak out before I did it."

"Yeah, you freak me out every day," Veronica said. She shoved him again and he shoved her back.

Before long, they broke into a contest. Andy fended off an onslaught of slaps and shoves, whilst continuing the conversation:

"The point is, Marv..." He shielded his face. "Sometimes you've got to say screw it and do something dumb." He playfully smacked Veronica's arm and she sprang at him. "Don't take things too seriously..." His adversary grappled with him. "Look at it like a videogame; you can always hit the reset button—*Oof!*"

They hit the ground. I wasn't sure about Andy's philosophy just yet, but the exchange definitely brightened my mood. I thanked him.

"Sure thing, man," he wheezed, Veronica's knee in his back.

Veronica wrestled him to the ground. "Say it! Say you give up!"

Boris snorted as the scuffle landed before his hooves.

Andy squirmed. "*Mrf!* Is this any way to treat your savior? *Ack!*"

She tweaked his arm.

The commotion stirred Murry from his meditation, and he swiftly broke up the dogpile. "Alright, alright, that's quite enough, you two."

Andy plopped down next to me, clapping the dust from his chest and flattening the wrinkles in his orange jacket. He winked.

"She'll find any excuse to get her hands on me."

Veronica snuck in another slap before Murry's stare steadied on her.

With the chaos subsided, the wizard eased back into his seat, retrieving maps and navigational instruments to figure our location. He cleared his throat a couple times, trying to work, although he was clearly preoccupied with other thoughts. Eventually he set the tools aside and rocked, glassy eyes downcast. Shamaul was his son, I reminded myself. I could only imagine how he was feeling.

In the midst of my examination, Murry's troubled gaze lifted to mine. Despite his current state, a grin cracked beneath his beard, and he reached for his rucksack.

"Let me show you all something."

He fished out the four crystals, each one wrapped in its protective brown cloth, and distributed one to each of us. I uncovered the one he handed me, the crystal from Veindai. It sparkled with beautiful, purple light. Veronica held out the one from Frost, glittering blue; Andy opened the red crystal from Meisio that glowed like fire; and Murry held up the one from Ravac. Four of the five.

The wizard glanced at his reflection in the shimmering, green stone, laughing a moment, then showed it to us. "Look at these. See what you've accomplished."

Dancing minerals flashed inside the purple gem in my hands, sheening its sleek surface where my reflection smiled back at me.

"You've all come so far. Everything that's happened..." His eyes trailed to the floorboards, now aglow with certainty. "It has all happened with purpose." He clasped the green gem. "These crystals are a testament to that." He rose in his seat. "Now, I promised I'd return you two home, and I will. And once you've returned, so shall I, with quite the story to tell no less."

Veronica smiled at him.

I wiped away saltwater that sprinkled onto the gem in my hands.

No one back home would ever believe this, I thought.

Andy rotated his crystal. "When I get home I'm gonna sleep for a month."

I chuckled with him and agreed.

Andy will know, I reminded myself. *And I'll know.*

We wrapped up our treasures and returned them to Murry's rucksack just as a strong breeze blew into the mainsail. The wizard rose to man the helm. And as the mast turned, Scooter scurried back down, leapt, and landed with a *smack* on my head, earning laughter from everyone. The little cephalopod clambered about, darting from my forehead, down to my solar plexus, then up to my left shoulder, and lastly my right, where he settled down and chirred serenely.

The sudden winds must have also swept away the clouds, as my view of the night sky was unimpeded this time. A twinkling array flashed with cosmic wonder in the starry firmament, one so marvelous and bright that it reflected off the surface of the ocean, making it look as though our small boat was sailing among the stars. I reached over the edge of the sloop. Ka glowed on my fingers and rippled the currents, once again drawing the intrigued school of variegated life upward from the depths.

A howling lament ricocheted across the otherwise silent castle, followed by sickening, ripping sounds. Gumble inched out from behind a stone pillar, spindly fingers clasping the cold, rough bricks as he peeked. Nothing in the dungeon. His shaky breaths steamed in the frigid air and bulging eyes raced to locate the source of the noise.

Another cry. And another.

Sounds of suffering were common in the Dark Lands, especially in the warlock's castle, but something was different this time. Shrieks such as these were usually reserved for the dungeon, but as far as Gumble could tell from the old, bloodstained cobble, ruined cage doors, and empty cells, they emanated from someplace higher in the fortress.

Normally he was able to find some enjoyment in such noises, but these shrieks were shrill, animalistic, and made his small ears ring painfully. He clutched them tightly and winced. The fate of this creature must have been slow and grisly. And for what reason? After the screams echoed apart, Gumble speedily bounded through the antehall on his knuckles. In a galloping hobble he checked each of the cell-holes for clues. Nothing. He raced up a flight of steps to a casement through which he could check the clouds. They were empty as well.

Gumble swallowed a thick glob of phlegm and shivered, hearing the grotesque noises again. By this time, they were muffled and gurgling. They were then punctuated by the distinct sound of tearing flesh which made Gumble lock up, frozen on the landing of the stairwell.

An eternal few seconds passed, and the goblin's ears twitched, alerting him to another din pounding from above. Slowly and awkwardly, his stubby legs shuffled, climbing up the spiraled staircase that led to the highest chamber. In between movements, a barrage of pounding notes resonated, pulsing through the goblin's tiny form and vibrating his bones. Four raps, metallic and sharp, yet at the same time heavy and booming. They seemed to grow louder and louder the higher Gumble climbed. Why he pursued them he had no idea. They were harsh, violent, and promising evil.

The goblin's own heartbeat seemed to sync with the raps for a sporadic moment, quivering, before submitting to the horrid howl they bent into against the uneven stone walls. He entered the chamber, his three-toed feet slapping against a stone that was sodden, and warm.

Gumble swallowed, and his nostrils twitched at the metallic stench of slaughter as his stare ventured to the ground, where he locked eyes with a rippling, dark reflection. Thick, fresh blood smeared the chamber, spattered over the floor and walls. Some even oozed from the ceiling. The goblin juddered as a drop hit his forehead, then balked when the thunderous rapping drew his notice to the stone arm of the throne, where Shamaul's long, armored fingertips, slathered in the same colloid substance, were drumming an impatient tone.

The nervous goblin sidled along the far wall, quivering with fear as his view expanded to include the body of a large, scarred gargoyle dismembered on the floor. His body was separated at the waistline, and his joints were savagely ripped from their sockets and strewn in several locations. Amid the dark puddles and viscera, the Dark Warlock sat, staring malevolently. His cloak was drenched; the spots where his hands gripped the armrests were especially seeping.

His mask too was smattered, ink-colored carnage blotting the silver. The fang-shapes that curved down from the bottom of his facepiece were also tipped with blood, like a predator post-meal.

Leaning against the back of his throne, the warlock's scepter was propped, the crystal pieces he sent for were still unattained, leaving two diamond-shaped sockets unoccupied, and his collection incomplete. His fingers drummed.

"*S-Sire?*" Gumble shuddered.

Shamaul didn't respond.

He edged closer, trying to repeat his question, but swallowed his words when the yellow, serpentine eyes of the ruler struck him like lightning, and the warlock's chamber rattled with whistling, whirling evil.

The goblin retreated back down the staircase, scales pale with dread, as his master sat back in his bloodied throne, drummed his stained fingers, and waited.

37

The Dark Lands

A film of snarled, viny seaweed and dead algae coiled the craft, and the briny scent of decay infested the air when pockets of stagnant sea foam were disturbed by our passing, freeing their noxious, fermented vapors. The thick atmosphere was occasionally cut by whispering breezes that sent chills up my flesh. They crept all over me and slung higher to assault the mystic, blue torchlights that guided our lonely voyage. The flames flickered atop their staves, nearly extinguishing, but managed to stay alight long enough to break the foggy haze and expose an encroaching, jagged landmass.

It had been a week or so without sign of land. Seeing the foreboding coastline drew me to my feet, neither excited nor shaken. Just present. Our sloop's exhausted hull made a final straining groan as it slopped through the last barrier of entangled muck, before its filthy prow ground ashore on the silty, gray littoral.

Much like our vessel, we too were haggard, eyelids heavy from irregular sleep and hair disheveled from salt and moisture. My tightened, reluctant leg muscles twitched achingly with each minor exertion as I crunched through mounds of colorless gravel. Some of the grit seemed to have been converted from seashells and fish bones that washed ashore, beaten into pallid, shapeless amalgams by the tides. They snapped apart beneath my graceless steps before I dropped into a sit atop a faded, warped driftlog.

Without having to exchange words the group naturally began assembling a rest area, cracking dry sprigs of driftwood in half and tossing them in a pile. I set the stack alight with the Inferna spell, the parched tinder igniting quickly in the heat, popping and sputtering. The spell's red energy dimmed in the spaces of my silver wand, and I holstered my trusty instrument in the loops of my vest as the group gathered for a meal.

The smoke of the fire rose in black plumes speckled with bright embers, and the toasting aroma offered reprieve from the

369

pervading mustiness of the coastline. Murry distributed sections of bread we brought with us from Xeev City. I let the orange flames lick my share of the loaf for a while, and the charred crust crumbled apart in my jaws as I tore away at it. The roasted mash coated my taste buds. I chased it with a swig of Garmut's broth. Even cold, the stew kept its strong, beefy richness. There were bits of spongy, mint-flavored herb that had been added to the mixture as well, meant for preservation I was told. Whether or not the broth was fresh or the bread had gone stale held no bearing on my meal, however. I was hungry, and the taste of any substance at all was blissful.

We were even spoiled with an extra course: a medley of dried exotic fruits and tree nuts. I had no idea Murry had collected them from Kardaac forest. Then again, I did spend a good portion of that trip knocked out. I partook of the assortment with gratitude. The tangy and earth-flavored mix was a fine dessert for us, and a rapturous main course for Scooter, who received the majority of it and swiftly vacuumed up every last morsel.

By the time my eyes rose from my serving everyone had finished their allotments. Andy patted his stomach with satisfaction, Murry gathered up gear, Veronica resecured her quiver, and Boris' muzzle was dusted with crumbs. The minotaur's blue tongue lapped up the remnants as he stood, and the rest of us followed suit, lining up to gape at what lay ahead.

Behind bands of fog, an immense wall made of stone stood imposingly on the horizon. The marvel of architecture dwarfed us, stretching high enough to fade in the strata. On our side of the barrier, the morning sun was cresting, casting its bright beams through a gauzy atmosphere and signaling dawn. But beyond it, a dome of night-colored energy writhed, failing to contain the evils within as plumes of unnatural, smoke-like matter funneled through the apex, assailing the sky and hanging there in an anvil-shape.

We're here, I realized.

The sight of it should have sent shivers up my spine. The barrier's brutal façade and dark energy promised unspeakable horrors. But for whatever reason we were eerily calm. I felt my friends' stares shift, exchanging silent regards. Mine landed on Andy, who was shaking his arms loose and bouncing lightly in place, as if gearing up for a big game. He kept his stare locked on the wall.

"Alright," he said, drawing his sword. "Let's go knock."

We marched. Strands of fog wisped apart as we waded through the lowslung murk, clearing to reveal skeletal remains. Left inanimate without its warlock rider, the bones of a dragon lay half-buried in the shards of rubble. Even less tissue remained intact since last I saw the corpse, its eyes now empty voids and wing webbing completely chewed away. I followed its vertebrae like a dotted line, slowing for a moment to gawp at a swarm of insects that had taken residence in its facial sockets. The skull had been converted to a hive. Countless squirming bodies writhed there, spewing from the hollows and gnawing at whatever remained.

I knotted at the wretched sight, but pressed on, following alongside a wing bone which pointed straight to a fallen section of the Dark Lands' barrier. Smoke-like blackness swirled in ghastly clusters, obscuring what horrors lay hidden within. My throat bobbed, eyes shifting between my friends.

"Stay close," Murry advised. He struck a light on his wand with the Luminiera spell. I did the same. Veronica drew her crossbow, Boris his club, and Andy clasped his sword with both hands. As Scooter's cool tentacles tightened around my neck, I took one last breath of the outside air, then stepped through.

I felt myself wheeze. The gaseous vortex stung my body like hot steam, as if suddenly afflicted by fever, and chilling breezes swept in to unstable me further. I clasped my mouth and coughed, eyes watering in the caustic wind. I pushed my head down and stumbled, escaping the two-foot tempest and crossing into a nightmare.

When I plodded through, it took a while for my lungs to refill. The air was oppressively thick; it felt like I was breathing through a straw. The atmosphere sat revoltingly in my chest as my blurry vision pulsed and adjusted to the lightless environment. I squinted, holding up my wand for clarity. It was unnaturally shadowed, so much so that life itself seemed to have drained from the land. There were no colors. No varying hues of any kind besides gray.

I jolted when Boris snorted at my left. I blinked quickly to distinguish his furry shape. The minotaur's nostrils flared, huffing in an attempt to purge the ruthless odor. The others followed soon after, similarly afflicted. While they acclimated, I scanned the area, dragging my wand side-to-side.

After a minute steeped in the Dark Lands' atmosphere, my field of vision expanded, allowing me to gauge what surrounded me: a dead forest with spindled trees. Their mangled branches were deformed and desiccated, their cracked bark dark and hollow. The twisted limbs of these giants curled inward in frightening patterns, like zombified hands reaching for salvation. We stood in a pathway that led straight to the barrier's gaping hole. The trail was littered with uprooted trunks and maimed branches, much of which looked to have been trampled into splinters by some kind of stampede.

Whatever caused the destruction had long since fled; this place was a wasteland, deserted and lifeless.

Still, I felt surrounded. I could have sworn I heard inhuman howls coming from somewhere. I chased them with my eyes, unable to find a source, but too cautious to assume it was the wind. The others heard it too. Murry followed the noise with his illuminated wand. Veronica looked down the scope of her crossbow. They echoed from everywhere, yet nowhere. There were no surfaces in the clearing solid enough to produce such calls. They dissipated and resurfaced, seeming sometimes far away and sometimes right behind. They possessed a supernatural quality.

My physical senses were betraying me. I had to rely on Ka to guide my first cautious footsteps into the barren field, sensing for danger at every angle. My friends followed. Together we moved as a unit, reacting to every crack or shuffle we detected beyond the framing trees, waiting, before trekking on. It wasn't long after we started again that I stopped, bringing the rest of the group to a standstill.

"What is it?" Veronica asked.

I wasn't sure myself. I waited and listened, and before I could interpret the energy a rustling drew our attention and the points of our weapons to the right. This time, the source wasn't so easily concealed.

A muffled, swine-like utterance, low and grunting. It emanated from a spot where two red eyeshines were visible through a mangle of dead shrubbery. Twigs snapped and rocks shifted, as a boar matted in black hair shambled through. Four overgrown, curved tusks framed the snout of its ungainly, stretched cranium. Its huge head bobbed with every stamp of its sharp hooves, and twiggy, tufted tail swung at its hindquarters. Fully exposed, I could see its emaciated torso was sunken in, ribcage pressed against thinning skin. The boar stopped, dirty mane bristling at our presence.

"It's some kind of pig," Andy voiced.

The boar's jaw unhinged, dropping to a near-ninety degree angle to bare jagged, overlapped teeth that virtually scraped the ground as it uttered a breathy hiss.

"I stand corrected."

It charged.

Veronica unloaded two arrows into the creature. Murry and I blasted it with spells. Still undeterred, the boar let out a pulsing squeal, but couldn't complete its cry when Boris clubbed it. The swine sputtered a grunt and spiraled skyward, then plummeted, its body snapping through a decayed canopy and scattering winged creatures from their perches. Boris lifted his head to the forest and snorted.

Scooter darted from shoulder to shoulder, on lookout for more threats. He ground to a halt on my left one, chirruping and retracting into his shell when what appeared to be a boulder stirred. An arm emerged, then a leg. We readied to fight again when a mammoth of a creature reared and sniffed at the air, something I would later learn was called a *traug*.

The traug's face was flat and square. A blunt mouth of pointed, external teeth was armed at either corner by lance-like, elephantine tusks. Its skin was also that of a pachyderm, rough and gray, with additional dermal plating running down its back, patterned like the shell of an armadillo but spined with lethal spikes and quill-like hairs that twitched as it assessed its surroundings. Slit nostrils flexed between the creature's brows. Unlike the boar, the traug's eyes didn't glow. Recessed in its sockets were two milky spheres that evidently failed to provide outstanding sight, as it bumped into nearly everything when standing from its nap. The traug snarled groggily and lifted itself.

Murry and I dimmed the glow of our wands just as the behemoth's attention swept our way. It sniffed—thankfully not picking up our scents in the fetid air—then stomped off on two-fingered knuckles like an ape. Rubble tumbled down its plating and low branches fractured as the traug left the glade. The didactyl toes of its stubby back legs, somewhat hoof-like, shuffled behind the strides of its muscular front limbs, dragging a pudgy, crocodilian tail while departing.

Steadily, the glow of our wands returned, shining and shadowing the faces of our group. We listened for a moment as the trudging sounds became fainter. Once gone, Murry and I nodded to one another, lifted our wands like torchlights, and walked on at the lead.

The trail of downed trees emptied into a rocky patch of land. There, the ruins of what could have been a fortress lay toppled in desertion. I raised my wand, squinting at the interlocking, knot-like filigrees barely visible in the weathered stone of the downed columns and foundation blocks. Atop an arch that stood without sidewalls, what looked like an oversized crow with a serrated beak sat and cawed at me. I ignored the bird and continued my search.

What happened here? I wondered, exploring the ruins. *How did everything turn out this way?*

"Check this out," Veronica said.

We gathered in the center of the ruins, where a life-sized statue of two warriors stood on a circular base, untouched amid the destruction. The figures were back-to-back. One was a bearded man in long robes, the other a slender woman in a flowing dress. From her pointed ears I could tell she was Eramiri. Both fighters looked to be shouting, locked in battle stances against an invisible army. The man wielded a staff and the woman's hands were curled as though conjuring a spell. Murry wiped away a layer of grit from the base, finding an inscription that looked to be carved in Trymbadorian lettering.

He read it aloud: *"Here stands Kraiden the Elder and Etheria the Sorceress. Just as the dawn shall never come, and the land by their spell was made confined, so shall they remain, forever sealed."*

I shivered. *Were their bodies sealed in that statue?*

I backed up, then raised my wand defensively when the crow-like bird swooped low. It cawed at the light and sped off. As I watched the bird flap into the darkness, I spotted the platy back of the traug descending a cliffside. Even though it lumbered a safe distance away, I crouched behind a brick stack.

In the distance, a light. Not unlike the one of my wand. The traug seemed to pursue it. When I blinked, it had vanished. The traug had also escaped my view. I stood. *What was that?*

I returned to the others. Murry slid his fingers over the diamond-shaped casement cut into a square pillar that had toppled. Perhaps at one point a crystal had adorned it, but now all that remained was dark, glittery residue.

"So far no good," Andy commented.

"We'll find it," Veronica assured.

Murry patted the dust from his vest. "There could be a natural deposit nearby. A cavern perhaps." He smoothed the wrinkles in his violet robes as he stood. "Although I don't look forward to whatever creatures may have taken residence there. Goodness could you imagine—"

A horrible screech rattled us, followed by a pounding thud that vibrated the ground. We exchanged stunned glances, then fled from the ruins, descending a snaking ledge to a low flatland where we saw the body of the traug, sprawled out amid dust plumes that had yet to settle. Tentatively, we approached.

The creature was dead, laid out on its stomach. Most jarringly, its skull had somehow been turned completely around, the back of its head resting on the rubble while its jaw, frozen open in mid-wail, faced the sky. My face curled at the gruesome image.

Andy looked disgusted. "*Yeesh.* Someone's having a bad day."

"How did this happen?" I thought aloud.

As if answering my question, a white light sparked in the distance. My eyes flashed at it. *There it is again...*

Without a second thought I started after it. The light swerved, taking off just as fast. I gave chase. The others followed close behind, calling to ask where I was going. But when they saw the light, they too locked on it in full pursuit. It must have been powerful to take down that giant, I wagered, and whatever it was clearly didn't originate in the Dark Lands.

The light took a sudden turn, racing for the mouth of a cave. I shook my head, bewildered by the spectacle. *Where is this thing going?*

Away! another voice seemed to answer me telepathically.

I locked up at the phenomenon. *What?*

Away! it repeated, even more frantic. *Now, away with you. Find shelter. But not here. Bad beasts. They are close.*

Who are you?

No time... no time...

In the entrance to the cave the light halted, swinging on a metallic ring. I now could see it was a lantern of some kind. In the lantern's bright white glow, a small, cloaked figure spun around, the sheen of pale blue eyes glinting from within a hood. We panted tiredly as we trotted to a stop in the gravelly plain, observing the figure with perplexity.

The voice returned in my mind, *Why do you stop now?*

I tilted my head, still trying to grasp what I was hearing.

"What is it, Marvin?" Veronica asked.

The voice continued, *First you run, now you stop. Why do you stop?*

I shook my head in disbelief. *How can I hear you?*

Could you not the first time?

What?

Bad beasts are near. Find shelter.

A crack of twigs sounded from a darkened patch of woodland.

It is too late...

A ravenous pack of wolves with bristled, black fur sprang from the shadows, snarling fiercely through salivating fangs, and attacked us.

38

The Lantern

They lunged. Boris swatted one in the midst of its leap, while droves more poured from the shade. Terrorwolves, I learned they were called, all snapping vicious-looking, foaming fangs, bristling black fur, and staring us down with cold, saurian eyes. The one Boris clubbed rolled back onto its paws and regrouped, lower jaw now hanging to the side and dripping with blood and saliva. I backed toward the cave, but knocked into something hard. I turned around and gaped in disbelief at a stone slab that had sealed the cave shut. The hooded figure had abandoned us.

The canines circled, growling. I lit up my wand to keep them at bay, but when one heedless wolf pushed through the light, I fired.

The Luminiera spell took on mass for a moment, bursting against the wolf's frame. The impact returned the dog to its feral pack, toppling two others in the process and initiating battle. One leapt over the downed creatures and roared, only to catch an arrow in the throat. Veronica fired off two more preloaded shots before alternating to her multiweapon. The staff periscoped from its compact handle, ends tipped with spears that slashed away her attackers in a helicopter motion. She spun and walloped one that charged from the left. The dazed wolf bounded into Andy's range and caught the edge of his blade.

The Sword of the Sun gathered warmth and luminance the more Andy fought, gaining a fiery, ochre glow. Wolves yelped as the searing point lobbed off sections of flesh. The pack broke apart and reformed, but severed again when Murry's spells zigzagged through.

The wizard lit them up with a barrage of spellcasts. Wind upturned attackers and fire dissuaded their return. Some retreated, but those who still dared to fight were met with a bolt of sapphire lightning that surged, arced between bodies, and reduced them to steaming, convulsing heaps.

The wolf whose jaw swung limply lunged at Boris, teeth cutting into the skin on his abdomen but unable to latch on. The minotaur roared and kicked away the predator, who skidded, clawed, and jumped again at throat-height.

Then, a bubble of white energy captured the wolf, rendering it frozen, levitating. Its jaw unhinged completely, legs curled, and body contorted in unnatural ways. I stood aghast as the animal twisted up like a wet rag, then flew backward in a flash, knocking over the remaining pack.

The sound of squeaking metal could be heard in the now-silent glade. Behind us, the cave remained sealed. But above, the small hooded figure stood high on the rock face, his lantern swinging on a large metal ring that he clung to devotedly. With his free hand he blocked gusts from extinguishing its mystic flame as he carefully descended, landing light as a feather. He unshielded the light when two of the terrorwolves stirred and stood, shaking their skulls. He held out his lantern, to which the wolves growled and circled, keeping distanced. The lantern seemed to make a faint ring as the white glow expanded, and the diminished pack retreated from the element and disappeared into the woods.

The small figure ambled past us.

"Uh... thanks," Andy panted.

The Ka wielder didn't respond. He was muttering to himself. The little being waved his hand as if greeting the stone slab, and angular carvings in its fascia lit up in a maze-like pattern, before the round blocker rolled, and he stepped inside.

He left the cave door open this time. Figuring it was safer than the outdoors, and hoping to gain some answers, we followed him. The quick-footed creature marched on, mutters echoing through the tunnel-like passageway. I wasn't sure if he knew we were following him; he was so wrapped up in the conversation he was having with himself:

"No... certainly not. Bad beasts never stop. Too much hunger and not enough food. No..."

He raised his lantern high to light his passage. In the white glow, I saw his robes were the color of damp sand, synched with a rope-belt and cloaked by a small hooded cape that was moss-colored. They bobbed and scrunched as he walked, dragging along the stone floor behind him.

"Something different today... Bad winds blowing today..."

378

We had to jog to keep pace with the mysterious being. As his lantern's luminance shimmered against the cave walls, scattered glyphs in the stone were briefly highlighted. I recognized the same symbol Grimmoch had painted on his forehead—the Eye of the Aevæs—showing up frequently throughout the hall. Short phrases lettered in Trymbadorian appeared as well, along with several detailed, pictorial carvings. Most of them were of castles, swordsmen, and battle scenes. However, one in particular caught my attention: a recurring symbol of a tree with a twisted trunk. As I followed our tiny guide I saw the image repeat with slight alterations between pictures. A taller trunk here, more branches there. It reached its greatest height just prior to the end of the trail. The penultimate image, tall and imposing, was promptly followed by one that was noticeably smaller. The picture looked incomplete, the top half of the tree undrawn with only the trunk remaining from the middle section down to its roots. I pondered it for a moment until a second slab rolled sideways and more light washed in, making me wince.

A closet-sized hovel with furniture made of shaved wood, cupboards, warm-looking blankets, a floor littered with scribbled parchment, and copious lighting fixtures lay hidden behind the stone slab. We filed into the softly-lit home, as the tiny creature set down his lantern and removed his hooded cape. He was the same species as Orin: small and frog-like with pointed ears, wispy white hair, and tufts of whiskers cornering his mouth. However, unlike Orin, his skin was orange and bumpy like a toad's, and his big, ovoid eyes were pale blue. They blinked at us in surprise as he turned around, rolling his cape in his webbed hands.

"Oh... hello," he said, as if seeing us for the first time. His voice was shaky and squeamish. He introduced himself as Gnuthe, as he hung the cape on a tiny coatrack, then cringed at the ground, suddenly panicky. "Excuse the mess!" The papers were swept up in a current of Ka, flowing around us like autumn leaves and filing themselves away in wooden shelves. "So few visitors anymore; little need for neatness." He laughed uncomfortably, then squealed when Boris ducked inside.

"No!" Gnuthe hollered. He grabbed his lantern and scrambled toward the minotaur, bounding atop a table and thrusting the light forward. "Bad beast! Back!"

Boris sniffed the lantern placidly.

Gnuthe retracted. "Oh... Good beast."

Boris sneezed, almost extinguishing the white flame.

"What are you doing?!" Gnuthe screamed. He carried the lantern away, shielding the dwindled light. "*Mad beast... Crazy beast...*" he muttered, resetting the lantern on a wall-mounted hook. He cupped his mouth as if telling a secret, and whispered into the glow:

"*Touric Enavelir.*"

I remembered the spell. I had read about it in Murry's spell book.

The light returned, behaving like fire but keeping a nearly perfect sphere-shape.

Recited when banishing evil spirits, the passage resurfaced in my memory. *Only known to have been performed by Ka Masters.*

The toad-like creature wrung his hands anxiously as the bright white glow swathed his home again. He breathed a sigh of relief. I couldn't imagine how Gnuthe found himself in the Dark Lands, or how long he'd been trapped there. But the powerful, arcane spell emanating from his lantern evidenced his wisdom and integrity. I felt more at ease when he asked us to sit.

"I feel like I'm back in preschool," Andy murmured. Our knees came up to our chins when we sat in the small wooden stools gathered around a circular table that was just as low.

"More tea?" he asked.

"Ehm..." Murry started. His cup was refilled before he could answer. He sighed. "Thank you."

Veronica's face twisted up as the wizard downed his allotment.

"More for you?"

"No thanks," she said.

He went to Andy, holding up his tea kettle.

"I'm good for now."

Gnuthe nodded and refilled his cup anyway. Andy looked to Veronica in confusion and she shrugged, as Gnuthe circled around to me. I had just taken my last sip when he arrived. Bits of stringy, fibrous plant stuck to my teeth, emitting an herby bitterness that coated my whole mouth. I set down my cup, feeling it become full again.

"There you go," Gnuthe said. He hummed as he returned to his kitchen area then brought back a platter of chopped mushrooms.

"They call these *cave buttons!*" He chuckled. "Well... I call them cave buttons. Here, try!"

The mushrooms smelled sour. I changed the subject.

"Gnuthe, we're looking for something. Maybe you can help."

He shoveled several cave buttons in his mouth. "*Mm?*"

"We're looking for crystals. Do you know where to find them?"

Scooter seemed to share his appetite for the cave buttons. Gnuthe gave some to the cephalopod and said, "Crystals. Yes."

Andy sat forward. "Really? Do you have some?"

Gnuthe licked his fingers, shaking his head. "Not here. No. Only caves."

Andy stared at him blankly, then gestured to his surroundings. "Isn't this...?"

"Sh-sh!" Gnuthe snapped, eyes wide. "Did you hear it?"

It was silent. I shook my head. "I don't—"

"Sh!" His cross-shaped pupils darted side-to-side. He got up and checked around the slab. Nothing. He darted to the opposite wall and parted a curtain made of moss, revealing the viewing end of what looked like a giant spyglass. He squinted through, then gasped and scrambled away.

"What is it?" I asked.

"Bad beast. *Very* bad!" Ka glowed, drawing the curtains and sealing the stone slab. He redonned his hooded cape just to pull its drawstrings and cover his face.

I exchanged looks with the others, then stood up, parted the curtain, and looked through the spyglass. Through the smoky, warped lens I caught a glimpse of a creature, similar in height to Gnuthe, but with sickly green scales, small horns, and ungainly arms compared to his stubby legs. His bulging eyes glinted through the night and mouth curled into a sneer as he hobbled by.

"Goblin..." Gnuthe shivered.

Andy took a look. "He doesn't look too scary."

"Not him," Gnuthe explained, his voice muffled by fabric. "But who he serves..." He shuddered and tightened the drawstrings on his hood. "*Touric Enavelir, Touric Enavelir...*"

I peered through the lens again. This time I could see he was carrying something. I grasped the eyepiece and squinted. It was a stone with glassy, black sides. The inner prisms rolled with a smoke-like substance that sparked crimson power. It was a crystal.

"We have to go," I said.

"What did you see?" Veronica asked.

"He has a crystal. Hurry!"

We all armed ourselves and ran for the exit, but the patterns on the stone slab glowed, keeping us inside.

"Let us out!" Andy cried.

Gnuthe shook his head. I went to him, repeating Andy's demand.

Gnuthe pulled his hood back. "The warlock... That goblin's his servant!"

"All the more reason to stop him." I went to the spyglass, seeing the goblin taking off into the night. "He's getting away!"

The glow on the slab faded for a moment as Gnuthe took hold of my pant leg, begging frantically, "You must stay! The bad beast knows where he is! *He* knows—!"

I couldn't listen. I waved my hand at the slab, illuminating the patterns with Ka and opening the passage. Gnuthe gasped in disbelief. He stood there like a frightened animal as we hurried back into the cave's tunnel.

Our racing footsteps echoed off the walls, pounding into a single, roaring note as we sprinted for the exit. Smaller steps patted behind us.

"Wait!" A white glow shined in my peripheral. "It's not safe!"

I kept running.

"Wait—*Oof!*" Something metallic rang as it struck the ground. I turned.

"No... no no," Gnuthe whimpered, clamoring for his lantern. The white light had gone out.

The others ground to a halt in the middle of the tunnel.

"Come on!" Andy called to me.

"It went out! Gone!" Gnuthe sobbed.

I knelt by him. On the charred, smoking wick I sensed something, and for a moment I thought I could see a white ember blink. I drew my wand. Gnuthe sniffed, his frightened, uncertain stare shifting between me and the lantern. The air warped, wriggling, and without thinking or saying any magic word, the globe on the handle of my instrument glowed, light running up the spirals, and a ray of white energy beamed from the point, reigniting Gnuthe's lantern.

His moistened eyes blinked in surprise, reflecting the white flame as it danced and steadied into a perfect sphere. I was just as confounded as he was, but I had no time to lose. Gnuthe held his lantern close, about to say something, but by the time he looked up, we were gone.

The patterns carved in the second stone slab glowed with Ka and rolled to the right. I closed it behind us as we dashed outside, weapons freed from their compartments and urgency pumping through our blood. I pointed.

"There!"

The goblin hadn't gotten far. In fact, he was treading nonchalantly with the crystal at his side until he caught sight of us racing toward him.

"Grab him!" Andy shouted.

The creature jumped as an arrow stuck in the ground where his foot had been. He let out a shrill and ran, zigzagging through a field of boulders. I stayed hot on his tracks, firing a few spells that crumbled the stones but missed their mark. Each blast was trailed by thunder that rumbled in the frothing clouds above. I glanced up for a moment at the brewing storm, hoping it would mask the clamor I was making.

The goblin squealed, hopping across rocks. I reached my hand forward, trying to sweep him up with my Ka, but my rapid heartbeat and frenzied thoughts made it impossible to concentrate. He was getting away.

For a moment I lost sight of him, but Scooter chirruped in my right ear, guiding my attention to a stack of platy rocks that the goblin was trying to scale. He hopped and scrambled, glancing back at me worriedly. His climb was hindered by the cluster of Dark Lands crystals tucked under his right arm.

There it is, I thought.

383

With one last burst of energy I darted across the field and leapt, grabbing the goblin's scaly ankle. He let out a panicked scream and kicked, his dirty, three-toed foot slapping my face several times until I released him, and he pulled himself to the top, taking a moment to look over the side and make a taunting, evil grin.

He disappeared. I growled. Andy, Veronica, Murry, and Boris appeared behind me.

"He's up there!" I reported. Andy found a toe-hold and climbed with me. Boris gave us both a boost.

"We'll be up right after," Veronica said.

"Be careful!" Murry added.

We reached the top. I pulled myself up first.

"Any sign of that creepy thing?" Andy grunted.

I couldn't find the words to answer. Andy grappled the edge and lifted himself, asking again, "Can you see—?" His exhausted words trailed, as he and I stood there, frozen.

The goblin hopped, jumped, and skipped over the boulders, then climbed another rock face with ease. His crazed squeals and screams transformed into cackles as he reached the summit and set down the treasure. He leaned on his knuckles and bounced in place. His purple tongue wagged and jaw dropped into a sinister grin, as a black aura surrounded the crystal. The rock shook, then levitated upward into a set of long, armored fingers.

Shamaul stood atop the platform, hand closing around the last piece we needed to get home, as a monstrous horde of Dark Lands creatures writhed in the basin beneath him, eagerly awaiting orders. The Dark Lands, a place I once interpreted as desolate and abandoned, now teemed with the likes of every nightmarish monster imaginable. Hulking soldiers with dark gray skin clutched heavy weaponry, flanked at all sides by throngs of other depraved forces. Wolves, boars, gargoyles, goblins, and traugs all stood at the warlock's command.

The goblin's squealing laughter blended with a trembling choir of roars, snarls, and shrills that rose from the ghastly legion below. They began to writhe impatiently, lusting for battle. And the warlock, with his piercing yellow, serpentine eyes fixed on Andy and me, lifted his heavy armored hand, and pointed.

39

Ambush

Somewhere in the distance I heard war drums. Or so I thought. My heart sent shockwaves through my body that fueled my escape with a rush of numbing chemicals. My feet pounded against the ground in sync with Andy's. I don't remember what warning I shouted to the others, but when the ground beneath them trembled and boulders collapsed, they joined in our flight.

Roars of prehistoric cadence shuddered the Dark Lands. Not to be outdone, the thunder above resounded like booming snares. My heart thudded in tempo, my feet provided percussion against the slaty gravel, and storm winds blew sharply like eerie, medieval flutes. A ghastly orchestra, which crescendoed when the parapet-like rock stack exploded into smithereens, and Shamaul's horde of depraved monsters charged through.

You've made a costly error, the warlock hissed. I couldn't tell whether his voice was transmitted through speech or thought, but it echoed everywhere. I ran, leading the group toward another rock stack I thought we could climb. But the formation was upturned as soon as we arrived by a massive traug that rammed through, roaring maliciously as its goblin rider cackled and directed its motions from the creature's back. *There is no escape now...*

The goblin kicked his feet with schadenfreude and hooted as he levered a spear embedded in the animal's shoulder, making his unwieldly steed roar and punch the ground. Its clawed hand broke the earth behind us as we went in another direction and scrambled up a hillside. Loose gravel made for a sloppy retreat. Boris was forced to all-fours to make the ascent. I scaled the hill first and reached down to help up the others, while Murry and Veronica provided cover with arrows and spellcasts.

From this vantage I could see the entirety of the dismal expanse. The Dark Lands looked to be squirming as a single mass as the warlock's horde marched. Beyond them, cracked earth and dead trees, and even farther in the distance, the jagged barbicans of Shamaul's castle. The highest tower punctured the cloudbank, the epicenter of a terrible storm which rippled and swirled, casting awful gusts down into the basins to flow over the monstrous army, where frigid, whispering winds delivered the warlock's will.

Veronica fired off three arrows before reloading. "There's too many of them."

I assessed the incoming horde swarming the base of the hill. Few were nimble or light enough to make the ascent easily. And those capable were swiftly picked off by our projectiles.

"This is good," I said.

"What?"

"This is good. If we keep the high ground we can take them out one by one."

The group agreed with the plan and circled. Spells burst from wands, arrows from crossbow, and rocks and boulders were shoved over the edge by Boris and Andy. No creature made it higher than halfway up the hill before they toppled under our ruthless barrage. At one point traugs resorted to throwing their goblin riders into the air to attack us. Most of them missed, slamming into the hill, rolling, and getting trampled. But some hit their mark.

"*Oof!*" Andy grunted, knocked flat on the ground by one of the scaly cretins. The monstrosity somersaulted and righted himself, made a gravely laugh, then bounded on his knuckles like an ape and kicked. "Ow! Hey—*Ow!*" Andy hollered. Veronica hurried to his aid and hammered the beast in the chin. I helped up my friend, who slashed at his attacker and severed an arm. Andy's sword steamed as the goblin tilted his head at the wound, which sprayed ink-like blood. He just laughed at the injury hysterically, then ran at us, only to be batted from the peak by Boris' spiky club. The minotaur snorted in aggravation, then looked to the clouds, where bat-like silhouettes circled against the deep, gray canopy.

Andy shook the blood from his blade, eyeing the new threats that collected in the sky. "We're toast."

"It's okay," I said, partially to myself. "We can hold them off like we did the others."

Bright blue flares of magic drew my attention to Murry, whose powerful spells cascaded down the hillside more frenziedly than before. Between shots he spoke, "Not to be the bearer of bad news, but..."

To his left, I glimpsed what had developed since the goblin attack. My heart sunk.

"Orks," Murry narrated, as Shamaul's soldiers marched up the hillside, stairstepping the bodies of fallen creatures for traction.

Evil brewed above and below. Screeches pulled my focus to the sky, grunts to the abyss. The orks were closer, I reasoned. I lined up beside Murry.

"Split up!"

The two of us blasted the insurgent orks with every spell in the book, while Veronica, the most accurate shot, took out gargoyles with her crossbow, and Andy and Boris hacked away anything that swooped too low or climbed too high.

The system was working. From behind, I heard gargoyles uttering dying squeals, and metallic slashing sounds were occasionally followed by a severed wing spinning by. Scooter lilted a nervous tone as ink-colored blood was sprayed. Some coated the back of my vest, and Scooter, unable to shake the substance from his cone-shaped shell, shimmied sideways, set down in a defensive pose, and made an uncharacteristic, growling noise.

With the gargoyles being dealt with, Murry and I focused on the terrors below. The wizard summoned a vortex of wind that halted the orks' hike. I cast a bolt of lightning with the Zyros spell, which arced like plasma and funneled into Murry's airstream. The spells combined to form a miniature electric storm, frying anything that came near. The sparking tornado swept, bolting with spasmatic blue light that condensed into a sphere, then detonated, sprawling enemies and slowing their climb a moment longer. But the orks were relentless. Many of them lifted from the ground with gritting teeth and smoking skin, regrouping to climb once more. I made a tired pant, then took aim. Another spell charged in the globe of my wand.

But before I could fire, I heard the sound of three arrows whizzing skyward in quick succession, gusting wingbeats, and panicked shouts.

"Marv!"

"Look out!"

I grunted. By the time I turned, I was airborne, tackled and carried into the storm by a giant gargoyle. My friends' screams faded as the monster flew higher.

Scooter went to the claws of my captor, biting but balking as if tasting something horrible. The talons remained latched, tightening and cutting my skin. The scent of rot had suddenly infested the air as well. In my struggle I managed to get an arm free and punch the monster's face. Its head turned backward, neck cracking, then rotated completely around to face me again.

I gaped in terror at the flying corpse. Its sunken, milky stare locked with mine. Its scarred, dark gray body looked frankensteined together with seared marks around every joint. Its jaw dropped like a puppet, and billows of smoke poured from its shattered smile. I coughed as the ghastly vapors covered me, and the haunting voice of Shamaul surfaced in the ripples.

You've had a long, arduous journey, he scathed. The dark strands of smoke hissed as if taking a breath, then roiled again. *All to deliver me what I require.*

I screamed as the smoke seeped in, assaulting my mind with images of Murry's rucksack and the crystals, followed by Shamaul's stinging, yellow eyes. The clouds thundered, lighting held captive in the unhallowed nimbus.

This is the end... the voices overlapped in sinister tones, some muted and some irate. *Your involvement is no longer necessary.*

The gargoyle's tattered, undead wings tucked in, and we plummeted to the earth.

Black smoke drained from the gargoyle's mouth as we fell. Scooter cheeped and clung to my neck. The ground closed in. My muscles clenched to brace for pain, and a cushion of my Ka manifested between me and the rocky plain, flickering just moments before impact. I held on to Scooter as the ground broke and I tunneled partway into the gravel, and the gargoyle's body broke apart like a fragile puzzle, strewing limbs everywhere.

My back ached, though not nearly as much as it should have. I was able to lift myself slightly, deep scratches stinging in the fetid air. Then, a soft ringing sound. Through the fabric of my shirt I saw a blue light. I checked my chest and found the talisman spinning on its chain beside my father's dog tags, lighting up and mending the lacerations. I took a few breaths to steady my dizzied mind, blinking away the fog in my vision to see a battle waging atop the hill in the distance. I couldn't believe how far away I had fallen. I gripped the shingled edge of my crater to try to get up, but froze when the surrounding pebbles bounced, jostled by an earth-shaking force.

Heavy footsteps and grunting breaths. I turned to the left and saw an ork—this one particularly musclebound—hoisting an enormous, spiked battle-mace. His square, tan teeth scraped together, jowls vibrating and wet nostrils puffing rancorous breaths. His beady eyes squinted at me as he stomped to a halt before my feet, snarling. His knuckles bulged under gray skin and veins throbbed as he lifted his mace, ready to crush me. I quickly went for the loops of my vest to draw my wand, but it wasn't there.

I seized, searching for the silver instrument. Nowhere near me. I soon spotted its sheen secluded on the ground some distance away, but it was too late.

Then, without prompting, Scooter leapt. Shrieking, the tiny cephalopod latched onto the ork's face, his saw-like maw biting repeatedly. The ork wailed and dropped his weapon. He grasped for his face, but his oversized biceps prohibited him from reaching close enough. The ork yowled helplessly, as Scooter continued to grind his flesh into a bloody mess. I couldn't believe it. I was both thankful and shocked by Scooter's bravery.

Careening down the hill, a plume of dust. Bodies of goblins and boars went sailing as the force pressed through. And, sensing the perfect time to bail, Scooter jumped back into my arms. The ork's hands caught the thick blood that poured from his face, and his insane eyes shone through the slop. He growled, spitting through his dripping mouth, and turned to retrieve his mace.

CRACK!

Boris' horns rammed into the monster, sprawling him out several feet to my left. Before the ork could stand, the minotaur guardian grasped the discarded mace. With unfathomable strength, Boris lifted it, roared, and brought it down, and the ork was slain with his own weapon.

Before too long, the others followed down the path Boris had made. Veronica praised her pet. Andy took my hand and lifted me to my feet.

"Gotcha," he grunted as he pulled me up. "You're a disaster magnet, you know that?"

"Apparently," I said.

Murry sighed in relief as he patted my shoulder, clearing the dust and gravel from my vest, and returned my wand.

I thanked them all and petted Scooter's shell, who settled in my arms and made a purring sound.

My focus floated. Across the plain, the Dark Warlock stood on a jagged cliff and drummed his fingers on the crystal cluster. The others traced my gaze, and we stared him down for a moment, until he tapped the point of his scepter. It made an eerie, metallic ring and drew the attention of every monster nearby. An ork, a traug with a goblin rider, and a pair of hungry terrorwolves marched, stamped, and skulked our way. The wolves growled and clapped their jaws, the ork's lip curled as he beat a war hammer against his palm, and the goblin cackled and levered the spears in his ride's shoulders.

"Forward, beast!" he laughed sadistically from his saddle. "Kill them! Eat them!" The traug roared and gained speed, and we drew our weapons.

From the sky, a misty trail of vapors plunged. We halted and backstepped when the traug wobbled in a daze, then fell over on the ground, a translucent sword embedded in its cranium.

The warrior to whom it belonged, clad in white armor, took hold of the icy handle, cold lifting off the weapon as it was pried, before the icicle-like blade broke off and remained lodged in the creature's skull. It was Arduuk. The first Elemental we encountered on our journey held out his fractured sword for inspection.

"What undignified creatures," he noted. A new blade made of ice cracked and snapped sharply as it reformed on the weapon's handle.

The defenseless goblin rider shook his head in pain, then shrilled at the sight of Arduuk and tried to escape, only to be frozen solid at the touch of the sword's point. His ice-covered body then ruptured when a violet streak of lighting surged through. The two wolves were taken off-guard by the next attacker. They were walloped, punched, and kicked from every angle, seemingly by an invisible opponent, until his momentum slowed, and we saw it was Zax. One wolf went soaring into a copse of dead trees that splintered apart on impact, and the other spiraled sideways into the body of the ork soldier.

"Threats resolved," Zax buzzed.

The snarling ork returned to his feet, only to be stabbed in the neck by a fiery sabre. Erah appeared. She twisted the sword brutally in the wound. Bones snapped and blood gushed, and the ork was instantly killed. The monster's heavy body collapsed at her feet as she steadied her breaths and fire rolled over the blade of her sabre to cleanse it.

"What he said," she replied.

Kail snaked through the air, touching down upon the rocky terrain as her rider, Grimmoch, unsheathed his grisly sword and dismounted. His blazing eyes swept the clearing.

"That went faster than I expected," Grimmoch said, relaxing his battle stance and petting Kail. "That's what I get for feeding you two meals' worth of snacks before takeoff."

Kail leaned into him and cooed.

Erah teased, "You missed all the fun."

"There will be plenty more opportunities," Arduuk said, nodding to a faction of the warlock's wicked horde that had stomped into the plain.

"Approximately forty within the immediate span," Zax calculated.

Arduuk sighed, "Yes, thank you for the statistic."

Grimmoch took a moment to greet us. He knelt. The Eye of the Aevæs shimmered in gold paint on his forehead as his flaming stare met ours. "Thought you could use the help."

Murry bowed in gratitude. "Thank you, grandson."

Andy rested his sword on his shoulder. "We were doing alright."

Veronica gave him an unamused glare.

He coughed. "But yeah, thanks for dropping in."

Spirals of wind sent pebbles chittering around our shoes. We shielded ourselves from the downcast breezes as the karv touched down, piloted by Orin the Ka Master. The vehicle whirred as it settled, and Orin hopped out, addressing the Elementals:

"What happened to staying in your seats, eh? Maybe a little warning next time you decide to jump overboard." He huffed and drew a crystalline wand with a silver handle from his cloak. "Hello again, Realmhoppers." He took a whiff of the air and hacked. "Goodness, it smells even worse than I remember!"

"Perhaps we should clean it up then," Arduuk suggested. His frozen sword cut the air as Shamaul's hideous horde crept nearer, ghoulish snarls and shrieks collecting in the wicked atmosphere.

Erah grinned. "Well said."

Zax saluted. "A fair objective."

Grimmoch held his sword with both hands, his blazing eyes reflecting on the metal's sheen as he watched his father's encroaching horde with brutal intensity. "I have waited many cycles for this."

Almost immediately the tides of the battle shifted in our favor. Although we were but a decuplet of fighters, the power of the Elementals and the Ka Master made us an unstoppable force. With their addition to our team, the horde was minced into more manageable factions, which we fought off with expertise.

Veronica sniped a gargoyle that strayed from his flock to attack us. The arrow stuck in his neck as he squealed and fell past the flight path of the windserpent, Kail, who roared and bit down on the body of another, scattering the rest. She spat out a bloody mouthful and pursued them. Beneath the dragon, her master slashed at ork assailants. Sparks flew from clashing metal as Grimmoch blocked every strike, landing a killing blow in the brute's abdomen before moving on to the next.

In perfect synchronicity Erah and Arduuk spun. Half the enemies they faced were burned to death; the other half frozen. Zax would occasionally speed through to finish off a straggler, before zipping across the plain in the same moment to take out orks that had yet to even reach our sight. And in the middle of the plain, no creature was safe from the might of the Ka Master. With just the flick of Orin's wrist, bodies lifted off the ground in a tornado of Ka and were chucked in every direction.

We navigated the exploding field as ork bodies came down like meteors. Scooter kept lookout from atop Boris' head-horns. He chirped to alert us to any threats that were left standing, and we proceeded accordingly.

Left and right, the horde was toppled with striking precision as we advanced the battlefield in unison. Whenever one of us reloaded or recharged, another would step in to strike. I cast an indigo flare from my wand that exploded against an armored goblin. Andy issued the finishing strike. Veronica unloaded her crossbow into the body of a charging ork. Murry disoriented him with a gusting spell, and Boris finished him off with a powerful club to the face. We sidestepped and parried, spun and lunged, in a merciless dance with our fiendish attackers. And before long we had emerged from the onslaught prepared to fight again.

"Everyone good?" I asked.

Veronica's crossbow whizzed as the central gear rotated and the string drew back. "Oh, yeah," she said, reloading three arrows from her quiver.

Boris smacked an audacious goblin that strayed too close, sending him screaming into the distance. The minotaur snorted.

Andy's sword glowed red hot. "I'm set for another round."

Magic coursed on the end of Murry's wand. "Ready when you are."

Scooter leapt onto my shoulder and chirped.

I raised my wand, glimpsing my reflection on its silvery surface. The globe in its middle glowed brightly with power, and the point of its shaft was aimed toward a steep, rocky outcrop, atop which a long stretch of stone that resembled a halved mountain lay. There, the warlock Shamaul stood and commanded his army, serpentine eyes sweeping the gorge below as thunder rattled the trembling overcast. His fierce pupils landed on me, and he lowered his head, the brow of his silver mask appearing to frown with hatred.

I stared right back at him and held my wand at my side.

Cold metal pressed against my chest. My father's dog tags clinked together like chimes as I stepped to the front of the group. The others fell into formation. Weapons keen and brandished, the fire of valiance alight in our souls. I felt the power swell in the Ka of my teammates, imbuing our march with steadfast resolve. We trooped in unity against the shadowy vastness and funneled into the barren xeriscape that preceded the warlock's jagged platform.

Shamaul remained there. His tattered, black cape blew in the breezes of the brewing storm. He watched us, yellow eyes burning with a blend of bestial maliciousness and loathing curiosity.

I treaded on at the lead, never breaking stride. "Let's keep going."

40
A Different Shade

Nothing in the battlefield was left intact. Rock stacks crumbled and crags in the earth deepened. It seemed that nature itself had turned against us in the final stretch of our fight. The storm assaulted us with stinging winds and the terrain quaked and separated to release searing gases. I hopped over a steaming crack and reached out, Ka fluxing in my palm and forming a shield to block the whirlwind.

Three crystals were affixed in the crescent-shaped blade of Shamaul's scepter, feeding sporadic luminance into a blue, glass sphere at its center. When the green crystal glowed he lased the ground and summoned more earthquakes, and when the blue one shimmered he shot a beam into the sky, strewing the already-freezing winds with sharp pellets of ice. The blusters pressed against our bodies and slowed our advancement, and the cracking earth separated our group.

I shielded my face as a massive fissure fractured beside me, breathed hot fumes, and bisected our team down the middle. Andy and I on the right; Murry, Veronica, and Boris on the left. With the group divided, orks moved in to pick us off.

"Oh, good. *More* bad guys," Andy said.

Three on our side, four on theirs. I stayed on guard. Murry and I readied our wands, Andy brandished his sword, Boris' head shook like an enraged bull, and Veronica traded her crossbow for her multiweapon. They attacked.

Axes, maces, and hammers struck the fragile ground, prodding us closer and closer to the edge of the crevasse. Andy slashed at one of our attacker's blades, leaving a glowing cut in the iron. The ork eyeballed it in surprise, then growled and lunged again.

"On your right!" Andy yelled. I blasted the Luminiera spell at a charging ork. It roared at the blistering light and missed, falling into the crevasse.

"Thanks," I said, then shouted, "Heads up!"

Andy ducked under a swinging mace and hacked at the culprit's legs, who staggered and tripped, joining his comrade in the abyss.

"Thanks."

Becoming aware of a stinging sensation more violent than before, I lifted my head to the impetuous sky. A pillar of blue energy coursed from the warlock's scepter and infected the clouds. They conjured winds laced with unnatural, cutting vapors. My sneakers shifted, legs buckling under the pressure. I dodged another swing of an ork's weapon. The bulky monsters were unaffected by the storm.

Thunder rumbled inside the thick strata as Shamaul pressed his weapon higher, making the cycloning squalls nearly impossible to bear. Then, a white flash disrupted his spell. Orin entered the fray and launched a heavy barrage of Ka at the warlock, dispelling the blue energy and leaving the clouds to writhe, unaltered.

Seizing the moment, Murry thrusted his wand skyward. "Solaos inverum!" he called.

The clouds answered with a rumbling timbre.

His instrument flashed with power. "Aeralisk!"

A bright beam surged high and pierced the canopy, flashing over the gray formations before returning with a fierce column of wind that reversed the direction of the gales. The immense, gusting force roared down, vortexing debris. Leaving us completely unscathed, the otherworldly power swept up broken rocks and propelled them at our attackers.

"Quickly!" Murry urged. While the orks were down, we switched positions and went on the offensive, blasting, slashing, fighting. One of our orks clumsily cleaved the ground with his axe, and Andy's sword—glowing red with heat—sliced clean through the handle. The ork looked dumbfounded at his useless weapon, its molten end dripping. I fired the Sphira spell into the beast's gut. He dominoed into one of his remaining brethren, and the two plummeted gracelessly into the crevasse.

The orks across from us met the same fate. Two were beaten senseless by Boris, then prodded over the edge by the slightest of nudges. Murry took out the next one with the swish of his wand, directing a windy vortex with fine precision. And finally, Veronica's multiweapon extended to its full length. In a terrifying display, the speared ends chopped the ground as she spun it like a propeller.

She gained speed. An ork, devoid of weapon, backed alongside the other remaining fiend as Veronica's momentum and ferocity apexed. Spears sparked on the cracking ground. Chains rattled as the weapon released into a three-sectioned staff. The two orks found themselves cloistered on the point of the rocky ridgeline, facing the drop-off of the chasm. They grunted in terror when the weak slab of rock snapped. Veronica retracted her weapon into a pole, wedged it into the fracture, and pulled back. The warlock's henchmen belted echoey roars as they reunited with their squadron.

I watched them disappear into the blackness, still hearing their screams long after their bodies vanished.

"That was something," I said. When Andy didn't respond, I turned to him. He was staring at Veronica in awe. She twirled her multiweapon, retracting it fully to its compact handle, then clipped it to her belt and redrew her crossbow.

"That was the sickest thing I've ever seen," Andy said. He was practically drooling he was so mesmerized.

I had to peel him away. "*Alright*, let's go."

Shamaul's platform was well under siege by the time we arrived, pelted by the Ka Master's light. From every direction, Ka rained down. Shamaul kept a shield of dark energy raised—the only thing he had a chance to conjure beneath the relentless onslaught—as his scepter glowed. Then, the third crystal in its blade drained dark patterns into the globe. The blue sphere washed over with black, and he tapped the scepter's metal point once.

A horrible ringing filled the air, one which seemed to only affect Orin and me. Orin buckled and I screamed, covering my ears as I crumbled to my knees. The pounding noise carried with it a confusing vision:

In my mind, I had returned to the ruins we explored earlier, confronted with the statue of Kraiden the Elder and Etheria the Sorceress. Orks, traugs, and goblins flowed around me, as though I were a ghost, and swelled against the statue. It tipped. The one labeled as Kraiden looked to me, his stone head swiveling on a rigid neck, and a morose, helpless expression forged in his features.   The writhing mass of monsters then upturned the statue, and the two figures shattered into a million pieces.

The vision released me. I panted and gathered myself as the faint ringing sound faded in my eardrums. Andy was bent over trying to help. Scooter was cheeping repeatedly in my ear. The others called to me from the other side of the crevasse. All their voices were muffled. I unclasped my ears and blinked. Staring across the plain, I saw Orin. His eyes were wet. He turned to see more than half the horde marching, filing through the woods en route to the statue of the two spellcasters.

The Ka Master's eyes streamed with tears as he scowled at the warlock. He knew Kraiden and Etheria, I realized. Shamaul stared back at him with scathing enmity. Orin's sneer twisted in anguish, and he took off, almost flying, toward the ruins in the woods.

Andy helped me to my feet, watching the Ka Master disappear in the distance, trying to outrace the horde.

"Uh... what just happened?" Andy asked.

"Where's he going?" Veronica questioned.

I found my balance and tried to answer them, "He has to—"

POW!

Steam exploded from the crevasse, rattling our stances as the split in the earth cracked deeper and stretched longer, further separating Andy and me from our teammates.

Andy's face flushed with rage as he turned to the warlock atop the platform, green crystal fluxing in his scepter. The Sword of the Sun glowed brightly in Andy's clenching fist. He ran.

I didn't have a chance to ask Andy what his plan of attack was, but I was fairly sure there wasn't one. I hurried after my friend, scaling the steep, makeshift steps that spiraled the stone tower on which the warlock stood. I tried to call to Andy, to get him to slow up a moment, but he was fuming. His sword trailed waves of heat as he charged ahead. I wheezed and sprinted.

Andy skidded to the top, sword outstretched as he checked every corner. I ran up behind him. Only the warlock's goblin subordinate stood before us, the crystal cluster resting soundly on a rock to his left. The goblin scampered away.

From this summit everything was visible; on the horizon I saw explosions of power bursting through the trees: fire, ice, lightning, and Ka. Orin and the Elementals were fighting a valiant battle to protect the statue. Down in the plain nearby, a structure lay hidden in the basin of two warped, rocky peaks. Five interlocked arches stood on the outskirts of the battlefield. *The Mesalon*, I remembered. No wonder Shamaul chose this vantage.

Andy was furious. "Where is he?"

My throat bobbed as an unnerving quiet overtook the summit. I checked on Murry and the others below us. The rucksack was still strapped to the wizard's back, crystals stowed safely inside. I edged closer to the fifth crystal that sat on a round, flat rock, waiting for us.

I wavered reaching for it. *I don't trust this.* I hesitated.

It won't be that easy...

I locked. That second thought wasn't mine. Andy and I spun around in horror and dodged the downswing of the warlock's bladed scepter. Shamaul's horrible, demonic form peeled from the shadows and attacked us.

Andy blocked the next swipe, clashing with the glass sphere. It made a low hum on impact and rattled the mystic vapors coiling inside. They fluxed deep blue. The next strike Andy dealt made a thin crack on the globe, and the blue fog seeped out.

Andy jeered, "Sorry for busting your mood ring."

Shamaul's head tilted down as the sphere's cloudy vapors bled into black.

"Someone's cranky—*Whoa!*"

Animate shadows crept up, wrapped his ankles, and twisted. Andy grunted as he slammed into the ground and the warlock aimed his weapon at his gut.

Ka glowed on my friend's body. I pushed him out of the way and he skidded to the left just as the silver spike transfixed the earth. Shamaul's venomous stare struck me.

He leapt, swinging his weapon high. I blasted him with light and Andy slashed from the back. Whenever he went for one of us, the other would step in to strike. Andy blocked. I fired. Ka deflected Shamaul's next swing. Andy's sword clanged against his armor. Enraged, the warlock pressed his scepter down and a dark ring of power rippled outward and knocked us flat. He went for Andy first.

As Shamaul loomed over him, an arrow stuck in his ram-like horn. He removed it just as another one tinged against the forehead of his silver mask. He growled.

Although the cracks in the earth prevented her from fighting at our sides, Veronica fired arrows from atop another pillar of rocks some distance away. She reloaded, as Boris fought off several gargoyles that swooped at her, desperate to defend their leader. They ragdolled left and right. The minotaur made a roar as he swatted them.

Veronica aimed down the rail of her crossbow. The limbs flexed with tension, then sprang. Another shaft embedded in Shamaul's shoulder, he snapped it off and raised his scepter, firing.

A blue sphere of energy whirred, exploding the ground beneath Veronica. She teetered as the section crumbled away, but Murry appeared in time to grab hold of her arm and save her from falling.

The wizard looked across at his son, fear blanking his stare as it met with the Dark Warlock's. Shamaul and Murry shared an eerie exchange as the clouds produced more thunder. I pushed off the ground and seized my opportunity.

Icy wind surged from my wand and swept up rocks, denting the warlock's body armor as they came down. The Inferna spell baked the stones to fuse them to his feet and the Zyros spell arced electricity through the metal sections of his armor, jolting him while he was confined. Smoke rose off his cloak. Andy jumped in and slashed at him, the Sword of the Sun gathering enough heat to melt sections of his armor.

He reeled and roared.

The next swing Andy took was caught in Shamaul's armored fist. My friend tugged futilely on the handle. Molten metal rolled in the warlock's palm.

Shadows condensed on his frame. They exploded. The sword went one way, Andy the other. Rocky debris pelted my chest. Scooter shrilled and held on as we flew back, skidding just inches from the edge. I took in pained, whistling breaths and peered through the scratches in my lenses at the nightmare standing before me: the warlock, unfettered and coiled with smoke.

Shamaul's anger was palpable. His yellow eyes smoldered with inhuman rage as he stepped forward, cold, blue energy spinning in his scepter.

"How foolish are you?" he questioned scathingly.

Scooter urged me to get up. I placed one knee on the ground and pushed, only to be struck in the jaw by the glass sphere of Shamaul's scepter. I slammed back down.

"How slowly do you want to die?"

Blood streamed from a gash on my lip. I winced at the sting and tried to get up again. My muscles quivered with ache as the warlock neared. From the ground I glimpsed the sideways image of Andy crawling, reclaiming his sword.

Shamaul loomed over me. "You should have never come here," he gritted. "This Realm is mine."

Andy lunged. His sword was on fire.

Shamaul sensed him. They clashed blades. Flame roared on the edge of Andy's sword as he swung. The warlock parried, guiding the flaming weapon into the ground where it left a deep, searing crack. Shamaul then stomped Andy's leg. It snapped sideways below the knee. He screamed.

"Andy!" I yelled.

A gust of dark aura slammed into my friend and sent him rolling down the rock face and into the basin. The same energy blasted me from the peak soon afterward.

Sharp rocks cut into me as I tumbled, landing in a patch of land covered with boulders. I shielded Scooter and myself with what little Ka I could conjure, as Shamaul sliced the air in a reaping motion, sending bright blue crescents of energy raining down. They sliced through boulders, revealing their sleek, mirrored interiors.

The warlock changed focuses when Veronica and Boris rushed to the aid of Andy. I wanted to call at them, but my voice came out in a rasping wail. They were too far away.

Shamaul stood at the peak, aiming at the three of them. Veronica positioned herself in front of Andy. The warlock's scepter drew back, its blade lethal as the fangs of a cobra poising to strike. The blue sphere at its center whirred.

"Mahl!" a shrill, broken outcry shattered his focus.

The Dark Warlock turned to see Murry holding his hands high.

"Mahlgrador! Stop this!"

Shamaul growled. Shivering winds hissed like rattlesnakes as he stepped through a portal of smoke, emerging just strides from his father.

"How dare you utter that name?"

"Stop this at once!" Murry pleaded. Tears welled in his eyes as the monster that ruled the Dark Lands strode just inches from him. Black vapors lifted off his shoulders as he stared down the wizard. A full foot taller, he watched him like a predator through the eyeholes of his fanged, silver mask.

Murry kept his arms outstretched, as if awaiting a hug. "You're not what made you," his voice trembled. "Come back to the world..." Tears streaked his old face. "Come back, my son. Leave it behind. Leave them be..."

Shamaul removed his mask, and Murry's face went pale.

"Your son is dead."

The air hummed, and the wizard was bludgeoned by a wave of dark Ka. He flew across the field and landed inside a cave-like structure, where dust and grit jettisoned on impact. We screamed for him as rocks crumbled over the opening. Shamaul turned around and redonned his mask. Snaking, bladed tendrils twisted from his sleeve and lifted the wizard's torn rucksack to his view.

I wanted to scream, but no voice came out. I sank behind a boulder to remain hidden as the warlock's glare swept over us. Scooter curled in his shell. Having secured what he wanted, Shamaul stepped through another smoky aperture and reappeared atop his peak. The Dark Lands' creatures cheered in resonant grunts and screeches as their leader stood tall atop his platform.

There has to be a way out, I thought, straining to find a solution. *There's always a way out.*

As I clambered through the disturbed rubble my knee pressed against something metallic. A shield. It was dark and patinaed, with a golden edge and a diamond-shaped symbol in its center. I dug it out, and beneath it was a tarnished, gold helmet with damaged, red plumage. And, the final piece that lay discarded in the shallow crater: a sword, one left abandoned in this battlefield from whatever war was waged there long ago.

I took hold of it. The unearthed sword looked like it was made of crystal. Its blade had a translucent, frosty tone. Its pommel was sharp and diamantine, its handle wrapped in green fabric. Its hilt was gold like the helmet it was buried with, and what looked like a sliver of Ravacan crystal was embedded in the ricasso.

I eyed it in wonder. Scooter emerged from his shell to spectate, as something willed me to turn it over. Along one edge of the blade, a word was neatly carved in the Trymbadorian alphabet. I couldn't read it. But, on the opposite side of the fuller, a word was engraved in a lettering I did recognize.

It read, *Areok*.

My eyes flashed upward, locking with my reflection on the surface of a halved boulder. My mind braced, trying to grasp the origin of the artifacts and how they all ended up here, but there was no time.

I had to act fast.

Andy held his broken leg in agony. Veronica knelt by him, holding his head. "It's alright."

Thunder crashed, drawing their focus to the Dark Warlock at the summit. His sharp tendrils cut at the rucksack's fabric and rifled through the bag. Veronica searched left and right for Marvin or Murry. Nothing. They were nowhere to be seen. Boris batted off goblins that crept near, cackling with renewed confidence after their leader's acquisition of the crystals. Shamaul held up the red one, set it on the ground and cleaved off a section, which floated into place on his scepter. Andy uttered another pained tone.

"It's alright," Veronica repeated. She swallowed hard, not believing her own words.

She turned back as Boris clubbed away at attackers. An ork challenged the minotaur, punching his side. Boris bludgeoned him, roared, and clubbed again, over and over until the wooden club splintered apart, then proceeded to beat the ork with his bare hands. The ork grabbed the minotaur's wrists, but he was promptly head-butted by horns and felled in a bloody heap.

A giant traug with mammoth-like tusks and curling claws stampeded in next. Boris snorted tiredly and turned, fists clenched. He blocked Veronica and Andy with his body, prepared to protect them at any cost.

The traug roared, then squealed as its head turned upside down in a flash of Ka. It quaked the earth as it slammed down, and lanternlight appeared from behind a rock.

"Bad beast," Gnuthe said. He hopped in front of Boris and set his lantern to full-glow, keeping the rest of the horde at bay.

The warlock's scepter shook with power and instability. One cavity remained unfilled. Then, the sound of shuffling rocks drew his notice. He halted his process, overly cautious, and turned to behold the shield of his old rival.

Andy sat up, seeing his friend crest the cliffside. He and Veronica watched with anticipation.

"*Get him, Marv,*" Andy whispered.

Across from them, the stone blockade sealing Murry's cave flashed. The barricade exploded and rocks tumbled as Murry plodded through, searching breathlessly. He caught sight of the duel atop the summit, where the silhouette of Marvin edged forward tentatively, brandishing a large shield. Just as the lightning flashed within the nimbus above, the warlock attacked.

The wizard went numb.

In one swift motion, Areok's shield was knocked from grasp, as tendrils burst from Shamaul's sleeve and pierced Marvin's stomach.

Shouts of terror echoed everywhere as Marvin's body was thrown aside. It tumbled down the cliff, rolling into the basin and pluming dust. Andy hollered and crawled, ignoring the pain shooting through his broken leg as he pulled himself to his friend's side. Veronica ran to them.

Shamaul watched the terror unfold, tilting his head callously as the fallen Realmhopper was swarmed by his teammates. He lifted his scepter to finish the job, but a surging, electric bolt overtook him.

"No!" Murry roared. Magic coursed from his wand with unbridled power, singeing Shamaul's damaged armor. Tears burned the wizard's skin as he screamed again, lightning blasting forth. The Dark Warlock had to focus all his might on blockading the blasts.

Andy knelt over Marvin. Veronica's throat knotted as she beheld the wounds. Boris snorted with concern. Gnuthe saw it last, gasping and then flashing his lantern at a wolf.

"C'mon man..." Andy choked.

Marvin was pale. He uttered gasps, head darting like a frenzied bird.

"Don't do this to me." Andy held on to his friend. "I *can't* do this alone. I need you!"

Scooter scuttled over the battlefield, strangely calm. In his tentacles he dragged the talisman. Andy blinked away his tears and grabbed it, hope suddenly renewed.

"*Good boy, good boy—*" he whispered. He held the healing stone over his friend's stomach, squeezing it in his fist. His voice was shaking. "Okay, here ya go, buddy. You're gonna be alright..."

Andy and Veronica waited anxiously for effect as the shimmering blue dust spilled from the talisman. The grains swirled and shined, but redirected in midair, flying instead into Andy's leg to cure the fracture.

"No, no! Not me!" Andy cried.

"*Rr...*" Marvin uttered a sound.

Andy turned to him.

"*Renora...*" Marvin uttered.

Andy and Veronica tilted their heads in shock.

"*Renora... Renora,*" the words spilled out nonstop.

Andy and Veronica stared in disbelief as the body became transparent, repeating the word as it faded away.

"*No way,*" Andy breathed.

Scooter chirruped and cheeped at them, hopping up and down as he tried to convey a message.

Andy's eyes, wild and disoriented, returned to the summit as the warlock deflected Murry's attacks and blasted the ground at his feet to halt the onslaught. The wizard fell backward in the rubble and groaned, and the Dark Lands exploded with shrills and howls as their leader stepped to the edge of the rock and held the rucksack that contained the final crystal. He stood above all of them to display his treasure victoriously.

"My power has no equal!" he roared, thunder rattling the land in congruence with his tone.

A tremor of calls echoed him.

"I cannot be matched by a child!"

Then, in a flash of white, a crystalline blade was swung, and the warlock's hand was severed.

Shamaul's hand twirled off the cliff and into the crevasse below, and the rucksack floated in a current of Ka back into Murry's arms.

"It won't be that easy," I said.

Shamaul turned to face me, grunting and leaving his scepter standing in a crack to hold his streaming wound. His serpentine eyes studied me, then looked over the edge of his platform just in time to see the body of my shade ripple with magic, before it disappeared completely.

"*Semblance...*" he uttered.

The scepter scraped as he levered it free and approached. I held Areok's sword high, gusts charged with Ka spiraling. Shamaul hesitated when they flared brightly, magnetizing the shield and helmet to me. The helmet crowned my head. The shield belted to my arm. The mystic whirlwind cycloned, buffeting my hair before my shining eyes, and rattling my father's dog tags atop my shirt.

Shamaul stared as if witnessing an impossibility. He lunged forward with his scepter and I deflected it. He lunged again and I swiped it into the ground. The blade sparked on a rock. Its globe discharged several flares that warped into nothingness against the bright aura channeling around my body.

I pressed forward and Shamaul backed. Each time our weapons clashed, Areok's sword rang out like a tolling bell, reviving the minerals that had lay dormant inside and releasing their Ka. They glowed.

I felt it. All of it.

In the midst of the fight it all became clear. My friends' spirits pumping with fervor, not giving up. The unnatural storm writhing in dismay, panicking. The elemental power residing soundly in Murry's rucksack. The hidden power residing restlessly in me. Everything changed to become the same. Both terrestrial and sidereal, physical and ethereal, unified all at once. And in a flash of bright, white light, I was set free.

Shamaul shielded his eyes from the Omni-Ka that illuminated my body. Its glow cascaded, reaching everywhere, linking everything. Areok's sword whirred as its minerals flashed with luminance, their Ka signatures imbuing me with the skills, instinct, and wisdom of the hero who had wielded it before. With expert precision, I struck the warlock's scepter once again, scattering the crystal shards in its blade, then swung for Shamaul. The sword clipped his mask, lifting it off his face and leaving it to steam, damaged in the rubble.

His visage was skeletal. His yellow, serpentine eyes and twisted ram-like horns were attached to a demonic skull, with thin layers of dark scales covering the bone. Overlapped, grisly fangs parted to breathe exhausted pants as he backed away from me. His snake-like eyes rolled in their sunken sockets, clicking when they landed on the sword, as I held it skyward and summoned a spell.

The crystal blade glowed bright. Although the warlock's face had long since burned away, and his muscles were frayed beyond repair, a single nerve ending remained alive beneath all the dead, irreparable tissue. Emotion jarred it from dormancy. And at the corner of his right eye, a near-imperceptible spasm twitched. Fear.

Shamaul made one last attempt to strike, but when he took a step, his foot caught in a crag and his ankle crunched to the side, spurting blood through the spaces in his armor from an unmended stab wound.

In my mind I thanked Zyvin.

I thrusted the weapon forward, its blade white-hot. The warlock roared, but his outcry cut off, when the superheated sword melted through the armor on his abdomen and emerged from the other side.

Shamaul rattled with rage, the winds about his dying corpse singing the lamentations of every life he had claimed. The sword glowed bright. I shouted the spell:

"Touric Enavelir!"

A white beam broke through him, escaping though whatever opening there was. Eyes, ears, mouth—they all burst with the irradiant flash, soared skyward, and freed the explosive lightning within the Dark Lands' clouds.

Several strikes of lightning. A final flash of light. The spell emptied. Shamaul's body became heavy on the end of my sword, falling to his knees and slumping forward. Those yellow eyes rolled and steadied on me. His dead stare was no different than his living.

The chaos quelled, the winds dispersed, and the Dark Warlock's horde went silent. Their leader slipped down the point of my blade, the crevasse howling for him. His terrible eyes remained, still staring, still unblinking. Finally, Shamaul slid down, fell, and tumbled into the shadowy pit below.

41

The Five Crystals

Almost immediately, a pinpoint of sun streaked through the murky overcast, returning light to the Dark Lands. The creatures who thrived on darkness made wails of fright at the foreign element as it rained down, and they slunk away. Most took to the woods, others to caves and caverns. I removed my armor and staggered down the hillside, where I was immediately intercepted by overjoyed friends.

I grunted as Andy tackled me with a hug. Veronica and Murry followed, Scooter cheeped and leapt up to wrap his tentacles around the back of my head, and Boris stomped in with a crushing embrace around all of us.

"_Thanks guys,_" I wheezed.

They released me.

"We thought you were dead," Veronica said.

"Yes." Murry cleared his tears with the sleeve of his cloak. He set a fatherly hand on my shoulder. "Thank the Aevæs you're alright."

Andy slapped my arm. "That was unreal!"

I laughed tiredly and set Areok's sword blade-first in the rubble.

"Where did you find that?"

"It just sort of appeared," I said. I was as blown away and elated as they were.

Andy chuckled to himself.

"What is it?"

"You hit the reset button," he said.

I nodded, looking to the spot where my shade had disappeared, the healing stone resting on the gravel. I mirrored Andy's smile. "I guess I did."

We collected all the crystals. Murry reclaimed his frayed rucksack, peered inside, and reported, "All here, except for the Meisio stone—"

"Got it!" Andy called a moment later from atop the summit. "Still in one piece." He brushed away soot and grit that had collected in its fractures. "For the most part."

Veronica shot up beside him and held the Dark Lands crystal. It was delivered to my hands when they descended.

"Congratulations," Veronica grinned. She gave me the final piece. I held it to my eye. The dark energy quelled within, dispersing like the clouds above to welcome warmer, lighter tones. I wrapped it up.

We walked together to the basin of the two peaks in which the Mesalon resided. There we crossed paths with Orin and the Elementals. They were returning from the ruins, with two new figures following in their tracks. I felt a tingling warmth wash over me as I beheld the new arrivals. There was something celestial and saintly about each of them.

Kraiden and Etheria, the two spellcasters we saw cast in stone in the ruins before, stood in front of us. Flesh and blood, with auras of golden-white light surrounding them. Their presence seemed to hasten the retreat of the looming nimbus, swathing the new land in purifying sunrays.

Kraiden and Etheria were both tall, beatific people. Kraiden was introduced as the Elder Elemental. He had a deep tan complexion, with long white locks and a flowing white beard, both of which seemed to shimmer. His eyes were pale green and his white robes were simple and undecorated. In his hand he clutched a staff made of a sprucy, spiraled tree branch. Although his long beard and wise eyes convinced me he had seen many years, his face seemed fairly young, and had very few wrinkles.

Etheria, his wife, was introduced as the High Sorceress. She was Eramiri, with pointed ears emerging from her beautiful, blue tresses that flowed far past her shoulders. She had stunning, azure eyes and fair features. Angelic, she projected a genuineness emanating from within. Her robes were fairly simple as well: cream-colored with knotting decorations around the edges. Her pink lips smiled gently, and with a single look I was cleansed of my pain.

Although I had never seen or heard of either of them until now, I sensed their significance, and understood why the Ka Master needed to rescue them. I felt compelled to bow, but Kraiden beat me to it.

"Stay standing, warriors," his voice was soft, but stentorian. "It is I who must bow to you."

He lowered to one knee, and Etheria, Orin, and each of the Elementals did the same.

I was honored and speechless by the gesture.

Andy puffed out his chest. "We *are* pretty awesome, huh?"

Veronica rolled her eyes.

Gnuthe edged toward us. His hands wrung, he looked around with uncertainty at the newly-lit environment, muttering to himself.

Orin's eyes flashed at him. "Gnuthe?"

Gnuthe's bushy eyebrows raised as Orin approached him. "Yes? That's me."

"It's me, Orin!" the Ka Master exulted, taking him by the shoulders. "Great Aevæs, I can't believe it! How many cycles has it been, chap?"

"Quite a few," Gnuthe said. He squinted at his long-lost friend. "Judging from the length of that 'stache of yours. Heh, heh."

Orin patted the dust from Gnuthe's shoulders. "Oh, you're a right mess. We'll take ya home to Veindai, bucko. Clean you up proper!"

Gnuthe chuckled, becoming livelier. "Hey now, I've spent my finer cycles living in a cave. What's your excuse, hm?" He tugged on his friend's white mustache.

The two shared a hearty laugh and Orin walked him back to the group with an arm around him. As they passed, I caught sight of something standing in the shade of the woods.

A pair of bright eyes belonging to a large wolf. Unlike the fierce canines we fought off earlier, this one looked peaceful. Her silken fur was reddish brown, her muzzle sleek and pretty. At her heels, a smaller, dark-furred one peeked around, followed by an even tinier, brown-colored pup. When my eyesight sharpened, I thought I could see a necklace with a wooden totem nestled in her fur. The mother wolf appeared to bow, then took off into the forest. Her offspring trotted after her.

The Mesalon was a stunning architectural feat. It was like being in the presence of a monument. Five smooth, stone arches intersected to form a dome-shape. At one point, some type of vines had grown over the bases of the arches, but they had long

411

since died, dried into what looked like a matrix of dark veins. The Elementals started securing each of the crystals into their designated positions. They snapped into place inside diamond-shaped cutouts, magnetized inward by the pull of the other crystals that were added to the formation, but held firm by their frame, allowing shimmering minerals to seep through smaller cutouts behind them. I marveled at the setup.

"This structure," Orin announced, "is the very same Areok once used to return to Earth. I designed it to combine the energies of the five crystals without..." He made a looping motion with his hands. "Y'know, any explosions."

Andy and I exchanged nervous glances.

"*And* most importantly, to maintain singularity of the Orb. The Mesalon will merge the energies into a portal like the one you took before. The distance at which the sources are kept will prevent the energies from taking physical shape." Orin shook his head. "Aevæs knows the last thing we need is another one of those spheres kicking around, waiting to fall to malicious hands. One is quite enough responsibility for this corner of the multiverse, hm?" We nodded as he shuffled to one of the Mesalon's beams, sniffing. "Yup. She's seen some cycles but..." He patted the upright. "She should do the trick!" A section of the vines disintegrated into ash. Orin waved it away and coughed. "Start her up!"

"That's... reassuring," I said.

Andy chuckled. He nudged me. "Let's get ready."

Grimmoch placed the final crystal in its arch, and as we waited for the energies to mingle in the center of the Mesalon, we said our goodbyes. Andy and I shook hands with Orin.

"Farewell, Realmhoppers," the Ka Master said. "Until we meet again."

"You are defenders," Zax saluted.

"Noble warriors indeed," Arduuk proclaimed.

Erah patted our shoulders. "Consider yourselves honorary Rogues."

"You freed my land," Grimmoch bowed. "Thank you."

"Don't mention it," Andy said.

Kraiden and Etheria approached us. In his hands, the Elder held a pair of large, ornate-looking gold coins centered with green gems.

"I want to give you these," Kraiden said. "I gave one to my dear friend, Alistair, when he left for the final time."

I tilted my head at the unfamiliar name.

Kraiden grinned. "You know him as Areok." The Elder channeled Ka into his palms and the coins rose. Chains manifested out of the light, made of the same golden metal, and turned them into medallions. They levitated over our heads and lay on our chests.

"Sweet, I've been meaning to bling out my wardrobe," Andy said.

"They're incredible, thank you," I added.

Kraiden laughed softly. "Yes well, Orin tells me these siv pieces are of no value anymore, so—"

Etheria smacked her husband's chest.

"Oh, ehm, but the *symbolic* value is incalculable! Uh…"

Etheria stepped around her floundering mate as he rubbed his eyes with embarrassment. She spoke for him, "What he is trying to say is that they are tokens of our gratitude. And that they will keep you connected to our world."

Kraiden nodded, laughing bashfully. "Yes. Spot on, my darling."

We thanked them again.

Next came the hardest part. We went to the friends who had helped us, rescued us, and guided us throughout the entirety of our adventure. Veronica, Murry, Scooter, and Boris waited for us as we treaded toward them.

Murry stepped forward first to hug me. "Be good. Do great things."

As Andy said goodbye to him next, Boris knelt to my height. I scratched him behind the ear and he snorted. Andy did the same.

"You're a good buffalo," he said.

Veronica cleared her throat.

Andy laughed. "I know, I know. Ronk."

Boris' big blue tongue licked his face.

As he wiped away the slime, Veronica stepped forward. "Take care, Marvin." She hugged me. "And stay away from furadons."

I laughed, "I will."

I had the most difficult time saying goodbye to Scooter. The hexapoid leapt into my arms from his perch on Boris' head-horn, chirping lovingly. I cradled him close and petted his shell.

"I'm gonna miss you, buddy." I didn't know when I'd be back, but I assured him I would. His big, dark eyes glimmered as he blinked at me. He seemed to understand. The cephalopod scampered all over my chest, tickling me and earning laughs from the rest of the group, before he jumped into Murry's hands.

"I'll take care of him," the wizard promised.

I thanked him.

Closer to the Mesalon, Andy and Veronica were sharing an extended goodbye. Andy's foot twisted in the ground awkwardly as he searched for words.

"So, uh..." he said.

Veronica crossed her arms and listened.

"Y'know, um... if we can come back... maybe I can, y'know, bring you to Earth sometime?"

Veronica's head tilted. Her periwinkle eyes locked with his.

"I mean, only if you *want* to of course. I think it would be cool to—"

His words cut short when she grabbed the lapel of his orange jacket and pulled him in, planting a kiss on his lips. Their hair wisped in the breezes tossed from the energy growing in the Mesalon's center. She released him and he stumbled back in shock. She pressed her finger into his chest.

"*When* you come back."

Andy's face stretched into a big, goofy grin. "Right right, of course, *when* I come back. That's what I meant." He scratched the back of his head as he swayed. He cleared his throat. "I'm definitely coming back."

They embraced.

Andy and I stood before the whirring Mesalon, minerals floating from their crystals and spiraling in the middle of the dome. We watched them merge.

"Just a moment longer," Orin said.

The Elementals circled the structure, each pointing their weapons at the crystals from their respective continents as though funneling additional power into them. In the absence of Areok, Kraiden pointed his staff at the Ravacan crystal. The ground shook.

414

A single spark went off and fizzled, no greater than a firecracker. Andy and I looked at each other.

Orin looked confused. The Ka Master hammered his fist against one of the arches.

Andy called, "Is that it—?"

FWOOOOSH!

A whirring blast went off as green, blue, red, violet, and white beams converged, then condensed into a fluxing sphere of Tyrian purple energy that floated in the dome, bathing us in its warmth and light. Andy and I took one last glance at Veronica, Murry, Boris, and Scooter. We waved to them. Murry and Veronica smiled and raised their hands in return, Scooter chirped, and Boris lifted his head to us with a hearty snort.

I took a breath, then turned to my friend. "Ready?"

Andy nodded. "Ready."

"One... two... three!"

We ran through.

The two Realmhoppers ran into the Mesalon and disappeared in its portal. Orin clapped, instigating applause and cheer from the crowds around him.

"Job well done, eh?" he rejoiced.

"Indeed," Grimmoch answered. "The heroes have returned home, and the Dark Lands is freed."

"Yes, well," Arduuk said, shading his eyes as she noted the sun, "it isn't so dark anymore."

"You'll need a new name for it," Erah nudged him.

"Oh!" Gnuthe spoke up. "Light Lands! Yes."

Kraiden chuckled and placed his hand on the shoulder of the white-robed warrior. "That task will fall exclusively to you, Elemental."

Zax nodded. He buzzed, "You are in charge. Rightfully so."

Grimmoch's orange-red eyes flared with dignity.

Orin agreed, "Yes. You can set up a colony..."

From around a tree trunk, the warlock's goblin subordinate, Gumble, peaked, listening in on the conversation.

The Ka Master went toward the Mesalon and reached, trying to remove one of the crystals. "You can fix this place up. Be in charge of the whole bloomin' lot."

Grimmoch said, "The first order of business will be to find my father's body, and destroy it."

Gumble almost shrieked. He contained his terror.

Murry turned toward the pit his son had plummeted into.

Veronica spoke, "He fell pretty far."

Grimmoch acknowledged the notion, but added, "This man knows ways around death. This is the only way to be sure."

Gumble bit his fist to contain his hilarity. His frenzied, bulging eyes searched the rumble for answers. When Grimmoch's fiery stare swept his way, he panicked and ran, disappearing in the shadows.

The plan was set.

Orin cleared his throat to gain the others' attention. "If you haven't noticed, I'm not exactly what you'd call *tall*. If someone could help me shut her down I'd—"

Orin wobbled and lost balance as the ground shuddered and fissured beneath the structure. Its arches began to crack as the energy surged more erratic than before. The Ka Master hopped back to the crowd and commanded them all to fall behind him. Once they circled, he threw up his arms and created a protective dome around everyone. Just in time; the Mesalon fractured and imploded. Crystals broke free and collided. An explosion sent shockwaves over them and collapsed the basin into a crater.

When the dust settled, Orin lowered his shield, and everyone stepped cautiously toward the edge of the pit, in which a new Orb lay glowing in the rubble. Orin covered his face and shook his head.

Gnuthe consoled his friend. "There, there, chap. Those cycles just did a number on the poor thing. That's all."

Etheria spoke, "We'll protect it. We have to."

"Far away from prying eyes, preferably," Orin sighed.

"In the Fortress of Alistaan," Kraiden said. The new Orb levitated in a field of his Ka, steadying above his palm as it steamed with heat. "It will be safest there."

"My dad works there," Veronica said. She stopped in her tracks, suddenly remembering her father. "Oh, right..." she muttered. "He's going to kill me."

"I'm sure he'll be proud," Murry interposed. "Besides, you did send him a letter beforehand."

"Yeah, but I may not have given him *all* the details."

Murry paused. "How long did you tell him you'd be gone from the village?"

Veronica searched her memory, then winced and answered, "About ten days?"

Boris snorted and Scooter chirruped uncomfortably. Murry's eyes flashed at the number. "Hm." His mouth shifted in thought. "That may have undersold it a bit."

We emerged from a flash of light, floorboards squeaking as our sneakers touched down on a familiar, wooden floor. The Artifact Room. We were back!

Pots, pans, and figurines rattled into steady positions on their shelves as the Orb's glow dimmed. Andy and I took a look around, then exploded in celebration.

"Yeah, woohoo!"

"Alright!"

We jumped, cheered, jigged, and high-fived.

Andy pointed at me. "Oh, dude! Your clothes!"

I looked down. They were exactly like they were when we left. Even my backpack and Captain Galloway book had returned somehow, and Andy just about lost his mind when he realized he had been reunited with his shark tooth necklace. We were no longer outfitted in any of our Enkartai gear either. In fact, the only remnant articles that transferred through the portal were the medallions Kraiden had given us. I felt mine resting on my chest and tucked it under my shirt.

I went to the window to see what season it was. The trees were lush outside. It still looked like spring. *Everything* looked the same, in fact. I could see yellow school buses lined up in the circle in front of the museum.

"Oh, sweet Earth," Andy got down on the floor and kissed it. "How I've missed you." He kissed it again, then got up and wiped his mouth. "*Blech.* That was a mistake." He turned to the

Orb. It shimmered on its stand. "So, do we take it with us, or...?"

"Should we?" I asked. I reached for it.

"Whoa, whoa! Don't touch it! Are you insane?"

I laughed, "I'm kidding."

"Don't joke like that, man. Seriously, after all that—"

Clunk!

We froze as the doorknob twisted. Mr. Connley burst through the door, his wild, emerald eyes landed on us. "You two!" he shouted breathlessly. Andy and I stood like statues, stares shifting between one another.

Andy wagered a lie: "So you said we *could* go in the Artifact Room, right?"

The tour guide stormed in, fuming with rage. "I specifically told you *not* to. This room is *not* part of the tour. It was *not* for you to see." He immediately went to the Orb. He reached for the relic. "How did you two even get in here—?"

"No!" Andy and I screamed at the same time.

Mr. Connley set his hand down on the Orb and lifted it. There was no effect. He stared at us as like we were crazy. Retrieving a handkerchief from his jacket pocket, he polished the glassy surface, continuing to gripe about our disobedience.

"Just wait until your teacher hears of this—"

His voice trailed off as I noticed a gold chain on his neck. Below it, a gold nametag was fastened to the lapel of his dark jacket, with engraved lettering. It read, *Alistair Connley.*

My eyes flashed at the words.

"*Areok?*" I whispered.

The tour guide stopped his polishing, eyes widening behind gold-rimmed specs. He returned the Orb to its silver, three-legged stand and ushered us out of the room. "Time to go."

I took one last glance at the relic that initiated our adventure, and smiled. The Orb glowed, seeming to return the salutation, before the old, wooden door creaked shut.

42
The Hummingbird

I boarded the bus. It was just as wild and rowdy as before. Our classmates chattered away in blissful chaos. Some shouted and threw wads of paper. I followed Andy as he plopped down in his seat. I slowly lowered beside him, mystified by our unchanged, unassuming world. I eased back into the familiar seating: dark gray vinyl with chipped edges loosely covering old sponge cushions. It was all still here. No time had passed.

"I can't believe Connley covered for us," Andy murmured as he found his backpack under the seat and dug through it.

Neither could I. I peeked over the heads of the 'Acy Sisters to peer out the cloudy, square window, where the tour guide finished shaking hands with our history teacher before strolling back up the steep, marble steps of the museum.

"What was it he said?" Andy went on, shoulder-deep in a backpack full of crumpled note pages. "We were late because of our 'advanced interest' in one of the exhibits?"

"Yeah."

"I think Mr. Barber believed *you'd* do something like that. But *me*?" Andy chuckled. "Connley made me sound like the best student ever—I'm probably getting extra credit thanks to him." He dug deeper, then found it. "Aha! There you are!" He displayed his handheld videogame and kissed it dramatically.

"Watch out, Veronica will get jealous," I joked.

Andy laughed and powered up his system. The sounds of lasers beeped from its speakers.

Across rows, Alison sat, still drawing in her sketchbook. Her dark eyes flicked my way and her freckled cheeks dimpled as she subdued her grin and exchanged drawing utensils from a black, zippered pouch.

I leaned in. "Hey, Alison."

Her brown hair swished as her head turned quickly. She flashed a grin. "Hey!"

Andy's game went quiet. He was eavesdropping.

"So, when we were talking before I didn't have a chance to ask—"

"Alright, class!" Mr. Barber announced, standing at the front of the bus with his hands held high.

I sighed. The clamor puttered to murmuring exchanges, with which Mr. Barber was still dissatisfied. "Eh-hem!"

They went silent.

"Better. I hope all of you enjoyed our field trip to the museum."

Andy called out, "Best field trip ever!" Some of our classmates laughed and whispered to each other in the back.

The teacher wasn't sure if he was serious or not. "Yes. Thank you, Mr. Bailey. When we get back to the classroom we'll have a short quiz."

Everyone made muffled, yet audible groans.

Mr. Barber looked annoyed. "It's only three questions. And you can leave class as soon as you're finished."

The class seemed pleased with that. Our teacher sat down at the front, the doors shut, and the bus rumbled back onto the street.

Alison turned to me. "What did you want to ask me?"

"I was wondering if..." I stopped, sensing something.

Alison looked perplexed. "Something wrong?"

I darted backward, dodging a paper wad lobbed by Eddie Seaver. It zipped by and hit Mr. Barber in the back on the head instead. Everyone gasped. The teacher shot up, face flushed red.

"Mr. Seaver!"

Eddie went pale. He sank down in his seat as our teacher lit into him, demanding he stay after class and that the ride back be completely silent. Cut off again, I whispered to Alison, "*We'll talk later*," and she agreed with a nod, then went back to her sketching.

She was still shading and coloring when we were back in the classroom. She sat in the back of the room so Mr. Barber wouldn't notice as he delivered a closing lecture regarding the museum's relevance to our class, which gradually became an inspirational message about adulthood and responsibility—one he gave often.

"You may not realize it, but you're all on the precipice of adulthood," he said. "Sure, right now all you may be thinking about is how to impress your crush, who to invite to prom—"

He was right. His words trailed off as I peeked across the room at her. She was looking out the window, daydreaming in the sunglow. The bell rang and everyone flowed into the hallway. I found her in the crowd. I tapped her shoulder.

"Alison."

She turned around.

"I wanted to ask you—"

"Yes!"

"What?"

"Oh," she giggled awkwardly. "Sorry, go ahead."

My confidence swelled. "Do you, want to go to prom with me?"

She beamed an excited, white smile. "Yes."

A rush of elation ran through me, and before I could say anything else she reached into her sketchbook and retrieved the picture she was drawing on the bus. She presented it to me.

"Here."

A hummingbird with bright green feathers centered the page, wings high in midflight. Its slender, black beak drank the nectar from a beautiful, three-petalled Iris flower, which she had colored purple. In the same color, she signed her name in the lower right corner of the page. In big, looping letters it read, *Alison Adair*, with hearts dotting the i's.

"You're giving this to me?"

She nodded. "I drew it for you."

I traced the detailed imagery with my eyes, absorbing every inch. "It's beautiful. Thank you."

Her shoulders lifted bashfully. She brushed her hair behind her ear. "I'm glad you like it." She swayed in place as I looked at the picture. We lingered there for a few seconds.

I started, "So, uh..."

"Catch you later?"

"Yeah okay."

"Okay, bye."

"Oh, should we exchange numbers?"

"Sure! I mean, we live on the same floor right?"

"Oh, true."

"I'll see you in the hall sometime."

"Okay, sounds good."

"Okay, bye!"

"Bye."

We laughed away our awkwardness and waved to each other. Her hair swayed as she speedwalked down the hall, clutching her books to her chest. I looked down at her gift again, just as an arm wrapped around my shoulders.

"Nice work, bro," Andy said, walking with me.

"How long were you standing there?"

"Long enough to hear my little Marvy's becoming a man!" He pretended to cry.

Alison was still within earshot. She flashed a bright grin my way and turned the corner.

"They grow up so fast!" Andy fake-sobbed.

I wiggled from his grip. *"Alright, alright."*

Andy chuckled. "This is great though! Now we both have dates to the prom!"

"Who are you bringing?"

Andy scrunched his brow at me. "Who do you think?"

"Macy? Stacy?"

"Veronica, duh!" He rolled his eyes as we walked.

"You're gonna bring her?"

"Yeah, man. I mentioned it to her before we left. At first she thought a 'prom' was some type of exotic fish or something, but when I explained it she seemed game."

"Nice, man," I said. We continued down the hall. "How's that gonna work though?"

"No idea. I'll cross that bridge when I come to it."

We laughed.

My sneakers clopped against the uneven sidewalk, hastened by both the rainclouds rolling in and the excitement buzzing in my chest. I acknowledged the brewing storm, smiling, as mist cooled my skin and inspired me to go faster. My backpack joggled as I turned a corner. I flew up two flights of the spiraled, iron staircase of my brick apartment building, then raced down the hall, turned the key in my brassy doorknob, and rotated it. It clicked and opened.

With her back facing me and her wavy, dark hair bobbing as she listened to tunes, my mom tended to her indoor garden of plants that forested the back wall of our apartment, spritzing them with water. She turned around, lifting a headphone from her ear. She smiled.

"Hey buddy, how was the field trip?"

I ran up and hugged her.

"Wow. That good, huh?" She hugged me back.

I hurried down the hallway to my room, hearing my mom call, *"There's some leftover pizza in the fridge if you want it."*

"Okay," I called back, opening my door.

Unfolded clothes coated the floor; pages of homework, my computer desk. My bed was unmade, the green sheets wrinkled and flipped to one side. The only neat thing in the room was a stack of books that sat on the far shelf, organized in the order I wanted to read them. Everything was exactly as I left it.

I sighed and shook my head. *I made it*, I realized. I propped up Alison's picture atop my dresser—one of the few viable surfaces in the room—then set my backpack on the floor. It thudded, heavier than I expected it to. I frowned and unzipped it, and gasped.

There in my backpack, the Orb shimmered at me, silver base and all. Its purple light shimmered through the shade of the bag, illuminating my stunned features.

It couldn't be.

My mind raced with questions. *Did Andy slip the Orb in my backpack? Or Mr. Connley?* I shook my head. *No. Impossible. I would have felt it. Besides, I saw it sitting in the Artifact Room before we left. I'm sure of it.*

I lifted it carefully by the silver stand, not daring to touch its surface a second time, and carefully carried it to the left and placed it atop my dresser beside Alison's picture. I grappled with my thoughts, crossed my arms, and stepped back to view the relic's mysterious energies glimmer and swirl like the stars of a miniature galaxy. One spot of light twinkled brighter than the rest.

There was no logical explanation. It had followed me.

My door swung open.

"Laundry delivery!" my mom called.

I tensed up and blocked the Orb with my body.

"Hot out of the dryer. Try not to let these end up on the floor, okay...?" Her voice trailed off when she noticed my apprehension. Her brow scrunched. "Everything okay?"

I nodded. "Mm-hm."

Her eyes flashed at what was behind me. "What is that?"

"Hm? Nothing." I tried to block it.

She worked her way around me. "Let me see."

"No, Mom, wait—!"

"Isn't this cute." She picked up Alison's picture, walking right past the Orb. "Did that sweet girl from down the hall draw this?"

She was completely oblivious to it. The Orb was invisible to her. I shook my head, unable to comprehend what was happening.

"Uh... yeah," I finally answered. "Yeah, we're going to prom together actually and—"

Her eyes grew wide. "You two are going to the prom?" She returned the picture to its spot on the dresser, clapping her hands ecstatically. "Oh, this is wonderful! Forget about cleaning your room tomorrow. Look up corsages online. I have to call Dianne, she's gonna love this."

"Aw, Mom, please don't call Aunt Dianne—"

She was already on the phone. "Dianne? It's Marion. Guess what? Huh? No. No, we're not getting a cat. I know they relieve stress, just listen..."

When she finally conveyed that I had a date to prom shrills of excitement sounded through the earpiece, and they were off talking for several hours about how "grown up" I was.

I took another glance at the Orb resting on my dresser, reminiscing on everything that transpired, as the storm rumbled outside my window.

43
<u>Destiny</u>

Rain pattered against my windowpane, and wisps of wind inspired the branch of a nearby tree to tap softly against the glass. I unlooped my father's dog tags, tilting them in my hand and watching the amber light of my lamp illuminate the letters of his name, before I placed the chain around the framed picture of him I keep on my nightstand. I smiled as I met his proud gaze, shaded by the brim of his uniform hat.

Next, I lifted off the medallion Kraiden had given me. Its green stone shined as it reached the light, sparkling with the wonder of Enkartai. I stowed it away safely in my drawer and climbed into bed.

Through the crack of my door I spied the warm, orange glow of candles, carrying the familiar, singular scent of bayberry. The scent of home. I clicked off my lamp and got under the covers, arching my back until I found my usual spot. The mattress was lumpy and uneven, and sloped down in the center where I usually lay. It was the most comfortable thing I slept on in a long time.

I took a deep breath of the sweet candle scent as the rain pelted, tree limb tapped, and storm winds sang their lullaby, filling me with a swell of enrapturing somnolence, and chrysalism. And as the night dreamily sang its chorus, I tucked my hands behind my head, and watched the Orb cast patterns along my ceiling in bands of soft, Tyrian purple glow, dotted with bright white specks. They looked like stars.

In the corner of my room sat the portal to another world which had changed my life, forever. And the friends I made there undoubtedly felt the same. I smiled, sensing their connection while I traced the splendid constellations that danced on my ceiling, as Orin's words resurfaced in my memory:

All the worlds are elements, I remembered.

And at that moment, I decided that I,

I was the greatest element of all.

425

About the Author

What began as daydreams and doodles in the margins of notebooks evolved into the world of Enkartai, and the debut novel of self-published author Michael Thompson. *World of the Orb* is the first publication to exemplify his love of science fiction and fantasy stories, as well as those featuring unique, dynamic ensembles of characters and the high-stakes challenges that elevate them into heroes.

For more on Michael and his books, visit worldoftheorb.com

Made in the USA
Charleston, SC
15 March 2017